DISAPPEARING

EARTH

DISAPPEARING EARTH

· ·

Julia Phillips

Leabharlanna Poiblí Chathair Baile Átha Cliath
Dublin City Public Libraries

SCRIBNER

LONDON NEW YORK TORONTO SYDNEY NEW DELHI

First published in the United States by Alfred A. Knopf, a division of
Penguin Random House LLC, New York, and distributed in Canada by
Alfred A. Knopf Canada, a division of Penguin Random House Canada Limited, Toronto.

First published in Great Britain by Scribner, an imprint of Simon & Schuster UK Ltd, 2019
A CBS COMPANY

1 3 5 7 9 10 8 6 4 2

Simon & Schuster UK Ltd
1st Floor, 222 Gray's Inn Road
London WC1X 8HB

Simon & Schuster Australia, Sydney
Simon & Schuster India, New Delhi

www.simonandschuster.co.uk
www.simonandschuster.com.au
www.simonandschuster.co.in

A CIP catalogue record for this book
is available from the British Library

Hardback ISBN: 978-1-4711-6949-6
Trade Paperback ISBN: 978-1-4711-6950-2
eBook ISBN: 978-1-4711-6951-9

Several chapters in this novel were originally published, in different
form, in the following publications: 'August' first appeared as 'Disappearing Earth'
in *Confrontation Magazine* (Fall 2016); 'September' first appeared as 'Anya' in
The Toast (January 2016); 'November' first appeared as 'Valentina' in *Vol. 1 Brooklyn*
(May 2015); 'February' first appeared as 'Galya' in *The Antioch Review* (Winter 2016); 'March'
first appeared as 'Nadia' in *Glimmer Train* (May 2016); 'April' first appeared as
'Nina' in *The Brooklyn Quarterly* (Fall 2015); and 'May' first appeared
as 'Lera' in *The Rumpus* (August 2015).

Map on p. viii by Jeffrey L. Ward

Printed and bound by CPI Group (UK) Ltd, Croydon CR0 4YY

PRINCIPAL CHARACTERS

THE GOLOSOVSKY FAMILY

Marina Alexandrovna, a journalist in the city of
Petropavlovsk-Kamchatsky
Alyona, her older daughter
Sophia, her younger daughter

THE SOLODIKOV FAMILY

Alla Innokentevna, head of a cultural center in the village
of Esso
Natalia, called **Natasha**, her oldest daughter
Denis, her middle child and only son
Lilia, her youngest daughter
Revmira, her second cousin, a nurse
Lev and **Yulia**, called **Yulka**, Natasha's children

THE ADUKANOV FAMILY

Ksenia, called **Ksyusha**, a university student
Sergei, called **Chegga**, her brother, a photographer
Ruslan, Ksyusha's boyfriend
Nadezhda, called **Nadia**, Chegga's girlfriend
Ludmila, called **Mila**, Nadia's daughter

THE RYAKHOVSKY FAMILY

Nikolai Danilovich, called **Kolya**, a police detective

Zoya, his wife, on maternity leave from her work at a
national park

Alexandra, called **Sasha**, their baby

Oksana, a researcher at the volcanological institute

Maxim, called **Max**, a researcher at the volcanological institute

Ekaterina, called **Katya**, a customs officer for the city's maritime
container port

Yevgeny Pavlovich Kulik, the major general of the Kamchatka
police force

Anfisa, an administrative assistant for the police

Valentina Nikolaevna, an office administrator for a city
elementary school

Diana, Valentina Nikolaevna's daughter

Lada, a receptionist at a city hotel

Olga, called **Olya**, a schoolgirl

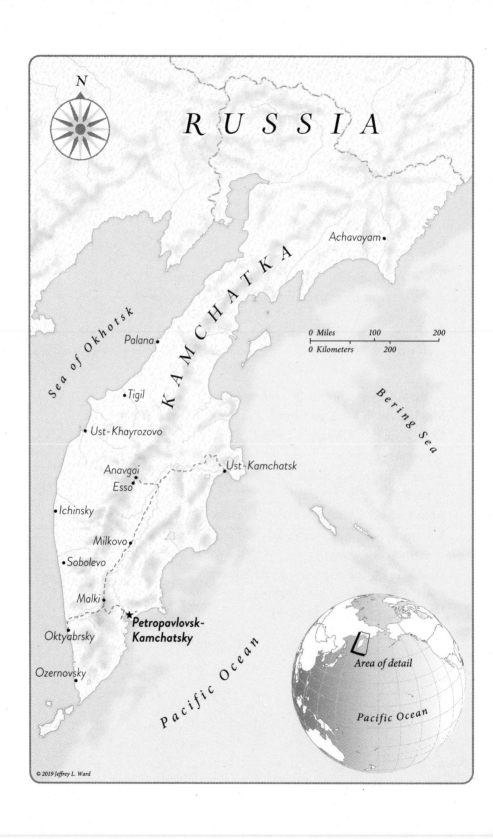

N

R U S S I A

Achavayam •

K A M C H A T K A

Sea of Okhotsk

Palana •

0 Miles   100   200
0 Kilometers   200

Tigil •

Bering Sea

• Ust-Khayrozovo

Anavgai •   Ust-Kamchatsk •
Esso •

• Ichinsky

Milkovo •

• Sobolevo

Malki •

★ Petropavlovsk-
   Kamchatsky

Oktyabrsky •

Pacific Ocean

Ozernovsky •

Area of detail

Pacific Ocean

© 2019 Jeffrey L. Ward

DISAPPEARING

EARTH

A U G U S T

S ophia, sandals off, was standing at the water's edge. The bay
snuck up to swallow her toes. Gray salt water over bright skin.
"Don't go out any farther," Alyona said.

The water receded. Alyona could see, under her sister's feet, the
pebbles breaking the curves of Sophia's arches, the sweep of grit left
by little waves. Sophia bent to roll up her pant legs, and her ponytail
flipped over the top of her head. Her calves showed flaking streaks of
blood from scratched mosquito bites. Alyona knew from the firm line
of her sister's spine that Sophia was refusing to listen.

"You better not," Alyona said.

Sophia stood to face the water. It was calm, barely touched by ripples that made the bay look like a sheet of hammered tin. The current got stronger as it pulled into the Pacific, leaving Russia behind
for open ocean, but here it was domesticated. It belonged to them.
Hands propped on narrow hips, Sophia surveyed it, the width of the
bay, the mountains on the horizon, the white lights of the military
installation on the opposite shore.

The gravel under the sisters was made of chips from bigger stones.
Alyona leaned against a block the size of a hiking backpack, and a
meter behind her was the crumbling cliff face of St. Nicholas Hill.
Water on one side, rock wall on the other, they had walked along
the coast this afternoon until they found this patch, free of bottles
or feathers, to settle. When seagulls landed nearby, Alyona chased
them away with a wave of her arm. The whole summer had been

cool, drizzly, but this August afternoon was warm enough to wear short sleeves.

Sophia took a step out, and her heel went under.

Alyona sat up. "Soph, I said no!" Her sister backed up. A gull flew over. "Why do you have to be such a brat?"

"I'm not."

"You are. You always are."

"No," Sophia said, turning around. Her tipped-up eyes, thin lips, sharp jaw, even the point of her nose annoyed Alyona. At eight years old, Sophia still looked six. Alyona, three years older, was short for her age, but Sophia was tiny all over, from waist to wrists, and sometimes acted like a kindergartener: she kept a row of stuffed animals at the foot of her bed, played pretend that she was a world-famous ballerina, couldn't fall asleep at night if she caught even one scene of a horror movie on the television. Their mother indulged her. Being born second had given Sophia the privilege of staying a baby all her life.

Gaze fixed on a spot on the cliff far above Alyona's head, Sophia lifted one foot out of the water, pointed wet toes, and raised her arms to fifth position. She tipped and caught herself. Alyona shifted her seat on the stones. Their mother always tried to get Alyona to take her sister along to classmates' apartments, but these little misdeeds were exactly why she would not.

Instead they had spent their summer vacation alone with each other. Alyona had taught Sophia how to do a back walkover in the damp parking lot behind their building. In July, they took the bus forty minutes to the municipal zoo, where they fed candy through the cage to a greedy black goat. Its slitted pupils swiveled in its head. Later that afternoon, Alyona pushed an unwrapped milk caramel through a chain-link fence to a lynx, which hissed at the sisters until they backed away. The caramel sat on the cement floor. So much for the zoo. When Alyona and Sophia's mother left them money in the mornings before work, the sisters went to the cinema, and split a banana and chocolate crepe afterward at the café on its second floor. Most days, though, they hung around the city, watching rain clouds gather and the sunlight stretch out. Their faces tanned gradually. They took walks, or rode their bikes, or came here.

While Sophia balanced, Alyona looked along the shore. A man was picking his way over the rocks. "Someone's coming," Alyona said. Her sister splashed one leg down and lifted the other. Sophia might not care who saw her act like an idiot, but Alyona, her forced companion, did. "Stop," Alyona said. More loudly. Heating up in her mouth—"*STOP.*"

Sophia stopped.

Down the line of the water, the man was gone. He must have found some clean place to sit. All the frustration that had been rising inside Alyona seeped out like a bath when the drain was unplugged.

"I'm bored," said Sophia.

Alyona lay back. The rock was hard on her shoulders, cold on her head. "Come here," she said, and Sophia stepped out of the bay, picked her way over, and squirmed next to Alyona. The smallest stones crunched together. The breeze had left Sophia's body as cool as the ground. "Want me to tell you a story?" Alyona asked.

"Yes."

Alyona checked her phone. They had to be home in time for dinner, but it wasn't even four o'clock. "Do you know about the town that washed away?"

"No." For someone who never obeyed, Sophia could be very attentive. Her chin lifted and her mouth pinched shut in concentration.

Alyona pointed down the shore at the most distant cliffs. To the girls' right was the city center, from where they had walked this afternoon; to the left, marking the mouth of the bay, were those black hulks. "It used to be there."

"In Zavoyko?"

"Past Zavoyko." They sat under the peak of St. Nicholas Hill. If they had kept walking along the shoreline today, they would have seen the stony side of the hill eventually lower, exposing the stacked squares of a neighborhood overhead. Five-story Soviet apartment buildings covered in patchwork concrete. The wooden frames of collapsed houses. A mirrored high-rise, pink and yellow, with a banner advertising business space for rent. Zavoyko was kilometers past all that, making it the last district of their city, Petropavlovsk-Kamchatsky, the last bit of land before sea. "It was at the edge of the cliff where the ocean meets the bay."

"Was it a big town?"

"It was like a settlement. Like a village. Just fifty wooden houses, filled with soldiers, wives, and babies. This was years ago. After the Great Patriotic War."

Sophia thought about it. "Was there a school?"

"Yes. A market, a pharmacy. Everything. A post office." Alyona pictured it: stacked logs, carved window frames, doors painted turquoise. "It looked like a fairy tale. And there was a flagpole in the middle of town, and a square where people parked their old-fashioned cars."

"Okay," Sophia said.

"Okay. So one morning, the townspeople are making their break-fasts, feeding their cats, getting dressed for work, and the cliff starts to shake. It's an earthquake. They've never felt such a strong one before. Walls are swaying, cups are smashing, furniture is—"

Here Alyona looked to the gravel beside her but there was no washed-up branch for her to snap—

"Furniture is breaking. The babies are crying in their cribs and their mothers can't reach them. They can't even stand up. It's the biggest earthquake the peninsula has ever had."

"Their houses fall on them?" Sophia guessed.

Alyona shook her head. The rock she leaned against pressed into her skull. "Just listen. After five minutes, the quake stops. It feels like forever to them. The babies keep crying but the people are so happy. They crawl toward each other to hug. Maybe some sidewalks split, some wires snapped, but they made it—they lived. They're lying there holding each other and then, through the holes where their windows used to be, they see this shadow."

Sophia was unblinking.

"It's a wave. Twice as high as their houses."

"Over Zavoyko?" said Sophia. "That's not possible. It's too high."

"Past Zavoyko, I told you. This earthquake was that powerful. People felt it in Hawaii. People way off in Australia were asking their friends, 'Did you bump into me?' because something was making them rock on their feet. That's how strong the quake was."

Her sister didn't say anything.

"It shook the whole ocean," Alyona said. "It sent up a wave two hundred meters high. And it just..." She held her hand out in front of them, lined it up with the flat water of the bay, and swept it across the horizon.

The air brushed cold on their bare arms. Somewhere nearby, birds were calling.

"What happened to them?" Sophia finally asked.

"No one knows. Everyone in the city was too distracted by the quake. Even in Zavoyko, they didn't notice how the sky had gotten darker; they were busy sweeping up, checking in on their next-door neighbors, making repairs. When ocean water came down their streets, they just figured some pipes had burst uphill. But later, when the electricity came back on, somebody realized there were no lights coming from the edge of the cliff. The place where that town had been was empty."

The ripples in the bay made a quiet rhythm behind her words. Shh, shh. Shh, shh.

"They went to look and found nothing. No people, no buildings, no traffic lights, no roads. No trees. No grass. It looked like the moon."

"Where'd they go?"

"Washed away. The wave picked them up right where they lay, like this." She propped herself on one elbow and gripped Sophia's shoulder, its bones shifting under her palm. "That's how tight the water was around their bodies. It locked them up inside their houses. It lifted the whole town and took it out to the Pacific. No one ever saw a sign of them again."

In the shadow of the hill, Sophia's face was dark. Her lips were parted to show the ridged bottoms of her front teeth. Alyona liked, every so often, to bring her sister to a place where she looked blank with fear.

"That's not true," Sophia said.

"Yes, it is. I heard it at school."

The water, opaque in the afternoon light, was keeping its pace. It looked silver. The rocks Sophia had been standing on appeared and disappeared.

"Can we go home?" Sophia asked.

"It's early."

"Still."

"Did I scare you?"

"No."

In the center of the bay, a trawler pushed south, heading for whatever waited out there—Chukotka, Alaska, Japan. The sisters had never left the Kamchatka Peninsula. One day, their mother said, they would visit Moscow, but that was a nine-hour flight away, a whole continent's distance, and would require them to cross above the mountains and seas and fault lines that isolated Kamchatka. They had never known a big earthquake, but their mother told them what one was like. She described how 1997 felt in their apartment: the kitchen light swinging high enough on its cord to smash against the ceiling, the cabinet doors swinging so jars of preserves could dance out, the eggy smell of leaking gas that made her head ache. On the street afterward, their mother said, she saw cars ground into one another and the asphalt opened up.

Looking for this spot to sit, the sisters had walked far enough along the base of the hill to leave almost all signs of civilization behind. Only the ship, and the occasional pieces of litter—two-liter beer bottles dragging their labels, peeled-back can tops that once covered oiled herring, soggy cardboard cake circles—floating by. If a quake hit now, there would be no doorway for the two of them to stand in. Boulders would fall from the wall above. And then a wave would bear their bodies away.

Alyona got up. "All right, come on," she said.

Sophia slipped back into her sandals. Her pants were still scrunched up to the knees. Together, they climbed over the big-

gest rocks and back toward the city center. Alyona slapped mosquitoes out of their way. Though they had eaten lunch at home before
coming here, she was getting hungry again. "You're growing," their
mother had said, mixed caution and surprise, when Alyona took a
second fish patty at dinner earlier in the week. But she wasn't getting
any taller; she remained one of the smallest girls in her class, stuck
in a child's body, a container around a limitless appetite.

Between the gull calls came the sounds of people shouting and
occasional car horns. Wet gravel rolled under the sisters' feet. Hop-
ping up on a knee-high boulder, Alyona saw their path curve ahead.
Soon the stony wall at their side would descend. They would emerge
onto a rock beach that was busy on one end with food vendors,
blocked off at the other with a ship repair yard, and teeming with the
summer's crowds. Once the two of them got there, they could turn
away from the bay to look onto the beaten grass of the city's main
pedestrian square. Past that, and the lines of traffic, were a statue of
Lenin, a sign for Gazprom, and a broad government building topped
with flags. Alyona and Sophia would be standing in Petropavlovsk-
Kamchatsky's heart, and seeing on either side the swing of the city's
hills, its long ribs. A volcano's blue top beyond.

A bus from the center would take them home. Television and
summer soup and their mother's best tales of work. She would ask
them what they had done that day—"Hey, don't tell Mama what I
told you," Alyona said. "About the town."

At her back, Sophia said, "Why not?"

"Just don't." Alyona would not be responsible for whatever nightmares Sophia did or did not have.

"If it's true, why can't I ask her?"

Alyona forced air out her nose. She climbed down, wound her
way around a few heaps of stone, and stopped.

Two meters away was the man she had seen walking along the
water before. He sat on the path with his legs stuck out straight. His
back was hunched. From a distance, he had looked like a grown-up,
but now that she saw him better, he was more of an overgrown teen-

ager: swollen cheeks, sun-bleached eyebrows, yellow hair that stuck up in back like the quills of a hedgehog.

He raised his chin to her. "Hello."

"Hello," Alyona said, stepping closer. "Hi."

"Could you help me?" he asked. "I've hurt my ankle."

She squinted at his pant legs as if she could see through cloth to the bone. Their green knees showed smudges from the ground. Funny to see a grown man sitting as scuffed up as a boy who fell too hard in the school yard.

Sophia caught up to them, and her hand came to rest on the base of Alyona's spine. Alyona shivered her away. "Can you walk?" Alyona asked.

"Yes. Maybe." The man stared down at his sneakers.

"Did you sprain it?"

"I must have. These damn rocks."

Sophia made a pleased noise at the curse. "We can go get someone," Alyona offered. They were only a couple minutes from the city center; she could practically smell the vendors' cooking oil.

"I'm all right. My car is close." He reached up one arm, and she grabbed his hand and pulled. Her weight didn't make such a difference but it was enough to get him on his feet. "I can get there."

"Are you sure?"

He was wobbling a little. Stepping tenderly with pain. "If you girls would just stay with me and make sure I don't fall."

"Here, you go ahead, Soph," Alyona said. Her sister went first, then the man, carefully. Alyona walked after and watched. His shoulders were curved. Over the low wash of the waves, she could hear his breath come with slow effort.

The path opened up to the center: the stone-covered beach, families on the benches, gray birds flapping their wings over hot-dog buns, and ship-to-shore cranes extending their long bare necks. Sophia had stopped to wait for them. The bulk of the hill was behind. "Are you okay?" Alyona asked the man.

He pointed to their right. "We're almost there."

"To the parking lot?" Nodding, he limped along behind the food stands, generators chugging exhaust around his knees. The sisters followed. An older boy in a fitted cap skateboarded past the fronts of the stands, and Alyona looked forward in shame—to be saddled with her little sister, to be trailing behind a weak stranger. She wanted to get home already. Taking Sophia's hand, she caught up with the man.

"What's your name?" he asked her.

"Alyona."

"Alyonka, would you take my keys"—he shook them out of his pants pocket—"and unlock the car door?"

"I can do it," said Sophia. They were already at the crescent-shaped lot on the other side of the hill.

He gave the key ring to the smaller girl. "It's the black one there. The Surf."

Sophia skipped forward and opened the driver's side. He got in, exhaling as he sat. She held on to the door handle. The side panel's flawless paint reflected her body, dressed in purple cotton and rolled khaki. "How does it feel?" she asked.

He shook his head. "You girls really helped me."

"Can you drive?" Alyona asked.

"Yes," he said. "You're going where now?"

"Home."

"Where's that?"

"Gorizont."

"I'll take you," he said. "Get in." Sophia let go of the door. Alyona looked across the street at the bus stop. A bus would take them more than half an hour, while in a car they'd be home in ten minutes.

The man had started his engine. He waited for their answer. Sophia was already peering into his backseat. Alyona, as the older sister, took her time: she spent a few seconds weighing the city bus (its starting and stopping, its heaving noises, the smell of other people's sweat) against this offer. His softness, his bad ankle, and his boyish face. How easy it would be to be driven. The car would get them home quickly enough for a snack before their evening meal. Like feeding zoo animals or telling scary stories, this would be another daytime thrill, a summer-break disobedience to be kept between her and Sophia.

"Thank you," Alyona said. She went around the front and climbed into the passenger seat, warm from the sun. Its leather was soft as a lap underneath her. A cross-shaped icon was fixed to the face of the glove compartment. If only the skateboarder could see her now—sitting in the front seat of a big car. Sophia slid into the row behind. A few parking spots away, a woman let a white dog out of the back of a van for a walk.

"Where to?" he asked.

"Akademika Koroleva, thirty-one."

He signaled and rolled out of the lot. A pack of cigarettes slid across the top of the dashboard. His car smelled of soap, tobacco, faint gasoline. The woman and her dog were crossing the line of food stands. "Does it hurt?" Sophia said.

"I'm better already, thanks to you." He merged into traffic. The sidewalks were clotted by local teenagers wearing neon and Asian cruise-ship tourists posing for pictures. A short-haired woman held up a sign with the name of some adventure agency. As the center of the only city on the peninsula, this was the first stop for Kamchatka's summer visitors; they were rushed from their boat or plane to see the bay, then rushed away, beyond city limits, to hike or raft or hunt in the empty wilderness. A truck honked. People kept stepping out into the crosswalk. The light changed and then their car was free.

From the passenger seat, Alyona took the man's features apart. A wide nose and a mouth underneath that matched. Short brown eyelashes. Round chin. His body looked carved out of fresh butter. He was too heavy, probably. That must be why he had stepped clumsily on the shore.

"Do you have a girlfriend?" asked Sophia.

He laughed and shifted gears, accelerating up a hill. The car hummed underneath them. The bay drew away behind. "No, I don't."

"And you're not married."

"Nope." He lifted his hand, fingers spread, to show.

Sophia said, "I saw already."

"Clever thing," he said. "How old are you?"

"Eight."

He glanced at her in the rearview mirror. "And you're also not married, am I right?"

Sophia giggled. Alyona turned to watch the road. His car was taller than their mother's sedan. She could look down on roof racks and along the pink lines of drivers' arms. People were sunburned after this one day of good weather. "Can I put the window down?" she asked.

"I prefer the air-conditioning. Straight through this intersection?"

"Yes, please." The trees along the sidewalks were fat and green from this rainy summer. They passed ragged billboards on their left and concrete-paneled apartment buildings on their right. "Here," Alyona said. "Here. Oh." She twisted in her seat. "You missed the turn."

"You missed the turn," Sophia said from the back.

"I want to take you to my place first," the man said. "I need a little more help."

The road pulled them forward. They hit the traffic circle, and he kept going, into it and through and out the other side. "Help with your ankle?" Alyona asked.

"Exactly."

She remembered she didn't know his name. She looked over her shoulder at Sophia, who was looking back the way they came. "I'm just going to let our mother know," Alyona said, slipping her phone out from her pocket. The man reached off the gearshift to pluck it away. "Hey," she said. "Hey!" He was switching her phone to his other hand. Dropping it in a compartment of his door. The thunk the phone made when it hit the door's plastic bottom. "Give that back to me," she said.

"You can call when we get there."

Fingers empty, she was wild. "Please give it back."

"I will when we're there."

The seatbelt was too tight on her. It might as well have been wrapped around her lungs. She couldn't take in enough air. She was silent. Concentrating. Then she lunged in his direction, reaching for the door. The belt snapped her backward.

"Alyona!" Sophia said.

She went to unfasten the seatbelt but the man moved fast again, clamping his hand over hers, forcing the buckle in place. "Stop," he said.

Alyona said, "Give it back!"

"Sit and wait and I will. I promise." Under his hand, her knuckles were bent almost to cracking. If they popped in his grip, Alyona believed she would vomit. Her mouth was already wet with it. Sophia leaned forward and the man said, "Sit down."

Sophia sat back. Her breath was quick.

He would have to lift his hand sometime. Alyona had never wanted anything in her life, ever, as badly as she wanted her phone. Its black back, its grease-marked face, the ivory bird charm dangling off its top corner. She had never hated anybody as much as him. She was sick with it. She swallowed.

"I have a rule," the man said. They were already at the tenth kilometer, passing the bus station that marked Petropavlovsk's northern border. "No phones while I'm driving. But when we get there, if you can both behave that long, I will give it back, and I will take you home, and you'll be eating dinner with your mother tonight. Understand?" He squeezed her fingers.

"Yes," Alyona said.

"Then we're agreed." He let her go.

She tucked her hands, one sore, under her thighs, and sat up straight. She inhaled through an open mouth to dry her tongue. The tenth kilometer. Before it, buses stopped at the eighth for the library, the sixth for the cinema, the fourth for the church, the second for the university. Beyond the tenth kilometer were limited settlements, scattered villages, tourist bases, and then nothing. Nowhere. Their mother used to travel for work, so she told them what waited outside the city: pipelines, power stations, helipads, hot springs, geysers, mountains, and tundra. Thousands of kilometers of open tundra. Nothing else. North.

"Where do you live?" Alyona asked.

"You're going to see."

Behind her she heard Sophia, breath in-out, in-out, quick as a little dog's. Alyona stared at the man. She was going to memorize him. Then she turned around to her sister. "We're having an adventure," she said.

Sophia's elfin face was overexposed in the sunlight. Her eyes were bright, wide. "Yeah?"

"Yeah. Are you scared?" Sophia shook her head no. Her teeth showed. "Good."

"Good girl," the man said. One of his hands was off the wheel and hidden in his car door. Alyona heard the falling chime of her phone shutting off.

He kept watching them in the mirror. Blue eyes. Dark lashes. He didn't have any tattoos on his arms—he wasn't a criminal. How was Alyona only noticing his arms now? When they got back, their mother was going to kill them.

Twisted around, Alyona pressed her chest to the passenger seat. A pair of work gloves, palms coated red with latex, was tucked into a cup holder in the car's center console. The gloves were dirty. Alyona forced herself to look at Sophia. "Want another story?"

"No," her sister said.

Alyona couldn't think of a new one anyway. She turned back around.

Gravel popped under the tires. Fields of clumped grass flashed by. The sun made shadows short on the road. They passed the sign, dark metal, marking the turnoff for the city airport, and kept going.

The car shook under them as the pavement got worse. The door handle on her side was jittering. For an instant, she tried to picture herself taking hold of it, pulling the latch, tumbling out, but then—it was picturing dying. The speed, the ground, the tires. And Sophia. What would Alyona do, leave Sophia?

If only Alyona had been allowed to be alone today. Their mother always made her take Sophia along. Now—if something happened.

Sophia couldn't take care of herself. The other day she asked if elephants actually existed—she thought they'd gone extinct with the dinosaurs. What a baby.

Alyona jammed her fists against her thighs. Don't think about elephants. The leather under her was still hot, her lungs were tight, and inside her mind was all shimmery, the air waving up off fresh-pressed tar. She had told her sister that stupid thing about the wave. The piece of earth that disappeared. She wished she'd thought of something else. But now she couldn't undo it—she had to focus. They were in this car. They were headed somewhere. They'd be home soon. She had to be strong for Sophia.

"Alyona?" her sister asked.

She made her face happy and turned. The muscles in her cheeks were trembling. "Uh-huh?"

"Yeah," Sophia said. Alyona looked at her. Not remembering. "Yes, a story."

"Right," she said. The road was dusty and empty, lined by skinny trees. Leaning forward, rushing them along. On the horizon, the cones of the city's three closest volcanoes were exposed. The mountains were a line of sawteeth. No more buildings stood in their way. Alyona thought again of the tsunami. Its sudden weight. "A story," she said. "I will."

Olya came home to an apartment that smelled the way it always did when her mother was gone: a little sweet, a little rotten. Maybe Olya didn't empty the trash enough. She opened the windows in the living room, so a breeze could clean the place while she changed out of her school clothes. Then she lay on her back on the futon. From that angle, she could see nothing but sky.

Blue bleeding up to heaven. Forget the news reports, the stricter curfews, the posters of the missing girls—today was a perfect day to spend outside with someone. After the last school bell rang this afternoon, Olya had tried to get Diana to hang out in Petropavlovsk's city center, but Diana said she couldn't, that her parents were still worried, that they wanted her home. "It isn't safe," Diana said, with her voice high and cold in an imitation of adulthood. Diana's mother's voice oozing out of Diana's mouth.

Besides, best friends, Diana reminded Olya, didn't need to see each other constantly. This had been Diana's refrain for the month since the sisters' kidnapping. Olya couldn't tell from Diana's intonation, which these days gave every pronouncement a grown-up spin, whether this was Diana's idea or her mother's, but Diana certainly stood behind it. After those girls got lost, Olya and Diana saw each other just about never. Even now that the school year had started, Diana insisted: best friends had to put hangouts on hold, understand if there were sudden foolish rules in place, and bite their tongues instead of getting into another looping argument about danger.

Olya's own mother was not worried. She trusted Olya to look after herself. An interpreter, she was up north with a tourist group from Tokyo, turning their official guide's speech from Russian to Japanese so the peninsula's rich visitors could learn how to spot brown bears, pick late-season berries, and bathe in thermal springs. Whenever Olya's mother left, there was less music, less perfume, no lipstick-marked mugs in the apartment. Before the sisters vanished, Diana would come by Olya's during solo weeks like this one to waste away their afternoons together, but now summer vacation was over and everyone had become paranoid. Olya had no one to make noise with until her mother came back on Sunday with foreign candies as secondhand gifts.

Strands of hair brushed Olya's face. It was fine enough here by herself, anyway. Familiar, sun-warmed. Last spring, their year-seven history teacher had called Olya's hair a rat's nest in front of the class, and she had boiled with humiliation. But over this summer tourist season, as Olya turned thirteen years old, explored the city beside Diana, and felt her tangles tickle her neck, she thought again and liked that—a rat's nest. She was a beast. This was her hollow.

She sniffed—even the smell had stopped bothering her.

A truck honked outside and another one answered. She rolled over to scroll through the news feed on her phone: selfies, skate parks, classmates in short skirts. Someone's girlfriend had commented on his status with a heart. Olya clicked on that girl's profile, looked through all its pictures, and moved on, finding mutual friends, scrolling, clicking, skipping. She went back to her feed and refreshed. She stopped.

A girl they knew had just posted a picture of Diana. Diana's smile suspended between gleaming cheeks. Diana in her home clothes: that ridiculous red T-shirt, rhinestones lining the Union Jack on her chest, and those pink leggings cut off at the knee. Diana sitting cross-legged on her bed, and one of their classmates lying down beside her, and another leaning over in her school uniform while flashing victory signs with both hands.

Olya sat up. Texted Diana: *What are you doing?* Couldn't wait. Sent another. *Can I come over?*

She shoved off the futon, found her jeans, grabbed her jacket, filled her pockets with her wallet and lip balm and headphones and keys. After class, Diana had told Olya she had to go home, but maybe she meant Olya should come with her. Maybe both of them had misunderstood. Olya looked again at the picture. There were four of them together? The girl who posted it didn't even live in Diana's neighborhood. Olya refreshed. Nothing new. She made sure she had her bus pass, slammed the apartment doors, then ran down the stairs.

Outside, the sun was bright enough to make her wince. She hadn't been at the apartment for more than an hour, but already she had turned fully rodent, blinking at the light. As she hurried, she pulled fingers through her hair to smooth it out. Strands dropped behind. Olya had suggested they go to the center this afternoon—did Diana think she wanted to go only there? Nowhere else? Olya would've agreed to any other plan; Diana knew that. Diana knew Olya didn't want to be alone. Best friends did not abandon each other.

Olya's building's long parking lot was pitted under her feet. She tried leaping over the biggest potholes so she wouldn't lose her pace. Through her sneakers came the warmth of the asphalt, the pinpricks where gravel crumbled. In sunshine like this, Petropavlovsk-Kamchatsky's bad roads softened as if to heal themselves. Even the billboard over the traffic circle looked like new; the model in its center grinned with her hands in a foaming sink. Residential buildings around the intersection showed off their many colors on squares of apartments outlined by dark concrete seams. There were flaking pink and peach façades on the units with owners who once had money, navy reclad balconies on the units with owners who had money now. In the gaps between buildings, Petropavlovsk's hills lit up with yellow leaves.

Olya's mother was somewhere far north of that foliage. She was on a tourism agency's helicopter over the tundra. She was repeating *arigato* in the sun.

Hearing herself, the desperate noise of her shoes slapping, Olya slowed down, felt the light stroke her face, then hopped when she saw her bus rounding the traffic circle and had to dash to catch it.

The bus lurched as she went down the aisle. On either side were rows of people dressed in uniform after uniform: coveralls, scrubs, police dress blues, and blotted military greens. The workday was already coming to a close. Most of the men Olya passed looked like potential kidnappers. Useless, Olya's mother said about the whispers flying through Petropavlovsk in August, which described someone heavyset, anonymous. Olya's mother said the police's witness probably hadn't seen anyone at all. All that description did was make half the city's population seem sinister. Olya found a seat and checked her phone.

Diana hadn't responded. Quickly, Olya typed *???*, sent it, locked the screen, and shut the phone between her hands like that would undo her message. To keep herself from anything else, she looked out the window.

"Golden autumn" her mother called this time of year, brief and beautiful as a picture. All the trees on fire. And the air still inviting. More summery, really, than it had been all summer. Way off on the horizon, the Koryaksky volcano was capped with its first snow. Cold weather was coming, but it wasn't here yet.

By now Diana must've figured Olya had seen the picture. Olya crushed the phone between her palms. Were they all over there laughing at her?

This was how it went: the closer you were to someone, the more you lied. With people she hardly knew, Olya could say whatever she wanted: "That hurts" to the nurse giving her an injection, or "Put it back, I can't pay" to the grocery-store cashier. On her own, Olya was honest. Even more distant classmates couldn't constrain her—when the kid who sat behind her bragged about getting the highest score on their first exam of the year, Olya acted on the urge to turn away from him. Swiveling in her seat was enough to send a flare up her rib cage. Telling the truth was a thrill not found with her mother, who needed Olya to take merry care of their household, or with Diana, who made Olya measure herself out by request.

Just this morning, before the first bell, Diana had required that Olya be sweeter and softer-voiced. "My head aches when you talk like that," Diana said, face buried in her arms on her desk. Olya didn't say *Like what?* Instead she touched Diana's shoulder and whispered when their teacher entered the room. Olya was nice even as the words piled up like pebbles in her throat.

Comparing their math homework at lunch, Olya nodded along with Diana's corrections, though in that moment her best friend was ugly. Smug. As a little girl, Diana had been stunning; Olya, darker, rougher, used to admire the back of Diana's head in line as they were led from class to class. Now that they were in year eight, Diana was still pale blond and oval-faced, and her mouth was red, bright red, exciting like the lacquer of a new car, but she had a belt of acne across her cheeks. Her eyelashes had faded from startling white to transparency. In one minute she was lovely and in the next she was a ghost.

Olya pried open her clapped hands to look at the phone. Nothing.

During gym this afternoon, they had jogged together like always. Olya made sure their feet matched. She could have run faster, but love meant making compromises. With the people that mattered, Olya did not want to be free.

Traffic gathered under Olya's window. Lining the street were fiery orange and red leaves, bleached birch trunks, the sooty sides of buildings that had not seen new paint in decades. The bus's walls were covered in block-letter safety warnings from its Korean manufacturer and fat-marker graffiti from its Russian riders. It rolled her steadily downhill.

They slowed at the outdoor market on the sixth kilometer, where old women sold trinkets and pastries beside the cinema, then turned left toward Gorizont. Olya sank in her seat. Next to her, the plastic window shook in its frame. She hated to picture buzzing Diana's apartment without an invitation. Didn't best friends still need to be told they were wanted? She shut her eyes against the day, opened them, and called Diana, but the phone only rang.

She called again. She called again. They were getting close to Diana's stop. Phone pressed to her cheek, Olya squeezed past people's knees, showed her pass to the driver, and stepped off on the corner she knew so well. The phone rang in her ear. Olya hung up.

All Olya's rushing had made her a little too hot. Standing beside the bus shelter, three blocks from Diana's apartment, she dropped her jacket back a little so the breeze could hit her shoulders.

The buildings in this part of the city seemed cleaner. The neighborhood was called Gorizont—horizon—because it did look, poised above a golden forested gully, like it was welcoming the dawn. Olya usually liked coming here. She refreshed her news feed, now crowded with music videos, and went to the search bar to type in Diana's name. When the phone buzzed, Olya almost dropped it.

"Hi!" she said.

"This is Valentina Nikolaevna," said Diana's mother.

Olya pulled her jacket up. "Hello."

"Listen, Olya, we can't have you over," Valentina Nikolaevna said. No girls' voices rose in the background. The four of them must have been hanging out in a different room.

Olya squinted up. "I'm actually nearby already," she said. "I can just stop in."

Valentina Nikolaevna sighed. "Please go home. You should not be nearby. Isn't anyone concerned about you? We're frankly not comfortable with you two contacting each other outside of school anymore."

"What?" Olya said.

"Diana won't be able to talk to you outside of school."

That exact way of speaking Diana's mother had. Diana had imitated it, crisp, clinical, only this afternoon. Impossible to reconcile what Valentina Nikolaevna was saying with how she was saying it. A couple was walking toward Olya, and to give them room, she stepped to the edge of the sidewalk, where the pavement fell away into grass. "But why?"

Valentina Nikolaevna said, "You're not a good influence."

Olya wasn't a good influence. "How?" she said. "Why?"

One of the girls in that picture with Diana didn't wear underwear beneath her school skirt and got her first boyfriend in year five. Compare that with Olya, who had never even smoked a whole cigarette. All Olya ever did was attend to Diana, and copy her new music onto Diana's player, and keep a box under her bed of the cheap translated romance novels Valentina Nikolaevna didn't allow Diana to read. As a joke, Olya sometimes kicked Diana's ankles under the kitchen table when she was invited to Diana's for meals. She copied Diana's math solutions. That was it—that was all.

"There's nothing to discuss," Valentina Nikolaevna said. "Your behavior this past month has been frightening. When Diana told me today you suggested going to the center, I could not believe it."

"But—it's okay. It's fine."

"It certainly is not fine. You know that. And your family structure— the lack of discipline. It's uncomfortable to watch."

Olya pressed a hand over her eyes. A dog barked behind one of the clean buildings uphill. "Family structure . . . you mean my mom?"

"Who else could I mean?" Diana's mother said.

Olya was well disciplined. By her excellent mother, by the needs of her best friend, and by her own daily efforts, she had actually become so disciplined that her mouth refused to form around the right response, which was that Valentina Nikolaevna was an overbearing bitch. Instead, Olya said, "Don't talk about her like that."

"We're talking about you and my daughter."

"Because that's not right. That's not fair."

"That's how it's going to be. You can see each other in class, under supervision, but please do not bother her anymore outside of that. All right?" Olya could not answer. "Do you understand?"

"Yes," Olya said, because that was the only way the conversation was going to end.

"All right," Diana's mother said. "Thank you. That's all."

After Valentina Nikolaevna hung up, Olya wiped her phone off on her shirt and looked at the smeared blackness of it. Unlocked it. She scrolled to her own mother's name and stopped.

What would Olya say to her mother? *Valentina Nikolaevna thinks we're a bad influence.* And what could be the response? Olya's mother couldn't fix what had already gone wrong.

Valentina Nikolaevna had always looked hard at Olya's family. Since year five, when Olya and Diana started their friendship with nightly phone conversations, the woman had had something to say. An administrator at one of the city's elementary schools, she took information from student files to use in little strategies. The last time Olya came over, Valentina Nikolaevna had interrupted dinner to point with the television remote to the evening news, which was again going through the endless cycle of the police's comments and the civilian search party's plans and the missing girls' school pictures. "This never could have taken place in Soviet times," Valentina Nikolaevna said. Diana sipped her soup. "You girls can't imagine how safe it used to be. No foreigners. No outsiders. Opening the peninsula was the biggest mistake our authorities ever made." Valentina Nikolaevna put the remote down. "Now we're overrun with tourists, migrants. Natives. These criminals."

Olya should have kept her tongue behind her teeth. But she asked, "Weren't the natives always here?"

Valentina Nikolaevna's face, the same oval as her daughter's, tipped up toward the screen. She wore mascara to make her eyes look more alive. "They used to stay in the villages where they belong."

The sisters were last seen in the center, the reporter repeated, which meant nothing in a city of two hundred thousand people and a peninsula twelve hundred kilometers long. These warnings had already faded to background noise. When the missing girls' mother appeared on-screen, Valentina Nikolaevna said, "There she is." She pressed her manicured hand between Olya's and Diana's place mats to make sure she had their attention. "It's awful, isn't it? Tragedy. That poor woman . . . it's only her, no husband, and she works all the time. I read in the younger one's class records that she didn't come a single time to meet our teachers." She glanced at Olya then lifted her chin. "No father, and the mother gone. That's how such situations happen."

And Olya did want to say something then, to say *how dare you* or *shut up* or *I know you're talking about me,* but she didn't try. Diana would not permit it. Instead Olya stirred the soup in her bowl. Valentina Nikolaevna left her job every day at three; she sat in her renovated kitchen, with her dumb husband stuck at his research in the volcanological institute uphill, and made up her mind that Olya had a flawed family structure—because Olya's mother had a skill, because she had to travel, because they didn't have the money to hang around painting their lashes and watching the evening news and fretting over two random little girls.

Olya's apartment was different. Olya's mother was fun. When home, Olya's mother took the best clothes—a Red Army garrison cap, a silk robe bought in Kyoto during student months studying abroad, a leather pencil skirt—out of her closet for the girls to try on. If another friend followed Olya and Diana over, Olya's mother greeted them in Japanese. Her cheeks rose as she spoke, smiling but trying to hide her smile, so Olya always associated the language's swinging sounds with her mother's flickering happiness. A couple months ago, Diana, full of phrases she learned from anime, tried to answer, and Olya's mother propped one hand on her hip and chattered away. Diana tried for ten seconds to look like she understood. Then her mouth stretched in distress. Olya's mother smiled and said, "I'm joking, sunshine."

Silly and clever and trusting and fun. Olya could not ruin that by calling her mother now.

She crouched and hid her face in her elbow. On the other side of the street, trees rustled. Wind was passing through the gully. Cars kept going carelessly by.

Diana was Olya's friend. Her best friend. They had known each other since the first year of school. No matter how odd Diana could be, distant in one second and overeager the next, Olya loved her, and for all Olya's rattiness, her fidgeting during lessons, the sharp things she said sometimes to their classmates, Diana loved her back. Diana used to sleep over when Olya's mother was out of town. She combed out Olya's hair and braided it into one brown tail that became skinny as a chewed-up pencil at the end. Every so often she borrowed Olya's T-shirts to wear to school, the less laundered the better, because she enjoyed having their intimacy pressed against her back—and Olya did not influence her to do those things. Diana tried hard with Olya for the same reasons Olya did with her: out of history, out of desire, out of care.

The sleeve of Olya's jacket was warm from tears. When she straightened out her arm, she found a starburst pattern in the crook of her elbow, the folded place where the fabric had stayed dry.

She stood and texted Diana again. *Can you talk?* Watched the screen. No response.

Even if Diana were allowed to text right now, she wouldn't have anything new to say. Another excuse. The missing girls, Olya told her at least once a week, had nothing to do with them: they were little kids, bobbleheaded, the older barely into middle school.

After their last class today, when Olya mentioned going to the city center, Diana had brought them up again. As if that place were responsible for their absence. Olya said, "Can't you just call home and ask if you can go?" So while the other kids were shoving toward the street, while the teachers were shouting at everyone's backs, Diana said into her cell, "Okay, Mama. I know she is. I will."

Diana hung up and Olya said, "You didn't even try." Diana shook her head. "I tried," she said, and Olya said, "You didn't." Diana dipped her head so her pupils were covered by blond fringe. She looked albino in those moments. "She told me she doesn't want us going there. I listen when people tell me what to do," Diana said. The *I* was made to sound like an accusation.

I listen, Olya had not said. Olya was an excellent listener.

For example, Olya heard the truth behind what Valentina Niko-laevna was saying. That the missing girls were strangers—they didn't matter. That Valentina Nikolaevna just hated Olya, hated her mother, for no reason, because they were brave enough to survive on their own.

Another bus chugged to a stop in front of Olya. The wooden board propped in its front window announced its route: this one went not back to Olya's apartment but toward the other end of the city, the repair yard district and Zavoyko. She touched the pass in her pocket. She could get on it. She could do anything she wanted. She was alone.

So she did. The bus took her down past the police station, the hospital, the lines of flower stands and bootleg DVD vendors, the brand-new grocery store with its apples imported from New Zealand, the lower campus of the pedagogical university. Pressed on all sides by grown-ups, Olya held on to a hanging strap. It was too crowded to take out her phone so she imagined the picture instead. Diana didn't look good in it. Rounded shoulders and high-contrast whiteheads. A classmate tipping into the frame with her skirt riding up one leg. All of them shiny from the flash.

An old lady down the aisle was staring at Olya. Probably thinking about Olya's so-called frightening behavior. Olya shook her head so tangles fell forward and hid her face.

When the bus pulled over next, Olya got out, elbowing against late commuters. She emerged from their bodies to find the city center still busy. There was the statue of Lenin, his jacket billowing out and high school boys on their bikes around his feet. The wide municipal building, the brilliant burning hills. The volcano—only its peak was visible from here. To Olya's right, a pebbled beach sloped into the bay. St. Nicholas Hill stood to the side. Car exhaust mixed with the smells of grease and salt water. The missing sisters had been imbeciles to get themselves lost from this place.

Olya checked her wallet and turned toward the food stands.

"I have eighty-six rubles," she told a vendor, who nodded toward the posted price list. "Can I get a hot dog, though?"

"That's a hundred and ten."

"Can I get a hot dog without the bun?"

The vendor rolled her eyes. "You said eighty-six? A soda and a tea are eighty-five." Olya slid her money across the counter and took back a coin, a handful of sugar packets, a can of Coca-Cola. After a minute, she got her soft plastic cup of tea. Drinks in her fists, one hot, one cold, she picked her way across the stone-covered shore to a bench.

Cars passed behind her. Tiny waves lapped the rocks. Olya drank the soda first, while she listened to the current and the engines and the back-and-forth shouts of teenagers by the statue. Then she shook three sugar packets in her tea and drank that, too, tipping her head back until the sludge at its bottom slid to her tongue. Sweet grit in her throat.

People thinned out on the sidewalk. Birds swooped toward the hill. Ahead of Olya, the water twinkled with sunlight. The rows of cranes farther down the coast were motionless. Their operators were long home, with family, with friends.

The phone lay heavy in Olya's jacket pocket. She did not want to check her news feed. She might discover more pictures of the four of them, temples pressed together, hands cupping each other's faces, and the captions underneath: *best friends!* More of a threat than any stranger.

Though there might be no new posts at all. After today's conversation, maybe Valentina Nikolaevna had taken Diana's cell away. Maybe she kicked the other girls out. Maybe Diana, hearing what her mother had said, was going to cry all night.

And tomorrow before their first class, Olya would ask, "Why did you let her talk to me that way?"

Diana would say, "I couldn't stop her. She grabbed my phone and pushed me away while she called."

"You never stop her. She's sick in the head." Olya would have permission to speak plainly because she'd been treated so wrong, and Diana, after years of pretending she had the ideal family, would finally have to agree.

Together they would come up with a plan. Diana could say she joined a club so they would have two afternoons a week to go to Olya's apartment. No one else would have to know. Olya's mother would not tell. Olya ripped open another sugar packet, poured the crystals into her mouth, and chewed. The sugar dissolved on her teeth. The club could be called the Everybody Hates Valentina Nikolaevna Group or Escape from Mother Monster.

Swallowing, Olya brushed her trash onto the ground and lay across the bench.

The bay made such soft noises. Its ripples appeared a meter or two from shore. Far across the water was the dark opposite coast, the lights that marked where nuclear submarines docked, the layers of mountains that grew paler all the way to the sky.

The club could be called the Olya-All-Alone Brigade because Olya knew Diana wouldn't do it. She knew that. No club was happening. When it came to love and lying, Diana put Olya last every time.

The yellow in the sky was leaching into the ground. Lights across the bay flickered. Behind Olya, traffic passed without a break.

Her temples grew wet and cold from tears. Olya wiped her eyes. Someone's big hand closed around her right ankle and she sat up, terrified.

The detective from the news stood at the foot of her bench. He was tall, wearing sunglasses, imposing in his uniform. He let go of Olya's ankle and said, "Alyona Golosovskaya?"

Olya drew her legs back. Her breath was quick. "Do I look like that girl to you?"

"Surname, name, and patronymic."

"Petrova, Olga Igorevna." Was this how the police conducted their search? Bench by bench where the girls were last seen? No wonder the Golosovskayas were still missing. "I'm older than they are. I'm in year eight. And I don't look anything like her." Olya wiped her face with both hands before staring up at the detective's sunglasses to show him. The Golosovskaya girls had been tiny things, small-boned and fragile. Not teenage rats. Not Olya.

The detective evaluated her, then waved in dismissal toward the street. A police car, engine humming, sat at the curb. "How long have you been here?"

"Maybe an hour."

"Have you seen anyone suspicious?"

"I haven't seen anyone. I've seen you, that's all."

"No one else approached you? No man in a dark car?" Olya shook her head. "Don't roll your eyes while I ask you questions," the detective said.

"I didn't." It felt surprisingly good to lie to a stranger.

"I hope you understand the risk of being out here by yourself."

"Oh, I'm not," Olya said. She smiled up at him. "My mother just got out of work. She's coming to get me—she should be here any minute." On her lap, under her folded hands, her phone vibrated. Olya started. "That's actually her calling right now."

The detective shifted his feet. Though his glasses and clothes made him look authoritative, his face behind them was smooth, young. He pulled a business card from his back pocket and handed it to her: LT. NIKOLAI DANILOVICH RYAKHOVSKY. A number below and a shield embossed in the corner. "Call if there's anything you want to tell me," he said. "And let your mother know when she arrives that this is no place to leave a little girl."

Nodding, Olya lifted the phone to her ear. "Hi, Mama. Yeah? Soon? Great." She watched the detective leave, rocks shifting under his weight. The phone kept vibrating against her cheekbone.

After the detective climbed into his car, Olya lay back down. She looked at the glowing screen. One missed call from Diana. Unlocking her phone, Olya cleared the notification, opened their text message thread, and waited for Diana's explanation to arrive. She pictured its letters, its sloppy dashes. Nothing appeared. She locked her screen again.

To tell the truth, Olya did not want to call back.

Olya all alone out here. She liked it more than she knew she would.

In the sunset, the pebbles on the shore shifted their color from black and gray to honey. Amber. They were brightening. Soon the stones would glow, and the water in the bay was going to turn pink and orange. Spectacular in the city center, where people feared to have their pretty daughters go.

When Olya turned her head on the bench slats, electric white and yellow lines appeared in her peripheral vision. Her hair had caught the light. Her jacket, too, was sun-soaked. Saturated.

Golden Olya. She concentrated on that light in the air. Even if Diana came to the apartment to explain things or arrived at school with a written apology from Valentina Nikolaevna, or if Olya's mother, home next week, announced she found a new job, well salaried, teaching grammar in the university, so she would never have to leave for long again, or if the kidnapped girls returned, or if the police stopped patrolling, or if Petropavlovsk went back to normal . . . even if all of that happened, Olya wouldn't tell them how the colors changed here. She would share nothing. They would never find out they missed the most beautiful day of autumn, while Olya, alone, had been in its very center.

How good Olya would feel to keep this secret. How safe it was inside herself.

OCTOBER

We forgot the tent," Max said, turning to Katya. The beam of her flashlight flattened his features. His face was a white mask of distress. The forest around them was black, because they'd left Petropavlovsk so late—his last-minute packing, his bad directions. His fault.

In the harsh light, he was nearly not beautiful anymore. Cheekbones erased, chin cleft illuminated, lips parted, he looked wide-eyed into the glare. Katya and Max had been together since August and as of September were officially in love. Yet the tent. Disgust rippled through her. "You're not serious," she said. She caught the tail of her repulsion before it passed; she had to hold on to it, a snake in the hand, otherwise she would forgive him too soon.

"It's not here."

Katya handed him the flashlight and started to dig through the trunk. Shadows lengthened and contracted against their things: sacks of food, sleeping bags, two foam mats. A folded tarp to line the tent floor. Loose towels for the hot springs, a couple folding chairs, rolled trash bags that unraveled as she shoved them. Katya should have packed the car herself, instead of watching his body flex in the rear-view mirror this evening. Pots clanked somewhere deep in the mess.

"Max!" she said. "How!"

"We can sleep outside," he said. "It's not that cold." She stared back at his outline above the circle of light. "We can sleep in the car," he said.

"Magnificent." We forgot, he said, *we*, as if they together kept one tent in one closet of one shared home. As if they jointly made these mishaps. As if she had not needed to leave the port early this afternoon, drive twenty minutes south through the city to shower and change at her own place, drive thirty-five minutes north to get to his apartment complex on time, then wait eighteen long minutes in his parking lot for him to come out.

He'd told her earlier in the week he would bring his tent. His car, a dinky Nissan, didn't have four-wheel drive, so they were taking hers, and he had loaded such a stack of stuff into the trunk—enough to merit a second run up to his apartment, a return trip with his arms full—that Katya told herself he had it handled. Instead of checking she tuned her car radio to local news of a shop robbery, an approaching cyclone, another call for those two little girls. She gripped her steering wheel. Once Max finally climbed into the passenger seat, she said, "That's everything?"

Nodding, he leaned to kiss her. "Let's get going. Take me away," he said then. She checked the time (forty-one minutes late) and shifted into reverse.

Now they were going to spend the night in her mini SUV. Dependable as the Suzuki was, bringing them these four hours north of the city over roads that turned from asphalt to gravel to dirt, it made terrible sleeping quarters. Two doors, two narrow rows of seats, no legroom. The gearshift would separate them from each other. Neither of them would have space to lie down.

Katya sighed and Max's shoulders bowed in response. She wanted to touch those shoulders. "It's okay," she said. Her disgust slithered off to wait for his next error. "It's all right, bear cub, it happens. Would you gather us some wood?"

Once the flashlight was off bobbing between trees, Katya moved her car over the flattened patch of weeds where a tent was meant to be staked. The mistake had been hers in not asking earlier . . . next time they'd do better. Max was simply the sort of person, like so many others, whom she had to supervise.

Soil shifted under her tires. She didn't turn the headlights back on. Slowly, her eyes were adjusting to the dark. She had visited these woods as a child, and though she must be seeing two decades of growth, the birch trees in the starlight looked to her exactly as they had when she was a girl: aged and grand and magical. The world outside had steadily warped, become less predictable and more dangerous, while spots like this were protected. Here, there was no radio news, no city stresses, no schedule to disrupt. The tent had served as the last opportunity for disappointment. There was no reason left to get worked up. Katya had to remember that.

When she opened the door, her keys chimed in the ignition. She pulled them out and the nighttime rushed in. Bats chirping, insects whirring. Dry leaves brushing against each other at the tops of the trees. Max, far in the woods, cracking branches for their fire. The steady waterfall noise of the hot springs.

Katya cleared her head with the sounds. Max's company left her overstimulated; back in the city, at his apartment, she sometimes excused herself to the bathroom just to sit on the closed toilet lid and cool down. Even having him give directions from the passenger seat overwhelmed. His clumsiness, his sincerity, the shocking symmetry of his flawless face lit her up.

"It's the honeymoon phase," her girlfriends told her. Oksana, who worked with Max at the volcanological institute, said, "He's an idiot. It'll pass." But Katya had been with other men, even lived with one for a while in her twenties, and never gone on this kind of honeymoon. Max activated a new sense in her. Just as the ability to hear lived in her ears, taste in her tongue, touch in her fingertips, a particular sensitivity to Max was now concentrated below her belly button. He reached for her and her guts twinged. Her sixth sense: craving.

He might be an idiot, but it wasn't passing.

Craving him distracted Katya from other things. Like the tent, she reminded herself, as she took her headlamp from the glove compartment. Strapping it on, she got to work—organizing the bags, unpacking their groceries, reclining the front seats as far as they would go.

She stood back to scan them in the thin light of her lamp. Not very far at all.

Max returned to a set-up camp. Peeled potatoes bumped in a pot filled with stream water. Katya had laid half a smoked salmon belly, alongside slices of radish, tomato, and white cheese, on a plastic bag on the hood of her car, so they could snack before dinner. Together, in the brisk air, they built the fire. "I fell out there," he confessed once they had the flames going. He turned to show her a smear of dirt down his back.

She pressed her fingers to his shirt, the heat of his skin underneath. Ripples of muscle. "You're not hurt, are you?"

"Mortally wounded."

She had to laugh at the length of the stain. "You're not much of an outdoorsman, cub."

"I am," he said. "Give me a break, Katyush, it's dark."

"I know," Katya said. Still. Over the fire, the potatoes were boiling. She took her hands away from him to stir the pot.

The firelight painted them both orange and black. Max's chin, his fine bones, the tip of his nose, the knob that ended his jaw. Too handsome. With one boot, Katya nudged a burning log into better position.

The only other weekend Katya and Max had spent away together was the one in August when they first met. Oksana had invited Katya as a plus-one on a work retreat to Nalychevo Park. Katya did not dare refuse; Oksana's terrible summer, spent going through her husband's phone as their marriage crumbled, had hit its low only days before when she managed to walk her dog past the abduction of those little girls. Oksana had spent hours with the police as she tried to describe a kidnapper she hardly remembered. "The only reason I noticed him at all," she told Katya on the drive up to the park that weekend, "was because his car looked so good. I thought, Where does he get that cleaned? My van looks like trash after one turn around the city, while his shone." Oksana checked her mirrors and shifted into the left lane to pass a truck. "I told the officers that when they find this guy, before they cuff him and beat him unconscious, they have to ask him for his best car-wash tips."

"My God," Katya had said. "Are you sure you want to do this right now?" Their route from the city to the Nalychevo cabin forced them to ford six shallow rivers; after they parked, they needed to walk the last half hour of their journey through marsh. Katya found Oksana's commitment to the trip disturbing. If Katya were in the driver's seat, she would have turned the van around.

In the first days after the kidnapping, Katya was nervous, touchy, about everything. She looked at her friends like they were aliens. She could not fit the missing sisters in with the crimes she knew. Bribery, for example, Katya understood—she encountered corruption all the time at her job. Just today, inspecting the cargo of a new Canadian importer, she and the other customs officers discovered thousands of live turtles, their yellow arms waving in the light. ("What'd you do with them all?" Max had asked her this evening as they left city limits. "Threw them in the bay," Katya said. "No. Come on. Seized them for destruction." He'd pouted and she'd laughed.)

So smugglers, sure. Or poachers, trespassers, arsonists, drunk drivers, mauled hunters, men throttling each other in the course of an argument, migrant workers falling off the scaffolding at construction sites, people freezing to death over the winter months . . . these were regular items in Kamchatka's news. Two stolen little girls were a different matter. Oksana had passed only ten meters from the crime as it happened but managed to joke about it; meanwhile Katya studied the missing-person posters and frightened herself by thinking of what abductors she might run into one day.

"I'm obligated to do this," Oksana had told Katya during their drive. "I'm not going to stop going to work because I happened to walk Malysh at a shitty time." She passed another slow car. "Besides, what else am I going to do? Spend all weekend relaxing in my happy home?"

Katya had known Oksana more than a decade. Even when they met, as graduate students, Oksana had been cold, guarded, but intriguing. A fine distraction on a long trip. She spent the rest of the car ride briefing Katya on her colleagues. Boring, sloppy, and pregnant, Oksana said of the three other institute researchers in the group. "Don't bother with any of them. At least we'll have each other." Then Katya followed Oksana into a park cabin to discover a man who looked like a film star.

"Who, Max?" Oksana said. "Ugh."

From the first night, he put that tug in Katya's stomach. Petropavlovsk wasn't that big and the number of thirty-six-year-old singles in town even smaller, but she had somehow missed him for all these years, until Nalychevo. The two of them kept slipping off to fumble under each other's clothes behind the woodpile. They could hear the group's voices through the cabin windows. When Max whispered caution into Katya's mouth, she only wrapped her arms around his neck and pulled him closer. She wanted his beauty to blot out all fear.

And now Max and Katya were well on their way to domesticity. Max's coworkers had moved on from their initial burst of gossip; even Oksana was too preoccupied with her home life to do much more than shrug when Katya brought him up. Katya's male colleagues had backed off on asking her to drinks, and her female colleagues treated her marginally less like an old maid. On weekends, Max and Katya cycled through the city together. They kayaked the bay and barbecued by the ocean shore. He took her a few times to his climbing gym. This autumn trip to the hot springs was Katya's initiative.

Max stood to fetch her a strip of salmon. The long shadow of dirt showed on his thermal top. *I love him,* she practiced telling herself. It still sounded strange.

Sloppy, Oksana had warned Katya about him during their car ride, before any of them knew a warning was necessary. Once they arrived at the cabin, Katya was too busy picturing him pressed against the birch logs to listen. The Nalychevo group, like the rest of the city, had been hungry for news about the girls' disappearance. Oksana's story did not satisfy them. They looked instead to Max, who talked up his role in the volunteer search parties.

"Oksana's giving herself too little credit. Thanks to her, we have a description of the guy and his car. We're going to keep looking until we find them," he said. He even passed around the girls' school pictures on his phone.

Their supervisor—the boring one—squinted at Max's screen. "What type was he?" he asked Oksana. "Russian, you think? Or maybe Tajik? Did he look dirty?"

Their pregnant coworker stared straight ahead. Oksana raised a loose hand. "He looked like any other guy. Nothing interesting."

The supervisor pressed on. "What about his hair color? The shape of his eyes?"

"The shape of his eyes! You're asking if I stopped to chat about his genealogy? Was he half Korean, a quarter Chukchi?" Oksana laughed, a noise pinched and bitter. "I saw a big man. A big car. Two little kids."

"She saw enough," Max said.

Katya had flinched from the force of her inappropriate desire: the more Max spoke about witness statements, police debriefings, and grieving mothers, the more she wanted him. A confident man volunteering to undo danger. To find this eager heart inside this immaculate body . . . she hadn't thought it was possible.

Well. It wasn't, not entirely. The Golosovskaya sisters were still missing, and Max hadn't gone out with the search parties since the first of the month.

The tent tonight was only his latest plan to fall apart between promise and execution. Usually there was something endearing about that pattern—Max's ideas, his excitement, his fumbled follow-through—but Katya had not found it cute to watch the sun set over the mountains when they were hours away from this campsite. The trees on either side of the road north had darkened while Max kept turning his phone to try to recover a GPS signal. In came Katya's private, slippery distress.

The more time they spent with each other, the more she learned. If, one day, Petropavlovsk was flooded with lava, Katya feared she would know exactly which handsome researcher at the institute must have overlooked every sign of an imminent eruption. Max could not always keep track of what was important. He did not seem as excellent to her now.

For the length of this weekend, though, it would not matter. The smoke from their fire mixed with the steam off the hidden springs, making the night dense. Charred wood, rich sulfur, and cold earth: the smells of nostalgia. Her family had loved this place. After the USSR collapsed, there were no longer any restrictions on travel, no stop to movement; the Soviet military bases that had constrained the entire peninsula were shuttered, so Kamchatka's residents could finally explore their own land. Katya's family had gone as far north as Esso to meet the natives with their reindeer herds, west to see steaming craters, and south to pull caviar out of what had become unpatrolled lakes. She spent her youth in the brief reckless period between the Communists' rigidity and Putin's strength, and though she had grown into a boundary enforcer, inspecting imports and issuing citations, within herself there remained a post-Soviet child. Some part of her did crave the wild.

Katya allowed herself to blend with the darkness. "My parents used to take us camping every weekend," she said to Max.

"Yeah?"

"Practically." She took her last bite of fish and he passed her a soft slice of cheese. "As soon as the snow melted, we were out in the woods. They would give me and my brothers projects—following animal tracks, or finding different types of trees."

He touched her waist. "They were probably giving themselves some time to be alone."

"I don't think so," she said.

"Probably, though, right?"

When she was ten years old, her parents were . . . She had to count it. Her mother had only been thirty-two. Younger than Katya was now. She pictured them then, their long limbs colliding, and shivered. "Stop," she said, batting Max's chest.

"I'm joking," Max said. "I'm sure their intentions were completely educational. How'd you do with the projects? Find all your trees?"

"Of course we did," she said. "I was the oldest. I told them we weren't coming back without a full catalog of leaves."

Over soft potatoes and seared sausage, they told each other stories. How Oksana had said she'd discovered texts to yet another woman on her husband's phone—"Everyone in the office is talking about it. He's an asshole," Max said with his mouth full.

"They need to end it already."

"Good luck giving that advice," Max said. "I try as much as possible to avoid telling Oksana what to do." Katya put her plate down and rested her hands on Max's pant leg as he ate. Under her palms, the swell of his thigh.

Through the woods came the drunk rise and fall of people at a neighboring campsite singing. The trees made a black wall. Those voices, the ash in the air, and the chattering night put Katya in mind of their first weekend together. "Any updates from the search?" she asked.

Max shook his head. "And there won't be any more volunteers going out after it snows. Lieutenant Ryakhovsky says now that the girls may have been taken off Kamchatka."

"Come on," Katya said. "In what, a passenger plane?"

"I don't know. A ship."

"A cruise ship? To Sapporo?" If so, Katya's colleagues would have found them. Customs inspected every vessel leaving by air or sea.

And air and sea were the sole options for leaving. Though Kamchatka was no longer a closed territory by law, the region was cut off from the rest of the world by geography. To the south, east, and west was only ocean. To the north, walling off the Russian mainland, were hundreds of kilometers of mountains and tundra. Impassable. Roads within Kamchatka were few and broken: some, to the lower and central villages, were made of dirt, washed out for most of the year; others, to the upper villages, only existed in winter, when they were pounded out of ice. No roads connected the peninsula to the rest of the continent. No one could come or go over land.

"A cargo ship," he said. "Maybe."

Katya had to laugh. "Aha," she said. The campfire flickered over Max's face.

"I'm only repeating what the detective told all of us. It's possible, isn't it? Because we looked everywhere else. We found nothing."

Everywhere else, he said, as though Petropavlovsk-Kamchatsky's borders marked the edges of existence. "Those girls didn't leave the peninsula," she said. "Couldn't he have hidden their bodies? In a garage, a construction site, the woods?"

"We searched those places," he said. "For weeks. Covered every neighborhood."

"Outside Petropavlovsk, then," Katya said. "You don't think he took them along the road to the western coast? Or north?"

Max set his plate down. "Maybe he hid them in a national park. Threw them into a geyser."

"Maybe so," Katya said. He grimaced. "He could've done anything, that's my point," she said. "Driven them six hours away and enrolled them as his own children in some village school."

"Well, yes. There's no limit to the possibilities. So the police asked us only to focus on what was most likely," Max said. "This was someone from Petropavlovsk. Oksana described a white man."

"Did she?"

"Normal-looking, she said."

Katya did not disagree with that. Instead, she said, "She barely saw him. Anyway, it's not all natives out there."

"She saw his car," Max said. "A shiny dark car, she told us. No one comes down unpaved roads from the villages without getting covered in dust. So think: how would this person, living in the city, desperate, maybe crazy, most likely leave? He would know ships come and go daily. The detective says he could have bribed his way into a shipping container."

"Or maybe *this person* does what is unlikely," she said. "Went to a geyser after all. This is a man who preys on children. Who knows what he might be capable of?" She was talking like a tabloid reporter, she knew, but that post-kidnapping touchiness had crept back on her. If the police had solved the case already, she would not have to speak about such things. She did her job at the port well—the girls couldn't have left Kamchatka. Did everyone else in the city do theirs?

"Katyush," Max said. "Please. They're gone. The search isn't useful anymore."

Max, of all people, announcing what was or wasn't useful. Katya shifted her fingers on his leg and he fell silent.

They stooped under her open trunk door to change into their bathing suits. Away from the fire, they had goose bumps. Their breath fogged. Katya adjusted her shoulder strap and Max grabbed her. He backed her up until her legs hit the car. They kissed for a long time under the metal canopy, where neither of them had room to stand up straight. They bent into each other like two praying hands, but Katya wasn't thinking of God. She forgot lost children. She was thinking of Max, his arms, his fingers, his mouth, his fine teeth, the urgency under her skin.

Eventually she had to pull away. She was in her bikini and rubber sandals, and the cold had numbed her feet. Max, in his briefs and old sneakers, shone in the dark.

He crossed his arms on his chest. "So where are we going?" he asked.

The hot springs were calling—hissing, bubbling. "Come on," she said and led him away from camp, along the stream, on a narrow path through the trees until they came to the clearing that held the baths.

Five rubber-and-wood structures, aboveground pools fed by hoses from steaming wells. The rotten-egg smell of the springs was thick here. Warm mud slid under their feet. Katya and Max left their shoes at the base of one bath's stairs and climbed in. The heat dragged up their bodies. Katya exhaled into the swirling air. "Heaven," Max said, and she sank next to him in the sulfuric water to her chin.

The steam unwound. Above them were a million tiny stars. The night was blue and black, outlined by autumn constellations, and Katya, staring up, found a satellite blinking its way across the sky. The longer she watched, the deeper the heat reached inside her. It bled into her organs. It cleared her mind.

Near him, she couldn't think of anything but him. But when they were a little apart she returned to herself, and she liked that woman she came back to. Someone . . . capable. Someone who maintained standards, who met commitments, who produced results. Someone who would be disappointed in a man who acted the way Max so often did. She should be disappointed with him.

Max slid through the water toward her. His skin was slick from dissolved minerals. Against her back, the wooden edge of the pool was slippery. He tucked his fingers into her bathing suit bottom, and she stiffened, holding on to that bit of her own brain.

"Not here," she said.

"Then where?" he said in her ear.

"In the tent," she whispered back.

He pulled away.

That had come out meaner than she meant. "I'm joking," she said. Now he was far away from her.

"Huh," he said, his voice separated from his body by a wall of steam.

"It was a joke."

"Funny."

"Don't—" she started, and then stopped. Should she apologize? Try to explain? If he made mistakes, though, he had to accept the consequences. She, too, should accept the truth in front of her: what had propelled her into a weekend's liaison in August wasn't enough to sustain a relationship through the fall. Let alone beyond. The snake slithered up her throat. Max could not handle responsibility. Each of them would be happier in the long run with anybody else.

Between them, heat puffed. The water hissed and trickled.

Back at the car, they changed into dry clothes, stepped into sleeping bags, and hopped into their seats: Katya in the driver's, Max in the passenger's. Both of them already sweating from the effort. It was going to be a miserable night. She peeled off her long-sleeved shirt. "Should we buckle ourselves in?" she asked, turning to him, smiling, but above his sleeping bag, his shoulders were still high and offended.

This was their romantic trip. She leaned across the gearshift and he pecked her on the lips. "Night," he said.

"Good night." She pressed her forehead to her window, her swaddled feet against the brake. How much longer could she do this? Max was sweet, he was gorgeous, but he was not the hero they had both pretended . . .

The world outside was muffled. The chirps from the forest were quiet, then quieter, then gone.

She woke to a screech.

Shadow at her window. There was a man. A huge man, a killer—whoever'd taken those girls—Katya had slipped her bare arms out of her sleeping bag overnight, and she froze that way, half-unwrapped, terrified. A pane of glass away from danger. Her shirt was twisted. Her chest was pounding. It was almost light out. Not a man—a bear.

A brown bear on its hind legs. Scraping noises came from the roof over her head. The bear fell heavy on all fours beside her door, and dust puffed from its fur. It stepped forward, reached the front of the car, and stood again, its paws pushed to the navy metal of Katya's Suzuki.

From the other side of the windshield, pressed back hard on her seat, she could see its claws, each one huge and yellow and savage, resting on the hood.

"Max," she said through stiff lips.

He was breathing heavily beside her. The bear lowered its enormous head and extended a white-flecked tongue. It gave a long lick to the car's hood, where she'd laid out the salmon the night before. Her fault.

Max was shifting. His sleeping bag rustled but she could not turn to see. The bear kept dragging its face across the car. Max took her hand, and her breath caught. She felt his heartbeat in his fingers, and her own pulse, in her throat, in her mouth.

Their fire was long out. The trees around them were black brush-strokes against a powder sky. In this grainy dawn, the bear was hyper-real, saturated with color, its face dirty and snout bleached and eyes shining through the dimness.

One massive paw drew back across the hood. From under its claws, the terrible screeching came again.

Max released his grip on her. Shifted his hand up. Touched the center of the steering wheel. They sat.

"Yes?" he whispered.

The bear hadn't yet looked up at them. She couldn't swallow. Max waited, his hand hovering over her lap, until she was able to speak again.

"Yes," she said.

He pressed, and the horn exploded in noise. The bear flew back from the car. It hurried away awkwardly on two legs—a giant baby— then twisted onto all fours and ran faster than she could've imagined into the trees. Before the horn had finished blaring, the animal was gone in the darkness. And Max was laughing.

He opened his door and fell out, dragging himself free from the bag. "Holy shit," he said from the ground, which was streaked white with frost. Katya was trapped in her seat. In his thin T-shirt, Max came around the front of her car to peer at the silver scratches in the paint. "Holy shit!" He looked through the windshield at her. His face was bright and brilliant. "Katyush, it took your antenna!"

She leaned forward, but the horn beeped again and she jerked back. "It—" She opened her door and reached up, feeling the snapped-off place where her car's antenna had been. If they had slept in the tent? "Oh my God," she said. She was trembling.

He couldn't stop laughing. He was moving so quickly. She, meanwhile, was stuck, she didn't trust her legs, she couldn't stand, but only Katya or Max needed to be competent at a time, and for now he was the one. He looked wonderful doing it. He pulled her fingers off the antenna socket. Her body was cold with late-arriving fear; his mouth was hot. With both arms around his neck, she clutched him. She touched without stopping. She lifted her hips off the seat and he pushed her sleeping bag down. Against his cheek, she said the word *love*, she said *love*, but he covered her lips with his. She let the rest go.

NOVEMBER

There was a blister on Valentina Nikolaevna's chest that never healed. Dark, it rested four centimeters below her clavicle, on the freckled plain of skin exposed by low collars. It had started as a spot, and then the spot swelled, popped, scabbed over, and continued to grow. Under the skin was hard with blood.

Valentina told herself the blister would fade in its own time. After every shower, she covered it with a small adhesive bandage. The blister didn't hurt, but the look of the thing, a bodily purple when exposed, unsettled her. During the first week or two she wore the bandage, a few people asked what happened, but once a month had passed, nobody noticed it anymore. That fabric strip became her affectation—like wearing a silly hat or whistling. Her daughter ignored it. Not even her husband was bothered as they moved past each other on their paths through the house.

She believed the spot came from working outside. Maybe she'd pinched her skin leaning over a shovel. After Diana was born, Valentina had encouraged her husband to spend as much time as possible at their dacha all together; those two little girls' abduction in August only emphasized the point she had been making to him for more than a decade. Family, she told him, over everything. A child raised in a close and loving family would grow up safe and healthy. Just look at the alternative—parents neglecting their duties, children wandering the city center, elementary school students vanishing. Now Valentina made sure that every weekend was reserved for the three of them. Her husband grumped over the forty-minute drive out to the countryside, and Diana, ever more teenage, got sullen, but Valentina would not have it any other way. She tended her garden there in satisfaction. Afterward, she always discovered some new scratch or bruise or scab. Wonderful as keeping a place outside Petropavlovsk was, the dacha held its risks, too: Valentina got to have her own space, her own chunk of hardened soil, along with all the wounds and inconveniences that gave. Only in late fall, when her vegetables were buried under snow, did Valentina look up from the sink in her office's bathroom and really notice the humped bandage in the mirror. She counted on wet fingers. She had been putting that strip on daily since April, the better part of a year.

At forty-one, Valentina was far from old, but she was not unused to the peculiarities of the body. Her wrists were weaker these days. Her leg hair was lighter, thinner. If she ate sweets, her stomach cramped—the other women in the school office made a joke of offering her chocolates during their breaks for tea, and Valentina shook her head in wider swings every time. She and her husband, who had maintained a good distance from each other even as newlyweds, entirely fell off having sex a few years before, and she had seen her breasts deflate as if in answer.

Still, she had remained confident. Watchful of budgets at work and Diana's school assignments at home. Valentina prided herself on taking care of her domains: the garden, the kitchen, the school office's file cabinets. Certainly her own skin, she would have said. The reflection of this brown and purple circle made her fear all her competencies were about to disappear.

Adding up the months shook her. That Friday at lunch she finally went to the doctor. He leaned over her chest to study the mark: high as a knuckle, hard as a screw. The blister was small enough to fit under her bandage, but not as small as it once had been. "This is serious," he said.

She raised her fingers to the top of her sternum. She had come to his office for a tidier answer than that. "How serious?"

"You'll have to go to the hospital." She hardly knew this doctor—

she had seen him three years earlier, for a tetanus shot after she stepped on a hand rake. He had only just received his degree then. She chose this clinic because it was private and so offered a class of service, prompt, discreet, that she admired. On both that visit and this one, she hadn't spent more than ten minutes in the waiting room. She hadn't told anyone else that she was coming in today because she expected to make it back before the end of her lunch break.

"Why?" she said. "It's just a blister—can't you take care of it here?"

The doctor stepped away. He had given no sign of remembering her when he first entered the room. He turned toward her file. "We're not equipped," he said. "You've got to have it out as soon as possible. We'll call the hospital and you'll head over there straightaway."

Valentina collected her things, followed him out to the front desk, and paid her bill. The girl at the desk took her cash and got on the phone. Valentina no longer had her bandage on. The blister, which for months had sat uncomplainingly over one rib, felt hot. She touched the skin around it but not the thing itself. It might have opened again but she was afraid to look down and check. Hanging up, the girl nodded at the doctor. The girl's face was rude, slack, careless. "Fine," the doctor said. "Go on, they're expecting you."

The walk across the parking lot left Valentina's eyes sore from snow brightness. Wet flakes rushed toward her car. She let the engine warm and scrolled through her phone past her husband's name. What comfort could he give her? He was no authority. Instead she called the school to say she would be out for the rest of the day.

"Is everything all right?" her colleague asked.

"It's nothing," Valentina said. Her voice was steady enough to convince even herself.

"Well, when you do get back, Lieutenant Ryakhovsky wants you to call him."

Valentina straightened. "Did he come in again while I was gone?"

"No. He called."

"Did he say anything about the Golosovskaya girls' father?"

"No."

Snow was piling up on Valentina's windshield. She flicked the wiper switch. "Try harder to remember," she said, as crisp as she could manage.

"I do remember," her colleague said. "The whole thing was very memorable. He asked you to call and then he hung up."

Valentina raised her hand toward her blister before gripping the steering wheel instead. This was exactly what she had feared—she allowed one disruption, a bandage removed, and her whole life crumbled after. She was missing important calls at work and allowing the younger women there to speak disrespectfully to her. She would have to discuss it with the principal when she returned.

"I suppose if there were any urgent matter the detective would ask for my cell number," Valentina said. "So I'll deal with it on Monday."

Her colleague wished her a good weekend and hung up.

Valentina shifted into gear, rolled into the wet lines made by other people's tires, and started to climb the hill that would bring her to the regional hospital. She would wrap this up then go back to her routine. Nothing to worry about, she told herself—just a chilly day, a task pending, a quick doctor's visit.

But the last did worry. Valentina had never had surgery. Scares like that belonged to other people. Over the years, her peers had lost gallbladders and appendixes; Diana had drainage tubes put in both ears when she was tiny; even Valentina's husband, dependable as he was, had to have his tonsils scooped out as an adult. Slices were made in all their bodies.

Now, after long luck, Valentina's own death was catching up to her. That was crazy to think—but wasn't it true? The clinic doctor said he couldn't handle it.

It was cancer. Was it cancer? If it were cancer, wouldn't he have said? It was cancer. Sometimes doctors didn't let their patients know. If the illness was untreatable, they kept that bad news private and allowed people to die in slow ignorance. Valentina's grandmother went like that, coughing up chunks of her own lungs. Valentina's mother shut the door to the bedroom and said, "The flu." The whole family knew and said nothing.

Cancer. But that was a different time, a different world. Back then

Valentina wore red kerchiefs, and pledged allegiance to the party, and practiced handstands in their building's courtyard, and came home to the hot mixed smells of boiling water and yeast. These days, they tell you. And there's treatment—and tests. And it wasn't cancer, because if it were, she would be sure about it. The blister throbbed. Signaling right, Valentina pulled into the hospital's driveway, under the painted metal arch that announced the facility, and into a half-full lot.

The hospital was poured from concrete. As a child, Diana had cried in this waiting room until her pretty face swelled up. Valentina and her husband dressed the girl in a clean set of pajamas for her surgery. Should Valentina have brought spare clothes for herself? No, that was excessive; they needed a set for Diana because she had to enter a sterile operating room that day. But Valentina's procedure would be brief. It did not compare. The mark on her chest was tiny.

The waiting room was saturated by the sweet, stale smell of liquor. Old men sat with their hands pressed to their bellies. A mother kept her arm around her daughter, whose leg was streaked with iodine and blood. Valentina moved past them to the desk of the admitting nurse. "Dr. Popkov called on my behalf," Valentina said.

The nurse squinted at her computer monitor and looked up. A native woman. Valentina wanted to return to her doctor's office, the good clean Russian service offered there. "Of course," the nurse said. She tapped a few pages together on her desk. "Sign these, then come with me." Valentina pulled her purse higher on her shoulder. Around them, the sick people groaned.

They took a corridor back, leaving the bleeding children, drunken men, and scuffed plastic chairs behind. The nurse led her up two flights of stairs. On the third floor, they emerged into a wide hall, tiled in green squares and lined by shut doors. The nurse opened one door, took Valentina past a row of red medical waste bins, and motioned her into a room. "Dr. Popkov—" Valentina started to say.

The nurse shook her head. Native as she was, she seemed responsible. Brows fading to gray, mouth unsmiling but not unkind. "Someone will be in to see you soon," she said.

The door closed. Valentina put her hand in her purse and felt for her phone. But who could she call? What would she say? "I'm at the hospital and I don't exactly know why," she'd tell her husband, and he would go silent, or question her, or laugh. The idea that Valentina did not know. It was laughable. It put her to shame. So she shut her bag again. The room was small, windowless. There was no chair, so she hoisted herself up to sit on the exam table. Her slacks snagged on its cracked vinyl.

She reminded herself to sit up straight. Over minutes, though, her spine hunched, her belly folded. All these months she had told herself it was a common blood blister. She couldn't trust her own judgment anymore. "Serious," the doctor had said. Her hands were shaking. To stop them, she crossed her arms over her chest and listened. The room made a clean case around her. No sound from outside the door.

The next person who came in, she would ask to explain the diagnosis. If they didn't know, she would say, "Call my doctor, please." She opened her purse again to find the phone number. The purse held her clinic receipt, filled out in pen by the front desk girl; her wallet, suede, rubbed shiny at its corners; a pack of mints; a tube of mascara; folded attendance records. She had forgotten she brought those papers with her. She took them out and smoothed their creases over her thighs. Tardiness and truancy. The student names in their columns wavered.

Valentina focused on the door handle. It did not turn.

The ground outside the dacha would be frozen after today's cold. Tonight at the apartment she would thaw pelmeni for her husband and Diana. Nothing too taxing. It would be dark by the time she got home; she might be tired, and a meal pulled from the freezer was the best she would be able to manage. That, a stiff drink, and a long sleep. In the morning she would call the detective at the police station for an update on his investigation. Then she and her husband and Diana would drive out of Petropavlovsk as a family.

For the first few weeks after the Golosovskaya girls' kidnapping in August, her husband fancied himself the expert on abduction. He worked at the volcanological institute with the crime's only witness. He came home with reports of black cars and no bodies as if neither of those things was communicated daily at the city's markets. But once the police turned their attention away from the fat ghost created by a distracted dog walker, Valentina became a better source of information. Lieutenant Ryakhovsky hung around the elementary school office to speak with her long after he had finished his interviews with the girls' teachers and classmates. Valentina would open the sisters' student files before the detective and discuss suspects while he reviewed their papers. He'd come by that very Monday, when the snow started, to tell her they were stopping the civilian searches entirely.

"Because of the weather," he said. "That, and the fact we haven't found a thing."

Valentina swiveled in her chair to face him. His broad shoulders were bowed over her desk as he flipped through Sophia Golosovskaya's file. "Did you look at airplane or ship logs? The city is so crowded in the summer."

"That's true," he said.

"A foreigner could have easily taken them." Valentina's parents had moved to Kamchatka in 1971 for her father's officer assignment, so she grew up knowing the region at its best. Military funding used to stuff the stores with food. There were no vagrants, then, no salmon poachers, and no planes but Soviet military jets overhead. The peninsula was so tightly defended that even other Russians needed government permission to enter. But when the country changed, Kamchatka went down with it. A whole civilization lost. Valentina was sorry for her daughter, for all the children, who would grow up without the love of a motherland. "My husband thinks a Tajik or an Uzbek," she said.

Lieutenant Ryakhovsky glanced up from the papers. He didn't bother to talk to the other women in the administrative office; Valentina, as the office manager and the keeper of records, was the sole person he had to consult. "You heard the suspect description?"

Valentina pursed her lips. He continued: "The witness didn't say a Tajik."

"That's what I told my husband. But she didn't describe a Russian, either," Valentina said. "She didn't describe anyone in particular. Just a man."

He shrugged. "That's all we've got. In any case, the girls probably aren't with anyone, foreigner or not, anymore. We've been dragging the bay for bodies." He flipped a page over. "My supervisors don't believe they could've been taken off the peninsula."

"People behave like Kamchatka is an island," Valentina said. "I have my doubts. If it's so secure, how do migrant workers keep showing up? Where do the drugs in our schools come from?"

"Are there drugs in our schools?" he asked.

"Most likely."

His head was back down. "We haven't seen any evidence of that."

Valentina crossed her ankles around the column supporting her seat. Week after week, the detective visited, studied the same folders, sought out her ideas. She must have something to provide. She asked, "You got nothing from gas station surveillance cameras?" He didn't respond. "How about people's dash cams? No one driving that day happened to record a dark car?"

"We asked the public. We reviewed all the footage turned in. Nothing."

"You interviewed the mother?"

"Many times."

"No boyfriends? Nobody hanging around?" He shook his head. "It must have been a stranger, then." Sophia's last school picture looked up at them from the file. The girl's pale eyebrows, skinny lips, sharp chin. Valentina could not remember the older sister outside news broadcasts, but she knew she had seen this one the year before in the school halls. Her narrow shoulders. Her high voice. Her colorful backpack thudding on her hips as she turned in to a classroom. Valentina could not bear to picture her in the hands of a sexual predator. "What about the girls' father?" she asked.

"We interviewed him by phone. He lives in Moscow."

Valentina gripped her fists in her lap. "But no interview in person?" she said. "How did he sound when you spoke to him?"

"As you would expect," Ryakhovsky said. "Upset."

Upset, the detective said. Distressed just as much as one might think he ought to be. Yet unwilling to come back to help search for his daughters. Valentina felt in her chest the welcome flush of certainty. She had always been able to know, to interrupt, when something was wrong. "Nikolai Danilovich, stop. This is it. The girls went with their father."

Ryakhovsky looked at her. "No one reported seeing the father. There's no record of him traveling in or out."

"Don't you know how easy it is to fake records or suppress reports? How much influence does this man have?" Ryakhovsky was listening now. She could tell from the narrowing of his eyes that he was interested in what she said. "Their mother works for the party," Valentina said. "You're aware of that, aren't you? The children of someone with those connections don't just fade away. But if their father is in touch with someone more powerful . . ."

"He's an engineer," Ryakhovsky said.

"An engineer living in Moscow," she said. "So he's rich. Everyone there is in someone else's hand. And he's from Kamchatka originally—he knows who to pay off here. He could've picked up the girls that afternoon, driven straight to a garage afterward, and arranged a boat off the peninsula. A private plane."

The detective's voice was low, focused. "Corruption."

"Nothing else," said Valentina. "After such a crime, a silence like this isn't natural. You have witnesses out there who simply decided not to speak. Their mouths have been stopped up by cash."

"Someone in this city knows something," Ryakhovsky said. "That's what I've been telling the major general all this time. And the father . . ."

"That's precisely it," Valentina said. "You're right, somebody knows. Look at the father's friends in Moscow, and start at the top, the ones with the power to pull a kidnapping like this off. That's how you'll discover the girls. They are right there in their father's house."

The detective's eyes tight on her. Even thinking of that look now, Valentina was warmed. Her husband had only carried gossip about the case from his office; Valentina had actually influenced the investigation. That fact was enough to remind her: she ran a workplace and a household. She was powerful.

Dinner tonight, the dacha, the phone call with the detective to follow up. The sisters found and her colleagues awed. Picturing her future, Valentina saw her chest clear, blisterless.

She concentrated on that. The return to routine. Skin left without blemish. Only the tiniest scar, which would fade away by next summer. The documents grew damp in her hands, and the vinyl cushion bent to her weight. She practiced telling herself that everything was going to be fine.

At last the knock. The vision she had of a world set right was shuttered. "Yes," Valentina called, as a doctor opened the door.

"Good afternoon," the doctor said and turned to the empty counter, the locked cupboards. "Undress, please. Everything off."

Valentina pinched the papers harder. Their edges were soft from her sweat. Then she stood up. She put the pages back in her purse and zipped it shut. Already half-naked without her bandage on, Valentina began taking off her clothes. She peeled off her boots and socks and put them in a corner with her purse, then folded her jacket and scarf and rested them on top. Then her sweater, her blouse, her slacks. Her back was to the silent doctor. The sooner she finished undressing, the sooner the exam would be over, the sooner she could go. She unsnapped her bra. The warmth from the lined cotton leached into her hands. Quickly, she took off her underwear, too, wrapped it with her bra into a neat little package, and set them on top of the pile.

She stepped back to sit up on the table. Her skin rubbed on it now.

As soon as Valentina was settled, the doctor turned around. She was dressed in white with a blue cap covering her hair. "No one's with you?" she asked. Valentina shook her head. "And you didn't bring clean clothes? A gown? That's all right," the doctor said. "It's not so important."

The doctor came close enough that they could smell each other: the doctor sharp with antiseptic wipes, cold circulated air, the waxed fruit flavor of lip balm tucked underneath, and Valentina slippery with nervousness. Valentina had skipped lunch. She was empty as a box bobbing in the sea. Bending, the doctor studied the blister; she touched it with her dry fingers. Then, carefully, she palpated Valentina's neck, jaw, ears. She felt the span of Valentina's chest and spent a long time pressing Valentina's right armpit.

"What's the matter?" Valentina said.

"We don't know yet."

Valentina studied the doctor's face to see if that was a lie. "Dr. Popkov said it was serious."

"Who?"

"My doctor. From the Medline clinic. He sent me here."

The doctor straightened. Even hunched on the table, Valentina was a little taller. The doctor's lips were pink and her cheeks were broad, giving her a sweet, apple-faced quality that belied the firmness in her fingertips. "He was right. We're going to take it out," she said. "Come with me."

Valentina pushed herself off the table. She moved toward her clothes.

The doctor said, "No, we have to keep it sterile there. Leave your things in this room."

But Valentina was exposed from her sagging neck to her frozen feet. Blister and breasts and ass and pubic hair. This was different from a bedroom or a bathhouse. Not even her husband had seen her like this—bare under fluorescent lights. Salt-covered. Filled with cancer—she could be filled with it. A naked patient in the regional hospital.

How many doors did she go through to get to this room? She could not remember. She wanted back the native nurse, who had looked at her humanely. The men waiting downstairs—had they also been shown into examining rooms? Were they sitting, round and jaundiced, just outside?

"I must have misheard you," Valentina said. Her teeth were chattering.

"It has to stay sterile and you have no gown. It's only a meter or two," the doctor said. "Come on." She was finished with Valentina's body, ready to move on.

Valentina was not. "Shouldn't I—"

The doctor was opening the door.

"I should bring my jacket," Valentina said.

The doctor shook her head. "This is no time to be modest. You are going into the operating room."

Naked, Valentina followed the doctor out into the short passageway with the red bins. If they walked straight, they would enter the hall, which had been empty before and now could hold—anything. Anyone. Instead they turned left, toward a double doorway. Valentina's ID, her money, her keys, her clothing: all her things were in the room. She covered her chest with her arms but air poured across her hips and thighs. The doctor didn't pay any attention.

Valentina held herself together as much as she could. Only two meters to cross. Under her feet, the passage's floor was gritty. The number of dirty bodies that must have gone this way before. Was this how everyone else she knew had entered surgery—naked, frozen? At the limited mercy of authority. Even Valentina's grandmother had died with more pride.

She gripped her own arms. Squeezed the muscle, stemmed the thought. Died. No. Yes, her grandmother had died, but Valentina was living, she had a job, a family, chores to finish, calls to make. She did everything right. Tragedy belonged to other people.

Yet she was going to the operating room. Her smallest toes were bent with age. Valentina's mother had raised her to wear slippers indoors . . . to keep their house clean, to keep them safe. Her mother warned her that cold traveled up a woman's feet to the rest of her body. That's how girls go barren, her mother had said. Valentina had repeated the same warning to Diana, along with cautions against strangers and lessons on friendship. Family over everything, Valentina said. But cold feet might not matter anymore.

A meter ahead, the double doors. The doctor silent at her side. The passage leading them to surgery was lined by red buckets. They contained . . . what? Blood? Gauze? Cut-out growths? They likely contained body parts, discarded nightmares. Valentina cast her eyes down at the floor. An animal smell, like dirt, waste, death, was thick in her face and on her bare skin. She did not deserve this. She was not prepared. Seized by fear, she looked again at the row of closed bins and pictured entrails.

Her feet moved her. Somehow, she walked. Her private clinician and the solemn nurse and this doctor here had directed her this way, toward these twin doors, so she continued, repeating to herself that this was what she must do. The passageway was already ending. The doctor put her hands on the doors. "Valentina Nikolaevna," she said, and Valentina looked up. A little kindness broke into the doctor's round face. "Don't worry. They'll numb you."

The doctor pushed the doors open. Valentina found a team of strangers waiting in gloves, gowns, and masks. Her life was left somewhere behind.

"Go ahead," the doctor said.

Valentina was so cold. The smell from the passage had sunk into her tongue, so she tasted soil, tasted blood.

She thought, In an hour this will be over; she thought, Everything is going to be fine. It will. It has to be. No more blister. No more cancer, if it was cancer—it'll be plucked out at the root. She told herself it would pass quickly. She thought, After this is done, I will never tell anyone about what has happened. No one at the office, and not the detective, not my husband, not my daughter. I will come back to the woman I was.

Ksyusha always knew about the dancers—growing up in Esso, she saw troupes perform at every minor holiday—but she was not interested in them for herself until her cousin came down from their village. Then Ksyusha's desires began to shift. The cousin, Alisa, had enrolled in the same Petropavlovsk university where Ksyusha was now entering her fourth year. For safety in the city, their mothers decided that the cousins should live together. The two girls rented a one-bedroom apartment at the bottom of a city hill and moved their things in: Ksyusha's neat from the tiny room she had kept in the dormitory, Alisa's dust-covered after the twelve-hour bus ride south from home.

The state of their suitcases wasn't their only difference. Alisa was only seventeen, with hair highlighted from black into orange-yellow above an adorable face. She had enrolled in school for philology, while Ksyusha studied accounting. During their first week of classes, Alisa met more people and learned more gossip than Ksyusha had over the last three years. And sometimes Alisa stayed out late. Once or twice, ignoring the missing-person posters that went up around the city that August, Alisa chose not to come home at night at all.

"I don't like it," Ruslan said.

He was still back home in Esso. This far into Ksyusha's long-distance study, she and Ruslan had worked out a system. They talked on the phone every morning, every night, and he made the long drive down to visit at the end of every month. They kept that schedule for both their harmony and Ksyusha's supervision; ever since she moved to Petropavlovsk, he had made sure to remind her how quickly a girl could get lost. His warnings got even louder after descriptions of the Golosovskaya sisters crept three hundred kilometers north to their village. Now Ruslan, in hearing of her cousin's social life, had one more reason for concern.

"Alisa's trustworthy. You know her," Ksyusha said into her cell. She was home in her pajamas, gray sweatpants and a navy tank top, though the sun had not yet set outside the apartment windows. It was early September. The fall semester had barely begun and he was already finding faults.

"Alisa was always a little loose. Maybe she's gone crazy in the city," he said.

"She didn't. She just has lots of friends."

"Is she out right now?"

Ksyusha was silent.

"Where are you?" Ruslan asked.

"I'm home," she said. "I told you." The line was fuzzy with his breath. She went over to the microwave, set it for one second, and let it go off. "See?" she said over the beeping.

"All right," he said, calmed. The microwave, the TV, or Ksyusha's guitar—these were the domestic sounds that now gave him comfort. When Ksyusha was in the dormitory he had relied on the voice of her roommate. In the days before this school year started, when the apartment was brand-new, Ksyusha had tried to put her cousin on the phone for support, but Ruslan never believed what Alisa said. "Is anyone over?" he would ask. "Is anyone over? Is anyone over?" So Ksyusha mastered different alibis.

.

In the middle of September, Alisa decided to join the university dance troupe. She had already gone to one practice and liked it enough for both of them. This group was small, far from the professional ensembles that traveled the country showing off Kamchatka's native folk dances to packed halls. It was more like a home troupe—it was just for fun. "We need this," Alisa argued to Ksyusha. It would be a way, she said, to spend more time together, to honor their roots. "And a way to get you out of the apartment in the afternoons."

"I can't dance," Ksyusha told her. They were in the kitchen waiting for their soup to finish simmering. The room smelled like hot cabbage, sorrel, salted butter, and chicken broth.

"Sure you can," Alisa said. "Even if you can't, it doesn't matter. You'll stand in the middle and look beautiful." She lifted her palms to Ksyusha's cheeks. "Look at you, Ksenyusha. You'll be our star."

Ksyusha withdrew. "Don't make fun of me." Ksyusha looked like their grandmother, pure ethnic Even, with bones broad, eyes hooded, brows faint, and nose turned up. Her face was too native, she knew, and hips too thick for stardom.

"I'm not." When Ksyusha shook her head, Alisa shook hers back without stopping, then started drawing her hands in rhythm through the steaming air.

"I don't know," Ksyusha said. "I don't want to." Even so she had to smile.

"You don't know or you don't want to?" Alisa beckoned, her fingers slim as little fish.

"I'm not good at that sort of thing."

"Neither am I!" This wasn't true—Alisa had danced as a child in one of the village troupes and knew the old steps. Having said this once, though, Alisa would never take it back. She did not accommodate.

All Ksyusha could do was make a face in response. "Stop messing around," she said, though she liked it, Alisa's stubborn body and skinny, quick arms.

"This troupe's all students. It's nothing special. Come on, let's see you give it a try."

Ksyusha, lifting the ladle, nodded along to her cousin's movements. Three years into university—classes each day on management or statistics, course work every afternoon, oral exams ending her semesters with the validation of top grades so she could maintain her scholarship, and her thrills relegated to summers in Esso, winter holidays in Esso, and the single weekend each month when Ruslan drove down—Ksyusha wouldn't mind trying something new. Still, she said, "I'm not going to."

"See you bob your head. You already are."

This was how Alisa changed her: not with invitations to go out but with the joy she carried in. "Ruslan won't let me," Ksyusha said, as her last protest. But as soon as Alisa's mouth twisted up, Ksyusha saw those words were a betrayal.

·

He was her first and only love. At night, Ksyusha passed into sleep by remembering his qualities. The scratch of his voice, the bunched cords of his muscles, the hair under his navel, the deepening creases of his eyelids. Seven years Ksyusha's senior, Ruslan used to come over to play video games with her older brother, Chegga, and she would sit behind them to stare at Ruslan's back. That sunburned neck above a baggy T-shirt. She used to dream about being old enough to kiss him, and now she was, and did, and it was everything she had hoped for.

The next Friday that Ruslan came, she wrapped herself around him on the futon. Alisa entered the apartment that night, unlaced her sneakers, and passed the couple on her way into the bedroom; she didn't shut the door fully as she changed out of her street clothes. "Did Ksyusha tell you about the dancers?" she called.

Ruslan tipped his face down at Ksyusha. His mouth was already thinner, expecting bad news.

Alisa came back out in leggings. "We have a university ensemble," she said over the noise from the TV they had been watching. "They're looking for more girls. Wouldn't she be perfect?"

"She doesn't know how to dance," Ruslan said.

"Oh, she could," said Alisa. "You just show up, anyway. You don't have to be any special talent for this one. They take whoever arrives."

He scoffed at that. "I don't remember any university ensemble," he said—he had studied in the city for a couple years, before he and Ksyusha started dating, when he was still Chegga's video-game friend and she was still a schoolgirl. Though Ruslan left before receiving his degree, he found himself a decent job with Esso's public utility, where he ran waste pipes and rebuilt the rotting wooden bridges that crisscrossed their village's rivers. Ksyusha's parents liked him now even more than they had when he was young.

"The group's been around a while, but it's not for white kids," said Alisa. "That's probably why."

"Alisa," Ksyusha said.

"He doesn't mind."

"So it's that kind of group," he said. "Drums and skins." He squeezed Ksyusha's shoulders, then released her and stood. "You don't think they'd take me?"

"Not unless you got a really good tan," Alisa said.

He squatted and held out his arms. "Even if I show them what I can do? Hey!" Stomped forward in imitation of the dancers they grew up watching. With one fist, he mimed holding the straps of a frame drum, and he swung his other hand out wide to pound its face.

Alisa jumped toward him. Her hands lifted. She twisted in place, head sliding one way over shoulders sliding the other, and so on down the length of her body, hips swinging, knees together swaying, heels lifting, and feet pivoting in harmony. She whooped while Ruslan stomped around, singing loud in a nonsense version of the Even language, and Ksyusha laughed because they wanted her to laugh, although the way they moved gave her pause. The way they looked—Ruslan strong and wiry, the stubble copper on his jaw, and Alisa synchronized before him. Natural partners.

Ksyusha reached out to grab her cousin's elbow. She stopped Alisa, without seeming to try. "Is that how the troupe does it?"

"Something like that," Alisa said, plopping down on the futon beside her. "You'll see for yourself." Alisa lifted her gaze to Ruslan. "Unless she's not allowed?"

He straightened. "What does that mean?"

"I thought maybe you wouldn't let her." Ksyusha stared at her cousin, but Alisa was refusing to turn from Ruslan.

"That's not how this works," he said. To Ksyusha, he asked, "Do you want to join this thing?"

She was struck, nervous, trying to measure the flush under his eyes. "I don't know. I thought you might—I thought it might be a good way to stay connected. To keep myself thinking of home."

"Do you need extra help thinking of home?" he said. "Fuck. Go on and do it, then. Who am I, your father? Have I ever told you how to spend your time?"

Every Monday, Wednesday, and Friday afternoon, the troupe met in a university music room. Ksyusha reported back to Ruslan after the first practice: "It was fine. Awkward." Alisa had made everyone shake Ksyusha's hand. Some of the group members were at the pedagogical university, like the two cousins, but a couple others studied at the technical university up the hill, and one boy was only in year ten of high school.

"How many guys in this group?" Ruslan asked.

Ksyusha didn't know how accurately to answer. "Maybe it's half and half," she said. Everyone indigenous: Even, Koryak, Itelmen, or Chukchi. Black-haired, brown-eyed.

"Watch out for yourself," Ruslan said. "They'd love to be company for my native queen."

He was the only white person who could tease her that way. He grew up with her family, after all. Her first week in the city, when she was Alisa's age, some other students had mocked her. "Where are you from?" one asked before class. "From Esso," she started to say. "From the reindeer herds," someone else said under her words. And then they laughed.

She sat in mortified silence for a moment before raising her fingers to her cheeks. Pressed them there, cold circles against flushed skin.

She, who won a gold medal for academic excellence at her high school graduation and earned a funded spot in the university's accounting course, was laughed at. It was her voice. The bouncing intonation of her sentences—she sounded northern. And her skin, her hair, the angle and narrowness of her eyes. They recognized her immediately, these city kids. They spoke to her like she was part herd animal herself.

At home, everyone knew Ksyusha and her brother not as a future banker and a photographer but as herders' children. Her family was one of too many sources in Esso for meat and pelts. Her grandparents and father lived in the tundra with their animals year-round, while her mother stayed with her and Chegga in Esso until classes ended. Then it was back out to the wilderness. Ksyusha had missed every school vacation when young, yanked with the rest of her family to work in the empty rangelands while the white kids in the village got to play soccer in the streets and duck under roofs when it rained. Esso in the summertime was beautiful—cottages were repainted in primary colors, gardens grew dense with vegetables, the rivers ran high, and the mountains that surrounded the village turned dark with foliage. Ksyusha did not get to appreciate the sight until she was seventeen years old. Instead, the demands of herding ruled her summers: kilometers on horseback, legs aching, back sore; mosquitoes crawling under her clothes and staining her skin with her own blood; hurried baths taken in freezing river water; Chegga's teasing; her mother's resentment; her grandmother's reprimands; the men's arguments over money they should've earned at last year's slaughter and debts they planned to pay off at this one; the way Ksyusha's mind itched for a book or a pop song or a television show, anything to break up the monotony of the landscape, grass and hills and shrubbery and antlers and horizon; the rich metallic taste of reindeer meat in her mouth for breakfast, lunch, and dinner, for days, weeks, for months, until they got to go home again.

Dirty. Stupefying. That herding camp stink—smoke, meat, mildew—had somehow followed her all the way down here.

At least she had Ruslan. The rest didn't matter. Ksyusha passed her days waiting for his texts, drifted away from other students when classes were dismissed, looked forward to two-hour-long phone calls, and fell into bed thinking of him. Her look, her sound, her smell—he was used to it. No one else would love her like he did.

·

The troupe's director, Margarita Anatolyevna, was a short Koryak woman who kept her hair pulled back with a scarf. The dances she taught were traditional ones, and she instructed the group as if they all led traditional lives; after she passed out leather straps to the boys for the herders' dance, where they squatted and kicked and spun the straps in the air, she yelled over the music to be heard. "Higher! How do you lasso deer like that?" In the tundra, Ksyusha's father, uncles, and grandfather stepped into a whirling herd of thousands, snared running bulls, and wrestled the animals to the ground. But some of these dancing boys had never lassoed anything. They let the leather go slack in their hands. City people, Ksyusha's father would say if he saw.

Yet not all of them were that way. There was Alisa, and a couple of girls from settlements near Esso. A graduate student named Chander from Palana, far north, beside the Sea of Okhotsk—Ksyusha's brother had met his current girlfriend in the fishing camps up there. One boy studying at the technical university came all the way from Achavayam. His face was flat and frown permanent. He hardly spoke enough for Ksyusha to hear his accent.

Being with the troupe was both engaging and awful. It was fun, for the first time since Ksyusha moved to the city, to tell Ruslan about something beyond her classes, even if that something had to do with a high school kid and a bunch of fake lassos. At practices, she took the spot behind Alisa and concentrated on matching her cousin's movements. Legs together. Toes planted. Heels raised. Knees bent. The music, recordings of drums and buzzing mouth harps, was just a little too loud, and Margarita Anatolyevna yipped along to keep the beat. In her jeans and knit sweater, Ksyusha, dancing, sank out of her thoughts. Into her body. Her breath, her muscles, the throb of her blood. Ahead of her, Alisa's sunny hair swished in time.

But the group also made things more complicated by swallowing her once predictable days. Margarita Anatolyevna had a no-distraction policy, so Ksyusha was forced to keep her phone in her bag through every practice. For the first couple weeks, Ksyusha kept coming back to a screen clogged with messages. *What are you doing now? Important. If you don't answer me . . .*

Hard to miss Ruslan's texts, hard not to check in with him, hard to let him pass out of her mind when the percussion started through the speakers and then let him back in when the music switched off. Hard to master the movements—Margarita Anatolyevna showed the girls how to fall to their knees, bend backward, arch their spines until their ponytails brushed their calves. The boys worked on making their drums thud in unison, and Margarita Anatolyevna shouted at them to work harder. In the evenings, Ksyusha and Alisa shimmied across their bedroom.

And hard to try to make friends. Alisa seemed as ever to manage fine, but Ksyusha couldn't remember trying before. Everyone else in the world Ksyusha cared about had known her since she was a little girl.

She liked them, though, the other dancers. Despite the gaps in their knowledge—the fact that some of them had never been near a wild animal and others had enrolled in university before seeing a public bus—the group members felt more familiar than the other people she'd met over these years in Petropavlovsk. Understandable in a way the white kids were not. And she liked Margarita Anatolyevna, who encouraged them to chirp like baby birds calling for food. Out of anyone else's mouth, that description might have sounded ludicrous, but Margarita Anatolyevna said these things without seeming silly. The dances had old names, pagan ones, about gods and nature, so Margarita Anatolyevna taught them how to move in pagan ways. This one requires that you all look like fish, she said, so push your arms back. Wriggle. Open your throat, wide, wide, and drink seawater down.

·

For the partner dances, Ksyusha was paired with Chander, the one from Palana. Of all the boys, he seemed the best. He was smart, earning his doctorate by writing a dissertation on Paleosiberian language families, and he paid attention when the director gave instructions. He was tall, he moved well. That first practice when Alisa pushed Ksyusha's hand into everyone else's, a few of the kids had tried to flirt: "Does every woman in your family look so good?" one had said. But Chander only asked where she was from and said the group was glad to have her.

Alisa, meanwhile, was paired with the student from Achavayam. They were an unlikely match, with him tense, taciturn, and Alisa so talkative she was studying German and English to give herself multiple languages to converse in. Sometimes she slipped steps from childhood into routines they were learning, and he noticed, and they argued, Alisa spilling out three defenses for his every critique. Alisa said she couldn't stand him, though Ksyusha believed that wasn't true. It probably flattered Alisa to have someone pay such chaste yet close attention.

Still, Ksyusha wouldn't have wanted to dance across from Alisa's partner, with his narrow-eyed focus and his disapproving mouth. Instead, Chander showed her the way. In one dance, the girls stood and the boys knelt before them. They bent into each other, the girls stroking the air to draw their partners closer to their waists. Through the minutes the music played, Chander kept the same easy look he'd had on the first day they met. His face, from smooth forehead to straight eyebrows to high lifted chin, was undisturbed. Once they went through the routine a few times, he got up, the knees of his jeans whitened from dust, and said, "You're getting a lot better, Ksyusha." She was practically panting from the movements. But she agreed.

·

"Tell me about today," Ruslan said.

Ksyusha was under her sheets in the dark. The phone balanced against her cheek and her hands rested on the little hill of her stomach. Her cousin's bed across the room was empty. "It was crazy," she said. "Margarita Anatolyevna yelled at Alisa, and I thought for a second Alisa might yell back. She had that look." The city around

Ksyusha was filled with what was sure to provoke him: those two lit-tle girls disappearing by the shoreline weeks earlier, photocopies of their class pictures tacked to the university bulletin boards, civilian search parties climbing the hills, and policemen watching Ksyusha on the street like she was the dark-skinned villain responsible. Ksyu-sha wanted Ruslan to think of her protected. She wanted the same with her parents, her brother, so she kept any calls with them mild. Better not to speak of what might worry them. Stories of school and dance were all she offered.

.

The afternoon break between classes ending and practice beginning lasted an hour and a half. Alisa and some of the other group mem-bers used this time to go to a café, where they shared a slice of cake or a pot of black tea, but Ksyusha couldn't afford that. Anyway, part of her understanding with Ruslan was that they informed the other person wherever they went. Visiting a café with others would lead to too many questions. So she came to the practice room early instead, and sat outside it doing homework until Margarita Anatolyevna arrived to unlock the door.

One October Wednesday, Chander also came early. Ksyusha saw two legs in athletic pants over her textbook and looked up to find him standing there. "What are you reading?" he asked.

"Nothing," she said.

He sat down next to her, his long body folding. His bag was dropped between them. He reached over to take her book. "Not nothing," he said, turning it in his hands. "Econometrics." He gave the book back, took out a notebook of his own, and started to work.

.

Chander was the son of a fishing family. In his hometown, they went out in the winter for seal, the spring for pollock, the summer for flounder, the fall for crab. "Anatolyevna would call it traditional," he said.

Ksyusha had never tasted crabmeat. Chander rested his head on the hallway's tile wall. They were alone as always outside the locked practice room. "Next time I go back," he said, "I'll bring you some."

She had never had a friend like him. So comfortable, so quickly—out of all the people Ksyusha grew up with and the classrooms full of student strangers, Chander became the exception.

During practices, he was polite to the other members. Margarita Anatolyevna liked him especially, and corrected him quietly when she would not hesitate to shout at anyone else. But he didn't seem close to anyone in the troupe but Ksyusha. When Margarita Anatolyevna switched on the music for the herders' dance, he glanced at Ksyusha and raised his leather strap, which he knew irritated Ksyusha, which he knew made her laugh. In moments like this, she thought, We're friends. The idea came as a surprise and a comfort every time.

She looked forward to tasting crab. She asked Chander for more stories about Palana: if he wished he were still living there, if his family ever came to Petropavlovsk to visit, if he had ever met her brother's girlfriend. No, no, and no, Chander said, though he softened those answers with tales from childhood. He described a place, four hundred kilometers north of Esso, with a population a fraction the size of Petropavlovsk's but apartment blocks built just as tall. It was cased in ice in the winter and had a windy avenue leading straight to the sea. Pylylyn, he told her, was the town's Koryak name. Meaning "with a waterfall." His language came from farther back in the throat than the Even she had grown up hearing from her grandparents. When she tested its vowels out, he smiled.

He talked to her about Esso, too. The one land route south from Palana was a snow road passable only from January to March, yet Chander had been in Ksyusha's village dozens of times, because the flights he took between Petropavlovsk and Palana were often grounded in bad weather at Esso's tiny airport. Chander had spent days in her village waiting for storms to settle. When she showed him a picture her brother had taken of the house they grew up in, he took her phone in both hands, zoomed in with his thumbs, and peered at the screen. The hall was warm. They were sitting on their jackets.

"I've seen this house before," he said. "Do you have a cat?"

Ksyusha squinted at him. "We used to."

"A black and white one. I remember."

She drew back. "No, you don't," she said to test him.

"I do." Infallible. Was this how all doctoral students behaved? He tapped on the screen to bring the picture back to normal size. "A blue house with a black and white cat sitting on the fence."

"And me inside."

"And a Ksyusha inside."

Letting him scroll through the rest of her phone's camera roll, she explained each image. "My mother, in our kitchen, making dinner . . . She doesn't like this picture. She doesn't like, in general, to be photographed. She doesn't consider herself pretty." Chander shook his head in silent comment on the wrongness of that, and Ksyusha was grateful once more for how appropriate he was. The picture only showed her mother's profile. Disagreeing out loud would have been too much. She flicked to the next image. "This is home, again, the same night, the meal she made." Chander looked hard at the food, the furniture, before flicking to the next. "Ruslan," she said.

In the picture, Ruslan was in a white undershirt, close to her camera, half-stern, half-smiling. She had straddled his lap to take it. She hoped Chander couldn't tell. Heat rose to her cheeks as she attempted to look at the shot like it was new.

"He's handsome," Chander said.

Again, the right response. Her nervousness left her. "He is." They went through her phone until Margarita Anatolyevna reached over their heads with the key to the practice room.

·

Chander, too, had dated a Russian. A white girl. In the city, while he was an undergraduate—they were together four years. "I loved her," he said. Ksyusha was looking at the side of his face, the line of his jaw, his high cheeks, and his blunt nose. "She was willful, though, and we would fight—she finished university the year before me, with a degree in international relations, and she wanted to leave Kamchatka for work, but I—"

"Nymylan," she said. Another Koryak word Chander taught her. It meant "settled"; he taught her "nomad," too, when she first told him how her grandparents moved with the deer. (He had asked her for Even words in return, but while she understood her family's language fine, all she could confidently pronounce was the vocabulary she'd been taught in elementary school. Asatkan, nyarikan: "girl," "boy." Alagda. "Thank you.")

Chander turned his head toward her. His eyes were dark gloss. "Exactly," he said. "I couldn't do it." His voice was as gentle as a finger down her spine. He turned back to face the tiles, which reflected spots from the overhead lights. "I was supposed to move into her apartment when I graduated, but she kept talking like that would only be the first of many moves. First Petropavlovsk, then Khabarovsk, then Korea or something, some new frontier. I told her I needed time to think. She said, Fine, take all the time in the world, we're done, and I said, Fine, if that's the way it is. I took my final exams and went back home to help my father. She and I didn't talk for a month and a half. As the summer was ending, I started to call her, but her phone was never on. I thought she'd blocked my number." His eyelashes were straight, short, dry. "Know where she was?"

"No."

"Australia."

"Australia!"

"Australia," he said. "She went to be an au pair. Her friends told me, eventually. One called me . . . I'll never forget that conversation. She's still there. In the end of ends, I heard she got married."

This girl was unimaginable. Ksyusha and Ruslan had not yet started dating when she applied to university, but if they had, she would've kept living in Esso and enrolled in distance learning instead. As it was, she thought of dropping out her whole first year. Her parents had insisted on her taking the scholarship, and she did want to get a diploma with honors, and Ruslan agreed to keep an eye on her—those were her only reasons to stay this far from home. Anyway, she was almost done. Only a year and a half until graduation.

"Australia," Ksyusha said. "Do you miss her?"

"No," he said. "I'm done with that."

"What, with dating?"

"With those girls." His calm look. A top lip with no bow, and stubble dotting black under the skin. "With Russians."

Ksyusha had heard her people talk like that before. She pushed her head back hard against a tile. "You don't mean it."

"I do."

"Well, you should be smarter."

"Uh-huh. You haven't noticed by now that you can't trust them? They don't care about us the same way they care about themselves." Ksyusha waited for Chander to voice an exception: Ruslan. He did not. In her thoughts, Ruslan slipped from a man she should defend to a man who might abandon—Ruslan could leave her so much more easily than she could leave him. Chander was talking about something other than love now, though. "Something happens in the north," he said, "and no one pays any attention. Then the same thing goes on down here and it's news. When we had the fuel crisis in 'ninety-eight—remember? At home we had a solid year without power. People froze to death in Palana. But the ones in the city talk like it was just three or four months of cold, like the rest of the time didn't matter because it only happened to us."

Ksyusha hadn't heard about this. During the fuel crisis, she was barely old enough to form memories.

"Or the two Russian girls who went missing over the summer," Chander said. "The media report on it constantly. They show us the police officers and the girls' mother until I know those faces better than I knew my own neighbors growing up. But what about that Even girl who disappeared three years ago? Who covered that? Who even thinks about her anymore?"

"The girl from Esso?" Ksyusha asked. "Lilia."

He paused. "You knew her."

"No," Ksyusha said. "Not really. Her brother worked in our herd one summer, that's all. How would you know her?"

"I didn't." Chander looked at Ksyusha with new care. "I heard about it when I flew through Esso that fall."

Ksyusha had just started university when that girl went missing. Lilia Solodikova. Though Lilia graduated from the village's high school only the year before Ksyusha, their paths at home had hardly crossed. Even Chegga, who had taken Lilia out on a few early dates, lost track of her in their teen years. Lilia got low grades. As small and sweet-looking as a child, she acted shy in public, but was rumored by classmates to be reckless with men. People said Lilia would let them touch her for money. The boys in Esso shouted after her as she passed. There were times that Ksyusha, up late on a school night, looked out her bedroom window and saw Lilia's tiny body crossing into the shadows of the village's athletic field.

Lilia and Ksyusha were nothing alike, yet for months after Lilia's departure, Ksyusha heard warnings from her parents, her brother, and Ruslan. *Don't go out alone. Guard yourself. Avoid temptation. Don't talk to strangers.* Chegga swore Lilia had been murdered by some jealous admirer. It was then that Ruslan first decided Ksyusha and he should stay constantly in touch.

"What do you think really happened to her?" Chander asked.

"She ran away," Ksyusha said.

"Is that true?" he said. "I heard that she didn't leave a note. She just vanished."

"She . . ." Ksyusha hesitated. "I was already living here in the dormitory when everyone in Esso started talking about it. I can't say what happened exactly. But Lilia wasn't so happy at home. Her brother, the one who worked that season for my grandparents, was crazy. Their older sister had already left because of it. Their father was dead, and their mother was . . . Lilia didn't have much to keep her living there." She smiled at him. "Maybe Lilia also became an au pair in Australia."

He did not smile back. "Did she seem like the type of girl to run away?"

"Who's the type of girl to do anything?" Ksyusha said. She shrugged. "I really didn't know her, Chander. I don't think we ever spoke."

"I see," he said. "I just think about her story when I see the city news."

"No, I do, too." Lilia, who was nothing more than a source of minor rumors when she and Ksyusha lived blocks away from each other, had changed the course of Ksyusha's life in the three years she'd been gone. The constant check-ins now. The scheduled calls.

Ksyusha supposed she ought to be grateful. If that girl hadn't left her life behind, would Ruslan have been so determined to hang on?

"The village police gave up on her instantly, didn't they? Meanwhile, the city sends out search parties for the missing sisters all the time. People here talk about those girls even when they have nothing to say," Chander said. "A white guy, a dark car, in the city center . . . that could be anyone."

Chander was right. In the city, Lilia might as well have never existed. Reporters behaved as though the sisters from this summer invented the act of vanishing.

But that obliteration was almost certainly why Lilia left. Ksyusha wasn't like Lilia, but she understood her. The belief that nothing better would come. The trap of family. The plan in secret for some desperately needed escape. Ksyusha used to feel that way, too, before Ruslan chose her.

Chander's hands hung over his bent knees. His voice was low. "A white guy and a dark car. They're everywhere," he said. "You know what I mean." She did. Chander wasn't insulting Ruslan. He wasn't even talking about his own ex-girlfriend. He was onto something else, deep common knowledge, an ache that was native.

·

Would Chander and Ruslan get along, if they met independent of her? They were only a year apart: Ruslan twenty-seven, Chander twenty-six. Ruslan was pricklier, fiercer, and Chander more studious, but if they'd gone to the same school or been called to a single army unit, they would have inevitably become friends. One white, one Koryak, each never doubting where he belonged.

.

Ksyusha skipped practice the last Friday of November, as she had the month before, to clean the apartment for Ruslan's visit. Alisa was staying at a friend's house for the weekend ("I don't want to hear your gross noises together," she'd said and laughed when Ksyusha squirmed). On her knees, Ksyusha scrubbed under the bathtub, while music blasted from her phone. The place smelled like synthetic oranges. She was aware of her kneecaps on the linoleum, the weight of her body warm with sweat, and all at once it hit her. She was happy. Really happy. Happier than she had ever been before.

All fall, small pleasures had come together. Now Ksyusha had everything: a boyfriend, a new home, good grades, a talent, and a friend.

Ksyusha's conversations with Ruslan were different from those with Chander. More about the neighbors they knew, the memories they shared, the desire that continued to knot them together. And when Ruslan was stressed, behind schedule on a project or harangued by his supervisor, he used their phone calls to search for her missteps. *Where have you been? Who were you with? Are you sure?* She squeezed out the sponge. The orange smell was sharp in her nose. She didn't mind his scrutiny, really, because she became better when he watched her, but how nice it was to spend three afternoons each week away, saying just what she thought to a person who would only sympathize.

How lucky to have them both. Ruslan in all his tempers, and Chander coming to her with no demands. After years of telling herself that Ruslan in Esso was enough—more than enough! she corrected herself—Ksyusha had discovered someone new in Petropavlovsk. Some people had nobody and nowhere; Ksyusha now had two.

By the time Ruslan arrived, it was nearly eleven. Before starting his drive he had worked in Esso all morning leveling dirt roads in preparation for asphalt. They had sex on the futon, his body electric, his duffel bag dropped on the floor and the air still sparkling from cleaning solutions. Ksyusha touched him with a fresh appreciation.

His voice afterward was rough in her ear. "Did you have a good day waiting for me?"

"I had a perfect day," she said.

He studied her. "What'd you do?"

She slipped a hand over his side to pull him closer. The smooth lines of his ribs slid by her fingers. "Nothing," she said. "Nothing at all."

They were quiet. "Show me one of your dances," he said finally, as he had the last time he came down, and she pressed her face against his chest and groaned but got up. The moonlight through the window lit her bare body. He rolled onto his side to get a better look.

Ksyusha chose a favorite routine. The paired one where Chander knelt. She leaned forward, beckoning. Shimmying. Her fingers pulled the air. She tipped toward Ruslan, then away, and stepped and spun and smiled. He watched her. For years, in bed with him, she had been shy, self-conscious, but she turned now in the white light without hesitation. Forward. Away again. Her body flowed into the next step, the next, as easily as a river following its course. She was dancing well. She knew it. She moved as if these steps didn't want a partner—as if she were fine on her own.

·

In the hall on Monday, Ksyusha was glad to see Chander coming. His sneakers and jeans and cheap waffle-weave shirt: they all made her soften. "I thought I'd see you here," he called.

"Where else would I be?" She had her book out to hold while she waited, but started to put the text away as he got close.

"Practice is canceled," he said, and she stopped. "Margarita Anatolyevna told us on Friday. Alisa didn't let you know?"

Ksyusha's fingers were on her bag's zipper. "No. I haven't seen her." The only communication she'd had with Alisa all weekend was when her cousin texted to ask how the visit was going, then sent kissy faces, winking faces, yellow dots of glee.

Canceled. She wouldn't tell Ruslan, because that would suggest that practices could be canceled on any day. That they weren't to be depended on. That she, by extension, was undependable. She dragged the zipper shut and drew her hands back to her lap.

"Is everything okay?" she asked.

"With Anatolyevna? Sure. She has a doctor's appointment." Chander sat down beside her.

Ksyusha tilted her head at him. "Why are you here, then?"

"To find you. How was your weekend?" he asked.

She told him about the visit. The movies watched, the news from home. Not the sex. Not the happiness. Still, maybe both showed.

"You must get upset when he leaves," Chander said.

"I do." She thought. "Not as much as I used to, though."

At a point not too long ago, saying that would have seemed like a betrayal. But she and Chander understood what she meant—she used to fear going out of reach of the microwave timer. Now Ruslan was growing more comfortable, and she, too, was improving.

"Bring him to practice next time," said Chander.

Ksyusha laughed. "I don't think so."

He leaned back, showing the easy curve of his throat. They sat in silence. The heater hissed down the hall.

"We missed you," he said. "I missed you."

"I missed you, too," she said.

He looked right at her. "I need to ask you something."

"All right," she said. And dread rose in her. Dread and curiosity, the two mixed up like sand lifted in seawater.

"Why did you join this group?"

"Alisa wanted me to."

"I know," he said. "But Alisa wants you to do many things you don't. She wants you to go to the café every day. You've never been. So why this?"

He was searching for some particular answer from her. His eyes moved in concentration from hers to her cheeks to her mouth. That sick mix swirled in her chest. "I don't know," she said. "I guess . . . I don't know."

"You wanted something different."

"Maybe," she said. "Yes."

"A change." He reached over to her. "Me, too. Don't be scared," he said, as he took her hand from her lap.

He held her hand. That was all. Still, she felt her pulse thud through her back on the wall. Chander. Her friend. She didn't want him to let go.

She had thought of him this weekend. Naked, fresh from the futon mattress, performing for Ruslan, she thought of Chander. She said she'd missed him. That wasn't a lie.

He was her friend but something more. Wasn't he? Coming to this hallway three times a week, she wished she could come five times instead. Their conversations, his seat beside her. She had wanted to find him here today.

They had already crossed some line together. He laced his fingers between hers. "Don't be scared," he said again, probably noticing the beat under her skin.

"I'm not," she said. Not of him. He kissed her.

·

When she was little, staring at Ruslan across the coated tablecloth during a family meal, she alternated between pretending to be his girlfriend and reprimanding herself for playing pretend. Their neighbor—her brother's friend—this sunburned boy. Something in that fantasy was mean, ludicrous. She felt it even then.

Then the summer after she graduated from high school, only a month or so before she moved away, Ruslan started talking to her like she was more than Chegga's little sister. On any given night, he asked where she was going, showed up at the spot she named, told her classmates she'd hit curfew, and led her home. Chegga had moved away the year before for his mandatory army service, and Ksyusha's parents had headed into the tundra for the season, towing along horses, sacks of flour, and handles of vodka to help them pass the time in the rangelands. That left Ruslan in charge. He took the responsibility seriously. They walked together over creaking bridges, past slatted wooden houses, and down dust-covered roads. The village black and abandoned. Ruslan finally kissed her under a streetlamp. He held her face as if she were beautiful.

That first month they were together, in the weeks before Lilia went away, Ksyusha kept wondering if this was pretend. It was too wonderful. Each time Ruslan came to the house, she opened the door to him in amazement. No matter where they met, she felt like she had on that perfect night, when they were alone on the streets they grew up on and their bodies were bathed in light.

And he wanted her even more after she left Esso. Checked in hourly, drove down regularly, and made sure she was avoiding risk in the city. Being his girlfriend still felt impossible. Ksyusha had tried for years to seem good enough to deserve his attention, but she really was not. She found little ways to slip out from scrutiny. She made excuses. She disobeyed.

After all this time, Ksyusha was showing her nature. It felt a base kind of good to know it: she was, in truth, the person she had promised Ruslan she wasn't after Lilia left—the person he feared was there. She was treacherous.

·

"I missed you," Chander said into her ear. His hair brushed soft against her cheek. His body, which she had been careful to move around for weeks, was close. "I kept picturing you with him on Friday." He kissed her jaw, her collar, and she lifted her chin so he could go on. He pressed his face to her neck. She put one hand on the back of his head and held him there.

·

Nothing should seem to change. No one could know. Ksyusha and Chander kept their same arrangement, meeting in the hall for an hour and a half before each practice, except now they pushed against each other as they talked. They shared secrets. "I wish I'd met you then," he said once, meaning when she was in high school. Before Ruslan, he really meant, but such a time had never existed.

Chander's mouth was sweet. Ruslan's was urgent, tasting of cigarettes. She knew Ruslan's mouth in the mornings, or from drinking, or like a hot iron pressed on her after an argument—all those times, good and bad. She loved it. But Chander's was sweet. Always. Soft. Lips full, teeth smooth, his tongue searching for and finding her, and then his breath coming in relief.

At times she doubted her affection for Chander, because it was so much slighter than her need for Ruslan. But she did love that puff of breath. One exhalation and she became powerful.

Was she happy? No and yes. Not in the same way she had been. She could hardly remember what had gone on inside the version of her that so diligently scrubbed the floor in November.

Instead she recalled other, older things. Coming home on the last day of school each year to find her father there. And being thrilled to see him, after his months out with their animals, but also knowing what his presence meant—that the next day he would take her and the rest of their family away from Esso to join the herd.

In early summer, the herders drove the deer closer to the village, so the animals could graze on mosses only thirty kilometers from home instead of three hundred. All the same, to reach them, Ksyusha's family had to ride on horses for hours through plains and mountain passes. When she was little, her parents tied her to the saddle with a rope around her waist, and every time she nodded off on her mare's wide back, her father yelled her name to startle her awake. The sun moved above them as they repeated that routine. At ten years old, she graduated to holding her own reins. The horses aged, their paces slowed, but the tundra kept the same shrill degree of emptiness.

Ksyusha dreaded those journeys. Her parents always ended them by fighting as they wandered the plains looking for signs of the herd. They would shout at each other about her father's drinking, her grandparents' health, their narrow wishes for her and her brother's careers, the weak market for venison, the deer's feeble calving and ragged pelts, the politicians who were killing the herding industry by refusing to subsidize it. During the rest of the summer her parents managed to keep their marriage together, as her father loaded the family's bags on their animals to move camp each morning and her mother set aside the best cuts of meat for him each night, but the long days they took to start and end the season only got worse every year.

At last, the summer before university, she told them she could not go out to the tundra with them again. Too much required reading to get through before school started, she said. Maybe because she had never refused before, they actually agreed to leave her home, and she was grateful, and then she was amazed, because that summer was her last one spent unsupervised. It became the season of Ruslan.

But now, in Petropavlovsk three years later, she thought of what she had missed in the tundra that last season. She thought of what she had seen out there all the years before.

The blue-lit black of nights. The limitless dry yellow of days. For all that she loathed about those summers, setting up camp in the rain and pretending not to hear insults spoken in Even and growing sick from the smell of singed fur, they had become some of the most vivid times of her life. The repetition of them: her father's arrival back in the village, their trip out together, the way when they finally got there that Chegga was folded into the men's shift schedule to watch the animals and Ksyusha carried water as part of their grandmother's kitchen crew, the ground the reindeer ate clean overnight, the early-morning packing of tents and bags that followed, and the daily moving of camp, on horseback, again, making their way along the thousand-kilometer loop of trails that took the herd a year to cover. The sameness of each day, each year, acted like the endless reopening of a cut, scarring those summers into her memory.

While the rest of the family slept in separate tents, Ksyusha's grandmother kept two spots for Ksyusha and Chegga in the yurt where the women did the cooking. After the evening meal, their grandmother banked the fire, spread the horses' blankets around its coals, and left the siblings to rest in the sudden quiet. The sun didn't set until almost midnight but the yurt would already be dim with smoke inside. Ksyusha and her brother lay there smelling the day's sweat with fresh crushed grass trapped underneath.

One time Ksyusha woke up in the middle of the night, not knowing why. The smoke hole at the top of the yurt was filled by the moon. A meter away, her brother, still a chubby schoolboy, was breathing.

The hearth's coals popped. She rolled onto her side to look. The coals were black, but still somehow crackling; she watched without understanding. Crackles getting louder. Only after a minute did she grasp that the pops weren't from the fire at all—the reindeer were passing outside the yurt. The men had taken the herd, for some reason, right through camp. The noise that woke her was the motion of eight thousand delicate hooves stepping just beyond the canvas wall.

Why return to these childish images? She had other things to think about these days. Course work, exams, the banking internship her brother's girlfriend promised her next summer, the phone calls she owed the people who were waiting at home. Ruslan, if she could bear it—or if she couldn't, then Chander, whose arms were around her. He pulled her close so her head rested on his shoulder. His lips brushed her hair.

Maybe it was because she was working hard at dance practices. Afterward came that same old soreness from the days once spent lugging wood, tending fires, building and taking down the yurt. Or maybe it was because she was around native people again; she hadn't been with so many since she was still living in Esso. Or maybe it was the troupe's herders' dance. Chander did look foolish holding his lasso. A tool like that belonged to her father and grandfather.

She remembered her family, their animals, lessons, and chores. The empty, rolling earth. Maybe it was that her childhood, seen from this distance, seemed simple. And that as much as she now loved these men's mouths on her, some part of her wished she could go back.

·

Ksyusha was idling around on her guitar, avoiding schoolwork, when Alisa came home. It was Thursday—no practice. Her cousin's face was red from the cold outside. "Scoot over," Alisa said, and Ksyusha made room on the futon. They sat with their knees touching.

Alisa's leg was chilly. Winter was here. Snow had been falling for a week straight, and the city beyond their apartment windows was heaped in white. The muted television showed the Golosovskaya girls' school portraits before their faces were replaced by a graph of the falling price of oil.

"Where do you suppose they are?" Alisa asked.

Ksyusha plucked a couple strings. "Who?"

"Those sisters. Do you think they're alive? Somewhere?"

To her cousin, Ksyusha did not have to pretend away danger. "No."

"Sometimes I imagine they could be in the next apartment over. You don't think they'll be found?"

"Not alive. I hope not." The missing girls were not like Lilia, old enough to run away. "Whatever happened to them, I hope it ended quickly, and they didn't have to suffer."

The news changed again to a weather report: continued blizzards. Stuffed cabbage rolls were heating in the oven. The smells of pork and onion filled their apartment. "Everything with you normal?" Alisa asked.

"Yes," Ksyusha said automatically. Once that answer came out, it didn't sound like enough, so she said it again. "Yes."

"Because you seem different."

"I'm not." Alisa laughed at the abruptness of that, and Ksyusha shifted her tingling fingertips. "How do I seem different?"

"You're nervous. I thought maybe Ruslan did something wrong."

Ksyusha glanced up from the neck of the guitar. "No."

"Okay."

"He wouldn't."

Alisa's mouth twisted. "Great." On cue, Ksyusha's phone vibrated underneath them. Alisa dug the phone out, looked at the screen, and handed it over.

"Hi," Ksyusha said. Her cousin stood up, off to their bedroom to change her clothes. "Nothing. I miss you." Ksyusha strummed a G-major chord for Ruslan. "Hear that? I'm here. I'm good."

In many ways, Ksyusha had improved as a girlfriend since joining the troupe. She was more patient, supportive, responsive. The worse she was in private, letting Chander trail his lips down her neck, the better she knew Ruslan to be. He had taken care of her all this time. So she texted him more, and asked for less, and when on the phone he got frustrated, she no longer tried to explain herself. She only soothed him until he settled down.

"I have wonderful news," Margarita Anatolyevna said. Her silk scarf gleamed under the music room's lights. "The university has agreed to send us to Vladivostok at the end of the month for the Eastern Winds ethnic festival. It's an honor. Truly an honor. We'll perform for more than a thousand people." Her voice swung. She paused, and everyone applauded, a noise rapid and furious. "We haven't gone for two years." This last bit was half-drowned by their excitement. "Chander, can you tell everyone more?"

Ksyusha caught Chander looking at her before he stood. "This is great," he said. "Right, they didn't fund us last year. It's for three or four days—"

"December twenty-third to twenty-sixth," Margarita Anatolyevna broke in.

"And we dance, meet other ensembles, see a real city. Stay in a hotel." Though he wasn't speaking in Ksyusha's direction, she knew he said that to her. "It's fun."

Alisa squealed, which set everyone off again. Even Margarita Anatolyevna was grinning. Ksyusha pressed her hands together to clap along with the rest of them, but she could not think of what to do next. Chander had told her that the troupe performed in public, but she'd pictured . . . visiting a local hospital ward, or taking the stage at an elementary school. Not missing classes to fly to Russia's Pacific capital. And so soon . . . What would Ruslan say? He wasn't planning to visit this month, as instead she would go to Esso to celebrate New Year's at home, but . . . staying in a hotel, in a different region, with people he did not and should not trust?

Ksyusha excused herself and called Ruslan from the bathroom. "What is it?" he said when he picked up. Men and machinery were noisy behind him.

She told him about Eastern Winds.

"Vladivostok," he said. "God."

"I know. I know."

"Just the name of the thing is ridiculous. 'Eastern Winds.'"

"I know," she said again, "but everyone else is excited. Alisa practically screamed when the director announced it."

"Of course she did," he said. "It's incredible. A free trip to Vladivostok. I told you this dance thing was a good idea. How long do you have to be there?"

"Four days," Ksyusha said. Even to her own ears, she sounded miserable. He clicked his tongue, and she understood that the more unwilling she seemed to take the trip, the more likely he would be to let her go.

That only made her feel worse. She had tried, since the first collision with Chander, to be better for Ruslan. But that effort—the tender questions, the caring noises, the more frequent promises that she loved him and home best—amounted to a strategy that paid off for her. Had she planned for this result all along?

"Drums and skins and Eastern Winds," Ruslan said. "I wish I could see you all perform."

She turned away from the bathroom's line of mirrors. She wanted to cry. "I wish you could, too," she said.

He didn't have the money for a plane trip. Neither did anyone else in their families. So saying that didn't matter—saying she wished for them to come together, though it would ruin them.

In the time before their next practice, Chander held her so tight she could not breathe. "Everyone else will go out at night," he said. "They won't expect you to come along. You'll stay in your hotel room, and I'll tell them I'm sick, or tired, or have to do research. Then I'll come to you."

"All right," she said. It couldn't stay kissing forever. Under her palms was his chest, the muscles tense in anticipation.

In their hall, they clung to each other, but once practice began they kept to opposite sides of the room. The knowledge of what was coming made her skittish. Margarita Anatolyevna announced an increase to five practices a week, and Ksyusha could not turn her head to look at him. She imagined he, and everyone else, knew what she pictured: his body above hers. The music started. Chander stepped forward and she flinched.

"When's the next time you'll see Ruslan?" Alisa asked. The two cousins lay in their separate beds. Ksyusha, who had been thinking of the university hallway, opened her eyes when Alisa spoke. Nothing but darkness above.

"New Year's," she said.

"Are you sad without him?"

"Sometimes." The guilt rose in Ksyusha. She stared up.

"Maybe he can come visit before we go."

"There's no time," Ksyusha said. She turned toward Alisa, who had her cell in her hand. The glow from the screen made Alisa look even younger, like a little girl at a campfire. "I'll see him soon enough. Don't worry."

Alisa's eyelids flickered. She was back to playing on her phone. A charm hooked to its top corner made a black line across her knuckles. "You're the one who's always worried."

Ksyusha was sick of her cousin's questions. Facing the ceiling again, she tried to return in her mind to the hall outside the practice room, but it wasn't coming as vividly as she wanted. How Chander spoke to her today. The way he touched her.

What would their first night in the hotel be like? Under Chander's patience was a growing force; he spent real effort unwrapping his hands from her as their time drew to an end each afternoon. If she agreed, he would peel her naked tomorrow and press her against the tiles. Ksyusha's stomach flipped at the thought.

She had lost her virginity to Ruslan that first summer on her child-hood bed. Afraid of making a mistake, she barely moved, and after-ward he called her a cold fish, fastened her bra, and kissed her. Now she knew what to do for Ruslan, but Chander might expect some-thing more, some great experience. Or he could be disappointed in her body. She looked better in her clothes than out of them. Soon he would find that out.

No. Chander, in his kindness, could never find her insufficient. She parted her lips in the darkness and imagined his face. Those brown-black eyes reflecting the hall lights. That quick breath, prom-ising to adore her.

.

The troupe spent most practices in costume now. Over Ksyusha's jeans, a leather dress hung heavy, with red squares embroidered from its bottom hem up to her knees. Strings of beads swung from medal-lions at her waistline. When she raised her arms, fur bunched at her neck. In less than two weeks they flew to the festival. After they got back, as soon as her last exam ended, she would take the bus north.

These were the days that would decide her. She would sleep with Chander, then see Ruslan. In doing these things she would learn: either one or the other. The cruel period of having both would end.

She wanted to be with Ruslan forever. But she did not know how that would go. For now, she played at being good enough on the phone that he didn't notice anything, but when she stepped onto their home pavement, wouldn't he spot betrayal right away? And even if he did not catch her— She loved Ruslan, she did, and always

had, but was it right for her to stay with him after what she had done
and what she was going to do?

.

Of all people, Ksyusha was honest with Chander, so she told him. "I
don't know what'll happen after this trip," she said. "Not the one to
Vladivostok, the one to Esso."

They were sitting cross-legged on the hall floor. He lifted her
knuckles to his mouth.

"It's possible—when I see him—everything will go back to the
way it was." Chander nodded. "I can't stay in the ensemble after
that," Ksyusha said.

When Chander spoke, his words came out warm on her skin. "It's
possible it could go the other way, too."

"I can't say. I don't know."

She studied his face, his stippled cheeks and serious brows. He
laughed, then, a short noise. "I can't stand it," he said. He tugged on
her arm and she folded forward into his lap. "In the hotel, they make
up the sheets all white and crisp," he said. "The mattress is like a
dream. Can you picture that? We'll be dreaming."

.

The next time Alisa came home while Ksyusha was on the phone,
Alisa took off her winter hat, pointed to the cell, and whispered,
"Ruslan?" Who else? Ksyusha nodded. "Tell him hi," her cousin said,
then spun to lock the apartment doors.

Ksyusha, watching the padded line of her cousin's back, said, "Hi
from Alisa." They never had a say-hello-for-me relationship. Ruslan
used to call the girl crazy.

"Okay. Remind me when you're leaving for the festival," Ruslan
said. At least he was always the same.

"Eight days." Not this Friday but the next. "And the week after
that, I'll see you."

Ruslan sighed, the sound coming thick from his lungs. "Wish it was sooner." Ksyusha shut her eyes. He didn't know what he was encouraging—what he was urging them toward.

·

Margarita Anatolyevna clapped for quiet. "Get in your pairs." Ksyusha stepped toward the center of the room; she knew, without looking up to confirm, Chander was near. Her mouth and cheeks had been kissed sensitive by him this afternoon, leaving her feeling like a tender extension of his body. Ksyusha pressed her lips together while she waited.

"My partner's missing," said the boy from Achavayam.

"Where's Alisa?" Margarita Anatolyevna shouted. Chander was already next to Ksyusha. The boy from Achavayam crossed his arms.

"We didn't see her before practice," a girl said.

The director jabbed a couple buttons on the stereo, making the music start and stop. "This is unacceptable," she said. "Do you understand the festival is in one week? Take responsibility for one another. Ksyusha!" Ksyusha jumped. "Where is she?"

Ksyusha's cell phone was tucked in her bag, but suggesting she call would only irritate things. *No distractions during practice*, Margarita Anatolyevna would scream. Ksyusha said, "She must be on her way."

Margarita Anatolyevna punched another stereo button. "Line up. Salmon dance." The boys gathered in the middle of the room. Ksyusha fell into place with the other girls, all of them in their costumes, leaving a spot for Alisa until the director motioned for them to tighten up.

Ksyusha tented her fingers in front of her chest. The song started, and the boys began to dance, lifting their feet to wade through a river that was not there. They squinted at the dusty floor to look for fish. Flexing her toes, Ksyusha waited for the girls' entrance. Her mind was with her cousin. Was Alisa sick? Had she missed today's classes? Their mothers had been texting them all week with worries about money after Tuesday's market collapse. Could they not make Alisa's tuition? Had she been called back to Esso? She had still been at the apartment this morning when Ksyusha left.

The recorded drums crashed. Ksyusha raised her arms with the rest of the girls and stepped forward. The boys pressed shoulder to shoulder, making a circle, and the girls swam around them. They turned until they found their partners. The boy from Achavayam frowned into space.

Chander grabbed at the air over Ksyusha's head, and she ducked. Bent at the waist, she spun into the next formation. She looked up. Margarita Anatolyevna faced away from the dancers. Relief: Alisa was at the door of the practice room, pulling a cap off her orange-streaked hair, gesturing in apology.

Behind Alisa, another person stood in the doorway. Alisa had brought a man.

She had brought Ruslan.

Ksyusha's hands, which should have been flat as fins, clenched. *He's cheating,* Ksyusha thought, wildly, because what were they doing together, but her cousin and her boyfriend were both smiling without guile. Alisa pointed at Ruslan, mouthed something to Ksyusha, and waved her palms in the air. These days of their echoing questions— how Ksyusha was doing, when she was leaving, when she expected to see him next—aligned.

Alisa had brought Ruslan to Ksyusha. They must have worked together to arrange this. Because Ksyusha had seemed to them nervous, Ruslan, who couldn't watch her in Vladivostok, came to surprise her before she left.

Through the speakers, a synthesizer blared. Ksyusha pivoted with the line of girls to face away from the door. She tipped her head up. She kept the beat.

Inside her was white and smooth, a frozen landscape, solid bone.

·

So this was the last time she would have both. Though Ruslan and Alisa could not see her eyes from this angle, Ksyusha did not dare look Chander's way. She had waited for the moment when her future would be decided. Only now when that moment was here did she know: the weeks she'd spent with both of them had been the best.

The best. Ruslan calling in the mornings to wake her up, his texts popping into her phone throughout the day, and then an hour and a half of Chander . . . those days were over.

Women's recorded voices rose high over the drumming. Underneath came the bass notes of men's growls. The steps brought Ksyusha back to her partner. She looked. Afterward, she knew, she would have to be careful, but she couldn't help this once—she glanced up at Chander and saw all his sweetness laid raw. His face was distorted with want.

Ksyusha stepped out of formation, away from him.

She turned toward the door so quickly her left knee twisted, and ran the few long meters that separated her from her boyfriend, the distance she needed to cross. Ruslan and Alisa might have allowed her an instant of shock after their arrival, but that instant was over. Ruslan could already suspect her. She had to get to him.

She pitched herself at Ruslan, her arms around his neck, and she only knew she was safe when she felt his body tighten under her, his hands grip her waist so the lines of beads there pinched, and his familiar mouth bear down.

He was saying something in her ear but the music was too loud to hear. She kissed him hard and pressed her cheek to his. He held her closer. She should have been thinking of her next alibi, but all she could bring up were memories: Chander in the afternoons, Ruslan on weekends, the pristine hotel bed she only ever heard described. The conversations she and Chander would never have again. The boys in this troupe practicing with their lassos. The first day of practice, shaking a dozen strangers' hands. Ruslan in his car in traffic, making his way toward her, and him as a boy playing soccer on their street with her brother. The summer they fell into each other. Her parents—her brother—their constant concern for her—their village lives. The horses they rode. The trails followed. The nights Ksyusha spent in the tundra, when she was younger and braver and slept alone, when her world was clear, smelling of smoke and grasses, and thousands of reindeer passed her by.

NEW YEAR'S

Though it was only eight o'clock, Lada was well on her way to drunk. She had helped finish another bottle before Kristina came back to the kitchen. Kristina returned to the group looking like a billboard model for cell service, with her phone propped in one hand, her bikini, and her blond bangs. "Guess who's coming?" she shouted over the music as she slid into place on the banquette. Lada was distracted by the tinsel flattened on the bottoms of Kristina's feet. Silver sparkles vanished under the kitchen table. "Masha."

"Who?" said a guy at the end of the table.

"Masha!" Kristina said. Her face was quick, pleased, her lips flushed brighter pink by vodka. Lada listened, not believing. "Masha Zakotnova."

"Who?" the guy said again, more sourly. A few people laughed.

Masha. The music was too loud. Lada wanted sobriety now as much as she had wanted festivity before. She focused on the food in front of her: cake, cured meats, salted and braided cheeses; ribbons of orange peel; pillars of boxed juice. An apple—she would have an apple. She reached over the tablecloth to take one. In the heat of their holiday rental house, which was slick inside with steam from the sauna down the hall, the fruit was surprisingly cold. Lada pulled the apple to her lap. "Give it," the man squeezed next to her said and plucked it from her bare thighs. He started peeling it clean with a paring knife.

Lada turned her attention back to Kristina. "So what," she asked, "tonight?"

"Yes, tonight," Kristina said. "Do you not want her to?"

"No, no," Lada said. "No. Why would I not?"

"Good, because she's already on her way." Someone uncapped a new bottle, and Kristina passed her glass down to be filled. "She's getting a taxi from her parents' place. I told her there are no extra beds but she said she would be fine on the floor."

"Is she cute?" Kristina's cousin asked. "My bed might have some room."

"You're not her type," said Kristina, as her glass was passed back. She raised the glass to the group. "Who has a toast?"

The man gave Lada her apple. Sliced and cored now. Lada popped a piece into her mouth and raised her drink after him. Her final one, she promised herself. "To the New Year," the man said. "May we meet tomorrow healthy and happy."

"May we have all our appetites satisfied," said the cousin, baring his animal teeth at the table. The girl next to him shoved him and made their side of the banquette jolt. Lada's shot burned down her throat. She took another apple slice. Around the table, people were talking over each other. Lada was heavy with alcohol, slow to comprehend.

How could Kristina say whether Masha liked any particular type? Masha was . . . they hadn't seen Masha in seven years, since after their first year of university. Lada and Kristina hadn't actually been friends with her since the summer before that. Masha had earned herself a scholarship spot at St. Petersburg State University. Before she left, the three of them spent weeks watching comedies in bed together and promising to call each other every day, but when Masha moved away for school, she disappeared. At first she replied to texts by saying course work kept her too busy to talk, then she stopped responding at all.

Once first-year exams were finished, Masha's parents had invited Lada and Kristina along to the airport to see their daughter in for the summer. They met a girl at security who was thinner, wary. Whose body was stiff in their arms when they hugged her. Who may have been coming home for a season but was determined not to stay.

And that was that. Masha ignored their messages all summer. By the time the fall semester began, they had to assume Masha had already flown back west to school. The New Year's holiday break came, then another summer vacation, and so on through all five years of university with hardly a word out of St. Petersburg. Kristina managed to keep in touch, but only scarcely; she chatted with Masha online then reported the most interesting bits: Masha had graduated with honors, found a job with a Western company that paid her salary in euros, moved with a roommate to an apartment just south of Nevsky. Meanwhile Kristina and Lada were living with their parents after wrapping up their provincial degrees. Kristina worked at a sporting goods store on the tenth kilometer and Lada was a receptionist at the Avacha Hotel. It wasn't practical, Kristina said, for Masha to come see them in Petropavlovsk. The long flight back wasn't worth it. Masha's rent in St. Petersburg was twenty-eight thousand rubles a month.

Lada had nothing to say to this shallow news. "Oh," she offered when Kristina tried. Or "Nice." She didn't want anything of hers, not even a tone of voice, relayed to the other side of the country for them to laugh over. *Ooh, our Lada's jealous,* Kristina would love to tell Masha—Kristina took any gossip she could get. How bizarre that, of all the people to stay connected to, Masha had chosen Kristina, with her whispers, her tales. Growing up, Kristina and Masha were not the ones bonded to each other. It was Lada and Masha who were close, carrying their hearts in each other's chests.

That was what it felt like to Lada, anyway. Like Masha had everything of her. They lived in neighboring buildings and sat next to each other in every class. If Masha found a good book, she read the entire thing out loud to Lada. Those readings took weeks sometimes. Lada lay on Masha's bedroom carpet while Masha's deliberate voice rose off the bed. Lada heard all of Sherlock Holmes that way: the investigator's words in Masha's mouth. *It is not for me, my dear Watson, to stand in the way.* Like that. When Masha left, she took Lada's love with her, and she never returned to give it back.

Oh well. Lada chewed on another piece of apple. Masha was coming. Here, tonight.

Maybe it was better this way—to see Masha once tonight, up close, instead of being surprised as she walked someday down their once-shared street. This way, Lada could greet her and get over her all in the year that was ending, and meet the New Year free of this old wound.

The song changed to something faster. The man beside Lada poured her another drink. "No, I don't need it," she said.

"It's all right," he said, sliding the glass her way.

The steamed-up windows behind him blotted out any stars, so the night beyond looked flawlessly dark. No lights streamed by from cars. Lada sighed. Her skin was softened from her trip into the sauna after she first arrived. The rounded muscle of this man's thigh was pressed to hers, and the seam between them was slippery. Lada leaned toward his ear: "Thank you," she said. Enunciating.

"It's nothing."

She could smell new sweat and old cigarettes. "Remind me of your name?" she asked. "Whose friend are you?"

He smiled at her. His bare chest was wide, showing the purple marks of old acne scars. "I'm Yegor. Tolik's friend." Lada shook her head, and he pointed across the table at a dark-haired stranger. "Tolik's my uncle's godson," Yegor said. "My uncle actually invited me. He's always pushing me to get out more."

"Funny. My family probably wants me to stay in more," Lada said. She took the shot and smiled back. "You live with your uncle?"

"I have my own place."

"In Petropavlovsk?"

"Up north."

"Oh, I remember." She'd forgotten because Yegor didn't look northern. But someone had mentioned the villages when his car first pulled in. Tolik, she supposed.

"Whose friend are you?" he asked.

"Kristina's." Masha's. Not anymore—but maybe again.

Masha was coming here. Strange. Lada herself knew barely any of the people in this house: Kristina and her boyfriend and her cousin. Two girls from Lada and Kristina's graduating class at university, one of whom had brought her detective husband along. Lada recognized the husband's face from the evening news. At the other end of the table, he was arguing about local politics through a mouthful of food. And Lada knew Yegor, now, too. Then the group spiraled out into friends of friends of friends. Beyond the nine of them at this table, another five were taking a turn in the sauna.

As a girl, Masha had never been much for parties. On Masha's twelfth birthday, she, her mother, and Lada hiked the Avachinsky volcano. That was ages ago. Still, Lada remembered the day perfectly . . . the acid-yellow leaves at the volcano's base, the raw rust-colored soil at its summit, the mineral taste from their water bottles, and the steady pump of their legs. After the Golosovskaya sisters disappeared last summer, Lada looked at the girls' school pictures and saw her own childhood. The hours she and Masha spent wandering Kamchatka as a pair. She could shut her eyes and pretend she still occupied that younger body. Flat-chested, weightless. Masha, ahead of her, so small.

Back then Masha wanted nothing more than time alone together. She changed in St. Petersburg, though. She had changed a lot.

The group was shouting over each other about movies when the taxi arrived. Headlights shone through the kitchen windows. Kristina jumped up to get the door. Left by herself, Lada understood that she was tipsy, nervous, nearly naked. She should have thought to change back into normal clothes. Crazy to be dressed in a bathing suit when seeing Masha for the first time in years. And Lada's bangs dry, curling—she touched her forehead. No way to help that now. No one else seemed to be bothered. Yegor, beside her, was an amiable slab. Lada tucked her hands under her legs and looked toward the hall.

"Everyone, here's Masha," Kristina called as she came back in.

"Mashenka, here's Zoya, Kolya, Tolik, Volodya, Ira, Andryukha, and Yegor. Don't worry. We'll remind you. Here's our Lada." Lada tried to rise, but she was stuck between the table and other people's bodies. She had to crouch up. If she were free, what would she do, anyway? Hug the friend who had forgotten her? It seemed—no. Lada sat back down. Masha dropped her backpack against one wall and slid onto the banquette after Kristina.

Masha had gotten more beautiful. Her hair ended blunt at her shoulders, her skin was pale as champagne, and she was not wearing a bra. She still had that look—narrow eyes and solemn mouth—that had made Lada's mother call her Little Auntie when they were growing up, but it had relaxed from childish primness into something more natural now. Her whole body looked fresh.

Masha stretched her arm across the table to reach Lada's hand. "Hi." Fingers cold from the air outside.

"Hi," Lada said. Warmth bloomed again inside her.

"Where are you coming from?" someone asked.

Masha pulled back. "Petropavlovsk," she said, at the same time Kristina said, "St. Petersburg."

"I was just in St. Petersburg last month," said one of the girls down the table.

"Oh, yeah?" said Masha. That same odd, low voice, coming out from behind teeth neat as a line of pearls. Teeth still as small and lovely and distinct as they had been when Masha was a schoolgirl.

"What do you do there?" asked the detective.

"I'm a programmer."

"I loved it," continued the girl, "but I couldn't live there. Too much craziness."

"Let's pour our guest a drink," Kristina said. In the back of the house, noise rose. The sauna door must have opened. Somebody in there was singing, stretching out each note. Yegor lined up more shot glasses for the friends coming down the hall.

They drank. Lada kept looking across the table. The last time she and Masha celebrated New Year's together, they were seventeen. They went to a club; Kristina kissed a boy on the dance floor, and

Lada threw up in the bathroom, and at the end of the night the girls took a taxi home together, Masha sitting in the middle. Under Lada's throbbing temple, Masha's shoulder had been cool relief. The city's sidewalks were filled with people, even at three in the morning, and the sky above their taxi burst over and over into new light.

Lada caught Masha's eye. "Did you bring a bathing suit?"

"It's in my bag," Masha said.

"Let's steam," said Yegor. The group that just got out of the sauna, shiny, thirsty, moved aside, and he pushed his way out from the table. Lada followed. The floor was wet. She stood in the kitchen doorway, letting other people squeeze past, until she saw Masha take an orange bikini out of her backpack. Then Lada turned toward the back of the house.

The sauna was shut off from the hall by a fogged-over glass door. Their group went in: Yegor, Kristina, Kristina's boyfriend, Kristina's cousin. Lada, who was trailed by one girl she didn't know. The air tasted like wood. It hit them hard. Lada swallowed to breathe. Splinters in her throat all the way down.

They took places next to each other on the burning bench while Kristina's boyfriend tipped a ladle of water onto the heater. Steam billowed up, squeezing their limbs and lungs. Masha came in through the fog. Lada squinted.

"Do you rent a place like this every year for the holiday?" Masha asked once she found a seat.

"My friend does," said Kristina's boyfriend. "Kostya. The skinny guy. But this is our first time. Nice, huh?"

"I like it," said Masha. She shifted to peel her legs off the planks.

To Yegor, Kristina said, "Your first time, too?"

He said, "I visit the city whenever I can, but this is my first New Year's."

Kristina's cousin laughed. "That's right. Our northern guest. You couldn't find a party closer to you?" Yegor leaned forward to rest his elbows on his knees. A rash of red was spreading across his back. "No friends at home?" the cousin asked.

"Be nice," Kristina warned.

"I don't mind driving," Yegor said. "As long as I get here and have a good time."

In the steam, Masha's head was bowed. Lada asked her, "How long have you been back?"

Masha lifted her face. "I got in yesterday morning."

The girl Lada did not know said, "I can't," and stepped down to the floor. She was blotched pink and white. Opening the door, letting in a current of cool air, she stepped out.

Kristina's cousin scooted over on the bench toward Masha. A fingertip touched Lada's thigh—Kristina, poking her to point them out. This cousin was a few years older. He probably met Masha when they were kids, but he wouldn't remember that bookish girl. In the bright bands of her bikini, her skin below yellowed ivory, her bobbed hair swinging, Masha looked sophisticated enough to have skipped childhood altogether.

Yegor leaned over to Lada. "More?" he asked. Sweat tracked down his thick arms.

"If you want," Lada murmured back.

He stepped down and dragged the ladle through the bucket of water. Though he didn't look around, he seemed to be doing it for her.

Just seeing him move gave Lada a base comfort. He wasn't attractive, no, but when she looked at his wide shoulders and soft waist, she resolved to like him. He looked like her father and her uncles and a hundred kids she'd stood behind in line at school. She would allow him many awkward moments for the sake of that familiarity.

Men might look different in St. Petersburg. More artistic. But a man like Yegor, from the north, lonely, who drank too quickly and did girls favors and would drive eight hours to attend a party, belonged only here on Kamchatka. He came from the humblest part of this place. When he turned the ladle, the room exploded in new heat.

He came back to sit closer. Their slick knees touched. Again, Lada felt that poke from Kristina, who was not saying anything. They were all paired up now—two by two by two. The cousin was telling Masha something quiet, so Masha bent forward to hear. Sweat trailed between her shoulder blades and spine.

Yegor's knee kept pressing on Lada. This was different from the kitchen, where they were crammed together. Here, Yegor was letting Lada know he was certain of her. If she wanted to sleep with him, she could.

Maybe she would. Yegor was a little sad, a little forced, but he had peeled that apple for her. He would be a fine choice for tonight. Lada pressed back.

It was good. Masha was home, and the return felt better than Lada had thought it would. Lada had pictured fearing the woman who came back to them. Instead, she found someone who was still recognizable. Changed but not entirely strange. Masha's voice, her mouth, her funny habits. Lada tried to see the situation with her buried sober mind . . . it was true, she believed that things were all right.

Anyway, now Masha had the chance to see Lada with this man, who was emphatic with his desire. Lada and Masha never kissed boys growing up—they never tried. Now they were women, and could do whatever, within limits, that they liked.

"Mashenka, how's your family?" Kristina asked.

Masha looked up. The skin under her eyes was drawn tight by the temperature. "Fine," she said. "Normal."

Lada's leg was hotter in the spots where Yegor's touched. "How's Vanya?" she asked Masha.

"Is that your boyfriend?" asked the cousin.

"My brother," said Masha. "He's good." She smiled, her teeth precise white in the room's mist. "He's graduating from high school this year."

"No!" Lada said.

"He's applying to university in Vladivostok. He wants to be a businessman." That little boy who used to follow them outside and watch them play. Once, when Masha's parents were out for the night, the girls told him ghost stories until he wet his pants. Now he was going to learn how to run a company.

"Good for him," said Kristina. She pushed her bangs back from her forehead. Her bare face was all cheekbones and lips. "Good for both of you world travelers."

"You're cosmopolitan, then, aren't you?" asked the cousin.

"I don't know," said Masha. "No. Not really."

"You don't miss Kamchatka life?" he asked. She shook her head. "You don't miss Kamchatka men?"

"No."

"You haven't met the right one."

Kristina's fingers trailed on Lada's leg. The steam lifted all the blood to Lada's head. Masha's discomfort was apparent in the line of her back—that beautiful back—her muscles, stripped and tensed and sleek—and Lada wanted to say, *Masha, it's New Year's, relax, let him touch you,* because Lada would let Yegor take her to bed tonight. *Masha,* she wanted to say, *just do it. Be with us again.*

The walls were hissing. Kristina slid down off the bench. Her shoulders shone with sweat. "I'm going outside."

Masha stood up fast. Lada, too, got to her feet, and the edges of her vision blotted black. The boys would follow. Kristina led them out of the sauna up the noisy hall.

Opening the house's front door, Kristina shrieked at the cold. It wasn't yet midnight, but the sky was black, black. Millions of stars blinked down. Kristina's boyfriend pushed her out onto the iced-over cement step, and they all squeezed after. People in the kitchen were shouting. The detective's voice rose above the rest. When the door shut, the racket from the house was muted.

Though Lada had braced herself, the outside air came like nothing. She couldn't yet feel it through the sauna's leftover warmth. From the clarity of the air, the crystals on the ground, she knew the night was far below zero. Her nerves must have sizzled out. On the base of her spine, a hand touched, steady. She looked down at her arms and saw them steam.

Yegor, behind her, leaned forward so his lips touched her ear. "You're so tiny."

She supposed that was a compliment. "I'm all grown up," she said and eased her weight back to press against his palm.

"Really. How tall are you?"

"One meter fifty-five." One meter fifty-four.

His hand rested on her back. "Have you ever been to Esso?" he asked. "I could take you."

Someone shoved against them. On the other side of the step, Masha said, "Stop it."

"Come on," Kristina's cousin said. "What's your problem?" Masha had moved away from the rest of them. The cousin was holding up his hands.

"I'm not interested," Masha said, in that flat tone. *My dear Mr. Sherlock Holmes.*

The cousin lowered his arms. He was tall like Kristina, with her same pout. On his face that mouth looked soppy. "Fucking lesbian."

He spoke like he was serious. People died for less. Lada felt the cold then. She was frozen.

"Don't say things like that to her," Kristina said.

"So what if I am?" said Masha. "At least I'm not a fucking pervert." She stepped down into the snow and gravel and pulled herself up into a different part of the group. Everyone was silent. Kristina's long neck bent forward.

The cousin said they made him sick. He was going back inside.

The other two men went, too. Yegor last, but he went. It was only them then—Lada, Masha. Kristina. Like it used to be.

Masha sat down on the edge of the step. Her bikini bottom wrinkled in back. "It's too cold to sit," said Kristina. "You'll go barren."

Masha did not answer.

A car flashed by the opening of the driveway. Its headlights lit up the trees. Someone was going late to another celebration. "Forget it," Kristina said and turned around.

The door shut again. Finally just the two of them. Lada lowered herself to the step, and the cement scraped the backs of her thighs.

"He didn't mean anything by it," she told Masha. "Are you okay?"

Masha looked straight ahead. Her arms were crossed on her knees. Everyone's cars were lined up on the driveway in front of them. "This is my last time coming here," she said.

"Kristina's cousin is an idiot. Stay the night."

Masha nodded at the iced-over yard. "Here, I mean. Home. Kamchatka."

The night was filling Lada's lungs with ice. "You just got back," she said.

"Yeah, well," Masha said. Her shoulders were raised. The way she sat was as it ever was. "My parents wanted me to come this winter. Now they say they don't want me to anymore."

"That's not true."

"That's what they told me tonight."

The sauna warmth was long gone. Masha's skin was raised in white goose bumps. Lada wanted to touch that skin—the impulse crested inside her. It had once been so easy to reach Masha. She was the girl that Lada knew, and she wasn't, all at once.

"But you're happy in St. Petersburg," Lada said. "Right? Kristina says you are—you have been."

"I guess," Masha said. She rested her head on her crossed hands to watch Lada. "I have to find a new apartment when I get back. I just broke up with my girlfriend."

"Oh," Lada said. The roommate. Kristina had said Masha had a roommate.

A girlfriend. Masha was so stupid. A girlfriend, Masha said outside the door, while all those big familiar men sat just on the other side of the wall. A detective. A police detective was in there. Underneath the frost, the steam, and the liquor, Lada's anger bubbled up, and she wanted to touch Masha now, but not gently, not with fingertips where Masha's fine arm hairs rose. She wanted to grab her by the wrist and shake. Brilliant Masha, with her scholarship spot, her tech degree. Perfect Masha, who got a job at a global firm. Gorgeous Masha, who paid twenty-eight thousand rubles a month to live with another woman. Masha had been treated her whole life like she was exceptional. If she, from that, now believed she could act this way . . .

Some people don't care if you're special. They will punish you anyway. Neighbors, for example, will report a girl, even a smart girl, with a girlfriend. The police will hurt you, if they get the chance. One person up the Okhotsk coast had been burned to death for this only a couple years earlier. Masha moved away from home at seventeen; when she thought back on life in Kamchatka, she probably pictured volcanoes, tasted caviar, remembered hikes on stone paths to the clouds. She didn't understand what happened these days to girls as innocent as she and Lada had been. They were destroyed for it. Any girl would be. The Golosovskaya sisters, who, walking alone, made themselves vulnerable—that one mistake cost them their lives.

If you aren't doing what you're supposed to, if you let your guard down, they will come for you. If you give them the opportunity. Lada could not believe Masha would be naïve enough to choose to have a girlfriend. They will hurt you, Lada had to say. You could die for this.

In the stillness, a pop song leaked through the kitchen windows. How could one person have studied so hard yet stayed so foolish?

Lada said, "You can't say that here."

Masha was silent.

"You could get killed. Why did you come back if you're going to be this way?"

"What way?" Masha said. "I'm the same. You know better than anyone the way that I am."

Lada folded her arms across her own knees, laid her cheek on them, and looked at Masha. She was trying not to be angry. "Mashenka," she said. "Listen to me. Can't you not?"

"No," Masha said and smiled.

Those teeth. Her tipped and lovely face. It made Lada's stolen heart hurt to see.

The stars scattered above them. Cold had sunk so deeply into Lada's bones that she felt her marrow must have frozen blue. After a while, Lada said, "Will you at least promise to be careful?"

"For you?" Masha said. "I'd do anything."

The mixed noise of people's voices came from the house. Bottles and laughter. Though sitting out so long was risky, because Kristina's cousin, in the kitchen, could be saying all sorts of things about what Lada and Masha were doing together in the dark, Lada could not bear to go. She'd waited years. So many parts of their friendship were lost forever, but Masha had spoken to Lada again, once, honestly, as if they were still the most precious people in each other's lives.

My dear, my dear. My darling.

"You promise," Lada said.

"I promise." Though God knew Masha had broken her promises before.

Lada shifted her seat to rest her head on Masha's shoulder. Under Lada's temple, Masha's cool, smooth grace. "I'd do anything for you, too," Lada said. "Anything I was able to do."

"I know," Masha said. "You would if you could. I knew that."

In front of their faces, their breath puffed white, curled up. Vanished.

"We should go in," Lada said.

Masha said, "Will you stay with me for midnight?" Lada nodded against her. "Just like this. It's silly to ask."

"No, it's not."

"It's my last night here."

Boys like Yegor had come before and would come again. "We can sit," Lada said. "That's easy. Really."

The night was an immense windowless room. The stars were impossibly far away. In the crisp dark, Lada pushed back against the alcohol in her blood. She willed herself to make new memories. This moment mattered in a way the trip she wouldn't take to Esso never could. She should not forget a second of this.

Masha may have carried Lada's love with her wherever she went, but that didn't keep anyone safe. Besides the hiking, and the reading, the games played in their courtyard and the movies watched in bed, Lada would hold on to this: her friend bare-shouldered, stubborn. Stupid enough to speak honestly. Sitting near midnight in weather that turned their toes white against the gravel. Smiling. Beautiful Masha, all grown up yet still childish. Unafraid of what harm was sure to come to her.

Roswell, 1947. The Tunguska event years before. The Travis Walton abduction, the Sassowo explosions, and the Petrozavodsk phenomenon. Height 611, along the Pacific, where witnesses reported the crash of an enormous red ball. The Voronezh incident, 1989.

Natasha started hearing these tales from her younger brother while they were still in school. Since then, aided by the arrival of satellite Internet in the Esso library, Denis had expanded his repertoire: Japan Airlines Flight 1628, Chile's El Bosque Air Force Base, Turkey's Yenikent Compound, and the opening ceremonies of London's Olympic Games. Outside the window of the International Space Station. The skies over Jerusalem, 2011 and 2012. The 2013 fireball that burned through Chelyabinsk. The purple lights, hovering, lowering, above the least populated parts of Kamchatka.

If aliens really did land on Earth, Natasha would ask them to start their world domination by erasing her brother's memory. Through fifteen years of study, Denis had absorbed an encyclopedia set's worth of information on UFO sightings, with mental volumes updated constantly. Four days into this new year, he'd already referenced every one of his false facts and started again at the top. Natasha had made her family pancakes with raspberry preserves for breakfast. Their mother was peeling an orange.

"The El Bosque Air Force Base," Denis said.

Natasha switched her knife and fork between her hands. She did not look up at him. Her brother and mother had arrived at Natasha's Petropavlovsk apartment the afternoon of New Year's Eve and were due to stay another week—Natasha would have to ration out her frustration to last the whole time. Difficult, though. Now that the celebrations were over, nothing distracted her from the desire to shake Denis until his eyes rolled. Concentrating on pancakes wasn't quite the balm she needed.

"The sighting was captured on film from seven angles."

"We know, honey," Natasha said, in the direction of her plate.

"The Minister of Defense saw it in broad daylight. An object—"

"An object was stalking their jets," she recited. "I said we know."

Their mother put her cool hand on top of Natasha's. The smell of citrus rose between them. "Don't," she said, then addressed Natasha's children: "You never do that, do you? Interrupt each other while one is trying to talk."

Natasha flushed. "Mama."

Their mother took back her hand. To Natasha's daughter, she said, "Yulka, you would never be so rude, would you?" The little girl straightened in her seat at the table. "So let's not pay any attention to the adults' bad example. Tell me, how's your reading going? What's the best book you read last year?"

"Yulka reads too much. She probably can't even remember them all," Natasha's son said. Natasha stabbed at a sliver of pancake. At thirty-one, a doctoral candidate, she was still getting reprimanded by her mother. Her family's every visit turned her into a teenager again. She had snuck enough holiday chocolate over the last few days to get a line of pimples across her forehead, and this morning, she had to style her hair differently to hide them. Her whole head felt sloppy.

"The Call of the Wild," Yulka said. "Babulya, have you read it?"

Natasha's mother propped her chin in one palm and managed to look terribly interested. "Jack London. Of course I have."

"Lev hasn't."

"Shut up," said the boy, and Natasha slammed down her utensils, and Natasha's mother called for order, and the morning was back to normal, just like that.

At least her kids seemed unfazed by Denis's strangeness. Lev and Yulka, after so many school vacations spent in their uncle's company, were used to following their grandmother's lead: keep it light, change the subject, don't engage. Even after the holiday's sparklers were extinguished, movies watched, gifts opened, they had not become bored enough to turn on Denis, who was picking at his food at the other end of the table. Waiting for a prime moment to mention the Chelyabinsk meteor, no doubt.

Did Natasha insist on nattering on about her interests? Her research on saffron cod populations? No. So why was her brother encouraged to talk endlessly? She burned to ask.

She would have liked to introduce her children to Denis as he was as a boy. Still shy then, still obsessive, but more engaged with matters on the ground than in the sky. Growing up, they had spent happy summers together, the three of them—Natasha and Denis dunking each other under the warm green water of their village's community pool, while their little sister sat on the side and screamed with pleasure.

Now Denis was single-minded, Lilia was gone, and Natasha could hardly make it through a shared breakfast.

Natasha cleared her throat. "I'm sorry I interrupted you."

"The footage is online," Denis said. "We can watch it, if you like."

Natasha took up her tea so she could widen her eyes at her mother over the rim of the cup. Her mother said, "We're not going to spend our holiday on the computer. Lev, your turn. What have you been reading?"

The alien stuff had started when Denis was in year nine. He spent his high school evenings watching space-invader movies. If she didn't have homework to finish, Natasha would sit on their couch beside him, take Lilia in her lap, and giggle at the cardboard ships suspended from wires. Denis, too, used to laugh when a scene got ridiculous. At the beginning of his shift toward outer space, he had been willing to participate in ordinary life.

Not anymore. Lev and Yulka knew a different Denis, a different family, a different world than the green-dream one in which Natasha grew up. Still, Natasha could make these days more comfortable for her children. They deserved better than a mad uncle and a self-conscious mother on her third straight morning of a champagne headache. "What do you two want to do today?" she asked.

"Ride horses," Yulka said.

Lev sighed. "You can't ride horses in the winter," he said, and Yulka said, "Yes, you can," and he said, "No, you can't," and Natasha interrupted them both to say, "Shhh." They continued the argument whispering. Natasha looked over at her mother, who looked back in expectation. Natasha always forgot her own household authority when her family came to town.

The absurdity of it: that Natasha, barely able to meet her obligations as a sister or daughter, was now in charge of school and work and two children of her own. "What do you think," her mother asked the table, "of ice skating?"

Denis tried next as Natasha parked them in front of the sports complex. "In 2008 at Yenikent—"

"Just a minute," she called over her shoulder. "I'm trying to concentrate." They were in her husband's car. Yuri was at sea again; he had sent her a picture, a full day late, of him celebrating the New Year in some Pacific port past the International Date Line. Beer in hand and a wink toward the phone's front camera. Natasha sent him back a selfie with her middle finger raised. Then she followed that almost instantly with a picture of herself lit by the lamp on their bedside table, her top lowered, her lips and cheeks spun by the low wattage into dark gold. The story of their marriage: a little love, a little rage, a lot of ocean water.

Shifting the gears with an ear for the same rising engine noises Yuri would attend to, Natasha eased the car into place. Her mother peered at the bumper ahead. From the back of the car, Denis said, "Yenikent."

"One minute," Natasha said, unbuckling her seatbelt and fully intending never to ask him to go on.

Once they were out of the car, though, she was not as convinced of silence as she had been. The children ran a few paces ahead. Her brother was subdued. He walked beside her and their mother with his back rounded. Natasha ought to ask him about the Turkish compound—she could ease him into the telling with his own words—*the most significant extraterrestrial image ever caught on tape*, she knew he would say—except she did not want to.

The tree branches stretching above the sidewalk were frosted white. Snow capped the iron fence that lined the skating rink. The ice today was busy with families, and young couples held hands while they glided in laps. "So crowded. I don't know how you stand living in the city," her mother said. She spoke in Even so the kids wouldn't understand.

Natasha made herself busy looking for her wallet. In Even, too, she said, "I don't know when you'll get tired of telling me that." Her mother snorted.

The prices above the cashier's head were taped onto a printed sign. Natasha would like to see what was under the tape—the entrance fees were probably twice as much as they had been before last month's devaluation. She paid for her mother's rental skates and laced Yulka's blades on. In his own bulky black skates, Lev stepped up to his uncle and asked, "Aren't you going to do it?" Denis shook his head. "Why'd you come, then?"

"Don't be rude," Natasha said. "Denis, are you sure you don't want to skate?" Another head shake. Her kids were already making their way onto the ice. She considered asking her brother if he wanted a hot chocolate, but he was a grown man. He could find his own refreshments. She knotted her laces and pushed off.

Flight 1628. Height 611. It went on and on and on.

The skates were snug around her ankles. She passed on one foot through a cluster of strangers, and once she had room, she surveyed the rink. There was Lev, with a couple classmates he had bumped into, and Yulka holding hands with Natasha's mother. Denis, at the rink's edge, caught Natasha's eye, and she waved. Then she looked across the ice for Lilia, like always. Just in case. Imagine finding

Lilia's face in the pale city crowds, only a few kilometers from Natasha's apartment, after more than three years. But Lilia wasn't there.

Natasha's limbs felt loose, liquid. She leaned to the left and glided past another group.

It was down to the two of them, then. Natasha and Denis. She knew that but somehow she forgot, searching for their sister every time she entered a crowd. It was down to them . . .

Making another turn, Natasha looked again for Denis's slouched body. He had propped his elbows on the rink wall.

The afternoon air was crisp on her skin. The sun was a cold, clear circle, a hole in a white sky. On what seemed like her hundredth loop, Natasha's husband called. His voice came through a second delayed. She waited for the connection to clear.

"Nice picture," Yuri said.

She grinned into the phone. "Thanks."

"I showed all the guys."

"The first picture or the second one?"

"The second one. I'm joking," he said before she could start. "How are the kids?"

She found them immediately. Yulka's knit hat and Lev's red-and-gray jacket. "Fine. Bickering, but fine."

"Is your mom helping?"

"Sure. She's perfect."

"You're perfect," he said. She touched light fingers to her blemished forehead. He went on: "I've been missing you."

"Turn the sub around, then. We're at Spartak. I want to be skating in circles with you."

"I want to be stuck in one warm place with you," he said, and she laughed. After twelve years of deployments, they were good at these phone calls. Better, in fact, than they were at living in the same cramped apartment. At home, Yuri got bored, bothersome; when he was on sea duty, he was only his best, with no time to show anything more.

Everyone looked better at a distance. Everyone sounded sweetest when you did not have to hear them talk too long. After her husband hung up, Natasha skated past her brother at the wall, their mother cleaning her glasses beside him. Loving someone close-up—that was difficult.

Lilia had understood. She left for just that reason, Natasha knew. After all, Natasha and Yuri had moved away from the village after high school to get some distance from their relatives—Yuri's drunken parents, Natasha's mother's strictures, Denis's rambling. Lilia must have done the same, only farther, beyond Kamchatka. And with no warning.

Natasha and Yuri were already living in the city by the time it happened. Natasha would get texts from her sister filled with small-town rumors, romantic troubles, the choicest Denis quotes. *Their mothership surveilled Earth from the outer atmosphere.* Or *Radar was tracking the pin-shaped crafts.* Natasha texted back invitations for her sister to see the kids, and Lilia said later, later, that she missed them, that she would come soon.

She never came. The fall before she turned nineteen, Lilia vanished. Their mother, not grasping why a teenager might want to flee Esso, went to the police, who agreed to spend a day or two chasing Lilia's shadow. Village officers showed her picture to the bus drivers in the area and knocked on a couple neighbors' doors. Esso's tiny police station was no more than an outpost of a regional branch of the force in Petropavlovsk, which in its turn responded to occasional directions from Moscow; they were not equipped for a missing-person case. Natasha's own search efforts—canvassing Esso, questioning airport security in Petropavlovsk, messaging her sister for months, *where are you, please answer*—seemed more promising. Though they, too, yielded no result.

"Lilia's eighteen, she graduated. She's restless like a lot of girls can be," Esso's police captain told Natasha's mother at the time. "She decided to go off to see the world."

Now, of course, Natasha knew the captain was right, but back then his words enraged her. To see the world, Lilia would have needed to leave the peninsula through Petropavlovsk. Would she really have come to the city without saying goodbye? Something must have happened at home to make Lilia turn her back on Natasha. Someone—and was it Denis?—had driven Lilia away.

Three years had gone by since then. In three more, or five, or ten, or seventy, Natasha would still remember every second of those first disappearance days. On the drive from Petropavlovsk toward Esso with husband and children in tow, the morning after her mother called with the news, Natasha had pulled over to dry-heave in the dirt. Lilia gone. Natasha was sickened by fury. When she arrived, she found that their mother had sobbed so much that her face had swelled, lizard-like. Denis told them Lilia did not leave but was taken. When he pointed up, toward the roof, toward the stars, Natasha slapped him.

It had been a waking nightmare. Lilia's things, her books, her rumpled clothes, were still scattered at that moment around the house. Natasha's children, then only five and seven, were asleep in the living room. In the kitchen, Natasha was watching her mother struggle to blink: behind her glasses, her lashes stuck out from sore eyelids. Yuri's hand weighed on the base of Natasha's back—he had not stopped touching her since they got the call that Lilia was gone. When Denis said that, Natasha crouched up out of her seat and hit her brother as hard as she could. The sound of the slap was a shock. His cheek was harder than she had expected. She made contact with his jawbone and two rows of clenched teeth.

To this day, Natasha felt awful about it. Denis could not have acted differently. He honestly believed their sister had been pulled away into the stars. Yes, there were times Natasha wished he had been more attentive, in the crucial months after Lilia graduated, to what Lilia was doing and who she spent time with. But Natasha had the same old regrets for herself. If she had returned to see their family more often—or insisted on Lilia's visiting her in the city—but it was impossible now to do those things, to go back or to say what would have saved them.

Anyway, Natasha was not angry anymore.

She skated up to her mother and brother to prove that to herself. "I was just telling Denis to wrap himself up," her mother said.

"That wind off the water. Lev and Yulka must get sick all through the winter."

"No, they're used to it," Natasha said. She faced half away from the conversation so she could watch her children pass. The bay beyond the rink was a silver dish. "Today's pretty calm, anyway."

Her mother lifted one hand to the scarf around her coat collar. "I feel the cold here, like a knife to the throat. It's barely below freezing but the wind makes you believe you'll die of exposure." For years after Natasha and Yuri moved, Natasha's mother had complained about city crime rates, but after their family's brush with the village police, she shifted to other subjects. The weather.

What Natasha's mother did not talk about was worse than what Natasha's brother did. Her mother harbored her own bitter theories. After the Golosovskaya girls were taken, Natasha brought them up on a phone call to Esso, and her mother said, "So now you're interested?"

"What does that mean?" Natasha asked. Though she knew. On the other end of the line, her mother stayed silent. After a long minute, Natasha said, "You've heard the news, then. It's frightening. Isn't it?"

"Now you're frightened," her mother said. "Yes. It's terrible. Their pictures are in our post office. But you are aware by now that these things happen."

"What things, Mama?" Her mother would rather despise the police, suspect their neighbors, picture her youngest child grabbed and murdered than admit Lilia had run away from them. "These are children. The older girl is only a year above Lev in school. They were abducted," Natasha said. "They aren't Lilia."

Her mother sighed. The sound crackled through the phone. "Tell me what Yulka and Lev need to prepare before school starts," she said. Then: "They were killed, I'm sure. Their posters here don't mention any abduction. But, Tasha, it's better not to speak of such things. What can we do about it all? Nothing."

After that, Natasha left the headlines out of their conversations. She did not ask how the village captain spoke to her mother, even now, years later, or what the neighbors whispered about their family while standing in line at the grocery store. Lev and Yulka swooped past her and bent on their blades for another turn. Her mother started to say, "Those gloves—"

Natasha raised her hand in greeting to someone coming over. "Sorry, Mama," she said in quick Even, and then in Russian introduction: "Happy New Year! It's so good to see you. My mother, Alla Innokentevna, and brother, Denis. They're visiting—"

"From the north, from Esso," Natasha's mother said.

"And this is Anfisa. Her son and Lev are in the same class." Natasha only knew the neighbor, a feline blonde, from chatting at the bus stop or the odd school concert. Denis, thank God, did not embarrass them. He made eye contact, said hello, stopped there.

"I'm thrilled you're here," said Anfisa. Under her winter cap, her eyebrows were arched and penciled to perfection. "We've spent the last few days stuck in the apartment. Look, they found each other." She lifted her chin toward the ice.

Natasha turned to see their boys skating in a cluster of year-six classmates. Yulka, cheeks red with effort, trailed behind. Natasha called her daughter's name, but Yulka didn't hear, or pretended not to.

"Is Yuri home?" Anfisa asked.

"Not until March."

"Excellent to have your family visit, then." Anfisa smiled at Natasha's mother. "Although Natasha's very strong—she handles everything—I'm sure she appreciates the company. Do you come down often?"

"Only for the winter holidays. They visit us in the summer," Natasha's mother said. "But once a year here is enough. Work keeps me busy—I run our cultural center at home. And Petropavlovsk overwhelms."

"I understand, I do," Anfisa said. "I was raised in the north myself."

Natasha looked in surprise at her neighbor. Anfisa's white skin and toneless accent. "I didn't know that."

"I was. In Palana. I only moved here after I had Misha."

"It's actually better to be away from the city," Denis said. "It's safest in a small town. At the London Olympics, the ships surveilled everyone. There's photographic evidence. Three lights in a row in the sky."

Natasha shut her eyes. She concentrated on the laced tightness around her ankles, the thermal leggings constricting her thighs. Low-level frustration sat trapped in her chest. But not anger.

When she opened her eyes again, she saw Anfisa. The neighbor reached out and gripped Natasha's elbow. "Come over this week," Anfisa said. "The boys can distract each other while we take an hour or two to ourselves." In her cat's smile, there was something small, recognizable, and secret, speaking to Natasha, saying: *You are not alone.*

Anfisa's apartment was in the same row of buildings as theirs, only a few entrances away. Two days after the skating trip, Lev tramped across their parking lot toward that door. "Slow down," Natasha called after him. She had Yulka by the hand to guide the girl over hills of unplowed snow. Under her arm, Natasha carried a box of chocolates, swirled dark and milk and white, each in the shape of a different seashell.

Her son overshot the entrance and had to double back when Natasha shouted. Since exchanging numbers on Sunday, she and Anfisa had been texting: first little things, *hello*s and *how are you holding up*s, and then jokes, memes, a picture Anfisa took of herself frowning next to a bottle of Soviet champagne. *You and Lev should come over,* Anfisa had written this afternoon. *Misha needs someone to play with and so do I.* When, fifteen minutes later, Natasha sent an apology—*we're trying to get out the door but my daughter*—Anfisa said to bring Yulka, too, just come already.

A buzz, and the building's door unlocked for them. Lev ran up the stairs. Natasha, climbing after, heard voices echo. By the time Natasha and Yulka reached the right landing, Anfisa stood alone, wearing a cream-colored sweater and leggings patterned with swirling galaxies. "They're in Misha's bedroom," Anfisa said to Yulka. "Down the hall, second door." The girl pulled off her boots, dropped her jacket, and dashed inside. Once Anfisa and Natasha were alone, Anfisa said, "Finally."

While the kettle heated, they sat at the kitchen table. The gift box lay between them. Anfisa held a white-chocolate nautilus; with one leg propped up on the chair, she looked like a teenager. Her eyes were outlined in gunmetal powder. "Tell me how long they're visiting," she said.

"Until the eleventh. Not that long."

"Long enough."

"It feels like forever," Natasha said. "When I got your invitation, I threw Lev's jacket on him so quickly I probably ripped a sleeve."

Water chugged in the kettle. Down the hall, the boys shouted what sounded like military commands. Anfisa popped the chocolate in her mouth and unfolded herself to get two mugs. "I get it, believe me. Last New Year's was the first we didn't spend at my parents' place."

"What excuse did you use?"

"Misha's music school. I can give you its name." Anfisa stirred their tea at the counter. The spoon chimed against the side of a mug. Below the hem of her sweater, her legs emerged narrow and dark. "It won't help you, though. Your family's already in the habit of coming down."

Natasha buried her head in her arms on the place mat. She only lifted her face when Anfisa put the teas down. "I slipped some whiskey in there," Anfisa said.

A lemon slice floated alongside the needles of tea leaves in each drink. "Thanks. Listen, I don't want you to think I'm some kind of ungrateful monster," Natasha said. "I'm just having an off week." She thought. "An off past few years."

"Don't worry about what I think. I'm a monster born and bred." Anfisa inhaled the steam off her mug. "Have you had lunch? Do you want something?"

While Anfisa microwaved two plates of rice and fish cutlets, while she spooned out salad from a bowl kept in the fridge, Natasha told family anecdotes. They came surprisingly easily. That morning, for example, Lev had interrupted one of his uncle's recitations to ask, "Why do you act like that?" And when Denis fell silent, mournful, Lev said, "See? There. Like that."

Anfisa shut the refrigerator door. "What was your brother trying to talk about?"

"You heard him."

"Only for a minute."

Natasha rounded her shoulders and widened her eyes. "Photographic evidence from London shows three unidentified ships. Three lights in a row in the sky." Thin guilt rippled through her. But she was having too good a time to stop.

"Oh, you're excellent," her neighbor said. "Keep going. What'd Denis say back?"

"He pretended it wasn't happening, I think."

Anfisa put their plates down. She fetched paper napkins and utensils. "Too bad, because it's a good question."

"It's rude. I made Lev apologize," Natasha said. The room smelled like dill, butter, warm salmon. "But yes, obviously, yes. It's not like I haven't wanted to say that to him myself."

"Invite me over before the eleventh. I'll ask him." Anfisa scooted her chair in, turned her chin up, and did a little playacting of her own. "Why are you the way you are? And can't you stop?" Natasha laughed, surprised, at the face across the table. Anfisa looked very young and very lovely. Very, for one instant, like Lilia.

Natasha had not ever noticed the similarity before. They had completely different coloring, and Anfisa was much taller, but there was some angle of the eyes, some bend of the neck, in common. Lilia, too, had been skinny, high-cheeked, funny. "How old are you?" Natasha asked.

"Talk about rude. Twenty-six," Anfisa said. She drew her head back and the overlap melted away. When Anfisa lifted her mug, Natasha raised her own, remembering. "May we get the answers to all our good questions," Anfisa said.

Natasha toasted to that.

The spiked tea spread through her. It tasted like pine and honey.

Walking back across the lot in the black evening, snow crystals crunching under her feet and traffic passing in a hush on the other side of their building, Natasha felt loose and beloved. Yulka and Lev chattered alongside. Out in the Pacific, Yuri was going off watch, going on maintenance, and Natasha did not envy him his lonely holiday. A person needed company. She carried a sense, wrapped in whiskey, that someone once more understood where she was coming from.

Over dinner, the kids told their grandmother about Misha's gaming system. Lev raised his arms to mimic the hold of a weapon in *Call of Duty*. Still warm inside, Natasha scooped mashed potatoes onto everyone's plates. She looked up to find Denis staring at her. Nothing in her was against him. Thanks to Anfisa, that necessary outlet. Natasha met his eyes and smiled.

The next morning, Natasha drove her mother and brother to the city ski track, where a cousin who moved to Petropavlovsk decades earlier had agreed to tour them around the cross-country trails. When they parked, Natasha's mother swiveled in the passenger seat to look at the kids. She was covered in nylon and fleece so she rustled. "Are you sure you don't want to come along?"

"They're going to their friend's house," Natasha said.

"To play that game again? It's not right to stare at a television set all day. You need some fresh air."

"Don't you keep saying this air isn't good for them?" Natasha leaned over her mother's lap to open the car door. "Bye, Mama."

"The harbor air isn't good for them. This is mountain air," her mother said. But she was already getting out of her seat. Denis, in the back row, climbed out in his snow boots.

"I'll pick you up at four," Natasha called.

Back in Anfisa's kitchen, the whiskey out, they talked about men. Like Yuri, Misha's father had been a military man, Anfisa said. She brought a photo album from her bedroom: he was a teenager, really, with buzzed hair that revealed big ears and a neck rising too skinny out of a student uniform. Anfisa turned the album's pages tenderly. All the photos had that yellow fuzziness that came from film. "Is that you?" Natasha asked, pointing to a pigtailed girl in a knee-length skirt. Anfisa said, "Fifteen when I got pregnant," and spun the album in place so Natasha could take a better look.

They talked about raising their kids on their own. Anfisa's parents still lived together, but Natasha's mother had done it herself, too. "I shouldn't even try to compare my situation to . . . I'm not really alone. Yuri's here for half the year," Natasha said.

Anfisa shook her head. "Tasha, are you joking? You do it all yourself. Yuri is a good man, but if he's not here all the time, he doesn't take care of the children the way you do." Natasha liked that—both the words and the way Anfisa said them, which was cozy, self-assured. Sisterly. Anfisa insisted, "I'm serious."

They talked, too, about their jobs. Natasha was one of a few doctoral students at the oceanographic institute. She and the other researchers spent their days in the laboratory, projecting the coming season's catch limits and complaining about their dissertations.

"You're so smart," Anfisa said. She wore less makeup today, and her cheeks were already pink from the alcohol.

Anfisa worked as an administrative assistant for the Petropavlovsk police. "So you know all about the Golosovskaya girls' kidnapping," Natasha said.

Anfisa shrugged. "As much as anybody does. Which isn't much."

"Well, what's happening?" At Anfisa's rolled eyes, Natasha said, "You must be able to say something at this point."

"Let's see." Anfisa sipped from her mug. "We took surveillance tapes from every gas station in the city. We tried to trace the older girl's phone—nothing. We searched all the abandoned cars at the dump. Did you hear that? We took dogs through to sniff for bodies."

"Oh, God."

"We only found a few old drunks who had to be escorted back to their wives. What else . . . Did you know our detectives were after the girls' father for a while? The man lives in Moscow, and we actually had officers there take him in for questioning. They acted like the whole thing was some kind of joke."

"It wasn't the father?"

"It was humiliating. He hadn't seen his girls in years. He never paid alimony, let alone the bribes it would take to arrange a kidnapping by private plane. Anyway, it would've been impossible to leave Petropavlovsk without anyone seeing."

"I don't know . . ." The empty, dusty roads around the city. The endless tundra. Natasha's sister had traveled that territory without a witness.

"Think about it. The alert for the sisters went up within four hours. Where could someone drive in that time? You can't show up in a village with two strange children in tow. And any other way you might want to take those girls—a dock, an airport—people would notice."

Lilia had told their mother she was sleeping at her friend's house the night she left, so she got a head start of two days. She went quietly, with only her purse. Later they discovered there never had been a friend she stayed with. Lilia had been leaving the house at night for her own reasons for years. "See, you're the smart one," Natasha said. "You're right."

Anfisa smiled at her. "The only answer that makes sense is that the girls must have died here that same day. Before their mother even notified us. The major general thinks they may have gone swimming in the bay and drowned."

Natasha edged closer to the table. "But didn't the police think someone took them? What about your witness?"

"That's what happens when you get your information from city rumors," Anfisa said. "The so-called witness . . . she saw a man, she *thinks*, with some kids, she *thinks*, in a nice car, *she knows*, for three seconds. The dog she was walking would've made a better witness than she did."

"She didn't actually see anything?"

"She admits as much herself. But the girls' mother is involved with United Russia, she works for the party, and our senior staff was terrified in the beginning about intervention from the governor. There was so much pressure to find some person responsible. They needed a big, scary kidnapper, so they made one up."

Natasha clicked her tongue. A made-up kidnapper—if only her mother could hear. "We can't trust a thing they report. I'll have to get my news from you from now on."

"Don't I sound authoritative?" Anfisa said. "When actually most of my time at the station is spent pretending I know nothing so the officers won't bother me." She sat up straight, laced her hands on the table, and arranged her features into placidity. Above blushing cheeks, her forehead was smooth. Incorruptible.

"Looking good while avoiding work? Really, you ought to be our major general," Natasha said. Anfisa unfolded her hands to pour them both another drink.

"Mama," Yulka said, making Natasha jump. Anfisa laughed. The girl stood, fidgeting, at the border where the living room carpet met the kitchen tile.

"What is it, bunny?"

"Can we go home?"

"What's wrong?" Yulka had her brave face on. Her eyes were wet but her chin was firm. Even this far into motherhood, Natasha found it extraordinary that she and Yuri had made two creatures who were so odd, so particular. During her practice run as a parent, tending to nine-years-younger Lilia, Natasha had been dazzled by the same thing: the raw dough of an infant shaping into a determined child.

These days Natasha pushed herself to see that quality fondly. A person's early sharpness. That insistence on being themselves. When their father died, Lilia was only five, and during the few days his body lay for viewing in their home, Lilia sat on Natasha's lap and asked questions. *Is he uncomfortable? Can he hear us? If we opened his eyes, what would we see?* "He's dead," Natasha told her, which was an answer that did not satisfy. For hours, Natasha rested her head on Lilia's back, in the space between her spine and the fragile wing of her shoulder blade. Natasha's arms circled Lilia's waist. Heat rose from her little sister's skin. There had been so much life inside her.

"The boys are arguing," Yulka told them.

"Boys argue," Anfisa said. "It's all right, sweetheart."

Yulka waited for her mother. Natasha sighed, stood, and hugged her daughter to her side. "Go tell Lev to get ready." Yulka hopped away with the news, and Anfisa sipped her tea. Inspired, Natasha leaned down to kiss her friend's cheek. Pink and smooth and comforting. Anfisa grasped her hand, smiled up, and let her go.

At home, Lev announced, "I hate Misha."

Natasha was filling a glass from the sink tap. She had an hour to sober up before she was due to retrieve her mother and brother from the ski base. "Don't say that."

"I do. He turned off our game because he was losing, and then he told me it was an accident."

"Maybe it was an accident," Natasha said.

"It wasn't," Lev said. "He did it. It was obvious."

·

On Thursday, her son refused to go back. "But they're expecting us," Natasha said.

"I don't care," Lev said. "I don't like Misha. He doesn't play fair."

They were sitting on their couch in front of the television. Yulka was the only one paying attention to the screen. In the armchair, Natasha's mother held a book but was clearly eavesdropping. "You'll hurt Misha's feelings," Natasha murmured to her son. He was too grown-up now to carry places. She could not make him go anywhere he did not want to go.

"Lev, honey, do you want to spend this afternoon together?" Natasha's mother asked. Natasha frowned.

Looking like Yuri in miniature, with the same round lower lip and black eyebrows, Lev pushed his body back against the cushions. "No."

"Tasha, don't make that face," her mother said. "Shouldn't we be together? We aren't down so often, are we?" Speaking in Russian so the children would hear.

"You're right," Natasha said. "You're right, you're right." Deprived of the release of Anfisa, she was tipping into nastiness. Natasha's daughter, lying on a pillow at their feet, turned up the volume on the television set. The screen showed a redheaded soap-opera star.

"What should we do, then?" Natasha's mother asked the room. "Our holiday's already half over. How about downhill skiing instead of cross-country?"

Denis said, "Where would we go?"

"Have you looked out the window?" Natasha asked. "Do you notice any hills in Petropavlovsk?"

His chin pushed forward. To their mother, he said, "You can take the kids out on your own."

Their mother pinched the pages of her book open. Her forehead was creased. "Denis, try not to be so sensitive. You know your sister doesn't mean to hurt you."

Natasha was trapped in this apartment with these family members. That truth was stunning. All the people she wanted to see were far from her. Even one day when their mother died, Natasha would remain stuck. No confidantes. Barely half a husband. She would have to look after Denis and hear his looped stories and nag her own children until they scattered.

Lev leaned forward. "Uncle Denis," he said, "if you're home today, I'll stay with you."

Denis turned in his direction. "Did I ever tell you about Travis Walton?" Lev shrugged. "An American. When Travis Walton was abducted, in 1975, his friends were witnesses. They were in the forest and saw a golden disk. The disk took Travis Walton and he was missing for five days. Finally he was returned to a gas station. When he came back, he described the Greys, who are short, with enormous heads." Denis touched his lower eyelid. "Big brown eyes with no white in them. Five times as big as normal. Travis Walton told investigators they look right through you."

Natasha stared ahead at the screen.

"That's not true," her son said.

"Lev," Natasha's mother warned.

"It is true. Travis Walton passed a polygraph test," said Denis. "They don't land in cities. But when you're not a threat to them, and there aren't many other people—I saw them the same way. In the wilderness. When I worked in the herds, the year before Lilia."

"Enough," Natasha said. Too loud. "Lev, I told you, they're waiting for us over there. If you don't want to come, don't, but understand how cruel you're being to your friend." Her son made a face, and she knew Misha wasn't his friend, not really. She got up anyway. "Yulka?"

Her daughter propped herself up on her elbows. "I'll stay here, too, Mama."

"Fine," Natasha said. "Fine." She went to the foyer for her coat. On the other side of the wall, the television squawked.

"Don't go," her mother called in Even. Natasha was sick of hearing her childhood language.

If aliens really had landed, they would have taken Denis, not Lilia, away. And didn't Natasha wish for that? An interplanetary exchange? "I'll be back soon," she shouted in Russian toward the living room. They were no longer children, happy to swim together in warm water—Natasha and Denis had no bond to each other anymore.

He wanted to talk about his spaceships. Tell them, then, and see.

.

"Denis claims he's hosted visitors from outer space," Natasha told Anfisa. The neighbor raised her eyebrows. Anfisa had not shown even that much surprise when Natasha turned up without Lev, although Natasha had not said she was coming, had instead wasted the short walk over on calling Yuri's out-of-service cell phone. He was somewhere off the coast of Canada. He would call on Sunday, if the sub stayed on schedule. For now, Natasha had to accept the rise and fall of their cell provider's recorded messages: *The number cannot be accessed. Hang up and try again . . .*

Anfisa rested her head on one fist. Their mugs were topped off with so much liquor that the tea in them was already cool enough to drink. Natasha said, "He worked one season in the reindeer herds." She explained it: the period in Denis's twenties when he kept losing jobs. He was briefly employed as a daycare attendant, a cook, a shop cashier. All that was before he found the position he held now, as a night watchman for the village school. Their mother had arranged a herding apprenticeship with another Even family that lived near them. Denis accepted it without fuss. He left that year in June, when the herders swung close to Esso, and returned in September sun-darkened.

Lev entered kindergarten that fall, and Lilia started her final year of high school. The week he came home, Lilia called Natasha to report Denis's experience of extraterrestrials. Her voice came through the phone amused. One night, out in the tundra with the herd, Denis saw a purple light overhead, she said. Simply spotting that light froze him in place. Meanwhile the deer kept grazing. The glow got bigger, filling his vision, and then creatures from outer space were on the ground beside him. They stroked his arms. They sent messages telepathically. When he thought how worried he was about losing the herd, that the deer might wander off into the tundra during this visitation, they told him not to worry, his paralysis was temporary, they had already put all the animals and the other herders back at camp to sleep.

The grasses rustling in the night breeze. The deer, barely a meter tall at the shoulder, hunkered down together to make a low, dark field of fur. The world so quiet that Denis could hear his own breath in his ears. The sweep of stars and satellites above.

"How considerate of them," Natasha said.

Lilia laughed. Natasha should have asked more questions, probed for Lilia's coming escape plans, but back then it seemed there was no other family sorrow to discuss. They turned the subject instead to Lilia's classes. Which kids planned to leave Esso after high school graduation to study. Lilia said she'd do that, too, but not right away. She talked about coming down to visit Petropavlovsk. Eleven months later, she was gone.

Returning home after her sister's disappearance was the only time Natasha ever heard that story direct from Denis. The same details: purple light, resting deer, alien mouths fixed shut while alien words in his head were echoing. He told her and their mother in the kitchen that first night. He was nervous. His breath came short. And he tacked on a new ending. "They told me they'd come back for me, but they came for Lilia instead," he said. "She's taken." Pointed up. "Lilia's safe," he said, in a promise that stemmed from a vivid dream, a promise neither he nor anyone else on this peninsula was capable of proving.

"Phoo," said Anfisa and shuddered. "So what really happened to her?"

"She ran away," Natasha said. Anfisa waited. "It was hard to figure out at first because she didn't take the bus out, she didn't have a car, and she never mentioned leaving permanently. But afterward we put it together."

They sat in quiet. The air around them was sticky with that pine smell, wet from steam. "My sister had secrets," Natasha said. "She dated people I didn't know about. She had a reputation our neighbors only mentioned after she left. Everyone at home says they saw this coming." Even Yuri, with his hands pressed to Natasha's back as reassurance.

"Please, these experts," Anfisa said. "They say that now. Don't listen."

"But they're right. Aren't they? It shouldn't have come as a surprise." Natasha wrapped her fingers around her mug. "My mother doesn't believe that, though. She thinks Lilia's like the Golosovskaya sisters—killed."

"Whatever happened with those girls is so different."

"My mother and brother don't grasp that," Natasha said. "No one needed to take Lilia. She left on her own. Because who could stand living with him? Talking incessantly about what does not exist. Hearing that, and only that, who wouldn't keep her own secrets? Who wouldn't go?"

After a minute, Anfisa said, "Take a sip." She took the kettle from the counter to top off Natasha's drink.

Natasha looked up at her friend. "You understand," she said. She was so grateful.

Reaching out, Anfisa wrapped her fingers around Natasha's wrist. That warm, soft skin. The kettle shone silver between them. Anfisa's hand eased back any anger.

"It must be so hard to have an invalid in the family," Anfisa said. "Which category is Denis in? The second?"

Natasha opened her mouth. Shook her head. "No, Denis isn't—None." She was startled out of her own words. Anfisa seemed sure that Denis fit into a government invalid group, that he received disability pay. That he was sick. "He's not."

"Oh," Anfisa said. "I thought . . . You were just saying he can't work."

"He can work. He has a job right now."

"But isn't that what you've been telling me? There's something wrong."

"Don't say that," Natasha said. "There's nothing wrong. Denis is strange. That's all."

"More than strange." Anfisa's fingers were still on Natasha's wrist. "It's like you said, isn't it? Hard to live with that. Who in your sister's place wouldn't go?"

Anfisa's hand still, still, still there. Still there. Natasha had said those things, yet repeated by Anfisa they were foul. They made her siblings into caricatures. Anfisa did not know. The memory came up inside Natasha like vomit: not Lilia herself, her wit and freshness, but the village women who came over after Lilia left to gossip about a teenage girl gone missing. How they hugged Natasha and her children, how they wiped their wet faces on her cheeks. Their appraisal of her household. The blow of judgment.

Natasha took her arm back. She was done with the taste of the tea. "It's time for me to leave."

"Come on."

"I've already been here too long. They're at home waiting."

Anfisa looked skeptical. "Uh-huh," she said. Though Natasha knew this situation was her own fault—she had given every reason, by sneaking away from her apartment to complain, for her neighbor to judge her family—she could not stand the look on Anfisa's face. Anfisa did not really look like Lilia. She was too old. Her jaw and cheeks and brow bones were highlighted in shimmering powder. She dangled herself like a lure; for the sake of a drinking partner, she had baited Natasha into intimacy.

Anfisa followed Natasha to the door. "I'm sorry if I offended you."

Natasha pulled her boots back on. "No. But they're leaving in three days. I should spend more time with them while I have the chance." Dressed for the cold, Natasha faced her neighbor. "Unlike you, I actually like being with my family," she said. Anfisa's expression kept that sly cat look, and Natasha wished she had come up with something more cutting. Or no—already she wished she had said nothing at all; already she regretted speaking. Always regretting. As if a comment made in anger was like another slap.

The building's stairwell was dark. The sun was already behind the mountains.

She had not told Anfisa details of Denis as a boy—the community pool, the way he spoon-fed baby Lilia cereal, how all three of them gathered grass together to feed the horses fenced in neighbors' yards—or Denis as a younger man. The herders that summer said that they wouldn't need his help in the future, but he had done well for himself in the field. Crossing the parking lot, Natasha swayed with guilt. Her coat was open. She dialed Yuri's number again. The recording piped into her ear, *cannot be accessed,* always *cannot be accessed,* like the thousands of times she had called Lilia with no luck, and she flung her phone down at a snow pile. It slotted sideways into the white. Quick, she crouched, scooped the phone back out, and pressed the home button—the screen still worked. Natasha wiped the phone over and over across one bare palm. For days, for years, she had been making the stupidest choices.

Anfisa was not Lilia. Lilia was kind and clever and had the wisdom to keep her views private. She was living in Moscow, or St. Petersburg, or Luxembourg. Natasha liked to picture her in Europe. Lilia was an elegant young woman now. Maybe she had finally enrolled in university. Maybe she had gotten married. Maybe she even had a child or two of her own.

Lilia, Natasha promised herself, fingers freezing, was traveling the world. And one day she might come back to them. For now, Natasha would have to deal with her brother without a sibling who could carry stories between them.

Denis was fine. He was just on the more idiosyncratic end of normal. He was all Natasha had at the moment, and so she needed to be kinder, not dismiss him, value having him nearby.

On her landing, with her keys out, Natasha could hear conversation. She let herself back in. Peeking around the corner, she found Denis and Lev still on the couch. Yulka had joined them there. The three of them in a row, holding her accountable.

Natasha turned away to hang her wet coat. Her fingers hurt from cold. "Where's Babulya?" she called to the children.

"She went out to meet her cousin again," Yulka said.

"How nice," Natasha said. Trying hard to sound loving.

"But we wanted to stay here."

Natasha went to the kitchen to pour herself a glass of water. She came out and took the armchair. Her face was flushed. "What have you all been talking about?"

Yulka glanced at her uncle. Lev said, "Nothing."

Natasha sipped her water. She put the glass down at her feet, leaned forward, and squeezed Denis's shoulder. He glanced at her with surprise and, she hoped, pleasure. "You only have a couple more days in the city," she said. "What would you like to do?"

"It's not safe to be out too much," Denis said. "Remember London. Petrozavodsk."

"I do," she said.

Yulka said, "Mama, Uncle Denis told us that he met aliens."

Natasha took her hand back and touched her forehead. "All right."

"Are they actually real?"

She only hesitated for an instant. "No, bunny," she said, then addressed her brother: "You know that, Denis."

His expression flattened. His eyes half-shut. Natasha felt it then, the familiar grief of looking for someone who would not be recovered.

"See, I told you," Lev said to his sister. Natasha watched her brother. She was listening.

Roswell. Tunguska. Chelyabinsk. Jerusalem. Natasha was waiting for Denis to change. And she, too, would be different—she was going to be an excellent sister. She would let go of this anger. She was not angry. She just wanted to hear what else Denis had to say.

Revmira woke up knowing it was February 27. The date bore down on her. She dressed slowly, sadly, under its weight, and came out to the kitchen to find her husband boiling their coffee. "Good morning," she said.

"Morning," Artyom said, and she knew from the line of his shoulders over the stove that he knew what day it was, too.

She got out cheese and ham for breakfast. While she prepared two plates at the counter, he poured their cups. The teaspoon clinked as he mixed sugar into hers. They had been together twenty-six years, nearly half Revmira's life, and still she was surprised by Artyom's kindness. He was the easiest man she had ever known. But then she had only known two.

"How'd you sleep?" he asked.

She shrugged, put their breakfast sandwiches down, and took her seat. "Are you on call today?"

"Twelve to twelve." Soon he would meet with the rest of his rescue team, stack their gear, get ready for any urgent flight to the mountains or the ice caves or the open water, but for now he was rumpled in his T-shirt. He had not yet shaved. Behind him, their kitchen window showed a clear sky.

She had slept heavy and dark the night before. She had not dreamed of Gleb. For years after the accident, she did—that Gleb visited her in her childhood home; treated her on her birthday; drove her down the bumpy road beyond the city limits to the ocean's black sandy shore. "This is impossible," she said in that one. "I know," he said and shifted gears. She wanted in the dream to touch his hand but was afraid to distract him at the wheel.

"It's going to be warm," Artyom said.

She looked up from her plate. "Is that right?"

"Almost zero."

"I'm not surprised," she said. "You only give yourself the best shifts. You'll probably spend all day picnicking."

"Having ice cream in the snow. Sure. More like we'll be called at noon on the dot for some novice getting sunburned off-piste."

"Just be careful," she said. He kept watching her.

"With weather like this, it could be a short winter," he said. "Lieutenant Ryakhovsky texted this morning. They want our boats to search for the sisters in the bay once it thaws."

The bread was dry in Revmira's mouth. "He never got back to me."

"I asked again about that. He didn't respond."

"He's a jackass," she said.

Artyom smiled at her from across the table. That look deepened the lines on his face.

"You told him about Alla's daughter?"

"I told him everything," Artyom said. "He's all business: the major general wants approval from the ministry for another round of water searches."

Revmira put her bread down. For months, Petropavlovsk's rescue team had been helping the police organize search efforts for the Golosovskaya sisters. Artyom's rescue work usually came in bursts—hikers unable to descend from volcanoes, snowmobilers cracking through thin lake ice, fishermen getting turned around at sea—but this case would not end. In the fall, Artyom had led civilians through the city to search for the missing girls; once the weather turned, he brought home occasional updates from officers.

How tidy of the police to throw all their efforts into looking for two small white bodies. That served as a good excuse to ignore the city's other corruptions, its injustice, its drunk drivers or petty arsonists. Why should Ryakhovsky answer Artyom's text messages about some northern teen? Preparing boats to drag a bay that was frozen must occupy all the lieutenant's valuable time.

Over the winter holidays, Revmira's second cousin, Alla, visiting from Esso, had said that her younger daughter was still missing. Alla had brought the subject up at the cross-country ski base's café after what was supposed to be a pleasant morning together spent gliding over snow. Listening, Revmira cut a cottage-cheese pastry into three portions, while Alla rubbed her temple and talked, and Alla's grown son watched those entering the base stomp their boots clean.

Revmira had never met this missing daughter. Alla came to the city only once a year, to see her grandchildren, and contacted Revmira with the same sadness each time. Their meetings came out of mutual obligation. After Revmira's parents passed, Revmira had stopped visiting the village. There was nothing for her there. Her cousin's gloomy annual updates were enough to confirm that choice.

"The authorities still have nothing to say about your girl?" Revmira had asked. Her cousin only shook her head. "Here the Ministry of Internal Affairs and the Ministry of Emergency Situations have been looking for these Russian sisters tirelessly."

"It wasn't that way with us."

"I imagine not."

"Natasha told me in the fall that the sisters were taken by someone," Alla said. "When Lilia disappeared, I begged authorities to look for the person responsible. All Esso's officers did then was spread rumors about Lilia's boyfriends. She wasn't . . . she had admirers, but that was exactly why . . ." Behind her glasses, Alla's eyelids lowered. Her nostrils flared.

Revmira sat in quiet with her for a few moments. Meanwhile Alla's son picked up his portion of their divided pastry. "Artyom could speak to the city police for you," Revmira said eventually. "He knows people. They might open a case for her, at least. Keep a description on file." Her cousin did not look hopeful.

Still, Revmira had collected a few details to pass forward. Lilia was small, too, and young, though not as young as the Golosovskaya sisters. Artyom had given Revmira the lieutenant's number, then himself messaged the lieutenant with a graduation photo of the teen, but they heard nothing back. No great surprise. Lilia was three years missing, Even, the child of a nobody.

Revmira should never have suggested a city investigation to Alla. This was how it went: no end to grief. Her cousin's cheeks had been hollowed out by absence. Revmira knew that expression too well.

"No shock Ryakhovsky didn't respond," Revmira said at the breakfast table. "Given the chance to assist an old native woman, our police would rather—" She stopped, turned her face from Artyom.

Rather die, she'd almost said. She had almost let herself forget what day it was.

"Well, he ought to try," Artyom said. She shook her head. He went on: "He's touchy these days about taking tips from civilians. He was reprimanded for it by the major general in the fall. But that's their job. These officers are too young to understand what duty is."

Revmira sipped the coffee. It tasted good. Sweet. She did not deserve it. Distracting herself, talking casually . . . even after all this time, it made no sense that she got to wake up and chatter and drink fresh coffee while Gleb could not.

She stood from the table. "Late, isn't it?" she said. Artyom glanced at the clock on the stove.

She went to brush her teeth. In the mirror, she saw herself dressed for work.

Had she ever been as young as she was when she met Gleb? All her days back then felt bright. When, at seventeen, she moved to Petropavlovsk, the city was filled with scaffolding, soldiers, polished monuments. She came to her first day of university and saw Gleb. She was thinner then, tanner, an emissary from Esso's Young Communist League, and he was as fair and glorious as a figure on a propaganda poster. His eyebrows furrowed under the classroom lights as he looked back.

What a lucky, stupid girl she had been in those years. Even the most difficult times she remembered from that age were nothing now. A month into her first semester, she received a package at her dormitory. The box was so light she thought at first it must be empty. She opened it to find dozens of dried pinecones; her father had gathered them to mail three hundred kilometers south to her. The box smelled like home. The forest, dirt, her parents' scratchy clothes. She shook out the seeds, chewed them, and cried. At seventeen years old, that was her most desolate moment: missing the people who sent her packages.

And that same afternoon she was able to bring a pinecone to class and pass it across the aisle into Gleb's hand. They were married before graduation. She had the whole world then, but she was only a child.

She applied her eyeliner. Revmira always took this date to repeat to herself Gleb's qualities: his patience, his charm. He waited by her desk after class and she prolonged collecting her books to keep him there above her. Once, in the park with friends, he knelt down to tie her shoes. He was that indulgent. That surprising. His fingers a little longer and thinner than hers. The weekend she, finally his wife, moved in with him and his mother, he brought home a two-liter tub of red caviar to celebrate. They ate out of the tub with spoons. The saline pop of those eggs on their teeth. She would never forget.

In the other room, Artyom was clearing the dishes. They rang against the sink. Each year, Revmira's recollections stayed the same—the tied shoe, the tub of caviar—while everything else, against her will, deepened, strengthened, grew. Gleb's letters and records were in a suitcase on the floor of her closet. She wore a white uniform, and kept a tidy house he would not see, and had been married again for so long that people said to her, "Your husband," without bothering to specify who.

She came back into the kitchen to give Artyom a kiss. "I'm off."

Wiping his hands, he followed her to the hall. He stood in slippered feet while she pulled on her heels. When she was ready, he held out her coat, wool and thickly lined. "Lunch this afternoon?"

"If you're not too busy," she said. "You'll let me know if you get called in?"

"Of course," he said. He always did. She kissed him again. His mouth under hers was soft and warm and living. It was not fair that he should be so good to her today, when she attended least to him. None of this was fair.

As she drew away, she saw his eyes had stayed open. He saw, somewhere in there, the woman she was when they first met—that destroyed version of her.

Revmira pulled her purse up on her shoulder. "Are you all right?" he asked.

"Of course," she said. She had to be.

All the same, she walked as though lost the four short blocks to the bus stop. The sky was washed blue. Melting ice broke under her shoes. Banks of snow propped up the buildings around her. The morning of the accident, Gleb's mother, still in her nightgown, came into their room. Sunlight was filtering through the curtains. Gleb had left for work almost an hour before. Revmira sat up, then, so the futon swayed underneath her. The frame was hard as bones below the mattress. "What is it, Mama?" Revmira said. She always thought of that question afterward—another recollection played and replayed. She should not have asked. Vera Vasilievna's expression already told her.

When Revmira found out, she screamed. Gleb's side of the sheets still smelled like him, but that would only fade. His clothes hung in the closet. On the top of their dresser, there were his childish prizes, his medals from the All-Union Pioneers and his school certificates.

At the funeral, there were photographs of him. A shut box that tormented her with what it did or did not hold. Revmira was ten when her grandfather died; his body had stayed for three days on display in her childhood home, and she could touch his skin, stiff as cardboard, which scared her and soothed her at once to feel. But Gleb, who had not been wearing a seat belt, had to stay in the state morgue until the service. Pieces of him could be missing. She did not know. She never would. Picturing him that way made her think she might go mad.

Vera Vasilievna covered all the mirrors in the apartment, like Revmira's family had in Esso—but Gleb was not an old man, he was twenty-two, he was immaculate. "You're my child now," Vera Vasilievna told her. "You're all I have left." Though when Gleb had first brought Revmira home his mother wept over his seeing a native girl. They threw fistfuls of dirt into his grave. It was impossible. His mother was shaking, and Revmira knew she should put an arm around the woman's shoulders, and she could not. Instead Revmira stood with her dirty hands folded. Everything around her was just an imitation of what he had been.

Revmira moved to a room in a friend's apartment. To keep herself sane, she had to keep going, so she gave away their wedding presents, the dishes they ate off, the clothes he saw her wear, until the only scraps left of their life together fit in one buckled bag. She finished her degree, found a job, paid her bills, made her dinners. She watched Gorbachev speak about openness and change on her television. And all the while she was screaming. She never stopped. In her mind, she was still twenty-one and ten months and two days, and it was just after seven in the morning, and Gleb had been lying next to her an hour before.

The bus delivered her to the hospital's triage desk by eight. The nurse getting off shift briefed her: this many beds open, this many appointments to expect, this or that piece of gossip that had surfaced overnight. Revmira draped her coat over the back of the desk chair and nodded along. There were only two men sitting along the wall of the admission department, which was no more than a corridor, really, a narrow green-painted hall. Any sick people who could afford it bought themselves seats in the waiting room of a private clinic. After the other nurse left, Revmira called one man over to the triage desk so he could state his symptoms. He opened his mouth and the sickly smell of booze washed over her. "Sit down," she said. She waved the other man up, reviewed his paperwork, and had him follow her upstairs for an exam.

Through the morning, patients came in clusters: brusque Valentina Nikolaevna for radiation therapy, a teenager whose appendix was near bursting, a snowboarder who broke his leg and was wheeled to the elevator with lines of snow on his jacket sleeves. Revmira assessed them all. She directed people for X-rays, for ultrasounds, and to the surgical floor. Doctors called down to manage prescriptions. Revmira called up about the patient flow. One man entered the admission department with a crossbow bolt through the meat of his right shoulder, and she had him fill out his papers with his left hand before she sent him forward.

As the hall thinned out to one or two again, she had time to tidy the top of the desk, lining up a stapler with the long edge of her notepad. She let her brain go neat and blank. Artyom texted her to say that he was being called in for a mountain rescue. She texted back good luck. Out the door, the street was sunny. The air was practically vernal. Eventually a trainee came down to cover her for lunch.

In the break room, Revmira picked up a magazine to read. Rather than attending to its pages, though, she held the magazine over her soup and recalled the summer day, before their last year of university, that she and Gleb got married. He in his suit and she in her plain little heels. Her hair braided over her shoulder. The way he held her after they said their vows—she had wanted to have his children that instant.

Good, probably, that they didn't end up pregnant. If she had stood at his funeral with a baby in her arms—where would she have gone afterward? What would she have done?

When Artyom, years after, found out he couldn't have children, Revmira had already lived too long for the news to surprise. That loss piled up with the rest. In any case, Kamchatka was no longer a place to raise a family. Just look at the hole in her cousin's life where a daughter belonged. The communities Revmira grew up in had splintered, making them easy places to be forgotten, easy places to disappear. Revmira's parents had raised her in a strong home, an idyllic village, a principled people, a living Even culture, a socialist nation of great achievement. That nation collapsed. Nothing was left in the place it had occupied.

Revmira stirred her cooling soup. Modern life had buried the lovers she and Gleb had been. She ended up back at the wedding registry office ten years later; though she and Artyom were married in the same building, they stood in a different room, before a different officiant, under the laws of a different state. All the spots she and Gleb went to as newlyweds—kissing each other before the Bering monument, at the city center, or on top of St. Nicholas Hill—were now covered in graffiti and trash. Even the university changed. Revmira had to stop by every fall to pick up student medical records. The first time, she went to the classroom where she met Gleb and found the space filled by strangers.

He died and the whole Soviet Union followed. Revmira's country, her young face, the entire course of her life had changed. Since she started at the hospital, she had sat next to more than a hundred patients to help them go, so she now knew death well: the release of breath, the rattle, the calm. Her parents went the same way, one after the other. And she missed them. She had resigned herself a long time ago to missing all the people who left her. There were many, many. Vera Vasilievna, too. But Gleb was the only one who had been perfect. He was the one whose death shocked her, who kept shocking her year after year.

It would have been easier if she had died with him. Not better, necessarily, just . . . easier. If she was in the car, too. She had imagined it so many times.

Back at the triage desk, she thought of that. His car, the road, the icy dark before dawn that day. Their wedding, his arms around her, the little boy they could have had, the little girl. February 27. Even when Revmira was awake, she was dreaming.

Her cell phone vibrated. The screen showed the name of the wife of another man in Artyom's crew. Revmira ducked her head to take the call. "Yes, Inna?"

There was a second of silence on the other end of the line. Inna said, "Something's happened."

Around Revmira, the people in the waiting room muttered and sighed and moaned. Under her forehead, the desk was smooth. Cold. Revmira kept her face down. She waited.

"They radioed in. They've been trying to reach us. Reach you. Artyom was hurt," Inna said. "I'm sorry, Reva. I'm sorry. I'm so sorry." Her voice continued.

Inna said a rock. She said his head. She said knocked out. She said no pain. The team medic tried to revive him. He was already gone. It happened too fast, Inna said.

Folded in her chair, Revmira looked down at her scrubs. Her cotton-covered knees. "I don't understand," she said.

Inna said a rock. There had been a rescue, a lost skier. She said they found the skier. And then a rock fell. She said his head. No pain. An accident. His skull. The curve of his neck, his jaw, his face looking at her this morning with the window soft and white behind.

"I see. I see," said Revmira.

She hung up. Someone came to the desk and she waved him away. She had forgotten to ask where Artyom was now. Should she call back? She unlocked the phone and looked at Inna's name in her call list. This was crazy. She opened up a text to her husband. Her fingers moved slowly over the letters. She had to tell Artyom what this woman had said.

Artyom was hurt. Inna told her that. But Revmira would take him as an invalid. She would take him weak. Diminished. As long as he was living.

She looked up and Inna was in front of the desk. Revmira looked at the clock on her computer. Time had passed.

"I came to take you home," Inna said. Her eyes were red. "They're still in the mountains."

"Okay," said Revmira. "I understand."

Inna went away. Someone touched Revmira's shoulder. It was the trainee, saying she would take over. Inna was there again. Revmira made sure not to forget her coat. They went outside. Artyom was dead.

Revmira concentrated on buckling herself into Inna's car. It was hard to do. Her hands were strange. She focused on her fingers, her bending knuckles. The parchment color of her nails against the seat belt.

Since Gleb's accident, Revmira had hated cars. Now she had to hate rocks, too. Rocks. Snow. The sound of her cell phone ringing. Sugar stirred into her coffee. The smell of breakfast filling their kitchen. She had thought she was strong, but she was not. She was not. Not anymore, not without him.

In the driver's seat, Inna started the engine and wiped her cheeks. She looked up through the windshield. Her jacket whispered as she moved. "It's this weather," Inna said. "Loose ice. Avalanche weather."

Revmira folded her hands in her lap. She could not get control of them. Cold air blew on her from the vents. It was February 27.

"This is fate," she said out loud.

Inna sniffed back tears at the steering wheel. "What?"

Revmira looked out the window at the heaps of blackened snow bordering the parking lot. Water trickled out onto the asphalt. The sun was high above them. She thought of the rock. His head. No pain. Last weekend napping on the couch in the afternoon, her legs pinned between his, their faces close together. His breath on her cheek. Once he woke up, he asked her if she was comfortable. They had talked about headlines, currency devaluations, parliamentary decisions, the Golosovskaya sisters. "If I were their kidnapper," she told him, "I'd bring them north. No one watches the villages. You could bury bodies right on your property in daylight hours without anyone noticing."

Artyom had kissed the creased skin below her eye. "My morbid, brilliant woman."

She carried death into their marriage, brought death with her up to this day. Quietly, into the glass of the window, she said, "Our suffering is fated." She should have expected this from the very beginning. She had met Artyom, that excellent man, and condemned him.

The parking lot rolled away, other cars gathered around them, city buses pulled over, traffic lights turned green. Inna took the long way home, past the cinema, and Revmira did not correct her. Snow piles rose and fell beside them like ocean waves. In front of her and Artyom's building, Revmira took out her keys. Inna plucked them away to unlock the doors. *I can do that*, Revmira wanted to say. *I know how to do all of this. I've done it before.* Instead she followed Inna into her own apartment.

The younger woman went straight to put on the kettle. Inna had decided to be capable. It was easy for Inna; the man she loved was alive.

"Excuse me," Revmira said. Her voice sounded so polite. She took her phone into the bathroom and called Artyom's sister.

"Oh," his sister said and started to weep. The sound of it, rhythmic, desperate, hurt. Revmira pressed the phone harder to her ear. She had not cried yet. She had to listen. "Have you seen him?" his sister asked.

"No," Revmira said. She knew how searches worked. "No, they're coming back from the mountains. It's quite— It's difficult. They bring the one they rescued first. It'll be a few hours."

"Maybe it's not true."

The bathroom sink was flecked with Artyom's hair. He had shaved this morning after Revmira left. This world was built for people to suffer. "It's true," Revmira said, and the sister wept harder.

Inna waited in the kitchen, so Revmira, after getting off the phone, went into the bedroom and shut the door. At the top of their tugged-up blanket was Artyom's pillow. Revmira touched it. Soft. On the bedside table, there was his book. His glass of water—she picked that up and drank it.

She put the empty glass on his side of the blanket, and the book there, too. They made little dents in the wool. Then she opened up the bedside drawer to find a pocketknife, his spare sunglasses, a bottle of vitamin D supplements. She put those on the bed. It was nice to see his things laid out. She could do that. She had nothing else to do. She went to their dresser and pulled out his sweaters, his pants, the white undershirts, the worn briefs. Artyom was in his house clothes when she last saw him. Navy athletic pants and an old T-shirt. She fetched those from the laundry basket. She did not know what he wore to work today, but she would find out soon enough.

She wanted to see his body.

The pile on the bed looked small. She went to the closet for more.

She should gather his things. She should stockpile memories. She met Artyom when she was twenty-nine, when her former classmates had already made themselves mothers and she, still young, had nothing but her job and her buried history. She frightened people. But Artyom was not disturbed. He was a friend of a friend; they were introduced at a party. He had trained as a biathlete outside Moscow and returned to Kamchatka after too many years of fruitless competition left him thin, fair-minded, strong.

They slept together sooner than a month after they met. In the blackness of Artyom's bedroom, his parents out and his sister a wall away, Revmira peeled off his clothes. His knees and shoulders were bound up in muscles. She ran her fingers over their cords. When she explored his chest, she felt his heart, that athlete's measured muscle, pounding. His breath was quick. His body betrayed him.

With her fingers tight on the closet rod, she began to cry. They last had sex on Wednesday. Today was Sunday.

How did Artyom want her, even then? How did he manage to survive for so long? For months after they were married, she appreciated him, his long legs, his service, and then all at once she fell in love. They were on the bus together. It was snowing the way it used to and never seemed to anymore, those flakes so dense that the driver followed the road not from sight but from habit. Three blocks from their stop, Artyom turned to Revmira, flipped up her collar, and pulled her jacket zipper to her chin. He tugged her hat down on her forehead and ran his fingers around her wrists to check the seal of her gloves. Then he took her hand and faced forward. Swaddled up, she felt herself—alive. Finally alive. The blood in her body was a rolling boil.

She had sat there warm and thrilled and terrified. She had believed new wonders waited. Her only bare skin was the strip around her eyes, and the world outside looked so fresh, so clean. So promising. After Gleb died, she was alone, alone, always alone, and suddenly, on a plastic seat in a crowded bus, she found that someone else was with her. She'd exhaled with joy into her jacket collar. Artyom.

Her husband. Her rescuer. He had done his duty. Now Revmira

was supposed to keep going without him. She wiped her face and went into the kitchen. When she entered, Inna stood up, phone in her hand, and said, "They're on their way."

"All right," Revmira said. She took his mug and plate from the drying rack.

In the bathroom, she grabbed his toothbrush, razor, cologne. The face lotion he used—she added it all to the pile.

For nearly all of the past twenty-six years, she had busied herself with Artyom's kindness, their careers, the mealtime conversations, the assistance they offered others. She looked at the rest of the country falling apart but believed that she and Artyom could last. She was wrong. Artyom's twelve-hour shifts, Revmira's work at the hospital, their appeals to authorities—those were the acts of an earlier age. Those things were useless. In the end, they did not protect anyone.

She went back to the closet, pulled out Gleb's suitcase, and heaved the case onto the blanket. Its bulk pressed on Artyom's belongings. She opened the case, snaps biting into her fingers, and saw some objects she had forgotten, some others she could not forget. She needed to be with these things of her husband's. All of it together was everything she had left. The letters he wrote her. Faded record sleeves. His winter hat, his civil passport. She emptied the old case out, then she put it down on the blanket and crawled onto the bed.

Boots, buckles, papers, and scarves. After Gleb's accident, she thought she would die. She thought she had. This date took him and pulled her down after, grief determined as gravity. But now she would live. She had to. It was what she did: live while others could not. There was no pleasure in it.

MARCH

Three wordless days after the kitchen flooded, Nadia and Mila took off from Esso's provincial airport toward Palana's. They had their own row to themselves. Mila, five years old, spent the plane ride eating cucumber slices and drawing figures with ever-larger breasts. She drew two big circles in her notebook and laughed, then drew two bigger circles around those and laughed again, then set her mouth in concentration to draw two even bigger circles. Peering over her daughter's head, Nadia asked, "No men?"

Quickly Mila drew another, wider person. She added two tiny nipple dots to the chest.

"I wasn't telling you to add one," Nadia said.

Mila put her pen back to the page and circled those dots with breasts. "Wonderful," Nadia said and looked out the window at the white ground.

They were already past the central mountain range that penned in Esso. Nadia had spent the last few days bartering with their pilot so this twin-engine turboprop, halted by a blizzard after leaving Petropavlovsk, would take her and Mila along for the last leg of its trip north. In the village they left behind was Chegga. His garbage palace of a rental house where they had spent the last three years. The newly broken radiator pipe, the tile floor yellow under ankle-deep water. The last sentence Nadia spoke to him—"Call the landlord," she had said on Tuesday—and the note she slid under the frozen honey jar on the kitchen table today.

She and Mila were starting over. Nadia put one arm around Mila's back. "My sweet," Nadia said, "let's not tell Grandpa and Baba about what happened this week, all right?"

Mila drew another loop. "All right."

"Pretend I'm Grandpa. Hi, Mila, what's new with you?"

"Nothing!" Mila said. "The other day a pipe broke and it made an ice rink in the house."

Nadia paused. "That's what we're not telling."

"I thought we weren't telling about you and Daddy being mad at each other."

"That, too," Nadia said. "All of it." She squeezed Mila's shoulder, took her arm back, sank in her seat. Pushed her knees against the seat pocket ahead.

It didn't matter what Mila said. In a month or two, their life would be good enough that Nadia would no longer have to misrepresent it to her parents. So instead of wasting words on what they were leaving, that iced-over shithole, Nadia unlocked her phone, scrolled to a Rihanna album, and put one earbud in. "Here, kitten," she said to Mila, who tilted the side of her face up. Nadia tucked the other bud into her daughter's soft ear and let pop music play them in.

They came at Palana from the east. The town was the administrative center of its district, but looked shabby from above: streets smudged gray, apartment blocks crumbling, rows of wooden houses trailing into the sea. Nadia hadn't been back since she and Mila moved south to Esso. She could not see any new structures from the air.

Her parents met them at the airport. Neither of them questioned Mila on what was new. Nadia's mother said, "I will not ask why Chegga didn't come."

"He's busy with work," Nadia said. "Not only the newspaper anymore—weddings, events." That wasn't the reason, but it was a flattering fact.

"He needed a break, I imagine. You're not easy to live with."

"And who raised me that way?" Nadia muttered. Her mother, too deaf to hear, was squinting at the other disembarking passengers in search of anyone she recognized. Her father was bent over and squeezing Mila's cheeks.

Mila had on a new coat, shining purple, that Nadia had bought her for New Year's. Thank God for Sberbank: it was Nadia's job that had landed them here. Seven weeks of paid vacation. She and Chegga had talked about using that time to go to Sochi for the summer, before one burst pipe, one final argument, and one firm conversation with her boss about what Nadia had called a "family matter" changed those plans permanently.

They had seven weeks now, which would take them into May. Long enough to find a quality place to live. Not in Palana, certainly, or in Petropavlovsk, where Chegga's sister was in university, but on the mainland—perhaps Kazan?—or even Europe. Istanbul? London? Without Chegga to hold them back, Nadia and Mila might become world travelers. Sberbank had branches everywhere.

In the car, Nadia took the passenger seat, while her father and Mila climbed into the back. Sitting close to the steering wheel, Nadia's mother continued to squint, though there was nothing but iced-over parked cars in front of them.

"Mama, can you see?" Nadia asked. No answer. Nadia twisted in her seat. "Can she see?"

"Of course she can," her father said. "She drove us here."

Nadia studied him, his knit cap, his own clouding eyes, and leaned over into the back to buckle Mila in. Her mother pulled into the line of cars leaving the airport lot. "Papa, I got a raise in January," Nadia said. "I'm a manager now. Sixty more an hour."

"With the way the ruble's falling, that's nothing," her father said. "Your mother's pension hardly buys our bread."

"Do you need help?" Nadia asked. Her father frowned. She had been away too long; she'd forgotten his habits, the complaints about money segueing into the same concerns about politics, bureaucrats, criminals clogging parliament. His lack of a wish to change. She took a breath. "Sorry. How's the catch these days?"

"What's there to say? Winter waters. How's—"

"How's our Chegga?" her mother asked.

"He's fine." Her mother didn't react. *"HE'S FINE,"* Nadia said. *"SAME AS EVER."* At this, her mother shook her head, her bun drifting from side to side across her scalp while her shoulders stayed fixed over the wheel.

The last season Nadia lived here was the first she spent with Chegga. He had finished his military service and decided to work a month in Palana's fishing camps, then extended his stay once they met. Nadia's parents fell all over him: a good boy, native like them, and from a place that was not theirs but seemed enough like theirs, meaning not too white, not foreign. Chegga was responsible, Chegga was talented. After Mila fell asleep with her mouth open each night, he and Nadia made silent love on the freshly laundered sheets. Next to them, Mila never stirred.

A month younger than Nadia, Chegga dreamed as big as she did. He already wanted to be a father. He loved that Nadia had Mila, who at that time was starting to speak, looking for someone to call Daddy. He talked up their future together. In his descriptions, Esso was the most beautiful village on Kamchatka, with carved log cabins and mountain air as fresh as an apple. After he went back, he called her every night: I found us a place, he said then, a temporary place, two rooms to stay warm in while we look for somewhere down the street to keep building our family. And while they saved for her and Mila's tickets south, Nadia walked around Palana flush with the knowledge that a better life was coming. Here were all the half-collapsed buildings, the flaking Soviet murals, the stained smoke-stacks, the mended nets, the tethered rowboats, the exes who no longer acknowledged her, the classmates who tittered when they passed Mila having a tantrum—and there, a flight away, was Chegga.

But in Esso, Nadia and Mila only found a half-collapsed shack of their own. *It's temporary,* he had shouted again on Tuesday morning as they stood in the flood. For three years he had been saying the same thing while pieces of the rental house fell off. Last fall, Nadia had approached her office about a home loan. She and Chegga argued about the bank for a month. No mortgages, he said, no debt. "We're not Americans. I won't live on credit." Goddamn it, she said to him, if we won't live on credit then we'll be stuck here—and still he insisted. So Nadia tried other methods. His parents had piled up savings from years of work in the reindeer herds; with Chegga's sister in university on a scholarship, their money just sat there. When the radiator began to leak this winter, Nadia went in confidence to Chegga's mother to suggest how they might see those savings spent. "Your generation always wants more," his mother said then. "Your avarice. Will that really seem good enough for you, to own someplace you borrowed and begged for? Will that satisfy?"

Nadia had not been begging. But now she saw his mother might be right: nothing in Esso would satisfy.

The village Chegga had flown them to was like the town they'd left. Over the January holidays, he had made Nadia and Mila spend their days with his sister and her boyfriend at Esso's public thermal pool. Whatever compromises Nadia suggested—*Can we pay for admission to a private pool, a cleaner one? Can we take Ksyusha, Mila adores her, but not invite Ruslan? Can we go out as a family, just the three of us?*—he turned down. Instead, they paddled in community waters, sweating, smelling sulfur, feeling the slip and give of algae on the cement under their feet.

In the pool, Chegga and Ruslan, his sister's sleazy boyfriend, had dissected the other villagers who came to swim—this one's mental deficiency, that one's weight problem, this one's unfaithful spouse. Chegga's sister, Ksyusha, only laid her head on the edge of the pool and shut her eyes. Once a man on the other side of the water waved in their direction. Mila dipped under, and Nadia clicked her tongue: "Mouse, don't get your hair wet. You'll catch cold." She stretched to grab a towel for her girl. Over her shoulder, she said to Chegga, "Someone's trying to say hello." Chegga glanced the man's way without acknowledgment. Ruslan, looking after, laughed.

"You're not going to greet him?" Nadia said.

"That's Yegor Gusakov," Ruslan said. "He graduated in Chegga's year."

"He's not normal," Chegga said. "A freak."

Nadia wanted to dip herself underwater, then, too. The man

across the pool was no hero—soft-bodied, sitting alone—but he was not monstrous. Chegga, meanwhile, was ignoring the misbehavior of his chosen child, who had undone her towel turban and let cords of hair freeze over her forehead. And Ruslan was about as agreeable as a feral white dog.

"You should feel sorry for him," Ksyusha said. Sweat glistened on her cheeks.

"I don't," Chegga said. "When we were kids he used to torture cats."

"That was a frog," Ksyusha said. "One time." Careful as always, this university girl. Ksyusha was restrained while her brother gave himself every liberty.

"A frog when we were watching. The cats, he did on his own. Lilia Solodikova told me Yegor left them in front of her house every week of sixth year. Her mother complained to all their neighbors because she thought someone was putting out too much rat poison."

"Oh, *Lilia* told you," Ruslan said. He nuzzled Ksyusha. When she turned away, he revolved to face Chegga. "Should we go ask Lilia what she thinks of him now?"

"You know she was probably murdered?" Chegga said. "You're an asshole."

Ruslan puffed his narrow chest up. "You're the asshole."

"Everyone's an asshole," Ksyusha said. "Let's talk about anything else."

Nadia was done with it all. If she wanted to hear family arguments, false superiority, and snide mentions of girls who fled the area years before, she could do that in her parents' town, where at least the heat worked and wallpaper stayed adhered to the walls. Nadia's mother drove them along a row of five-story apartment buildings. Blocks like that, half a century old, might not look as appealing from the outside as Esso's cottages, but their inhabitants could eat together without having to wade through chunks of ice.

Chegga used to swear that apartment blocks had no place in beautiful Esso. Kamchatka's Switzerland, he said. What did he know? None of them had ever been past Moscow.

At the house, Nadia's mother served fish soup. She insisted on giving them all a second helping as soon as the level of their broth dipped. Mila pushed her bowl away, and Nadia's mother pushed it back. "I don't want any more," Mila said.

"What?" Nadia's mother said.

"SHE DOESN'T WANT ANY MORE," said Nadia.

Clicking her tongue, her mother took the bowl to scrape back into the pot. Boiled potatoes fell splat, splat. Onions sprouted out of old mayonnaise jars on the counter. "It's because you're not eating. You don't set a good example for her."

Nadia flushed. "It's because she ate on the way."

"What?"

"IT'S BECAUSE SHE ATE ON THE WAY."

"That's not why," her mother said.

Nadia ducked her head so her hair made a dark wall between them. "Papa, doesn't she wear her hearing aid anymore?"

"Your mother's an excellent woman," her father said. He was lifting his spoon.

Nadia's nose prickled and she raised her face in surprise. She wasn't going to cry! Silly. But the way her father said that reminded her of the best of Chegga. The compliments Chegga delivered to Nadia through Mila—*Isn't your mama funny? Aren't we lucky?* The way he did show he loved her when he remembered to try.

She was simply getting sentimental because she was worn out after days of mutual silent treatment. Exhausted from the coordinating it took to get Mila out of preschool and herself away from the currency-counting machines.

Tired, too, from covering for the insufficiencies in their household. She could only imagine how people in Esso talked about their situation. That Chegga Adukanov, who lived in a dump, couldn't afford to fix his rented pipes. Maybe they did not even say "couldn't afford"—people could assume instead *didn't care.* They might think, There's a certain type of man, indigenous, probably drinks too much, seems polite when he's on the job but then see how he acts at home. Lives with a woman but doesn't follow through with marriage. Acts sweet enough to take on another man's baby but lets that child freeze. Except for the drinking, all those potential whispers were true. And Nadia could not stand being subject to more gossip.

This month and a half would give her the time to sort out what propelled her toward him in the first place. If she had been willing after high school to spend a few more days here, instead of getting pregnant by the first man who approached her, would she have ended up a couple lovers later in an even tinier village than where she started, with someone who took her and her baby on double dates to a communal swamp?

Once the lunch dishes were cleared, Nadia opened their suitcase in the living room. Mila's things were microscopic, rhinestone-dotted. "You're a very brave girl," Nadia told her daughter. Mila wrapped her arms around Nadia's neck and leaned into her lap. The girl smelled soupy: dill, black pepper, lemon juice. Nadia hugged her tighter.

Nadia shouldn't, but she could not resist. "We don't miss Daddy, do we?" she asked against Mila's cheek.

At first Mila was quiet. Then she turned her face in to Nadia's shoulder. Sniffed. Sniffed again—Nadia had made her daughter cry.

"Oh, my duckling," Nadia said. "I'm sorry. I'm sorry." She held her daughter hard, trying to squeeze the tears back in before Mila really started to go off.

"He's not coming?" Mila asked. Her voice was all choked. Nadia released some of the pressure around her daughter's ribs.

"He's back at home. Remember? We're staying with Grandpa and Baba for a while." Mila got louder, saying *no—no-o-o*—Nadia tried to talk over her. "Don't you remember how he broke the kitchen? He has to stay to fix it." Nadia had put Mila in this position, she'd asked her daughter about Chegga, and still she was getting angry at the girl. Nadia wanted to ask her, *Remember Tuesday?* Leaving the house cold and sobbing? The frost up the walls—the school attendant's pity—the way Chegga afterward had acted so defensive and put-upon? For once, couldn't Mila remember whose side she was on?

Nadia pushed her nose into her daughter's round cheek. "Do you want to watch TV?" There. Snot sucked back up into little sinuses. Cheburashka cartoons could undo any tragedy.

A swollen-faced Mila curled into Nadia on the couch. When Nadia was growing up, this was the spot where she slept, did her homework, fantasized about freedom; now she came back to this place as a mother and a professional. Together, she and Mila watched animals dance on her laptop. The light faded overhead.

When her phone buzzed, Nadia slipped out. In the hush of the hallway she looked at Chegga's picture on the screen. Then she silenced the call. The vibration stopped, but his face remained, back-lit by last summer's southern sun. His smile.

She felt that old tug he put in her. A finger hooked under her ribs.

The phone screen went black for a second, then lit up again. Another call. She knew exactly the conversation that was going to come—*why didn't you, when are you, why not,* and so on. She silenced the call again and pulled up their text message chain. *In Palana,* she sent. *Will call when I'm ready.*

The phone stayed silent. She watched the screen until she had to close her eyes against it. From the living room leaked the tinny sound of a song about trains.

Picture that hovel in Esso. Her daughter's breath fogging as she dressed. His barrel of a body looking ridiculous in gym shorts as he stood with his feet in ice water. Imagine anything but his voice rough at night, the toast and jam he prepared for Mila each morning, his breath over Nadia's shoulder as he showed her his latest work on his computer, the way his mouth must have fallen when he came home today and found his family was not there.

Again the phone vibrated. The tug was a yank, and she rocked with the urge to answer. The number coming up was unknown. Maybe he'd bought a new SIM card . . . Impressive, Chegga. She exhaled, picked up. "What is it?"

There was silence on the other end. A guy she didn't recognize: "Nadia?"

She pressed her hand to her forehead. "Yes? Sorry. Hello?"

"It's Slava Bychkov."

"Ooooh," she said.

"You don't still have my number, huh."

"I'm surprised you still have mine."

"Nadechka, it's not a question. So. How does it feel to be home after this long?" Nadia narrowed her eyes. Had her mother told the neighbors she was coming? But then he said, "My aunt saw you at the airport. You can't hide anything from anyone in this town."

"I guess I forgot."

"Don't worry. I'll remind you."

"Uh-huh," Nadia said. "We're having a great time here—my daughter and I." She lay on *daughter* a little harder than she needed to, probably, but she would like to hear him lose that ease in his voice. She and Slava had been seeing each other when she was pregnant. He left once she really started to show.

"Do you ever tell her about me?"

Nadia laughed. "No, Slav."

"Maybe she's too young to understand fairy tales." Nadia chose not to respond. "Does she like hot chocolate?"

"Yes, Prince Charming, she does."

"Would she and her mother like to be taken to Palana's finest café?"

Palana's only café. "Unfortunately, she can't make it. She has plans with her grandparents."

"And her mother?"

She still hadn't gotten a text back from Chegga. "Her mother," said Nadia, "is free."

.

The next morning, after she and Mila woke to the slam of the front door from Nadia's father leaving, after their bed linens were folded, the couch cushions rearranged, and the breakfast dishes washed, Nadia called the Far Eastern headquarters of Sberbank about an international transfer. A manager provided the number of the main office in Moscow, which, because of the time difference, would not open for another nine hours. Mila was sitting in Nadia's lap drawing. Nadia tapped her daughter's fist, pulled the pen out of her hand, and wrote on the top of one notebook page the phone number that would change their future.

After she hung up, she gave Mila the pen. Mila scribbled in the bottom circle of an 8 Nadia had written. "Don't," Nadia said and flipped to a blank page. To her mother, Nadia said, "Can I take the car today?"

Her mother hesitated, and Nadia leaned into Mila's back. *"CAN I TAKE THE CAR, I SAID?"*

"Where?" her mother asked.

"OUT."

Nadia's mother twisted her mouth up. "Okay," Nadia said to that knot of disapproval. She got up and plucked the keys off their wall hook beside the portrait of Stalin.

"Mama, I'm going with you," Mila said. She held on to Nadia's thighs as Nadia put her coat on.

"Your grandmother misses you too much to let you go, Milusha. I'll be back soon," Nadia said. "Be good." And Nadia was gone.

The cold grabbed her lungs in two fists. Wind off the Sea of Okhotsk polished the streets here with dark ice. In only a few years, she had gotten used to Esso—its clean puffs of snowflakes, its mounds of spotless snow, its seeming calm. Wooden fences lined garden plots in people's backyards. Horses had brushed their noses against Mila's palms when Nadia took her out walking. Palana, facing open water, looked vicious in comparison.

Nadia might like that viciousness now. Before moving again, she would need to research her options, collect a few paychecks, call landlords across Europe. While she waited for the car's engine to warm up, she experimented with the idea of pausing for a bit in Palana. Why not? Let the town see what she had made of herself. Spend some time at the edge of the sea.

Slava was waiting at a table when she got to the café. Five years on, he looked okay. Just okay, she told herself, glad for it. Time had carved lines around his mouth and on his forehead. His skin was darkened in a stripe over his eyes—he must be out on the snowmobile these days. And his hair was too long in the back. Compare that to Chegga, whose hair Nadia buzzed in their bathroom monthly.

Stop with Chegga, already. Nadia was moving on. She had evaluated herself in the bathroom mirror this morning, and felt herself attractive, or no more unattractive than she had been. She stood a little differently since having Mila—her pelvis pushed at a new angle—but the change was nothing stark. And her clothes had improved.

She took the empty seat. Slava stood up too late to pull it out for her and settled for kissing her cheek instead. "How many summers, how many winters. Hello, beautiful," he said.

"Hi. Tea?" He signaled to the waiter. "You don't work today?" she asked.

"I work nights. This is late for me to even be up. Two black teas," he told the boy.

"Mine with lemon," she said, and the boy nodded.

"How have you been?" Slava asked.

She opened her hands under the table. Since they last saw each other, Nadia had turned eighteen, had a baby, fallen for Chegga, moved to Esso, started at the bank, taken charge of a household. Gotten engaged—or at least talked a lot about marriage. "You first," she said.

He laughed. "You heard it all. I work nights. Not much else. I was married for a bit—did your mother tell you?—but we're separating. You don't know her. She came after you left."

After Slava broke up with her, Nadia had, for the first and only time in her life, cried so hard she vomited. There was a particular period of teenagehood when she behaved more childishly than Mila did now. Pregnancy certainly had not helped. Her heart had been fragile, its chambers shifting as easily and dangerously as volcanic earth. Slava got in there before the ground hardened.

Hearing about his marriage did hurt a little. Despite the length of his hair. Once in her life, one time, she would like someone to love her completely, with no room left for anything else.

"In Esso I live with my man," she said. "We're very happy. He's a photographer." The waiter came with their glasses and she busied herself for a few seconds by stirring.

She glanced up to see Slava appraising her. "So happy you came here to meet me?"

"Well," she said, then ran out of words.

He sipped his tea, steam rising. "How's your mother?"

Nadia squinted and leaned toward him. "What?"

"How's your— Oh," he said and laughed. Just that, the deep noise, unlocked something in her again. She looked away.

"She's the same as she was," Nadia said, "only more."

"Aren't we all?"

"Not me," she said. "I've transformed."

He smiled at her over the lip of his glass.

This was an adorable affectation—the café. When they last knew each other, Slava was all cheap beer and cheaper spirits. He might have knocked someone to the ground for suggesting he had ever been in the proximity of a moka pot. And Nadia used to like his posturing; like Chegga with the infamous Lilia Solodikova, Nadia had her own youthful fixations, her embarrassing things to adore.

But Nadia had matured. Girls younger than she were already graduating from university, for God's sake. They were grown women. Nadia herself was adult enough to have a half-grown child.

"How's your daughter?" Slava said, and Nadia started in her seat. If he could read her mind, she would have to stop thinking about his hair.

"Precious. Five already. Do you have any of your own?"

"I don't know," Slava said. Grinned. "I'd like to meet her."

"Hmm," Nadia said. She changed the subject to his parents, his brothers. The animals he was trapping these days. When he smiled, he showed those familiar teeth, the top two angled in toward each other to make a crooked gate. She let that old sweet sight wash over her until their teas were drunk and done.

In the car, though, Nadia was glad to be alone again. Sitting beside Slava had made her recall herself at her clingiest. In Esso, surrounded by family and old friends, Chegga had relished going over his school years, but Nadia did not want to soak in the memory of who she used to be.

A local embarrassment. A girl who sought her joy in other people—in men. She began to learn her error only after Mila's father left, when from him, reeling, she stumbled into Slava's bed. She had never wanted to get out. After that ended, she sincerely thought of dying.

She had been seventeen, four months pregnant, in love twice over with nothing to show for it. Sobbing into her pillowcase while her parents watched TV in their bedroom. She used to ask, *How can I go on?*

Then she figured it out. She could go on. She had loved Chegga, his big heart, his bigger promises, but what brought true joy in this life was a climbing salary, a full belly, a firmly connected radiator pipe.

.

Neighbors' dogs lifted their heads to watch her drive down their street. The animals sat in sockets of ice under fence posts. Nadia pulled up to her parents' house, turned the engine off, and heard a child crying. Taking her purse under the puffed arm of her coat, she got out—yes. Mila. "Where's my girl?" Nadia called, letting herself inside.

"Mamochka!" A wet-faced Mila pitched around the corner toward her.

"Hi, kitten," Nadia said. "Hi, turtledove. Have you been torturing your grandparents?" Her daughter shook her head. Mila must have taken her hair out and retied it herself; before breakfast, Nadia had arranged it in a clean braid, but now Mila wore two lopsided pigtails. Great lumps of black hair rose across her skull. Nadia took her hand. "I think you were."

"In here," Nadia's father called.

Mila led Nadia down the hall to the bedroom. The sound of the television drew them along. They found Nadia's parents sitting up on the bed, her mother darning a pile of already mended socks. A news program played at top volume: results of a Euro qualifying match, cease-fires called for the day in eastern Ukraine, rail service restored between the Donetsk and Luhansk People's Republics. "Happiness, it's happiness," a Ukrainian commuter told the reporter. Light from the screen flashed across the fleece blanket under Nadia's parents' feet.

Five years from now, or fifty, Nadia expected she would enter this room to find her parents this same way. She bent down to her daughter. "Your notebook is in the front pocket of my suitcase. Want to bring it?" Mila left and Nadia checked her phone. No missed calls. Chegga might not try again until the evening.

Mila came back with the breast-filled notebook. "Go get a pen out of the drawer in the kitchen table," Nadia said. Her mother looked up, questioning, but Nadia did not repeat herself. Instead Nadia sat on the rug to wait for her daughter to return.

One day soon Nadia would have her own television. A bedroom with tall windows for Mila. Fine new socks, machine-made in Europe, that she could ship by the carton back here. While Mila drew smiling faces, their eyes and cheeks and mouths decorated by ink flowers, Nadia finger-combed the girl's hair and put it in place. Nadia's father snored above their heads. A tiny, soothing noise.

The afternoon drifted away, at once quiet and too loud. A few minutes before five, Nadia plugged in her phone to charge and went to the kitchen to help with dinner. They were having buttered macaroni and fish. Nadia's father played with Mila while the room steamed up. Once the time to eat came, Nadia's mother portioned out servings, as she had when Nadia was little. Mila kept eating noodles with her fingers until Nadia smacked her hand.

Nadia did not miss Chegga. She and Mila were doing fine. So when she got back to her phone and saw he had called twice, she decided she should let him know.

He picked up on the first ring. "What were you thinking?"

She tucked one arm under the other. "Hello to you, too." Almost a week had passed since they heard each other's voices. He did not sound like he was savoring hers.

"You're really at your parents' place?"

"Where else would I be?"

"How much did those tickets cost us?"

"Christ, Chegga," she said. "Twenty-five thousand." Nearly all her cash. He let out a goose's hiss at that, *kkkh,* air forced from the back of his throat. "Mila flew half-price. And I took all my time from work, because we weren't going to use it together, anyway. Right? We weren't?"

"Unbelievably selfish," he said. "We were. Why weren't we?"

"Oh, I don't know," she said. Full of baked fish, half a meter from her framed graduation portrait on her parents' dresser, she knew again the cold clarity of that early-morning flood. She had followed him, his feet bare, hers in rubber boots, through the dirty water. He carried Mila, who clung to his shoulders like he was some sort of savior. Meanwhile Nadia, behind them, stared at his neck. The neat bottom of the haircut she had given him. The white rectangle of the open door ahead. The silhouette of some passerby already loitering to ask what their trouble was. "I don't think a cross-country trip was going to work out for us. You couldn't even put a roof over our heads."

"There was never an issue with the roof," he said. Now she was the one making exasperated noises. "Don't you act like that," he said. "I have done everything for you."

"Everything for me!"

"Without me, you would've still been living at home, fighting with your mother, working some ridiculous job to support Mila. Shoveling coal at Palana's hot-water plant."

"Fuck you," she said, just to hear him sputter. Nobody liked it when a woman cursed. "I'm supposed to be glad that you brought me to Esso? So I could fight with your mother instead?"

"Don't talk about my mother."

"Don't talk about mine."

"Don't . . ." He fell quiet. When he started again, he spoke more slowly, deliberately. "Do you know what I thought? Before I found your little note. That something happened to you two. That you had been hurt."

"You're out of your mind," she said.

"That I would have to show Mila's picture around the village. There's the gift you spent twenty-five thousand to give me. You don't remember Lilia?"

·

All of his worst qualities were coming back to her: his cheapness, his stubbornness, his eagerness to insert himself into other people's lives. Even his little sister had warned Nadia about this; in the wooden changing stall after swimming that January day, while pulling down Mila's bathing suit straps, Nadia had asked, "Was he in love with this Lilia or something?" Ksyusha shook her head. "Then why bring her up?"

Tugging on her jeans, Ksyusha kept her eyes down. She had come back from university for the holidays with muscled legs from dance classes and a tense jaw, Nadia thought, from too much schoolwork. How exhausting it must be to be as smart as Ksyusha. All that possibility held tight under Ruslan's arm. Ksyusha said, "Chegga likes the drama. The disappearance. He has fun making up theories instead of admitting she ran away." She stuffed her swimsuit into her purse. "Can I tell you the truth?"

Nadia nodded.

Ksyusha reached out to cup her hands over Mila's ears. "Lilia was a whore," Ksyusha said. Her expression was harder than Nadia ever remembered seeing before. "She was sweet, but she slept with everyone. Chegga didn't love her. He just loves talking about people, and she's the easiest to talk about, because she's not here anymore."

A whore, Ksyusha said. And Nadia had thought herself sufficiently humiliated when she saw herself in the cat-killing classmate swimming near them. Chegga had devoted himself to Nadia so quickly, so fully—was that because he loved her drama? When they met, she was barely out of school, raising a child on her own. And he had coaxed her and Mila into moving. Sworn he cared. Promised happiness. All that because he saw her as what she used to be? Had he only swapped her into Esso to fill that place?

·

"I remember," Nadia said. The words were raw. The phone beeped and she drew it away to look at the screen. "You're right, Chegga. Mila and I are exactly like your Lilia. We would rather get ourselves killed than live near you anymore." Again the beep. He was going to shout. "I've got to go," she said. "I'm getting another call."

"Slava?" she said when she switched over. Her voice was too loud.

"Hey. What are you doing?"

She waited to collect her breath. Then: "Nothing."

"I thought I could come over," he said.

Five years ago this offer would have been a firework. It did not burst and burn the same way now. "No," she said. "It's late. Mila's bedtime's soon."

"That's fine. I told you, I'd like to meet her."

Alone in the room, Nadia shook her head.

He said, "I've been thinking— You know, we were so young." Nadia didn't respond. Her high school picture on the dresser smirked back at her. ". . . I wondered if I might be her father."

"No," Nadia said.

"No?"

"No."

"Why not?"

"Because you weren't. And you aren't. My period was three weeks late when we first slept together." Mila's father was older, married. He was someone who was glad to make love to Nadia in his car by the coastline but stopped picking up her calls after she told him the blood had not come. She went for Slava then in the hope he could undo what had already happened.

Slava was silent. "All right," he said. "That doesn't change, though—I was there. And I still . . . I could have been there all this time."

"Well, you weren't," she said.

"Listen, I was a kid," he said. "I acted like an idiot. But I've grown up. I want a family. Please don't punish this little girl now for the mistake I made back then."

She could tell he had rehearsed that line. "My God," she said. "Tonight's not a good night for us, okay? Forget about it." He was not finished, she knew, but she was hanging up.

The whole thing made her want to laugh. Or scream. She'd felt the same way when she saw her positive pregnancy test: this must be a joke, this must be a joke, the feeling bubbling in her throat. Slava called again and she silenced the buzzing phone. His voice, his words, the suggestion (*we were young*) churned inside her.

Too bad she had nowhere for this hysteria to go. She could not call Chegga back, she would never tell Mila, and she had made no real friends from school to now. Some girls shared such things with their mothers, but not Nadia . . . just imagine screaming this phone conversation into her mother's crumpled ear.

Nadia did laugh then, loud and bitter. It was impossible to tell how much her mother perceived (the affair with Ivan Borisovich, the liquid few months with Slava, the late-night anguish, the growing belly) and how much was lost in background noise. They never even had a real conversation about the baby coming; in Nadia's second trimester, her parents simply started to make little comments—how soulless it was to raise a child into capitalism, how much better communal living had been for families, how important it was never to lift one's hands over one's head during pregnancy.

It was understood that Nadia had done a bad thing but that thing itself was never discussed. Her mother had not even looked directly at Nadia's enormous stomach when Nadia was admitted to the town hospital's maternity ward. And after the birth she certainly never suggested that Nadia would be a fit parent. That one generation might pass on any skill or knowledge to the next. Instead, her mother fussed about the nurses, the neighbors, Nadia's diet and vanity and laziness.

Nothing had changed. When Nadia came back out to the living room, her mother was there scowling. "Where have you been? I've had to set you up all by myself." Her mother bent, back stiff, to smooth the last corner of a sheet over the couch cushion. Nadia scooped up Mila and felt her waist warmed by her daughter's legs.

"Mama, I'll do that," Nadia called. Mila in her arms, she crowded close to the cushion until her mother was forced to step away. "You could've waited ten minutes for me," Nadia said, though she knew she spoke only to herself.

Her mother hung over them for a few more minutes. Nadia concentrated on kissing Mila's neck to make the girl giggle. Her darling girl. Everyone had something to say, doubts and whispers, but look at her daughter—Mila's long legs, her belly-out posture, her little fingernails, the wisps at her hairline. Her cheeks so round they swelled her profile and hid the corners of her smile. Look at what Nadia had done for Mila and what she was going to do.

.

Nadia phoned the main Sberbank office in the morning. It was closed, but even hearing its prerecorded menu of options, its vowels stressed with a Moscow accent, felt promising. After that she called the Far Eastern branch for an email address, too, so she was able to write to headquarters from her laptop. To pass the day, Nadia's parents took her and Mila to a fairy-tale puppet show at the Palace of Culture. The four of them sat in a row on a wooden bench. The lights in the auditorium went down. A curtain rose, and there appeared papier-mâché heads, ruffled costumes, hands lifting to make frogs and foxes and roosters fly through the air.

"Let's see a movie," Nadia said to her daughter afterward. To her parents, she explained, "There's no cinema in Esso."

Nadia's mother frowned. "There are films to watch at home."

"Don't wait for us," Nadia said. "We'll walk back when we're finished."

The cinema sat a floor above the puppet theater. When she and Mila got up there, they found the place dark. Mila started getting weepy. "Cinemas don't work in the morning," Nadia told her. "I'm so sorry. I forgot." They wandered back downstairs, where they found a booth selling berry hand pies, and Nadia peeled off a bill for two of those instead.

Sticky with berry juice, Nadia and Mila moved through the halls to study the murals. Nadia's cell vibrated, showing Slava's number. She silenced the call and took Mila's hand.

The paintings on the walls showed a swirl of men in wolf skins. Nadia's parents had brought her here as a child. "Milusha, do you want to go fishing tomorrow with Grandpa?" Nadia asked. "I used to go when I was your age."

Mila squeezed her fingers. "What's it like?"

The rich rotten smell of low tide—the endless flatness of the sea. And her father, hooking the bait, blood running thin down his forearms. "It's nice," Nadia said.

"I'll catch a dolphin. But we won't eat it." Mila shook her head at the thought. "It'll live with us."

"Great idea." Nadia squeezed back. "You know what? I'm going to get us our own house soon."

"For us and Daddy?"

"For us and the dolphin," Nadia said. "We'll buy a place on the beach so it can visit all its friends when it likes. And we'll have a fancy bathroom. We'll put in a tub big enough for it to live."

In the building's lobby, Nadia zipped Mila's coat, then belted her own. They pushed out into the cold together. Snow crystals in the wind brushed like fine-grit sandpaper across their exposed skin.

A familiar white hatchback was parked at the curb. Nadia moved toward the car cautiously. Her father was napping in the passenger seat. Her mother, as Nadia got closer, tipped her head in their direction, lifted one hand from the steering wheel, and waved.

Nadia boosted Mila into the backseat and climbed in after. "I told you *WE WOULD WALK*," she said. The car smelled like salted fish inside. Her father blinked awake.

"Mila will get sick in this cold," her mother said. "You should know that."

"She's fine. She's all wrapped up."

Her father turned in his seat and reached out to stroke Mila's purple sleeve. "These new coats," he said. "Manufactured in China. Terrible."

The prickling in Nadia's nose was back. "No, this one's quality, Papa. It's well made." He shook his head.

Nadia put her own fingers on Mila's sleeve. The refined slip of it. She ran her hand down to reach Mila's damp palm. Pushed back against the headrest and widened her eyes against tears.

More and more and more, Chegga's mother had condemned her for wanting. As though everyone in their generation was not already enjoying all they had taken for themselves—pensions, marriages, friendships, history, the values they were sure were wasted on their children, the sweeping moral high ground.

"What movie did you see?" her mother called backward.

"Communist Killers from Outer Space," Nadia said. They were not listening anyway.

Nadia did not pick up either Chegga's or Slava's calls that night. She had no energy for conversation. On the couch, Nadia read Mila a story about a bear cub, watched her drowse off, and folded herself around the girl to wait for sleep. Tomorrow they would go to the library. They would keep themselves busy until Nadia figured out where to go next. And they would have fun doing it—because they had each other, which was what mattered—Nadia and Mila, forever.

.

She woke with her pulse thudding. Someone was pounding on the front door. The room was silvery, divided into strips of light and dark, and Mila lay on her stomach in the crack between the cushion and the couch back. The sound of a man's voice outside. Nadia's father's feet coming down the hall.

Opening the living room door, Nadia found the shock of her parents and Slava. Her parents in their pajamas. Slava, by the smell of the hallway, drunk. The overhead light was on. Slava's face was red. That color in his skin, the slur in his speech, brought her right back to high school.

She shut the door behind her. "What are you doing here?" she hissed. "Go home!"

"Nadia, this—" said her father.

"I'm sorry, Papa," she told him.

"I've got to ask you something," Slava said.

Nadia threw her hands up. It had to be two in the morning. "You haven't heard of a text message?"

Her mother, soft in a worn nightgown, squeezed against her to get a better look at the scene. "Is that Vyacheslav Bychkov? What is he doing here so late?"

"I'm very sorry to wake you," Slava said. He was overenunciating. "I needed to talk—"

"I know your brother," Nadia's mother called toward him.

Slava blinked at her. Nadia waved in the air. "Enough! Leave!"

"Nadechka, you're not listening, you're not hearing me," he said. "I wanted— Okay, I was thinking. You could come home with me. My wife— No, it's my house, you know, it's only me now. You and your daughter could stay there with me. As long as you like. You look just the same as you did," he said. Speaking much too loudly. "You could come there. And our daughter."

"Who, Mila?" Nadia's mother asked, and Nadia turned.

"Mila is—" Nadia halted. "Get out," she said, "get out, get out." She pushed forward, past her parents, to Slava's stinking chest. Citrus and vodka. She hoped he'd choke. Pressed too close to Slava's jacket, that smell, the chill carried in from outside, she said, "Mila isn't yours." Still he did not leave.

Nadia kept talking. Let everyone go deaf together. "I told you I was already pregnant when we met. Can't you remember? Or have you drunk yourself too stupid to recall?" The other day's smile was loose on Slava now. "You were a fling," she said. "Not a very good one. If I were you, I'd be ashamed to show my face in this house."

Slava sneered. She used to want to hurt him, then to make him jealous, to cause him regret, but seeing this look gave no satisfaction now. "If I were you," he said, "I'd be ashamed to show my face in this town."

.

Her father pressed on the front door before locking it. Slush on the floor. Alcohol in the air. Slava was gone.

"I'm really sorry," Nadia said again. Her father wouldn't look at her. He was dressed in his pajamas, dark sweatpants. His mouth made a slit. Disapproval.

Nadia was vibrating in the silence. If they would just look at her— she was no longer a disobedient child; she had a job at a bank; she walked her daughter daily to preschool in a scenic village. She was not a whore. Not Slava's, not anyone else's. She had tried to make of herself someone beyond scandal, beyond shame.

"Go to sleep," her father said. Her mother, one hand on the wall, walked back toward their bedroom.

It had been a mistake to come back. A mistake. Nadia in Palana had been her worst—her most vulnerable—people saw that and took advantage. Chegga had spotted the same thing five years earlier. And yet she had spent her savings on the plane tickets back here.

All Nadia could do was return to the living room. She loathed herself so much her teeth hurt. She took extra care in closing the room's door. A strip of light touched Mila, who could not have slept through that, but whose eyes were shut. Awake or not, the little girl did not want to be any further disturbed.

Nadia put her hand on Mila's back, which rose and fell in the half-light of the moon. "I'm sorry," Nadia whispered. Her head ached. She lifted her hand, crawled in beside her daughter, and took out her phone to call Moscow.

"I want to go home," Mila said.

"That's what I want, too, dove," Nadia said. "I'm trying to find a home for us."

"No," Mila said. "Home. To Daddy."

He's not your fucking daddy, Nadia almost said. But she was looking at her daughter's perfect, stubborn face.

Nadia had gone to bed on this same couch as a child. Her own mother, coming in late some nights to load laundered clothes into the wardrobe, would stand there with her arms full of folded cotton. Always almost speaking, but never opening her mouth. And Nadia, not knowing what else her mother could want to say after days of nagging, would pretend to be asleep. Nadia must have had the same set look then as Mila did now. Cheeks fat with youth, eyebrows tense, and chin set. Pure unwillingness.

When Nadia got pregnant, years ago, she promised herself she would become better. She had not been and did not know how to start. Now she'd brought Mila to this house, this town, these old grudges, and it was clear they had to leave but she did not actually know where else to go. A city abroad? Where? How would they pay for the move? Another paycheck or two wouldn't cover the fact that Nadia had no real support. She knew no one off the peninsula. She was still the lonely child, the desperate teenager, who slept in this room with illusions.

Wherever she moved, she would be the same person. But Mila could grow up to be anyone. Mila could be encouraged by two parents, attend university, become a scientist, find a husband, buy a home, maybe even live in London. Or in the real Switzerland. She could be raised in Kamchatka's version and move to the other. And wherever Mila ended up in the world, she would know that someone—her mother—loved her most.

Mila's eyes were pinched so tight her lashes looked shortened. Nadia navigated to her phone's contact list. When Nadia spoke again, her words came higher, fainter. "Then let's go home," she said.

Back to Esso. Because all the joy in Nadia's life came from her daughter. The woman this child would one day be. Between the hard places in Nadia, some part, for Mila, was always open. A pipe thinned from pressure until the flood burst through. A chunk of dark stone worn down, broken off, washed free.

A P R I L

The men were already at work. Zoya watched them from her kitchen balcony as she smoked. They appeared and disappeared in the window holes of the unfinished concrete building across the street. Four floors below, they looked as small as the fingers on her hand. She still recognized them. Their muddy boots; their black hair shining over the collars of their coveralls; the way they walked, muscular, strange.

Her husband knocked at the glass of the balcony door and she jumped. "What are you doing out there?" he asked.

Zoya stabbed out her cigarette. "Nothing."

Kolya was knotting his tie. In his police uniform, he always seemed so serious. Different from the person she'd just watched finish a plate of fried eggs. She slid the door shut behind her and came over to touch his clean clothes. Smoothing her palms across his epaulettes, she said, "Handsome man."

"All right," he said, pleased.

The smell of his toothpaste glittered between them. Zoya raised herself on her toes to kiss him, and Kolya turned his face. "You stink," he said. She stepped away. Ever since the baby was born, he did not like Zoya smoking. She became less bothered by this criticism when she kept a pack nearby.

The sky over Petropavlovsk was gray-pink. Kolya had half an hour before his shift started at six. Though Zoya was months into maternity leave, she maintained the habit of waking with him, making his breakfast, and seeing him off. It was as if they were both getting ready for work—as if she, too, would soon walk out into the city.

Kolya was dressed and leaving. "Good luck today," she said. After their apartment doors shut behind him, her head cleared, her heart emptied. Sasha, freshly fed, would not wake again for two more hours. This was Zoya's time now.

This was theirs.

Zoya was not headed for the balcony just yet—she could credit herself with that much patience. Instead she washed her husband's breakfast dishes. Then she set the electric kettle, filled her teacup, and sat down with her phone, scrolling through pictures of other people's pets and weddings and vacations. One of her coworkers had posted about a route for ecotourists through icy central Kamchatka.

Zoya put the phone down. She had not left her neighborhood since Sasha's birth. Across the table, the kitchen wallpaper showed overlapping palm leaves.

She shook out another cigarette and slid open the door.

The men below were finished with their site walk-through. They had come from Uzbekistan, Kyrgyzstan, Tajikistan, to gather in the doorframe across her street. Their building was a concrete husk built level by level by their gloved hands. They had ripped up the side-walk around the structure and erected scaffolding. At the edge of the lot, they had made a shack from scrap wood with a roof of corru-gated metal. Zoya wanted to see inside. Their five-man crew ducked in there every few hours: when they all arrived, to break for tea, for lunch, to rest, and when the day was done. On the evenings her hus-band worked late, Zoya could catch them holding the shack's door open and filing out in street clothes. The last man would close the door behind him. The shack, the building, and she would all be left waiting for them to come back tomorrow.

She took another drag on her cigarette. The men broke away from each other. Their generator coughed, whirred.

The air on her arms was fresh and cold. The streets below were zebra-striped with melting snow. Four kilometers downhill, the city center spread out, its buildings dark, parking lots empty, ship repair yard motionless. Early last fall, before Zoya's leave started, she stood here watching the flashing blue lights of emergency vehicles. She'd imagined Kolya finding the Golosovskaya sisters on those far cliffs. He would be celebrated on television and get promoted to senior lieutenant, maybe captain. At work, her colleagues would gather around her for all the details. Then the blue lights turned off, the snow fell, the searches stopped, and Sasha was born.

These days, Zoya turned her thoughts to nearer fantasies. The men below lugged buckets of mixed concrete. They used a crane last month to stack slabs for floors, walls, and ceilings. Now they were tending to details—pouring staircases, ripping out support frames. They bent their necks in concentration as they moved. Looking down at them, Zoya bent her neck the same way.

The sun shone white above the distant water. Tossing the butt over the balcony railing, Zoya went back inside, where she washed her hands and smelled them. The smoke hung on her skin—so what? It flavored her. She brushed her teeth, applied perfume, and stroked on makeup as carefully as she used to on those mornings before she left for class or work. Foundation, concealer, bronzer, brow pencil. She ran texturizer through her hair and braided it into a yellow fishtail. Above the collar of her robe, she rose beautiful as a newlywed.

Until November, Zoya would have gotten dressed, driven to the park office, greeted her colleagues in ecological education, and started the day. An inspector might stop by, bragging of poachers apprehended. A movie producer might call from Germany for a permit to film in protected territory. The park director might announce a team visit to a far base, so all of them, research and protection and education and tourism, would have to shut off their computers and hurry to their cars and drive to the airfield, where they'd board a helicopter bound for the Valley of the Geysers or Kronotskoye Lake.

Now, instead, Zoya took her flawless face into the kitchen to wipe the counters clean. She reorganized the row of shoes in the foyer. When Sasha woke up crying, surprised all over again at the world in front of her eyes, Zoya nursed her. "How'd you sleep?" Zoya asked. "Any nightmares?" Sasha's tiny mouth worked against Zoya to tug milk forward. The leaves printed on the kitchen walls were frozen tropical.

At eleven o'clock Zoya called her husband. He did not pick up. With the permission that gave her, Zoya called Tatyana Yurievna on the second floor to ask if she could watch Sasha—"I'll be quick," Zoya told her. "No more than an hour." Groceries, Zoya explained, but it did not matter. Tatyana Yurievna loved the baby. The neighbor made up games with spoons and songs and measuring cups, and when she came over to babysit, which was often, three or four times a week, she never minded if Zoya took too long to wend her way back home.

The day cracked open. Zoya rushed to dress—satin button-down, smooth belt, dark jeans, and tall heeled boots—and stood by the door to wait. Her lungs expanded to breathe the air outside. The baby began to cry. Zoya tugged off her boots, unbuttoned her blouse, and lifted Sasha to feed. Sasha's head rested against Zoya's satin sleeve. Sasha had Zoya's same eyes: pale, glacial. The blank eyes of a drowned girl. Zoya kissed her daughter on the forehead to undo those thoughts.

The knock. "There's my darling," Tatyana Yurievna cooed when Zoya opened the doors.

"An hour," Zoya promised. She pulled her boots back on and stepped out the door.

She could do anything now—anything. She emerged from her apartment building into the cool light. Her boots were snug around her calves. Her skin was tight, too, with expectation. Across the street, the building hid the workers. Zoya walked forward to line up with the hole of its doorway. Then she stopped to take out a cigarette. Only a minute outside, and her fingers were already cold, stiff. She flicked her lighter, but the flame did not catch.

The building hummed with machines inside. Zoya was too early. Prickling with wasted anticipation, she put the cigarette back in its pack. The men were not yet on break.

So it was the grocery store. Zoya went there flat and frustrated. After she paid, she checked the time—still a few minutes before noon. Instead, then, of turning left out of the store and returning to her apartment, she headed for the end of the block. A set of marble stairs brought her into the courtyard of the city church, which shone, gold-domed, like new money. She chose a bench, took out her phone, and navigated to the profile of the girl she met at New Year's who lived in St. Petersburg.

At that holiday rental house, Zoya's husband actually felt sorry for the girl, who had seemed serious, even standoffish, refused the men, and left in the morning without saying goodbye. "There's the old maid you could've been if you never met me," Kolya whispered into Zoya's ear. Nine days later, Zoya went into labor.

The world-traveling old maid. Her stomach flat, her orange bikini. Locking the phone, Zoya shut her eyes.

She could live another life. It wasn't too late. If she boarded the bus to the park office, she would make it there in time to surprise them all in the middle of their lunches. The building would smell like it always had, that mix of paper, rags, and bleach. The eco-education girls would kiss her cheeks and the park director would come over to squeeze her hands. They might say, *Zoyka! What perfect timing. We've got an extra spot for you on today's trip.* A flight over the Klyuchevskaya stratovolcano—a helicopter to South Kamchatka Sanctuary. Her coworkers would treat Zoya just as they did when she was newly graduated, a tour leader through the park's visitor center. When she was young and unburdened.

But there wasn't really time to get to the office and back this afternoon, or any. They would ask her for stories, for pictures of the baby. And what did Zoya have to show, beyond her infant's blank expression? Almost half a year spent indoors. What could she say to them?

So instead she could choose something solitary. Go down to the city center, buy a sausage from one of the stands by the bay, and sit to eat her food on the shore. The water steady, the mountains beyond layered in dark blue, light blue, white. Looking like cut paper. Rocks pressing under her heels. She used to loiter there when she was a schoolgirl. She and her friends stayed late, drank on the beach, watched the horizon flatten, saw the night ships pass . . . But what if her husband drove by and saw her?

She could . . . why didn't she tell Tatyana Yurievna that she'd be gone three hours? An hour was not enough. Neither was a day or a week. Zoya could move to St. Petersburg, too. She could get away from this. She could leave.

But she wouldn't. She couldn't, really. Her chest tingled with milk letting down. She couldn't.

She exhaled fog. When she first moved to this apartment, the church was shut up in scaffolding. This courtyard was a stretch of gravel, no trees. Zoya was nineteen, and her mother's new man bought this place for Zoya so he and her mother could have their privacy. That was before Zoya met Kolya, before they fixed up the apartment; the wallpaper was stained, one stove burner did not work, the washing machine shook so hard that it jostled its plug from the outlet halfway through a cycle. And Zoya loved it. Some mornings before she left for class, she walked circles around the bedrooms, just looking. Anything seemed possible.

Things were different now. Zoya checked the time on her phone and picked up the groceries.

As soon as she got to the bottom of the courtyard stairs, she saw the workers. They stood together on boards over wet earth and sipped steaming cups of tea. Oh—her stomach twisted. These were the few minutes of their lunch break. She came toward them slowly, measuring out her steps to make the walk last, and as she approached, they broke off their conversation. To watch.

One said, "Hello, miss," in that half-swallowed way he always did. His accent made the greeting dirty.

A cord of tension extended from Zoya's eyes, her sinuses, the back of her throat, through her body, out her ribs, to the men. So close. The line was taut. She swallowed. "Hello," she said to the street ahead of her. She was almost past them now. The men said nothing in return. She kept her head up, tightened her fingers around the grocery bag, and let herself in the door of her apartment building.

The hall was cold and dark and left her alone again. If some neighbor brushed past her right now, she would thrum. Only two words—and still the migrants did this to her.

The locked joints of her knees. Her neck tense, her jaw hard. A thousand things to say behind her teeth. She pressed her back to the wall and listened to her heart pound them out: *I want you,* it said in the dark. There was no one around to hear.

Climbing the stairs, Zoya pressed herself down, holding fingers on her fantasies so they settled. Be still. Tatyana Yurievna met her at the apartment door with the baby in her arms. "We knew you were coming home, didn't we, Sashenka? We saw you from the window."

Zoya kept her face down as she pulled off her boots. "Is that right?" She took the bag into the kitchen. They followed her.

"Did those men say something to you?" Tatyana Yurievna asked.

Zoya was already putting the food away. Hidden behind the refrigerator door, she said, "Who? No."

"The migrants. It's dangerous. Nobody keeps an eye on them," Tatyana Yurievna said. "I heard on the news this morning that the police found a body in the bay."

Zoya shut the door to look at her neighbor. "One of the Golosovskaya sisters?" The lights, the boats, a child's slack limbs bumping along stones.

"They said it was probably an adult. But who knows? I get my information from other sources." Tatyana Yurievna winked. Zoya returned to her groceries. "What did Kolya tell you? Do they have any suspects?"

"I didn't know the searches were back on," Zoya said. "He didn't tell me anything."

"Because you're busy with this little angel." Tatyana Yurievna's voice rose and fell as she bounced Sasha. "I'll ask him myself. Those men outside, I wonder . . . any one of them could have taken those sisters. You're too young to remember what it was like before the collapse. It's only after Kamchatka opened to outsiders that we started to see any crime."

"They're just construction workers," Zoya said. "Not child molest-
ers."

"We don't know who or what they are. Why would someone come
to a different country if he didn't have something to get away from
in the last? You be careful, Zoyka. Who knows what they might do
to a girl like you?"

Her back to her neighbor, Zoya rinsed the vegetables. She, too,
believed in the migrants' power—not the power to steal children,
but the power to take a woman, to transform her, to turn her life that
was growing smaller all the time into an existence that was dark and
mighty.

That they came here from somewhere else only made Zoya hun-
grier. The workers' dirtiness, their ignorance. That they hardly spoke.
The way, when she was in school, they stood over her on the bus
and looked down. Her neighbor was right: this was not their country.
They had nothing to lose. Zoya wanted to enter that little cabin,
which must smell like sweat, mud, gasoline. A white woman's picture
would be stapled to its wall, and she would be the white woman in its
center. She needed to find out what these men might do to a girl like
her. She craved that knowledge; her hands, her mouth, wanted it like
they wanted cigarettes.

Tatyana Yurievna talked on. Zoya took cheese, cucumber, and
tomatoes from the fridge, sliced them up, and set out a platter. She
poured them both cups of tea while Tatyana Yurievna, holding Sasha
on her lap with one arm, picked up a bite. "At least we have Kolya
here to protect us. Zoyka, you don't know this, but our building used
to be full of humble people like us. Real Russians. The whole nation
was. No one was a stranger. We were united by our common ideals,
we believed in greatness. That was a different era, wasn't it? A better
time." The older woman looked down at the food as she spoke. Her
eyebrows were thin, her mouth loose, her bottom teeth lined with
stains like the shore when the tide goes out. The baby chewed on
her fingers. Tatyana Yurievna would talk about the way things were
until her stomach was full, then she would ask Zoya about Kolya,

compliment his service, squeeze the baby one last time, and return to her own floor. Three times a week and sometimes four. This was Zoya's life.

Zoya took a slice of cucumber. When she bit, freshness burst across her tongue.

The afternoon grew late before Zoya was alone again. Sasha lay in her crib. In the palm-leaf kitchen, Zoya scrubbed two beef tongues clean and slid them into boiling water. Garlic, onions, sugar, celery. She covered the pot. While the meat simmered, she chopped columns of carrots. The windows steamed over. She was a universe away from the park territory, its rainbow rivers, its puffing fumaroles. They used to go out there in the summer when the lakes churned with salmon. Bears gutted fish and scattered shining red roe across the ground. She wouldn't see such dangerous beauty again for years.

She let her mind wander. It wandered downstairs.

The baby at rest. The food on the stove. The air in the apartment sticky with starch and the walls beading. Hurrying out of her building, she'll find empty landings on every floor. The railing under her fingers will be rough from layers of chipped paint, blue and gray and yellow. She will press the button, release her building's front door, and go out into the sun.

An afternoon washed in greenish light, the whole city like a bud about to open. A hundred meters away, beyond the church, traffic will rush by, but no cars will turn down their street. As she comes closer to the building, the workers will lift their chins. They will bring her into the shack. They will take her out of her old body. They will make her new.

Zoya peeled the tongues, salted the vegetables, dressed the salad, sliced the bread. When Sasha woke up, Zoya fed the baby in the kitchen while skimming through the photo feed on her phone. Kolya was supposed to be back at half past five. Fifteen minutes past that, with no Kolya in sight, their daughter began crying. Baby on her shoulder, Zoya walked a loop through the apartment: from Sasha's room, wallpapered with ducks, to the master bedroom with its shining television screen, into the bathroom, out again, a hundred thousand times.

Her husband unlocked the doors at ten to seven. Kolya had people with him—two other officers and one of the female assistants. Thudding feet, happy talk. "Look how big she is," the assistant cried as soon as she saw the baby in Zoya's arms. Zoya said hello. She was flayed. How pathetic she must look, with the table set, the meat on the stove, her baby fussy, and her whole day displayed for ridicule. Kolya had brought three guests home to see how Zoya waited for him like she had nothing else to live for. Zoya could have run away today. They didn't know. She could have flown over a volcano. She could have moved to St. Petersburg.

Kolya shook off his jacket. When the assistant held out her hands, Zoya, shiny-eyed with shame, put the baby in them. Then Zoya slid back into the kitchen and whisked the dinner plates away.

Before they finished lining up their boots in the hall, Zoya took out a bottle, five shot glasses, and the platter of food from this afternoon's tea. "What a hostess!" her husband said when he saw. She held up her face to be kissed. This time she could smell him, a sharp, sweet booziness. "Pour us a round, my queen," he said, and she did.

"Queen," one of the men said, "do you know what your king accomplished today?" The other man snickered. "He earned himself a letter of reprimand."

"Ah, Fedya, you ruin a woman's mood that way," the assistant said. "Don't tell her such things." In her uniformed arms, the baby squirmed.

Zoya faced her husband. "What happened?"

He smiled at her. His collar was less crisp than it had been when he left. "They pulled a body from the bay this morning. Yevgeny Pavlovich congratulated us for finding one of the Golosovskaya girls. I told him, *Sir, if finding a corpse that size makes you hopeful, just wait, we'll drag in a sea lion.*"

The assistant sat up straighter to imitate the major general's voice. "*Bodies swell in water.* Didn't you know?" Fedya and the other man laughed.

"So I heard. Swell to a meter taller than where they started," Kolya said. "Swell enough to turn from a twelve-year-old girl to a middle-aged fisherman."

"You can't talk that way to your supervisor," Zoya said. "Even if he's wrong, you should work with him, respect him . . ."

The guests were already picking up their drinks. "A toast to our major general," the assistant said, one hand supporting the baby and the other around a glass. "And to you, Kolya. Your many accomplishments in this career."

Kolya passed Zoya a shot. "To my success," he said to her. His voice was rough. Everyone drank; Zoya, too, vodka singing in her throat.

"One day, Kol," Fedya said, "I'll write you a letter of commendation." He collected their glasses on the kitchen table and poured a second round. "You're right. Dragging the bay is pointless. The bodies of those girls are floating off Fiji by now."

"Cheers to that," the other officer said.

Zoya shook her head. "That's no good toast."

Kolya took his glass anyway, clinked it, tossed the alcohol back. He wiped his mouth. "Pointless, yes, but only because the sisters didn't drown. They were taken."

"This again," the assistant said. "Don't interrupt," said the other officer, and the assistant said, "Dima!"

"They were absolutely taken," Zoya said. Her husband nodded. The baby whimpered. "There was a witness."

Fedya's face was soft and scornful. "You call her a witness?"

"She saw something," Zoya said. Her husband used to come home energized about this case, excited. Zoya remembered: *two kids, a big guy, and a shiny dark car,* he reported the witness saying. That, and *I want his car-wash tips.*

"They were taken by someone off the peninsula," Kolya continued. "That's why we haven't uncovered any trace of them, dead or alive. They're not hidden in a garage or buried in the woods or floating in the bay. They're gone. That's what I've been trying to tell the major general for months now."

Fedya took up the bottle again to refill their glasses. The vodka glugged. "If that's so, if they were killed somewhere on the mainland, then what does it matter? Let this drowned body be called one of the girls. Listen to your wife. Stop arguing with your superiors. Otherwise you'll wind up where you did in the fall—"

"Enough," Kolya said. The assistant giggled at the end of the table.

"Looking at Moscow got you nothing but embarrassment," Fedya said. "In the future, you'll be wiser to keep any ideas to yourself."

"Hear that?" Dima said, leaning over to pinch the assistant's slim waist. His hand bumped Sasha's head and the baby howled.

Kolya's mood was darkening. Zoya waved away her glass. "Is that what you're going to write in my letter of commendation?" Kolya asked. "How good I'll be at shutting up?"

"What else would I write about?" Fedya said. "Your failure to find an imaginary kidnapper? Your years of monitoring the speeds on city boulevards?"

Sasha was really worked up now. Kolya was raising his voice. Zoya took the baby from the assistant, who smiled as if they knew each other well, and excused herself into the bedroom.

The baby didn't want to eat, so Zoya walked her until the girl's unhappy mouth relaxed again. With talk like this, Kolya's side of the bed was sure to stay empty past midnight. Zoya set down Sasha on the orange duvet and lay beside her. On her stomach, the baby lifted her head, arms, and legs, paddling through the air but going nowhere.

"That's not how you crawl," Zoya said. Sasha went on. Zoya watched her fat limbs work. After a minute, the baby looked wide-eyed at her. Zoya put her hand on her daughter's back, where her palm fit warm in that arch. "Sasha," she said. "Sashenka. I wish you could talk to me."

The sisters were taken. Their bodies could be somewhere near. Before the baby, Kolya would talk to her about his work, but since Sasha's birth, Zoya seemed to have lost her curiosity, lost nearly all her appetites. She used to have theories about the girls for her husband: the man that abducted them drove them west, to the villages on the coast of the Okhotsk, and kept them alive in his root cellar. He lived too far from his neighbors for anyone to notice. His car wasn't on the footage from gas station surveillance cameras because he'd carried fuel in his trunk. Those theories had disintegrated from disuse, and now all Zoya kept were images: a shining car, a round face, a floating child. Picturing those things gave her no relief.

What did was picturing pleasure. If only these guests would drink faster so the end of the night could come. She did not especially like talking to the detective version of Kolya anymore, but after people came over, he was always sweet with her. A tipsy Kolya reminded Zoya of the months before she graduated: going to parties, flirting with friends, winding up with him in these same sheets. She turned the baby stomach-up and cupped Sasha's small face in one hand.

They first met when Kolya pulled her over. Not yet lieutenant, he was Sergeant Ryakhovsky then, watching for traffic violations. She had been going too fast down Komsomolskaya. She was twenty, in the summer before her last year of university, leaving work to stop at the apartment before heading back out to a birthday dinner. And he was twenty-four and seemed so much older. On the gravel-rough side of the road, he watched her from behind his sunglasses. Her cheeks burned under her foundation. He was tall, broad-shouldered, unimpressed. He held on to the sill of her car door with one hand and looked down the length of his arm. She tried to tell him she was in a rush, going to an engagement. The cars behind his back whooshed by. Finally, he said, "Go on, then." No ticket.

The next week, on her drive home, lights flared again in her rear-view mirror. She pulled over with her heart quick and hands sweating. She had not been speeding, or she did not think she was. After five agonizing minutes, her passenger door opened, and he slid into the seat. His sunglasses were off. He smiled.

Six months later he moved into the apartment. They got married a few weeks after her final exams. By then, she was full-time at the park, and on her first day back after the wedding her coworkers kept bringing her champagne in a mug to celebrate, while their director pretended the drink was only milky tea. Zoya and her husband stayed happy for a while; when she found out she was pregnant, he held her and kissed her cheeks. She was crying. He did not ask her why. Now he took her car to and from the police station, while she stayed home and would for ages more. Two years, at least, Kolya said. That was what the baby needed. Enough time had passed that Zoya no longer wrapped herself up in romance over their second meeting, when he slipped into her passenger seat. His unfamiliar body strapped into its uniform, looking so adult, so sure, and hiding the man she would marry.

She had been away from the guests too long. Zoya carried Sasha back through the dim hall toward their voices—still arguing. Then someone in the kitchen said, "Illegals."

Zoya clutched the baby to her. The workday was over. The migrants were gone—but maybe one of her husband's guests had stepped out on the balcony in time, looked down on them leaving, seen Zoya's ashes, and found her out—

She came to the kitchen doorway. "Waste of our time," her husband said. "They call us then say nothing when we arrive."

"They're not the ones who call," Fedya said.

"Then who? Who else gives a shit? Over nothing. Paint and five thousand rubles' worth of fuel. They stood and looked at me like they had nothing to do with it," Kolya said. "Scuttling off afterward like a pack of rats."

Compact and dangerous, lifting mixed concrete. Black hair shining. And their accents. Zoya could go for hours on a single word. All day . . . if she had to be alone all day, why couldn't it be with them, in the cold, by the unfinished building, on the other side of the street . . .

Sasha wiggled. Zoya waved her hand in front of the baby's eyes to keep her quiet. She forced herself to ask: "What are you talking about?"

"Nothing," her husband said.

"Vandalism," said the assistant.

Fedya corrected her. "Just kids being kids. Graffiti at a construction site. Broken bottles, stolen tools."

"Where was that?" Zoya asked.

"Nowhere," her husband said, filling up their glasses. Then he relented. "On the eighth kilometer." By the library and the volcano-logical institute. Far from here.

She pictured those workers on the eighth kilometer—like hers but not. The kind of men not strong enough to protect themselves from petty crimes. "So what—" she asked, and as she did, Dima started in saying, "To our—" He stopped, lowering his glass. Zoya waved him on. "To our long days of work," Dima said, "and our lon-ger nights of pleasure."

"Good to hear it's going well," said Fedya after they all swallowed.

"So fucking rude," said the assistant.

"Watch your mouth," said Dima. He put a hand over the assistant's lips. To the rest of the table, he explained, "Anfisa's insulted because it's not just nights with us anymore. She's good for mornings, too."

"What a gentleman," said Anfisa from behind his fingers. Fedya refilled their glasses. "What honor. What chivalry."

"What did you do," Zoya asked her husband, "about the vandals?"

"There was nothing to do," he said.

"My gallant prince," Anfisa said to Dima. "See what happens if you keep speaking so sweetly to me. Our nights can get much shorter."

"Long lunch breaks, too," said Dima. Fedya snorted. "Our Anfisa is a twenty-four-hour kind of girl."

Zoya said, "But if things were taken. If tools are gone. Don't you have to catch whoever took them?"

"Why do you suddenly care?" asked her husband. He looked like the tired version of the officer she first met. At her car window, in her passenger seat—unpredictable. "Why should you tell me how to do my job? Do I tell you how to do yours? 'Sit at home, get fat, and tend to the baby'?"

"Kolya," Dima said.

"Ridiculous," her husband muttered to the table.

This wasn't her job. Or it shouldn't be. The dinner Zoya had cooked for them sat on the stove. Her husband did not know what she was capable of. Outside, the construction site was empty. The ground there was a mix of mud and snow, and four floors above, Zoya held her child, kept quiet among strangers, waited for tomorrow.

In bed later, Kolya was tender. His cropped hair brushed against her jaw. "Forgive me?" he asked. She hummed, a neutral noise. "They treat me like a child . . . they make me lieutenant, put me on this case, then treat me like I'm inferior." His breath on her neck. "I wish I'd never heard of these sisters. I could simply stay home with you."

She stared up into the dark. "Don't be angry," he murmured.

"It doesn't matter," she said. He held her tighter and she kissed his forehead.

Hello, miss, the migrant will say.

The sound of his voice will wet her mouth. She will say back, *Hello.* She will check that no one's watching. She will point to the shack. *Take me in there,* she will say.

Inside, she will back up until she hits a table. Then she will reach, grip the surface, scoot herself up to sit. His eyelids will be heavy as he watches her body. His pupils will dilate. Shining black. Forearms thick with muscle, jaw clenched, he will be ready for her. Beyond the thin wall, she will hear the others. She will open her hands.

Zoya had always wanted them. Always wanted, and never touched. Before she found these workers, there were others, the men pushing carts through the market, the ones sweeping the block where she was raised. Long before she met her first blond boyfriend, she watched the migrants. And even lying next to her husband, she wanted them still. This was not some fetish, she believed. This was something more. She was not a woman made for sitting home and nursing. She craved things darker, stranger, out of bounds.

Tomorrow. She will give herself three hours. If she can find a sufficient excuse—a doctor's appointment, maybe. No one will know. One afternoon, and then Zoya will return home, tell Tatyana Yurievna she's sick, go to the shower and soap away the marks left by the workers' fingers. She'll wash slowly, wishing they could stay. And after that she will make it as Kolya's wife and Sasha's mother. No more visions of dead children. No desires to undo herself. After tomorrow, she will have enough to make it through.

Zoya fell asleep into that fantasy. She dreamed of geysers and woke to the sound of running water. Her husband was already in the shower. In the kitchen, she brought out eggs to boil, bread to slice, white cheese from the refrigerator's bottom drawer. The room smelled like a charred pan. Beyond her balcony, the morning was getting so bright.

The kettle was almost bubbling. The bathroom door opened, the bedroom door shut. Watching the sky, gray shot through with yellow, Zoya took her pack and lighter off the top of the refrigerator, slid open the balcony door, and stepped outside.

The morning was cool. The men were there. The rippled sheets of the roof of their shack were on the ground where that little structure was supposed to be. The workers stood in a circle around the spot. One had his coat in his hand.

They were standing over ash-black wreckage. A couple of charred planks, and what looked like the metal base of a table. Zoya understood. Their shack had been burned down.

She tapped out a cigarette, put it paper-dry between her lips, and flicked at the lighter. No spark. She wound her trembling fingers around the lighter, tried again. The flame flared. The sun was not yet up. That yellow in the air was the leftover glow from them, their ruined shack, the blackened ground, metallic ash in the smoke catching whatever brightness reflected off the bay.

Do something, she was begging them in silence. Shout or smash something or start to rebuild. Zoya would make up their day together, change the setting, put them all in the dark half-constructed building, if they did *something*—but they just stood in a circle and stared.

Vandals, the officers said last night. Stolen tools, petty crimes, and arson. The shack had been an easy target. And the men across the street, these foreign workers, the migrants who were supposed to transform her life, were powerless.

Zoya lifted her fingers to take the cigarette from her mouth. She nearly could not get a hold on it. One of the men—she could not tell which—put his hands in his hip pockets. He looked down the street where no police car was coming. Then he turned around toward her.

She drew back against the glass so she couldn't see them anymore.

The water was probably boiling. Zoya had to finish breakfast or

Kolya was going to be late. Carefully, keeping her arm close to the wall, she tossed her cigarette off the balcony. Then she gripped one hand tight with the other. It only took a few minutes to settle down within herself. When she was ready, she slid the door open and went back inside.

M A Y

Oksana knew something was wrong when she saw the door. Her security door stuck into the hallway like a dislocated finger. Behind that metal panel, a line of white light shivered out. Both her apartment doors, the outer steel and the inner fiberglass one, hung open.

She was half a flight below, alone on the landing, and heard the blood in her ears. The double-layered entrances to other apartments were shut tight. Oksana held on to the railing for one second, looking up, and then called for her dog. "Malysh?" No one answered. "Malysh?" Oksana said, climbing now. Running. She pulled the security door the rest of the way open and pushed back the inner one to find her apartment quiet, clean, frightening. Her laptop rested on the coffee table. So she hadn't been robbed.

Oksana called the dog's name again. She went first to the bedroom to see if he was asleep in there—"Malysh, come!"—then to the living room, kitchen, bathroom in turn. She got on her hands and knees in case he had somehow squeezed under the tub. Feeling a bite on her palm, she turned a hand over to find her unused keys still looped around one finger. She pushed the keys into her pocket and bent deeper on her elbows. Malysh was not there.

The dog had gotten out. Her building's entrance door always stuck either open or closed, so it had been open for months, all winter long, as snow blew in and mounded ankle-deep over the ground floor. There was nothing to stop Malysh from running. He could be anywhere. Oksana hurried back to the landing and down the flights of stairs—"Malysh, Malysh," she shouted. The stairway was cool blue, its concrete walls washed by spring light. Up on the fifth floor, the apartment was open for the dog's return. Oksana was already at the building's entrance. She was already bursting back into the world.

She had no time to pause and take her panic in hand, so instead she rode it, shock turned to speed in her legs. The day's strains, the last decade of stiff work in a sediment laboratory, were subsumed by fear. She was moving quickly as a child. Out the building's door, she ran downhill. Toward the playground—Oksana and Malysh went there each morning before she left for the volcanological institute, when the neighborhood was draped in shadows and empty enough to let Malysh off-leash. Please, she thought, looking into the alleys between apartment buildings as she ran. Cables, trash bags, early patches of grass. She watched the ground though she was sickened to picture what she might find. Beyond the playground was a row of vendors, fruit and bread and flower stands, so there were always cars coming down these streets. Always trucks. Oksana's shoes flew over the pavement. She thought, Let him be there.

Why did she lend Max her keys at lunch? Why did she ever allow him to stop by? All those instructions she gave over their two trays and the speckled plastic table—"Turn the lock on the security door three times," she told him expressly—and the confirmation she asked for when he returned the keys to her desk this afternoon. "Everything good?" she said. Something like that, she could not remember now, her mind couldn't track the details, her breath was short. "Max. Found your papers? All good?" She only knew that he had smiled, agreed, asked her some facile thing about sulfide ore. He certainly hadn't mentioned he left both her apartment doors open. And now Malysh was gone.

Her heart, that distractible creature, raced inside her chest. As amusing as Max was with his big talk, his optimism, Oksana never really trusted him. Why did she not remind herself of that this afternoon? Of all people to put her confidence in—Max. Oksana's ex-husband used to roll his eyes during the evenings they spent with Max and Katya last fall. "At my climbing gym, we're organizing a trip to Kathmandu," Max once told them. "You should come with us. Haven't you ever wanted to climb the Himalayas?" Even Katya, sitting beside him, had looked embarrassed. And the way Max talked of their work at the institute was delusional. As if he would become deputy research director, then supervise the department, then lead the Russian Academy of Sciences. "Romanovich told me I just need to wait a few more months for my promotion. He told me, 'As soon as we permit you to begin rising, you'll never stop.'"

Oksana's husband had made to pull out Max's chair. "So go ahead and rise," Anton said, not really joking.

If someone had told Oksana then that in six months, Anton would be gone but Max and Katya would still be together, and that the two would come over for dinner, Max would leave his notes behind, and Oksana, trusting in her long friendship with Katya, would momentarily believe in this cretin enough to share her keys, she would have poisoned the ice cream she served them all that night for dessert.

The playground held a few schoolchildren, two elderly women, no Malysh. Oksana spotted the dog's absence from a distance. There were no walls for him to hide behind, just rods, ropes, and slivers of rubber. She circled the little park to make sure. "Malysh," she called. Her voice was faint behind her pulse.

Once she came back around to where she started, she chose the plumper of the pair of women and said, "Auntie, have you seen a dog?" The other one stared ferociously at Oksana's exposed knees below her skirt. "He's white," Oksana said, holding her hands apart to show Malysh's length. "A Samoyed. A big, handsome beast, a sled dog, very clean, well fed, strong."

"No, sweetheart," the woman said.

"We don't look after street dogs," said the other.

"I'm not talking about a stray," said Oksana. All the blood in her body collected, turned, slammed forward in rage. Her feet stayed planted but her hands wavered.

She could shove the old bitch down. A street dog—a street dog—if this hag had pulled her head out of her own ass for one minute today and seen Malysh, she would not speak this way.

Oksana herself had been a witness to a disappearance; she understood from experience what drew the eye. Ten months ago, Oksana noticed a well-polished car. These days on the street, she looked after smiling women or too-affectionate couples. God knew Oksana was not the most attentive person in the world, but she turned her head in public often enough to know what looked exceptional.

Arms crossed over her chest, Oksana turned away from the women to shout. "Malysh!" Identical apartment blocks filled her view. Behind her, kids giggled. Oksana chose the wide avenue to her left and started running.

By the time she crossed Akademika Koroleva, where true street dogs tricked her with their movements, she burned. Sweat slid down her spine to collect at her waistband. Her dog was nowhere. She called Katya from her cell. As soon as Katya picked up, Oksana said, "Are you with Max? Does he have Malysh?" Katya's voice drew away from the phone. Oksana shouted, "He left my doors open!"

Max came over the line. "The dog? But—"

"Both doors! What were you thinking? Idiot! Both doors open," Oksana said, and she was not weak enough to cry, but her voice was cracking. "Didn't you know Malysh would run? How could you?"

"Oksana, slow down, I don't know what to say." She could hear Katya talking in the background. "I didn't—I couldn't figure out your locks, so I just pushed the doors shut behind me. Shouldn't they have stayed closed? Could they have swung back open? Malysh was in the apartment when I left."

She stared down the road. "He's gone now."

Katya, distant, said, "Ask where she is."

"Where are you?" Max asked. "What can we do?"

Oksana did not respond. They did not understand. Even Anton hadn't appreciated her bond with Malysh, not really—Oksana had met the man who would become her ex-husband when the dog was two, and Anton moved out when the dog was seven. A few months ago, during one of those calls she had come to expect from Anton, those after-midnight ones, those his-new-lover-is-sleeping ones, Oksana told her ex, "Malysh almost caught a fox today. He ran off in the forest and came back to me with red fur between his teeth."

"I'm not interested in what's been in the dog's mouth," Anton said. He lowered his voice so the sound stroked her ear. "I'm more interested in what's going to be in yours."

No one in this world cared enough about what Oksana treasured, but only Anton's disregard ended up feeling like love. Nightly, as Malysh slept beside her, Oksana listened to her ex swear over the phone that he still wanted her most of all. No matter the woman he was staying over with—Anton's tongue and teeth waited for Oksana. He came back to the apartment every few weeks to fulfill that promise. The dog laid his white head on Anton's lap in celebration; the dog huffed with pleasure outside their bedroom door.

Oksana looked out across the roaming strays. Through the phone, she heard jostling, before her friend came back to the line. "We'll pick you up," Katya said. "We can search for Malysh together."

"Don't bother," Oksana said. Katya sighed. To ward off any accusations of coldness, Oksana said, "We'll cover more ground in separate cars."

"No, we'll come get you. You should focus on looking for him without also being at the wheel."

"All right," Oksana said finally. A truck rolled past and she shut her eyes against its bulk. "Anyway, I might find him here, by foot, in the next minute or two."

"Okay," Katya said. "I'm sure."

Max's meaningless words were rising in the background. Katya hung up.

Eight years ago, one of their coworkers had come into the office with a picture of four pups lined up, as soft and squinty-eyed as polar bear cubs. Oksana kept returning to his desk that day to look. "I need one," she said at last, as the coworker packed his bag to leave. She brought Malysh home that night.

Oksana threw out her best shoes after the puppy got to them and stopped wearing dark colors because they showed his fur too well.

Though she called him naughty, squeezing his face between her palms, she adored those little inconveniences. She lived for them. With Malysh, she—who grew up an only child, lying on the pullout couch and hearing her mother through the wall, who maintained friends she could intimidate and lovers who broke her faith, who had never been chosen for marriage and was told she was too old for babies, who was always apart from herself—was not alone anymore.

They went to the playground, the city center, the woods that lined their neighborhood, and the mountains beyond. Their legs grew the same muscles. After Anton came and left, Oksana returned to the habit she'd formed when the dog was small. She slept on one side of the bed and Malysh slept on the other, and when she woke up in the silver middle of the night, she turned toward him for comfort. They lay facing each other like two parentheses. His paws pushed across the blanket. Oksana reached out to touch the fine hairs that snuck between the pads of his feet, and in his sleep Malysh drew away, lifted his head, sniffed around, then relaxed back toward her.

Loving the dog best had become simple. Who else was there?

She described him to vendors at the fruit stands while the sun cooled above. She looked behind parked cars, in truck beds, into echoing lobbies. Other building doors, like theirs, were left propped open—Malysh might have gotten confused and ducked inside. If he were hurt . . . She peeked, mouth dry, into a dumpster, where someone might have heaved him . . . Reaching the edge of her neighborhood, she crossed into a patch of forest. Trees crowded her along the path. "Malysh," she called. Her footsteps were the only ones around.

At every crisis over the past year, the dog was her companion. When Anton betrayed her, when he moved out, when he started calling again, Malysh listened. When the ruble collapsed, and the institute's funding was frozen, so she no longer could do any field research and had to halt a two-year-long project on calc-alkaline rocks, she left work with the excuse of walking her dog and used the drive to pound her palms against her car's steering wheel.

When she had the bad luck to walk by the Golosovskaya sisters at the moment of their abduction. When she saw their school pictures appear on the television that night. When she sat up on the sofa and said, "I saw them," a declaration, and her husband said, "What?" and she said it again, "*I saw them,*" now a shout. The feeling inside her was dense and swift and devastating. She was the one who could have stopped it—she was the one who now could help. She called the police, and as she waited for an officer to pick her up, Anton followed her around the apartment promising she was doing the right thing. He told her they had every reason to be hopeful. The dog trotted alongside, grinning.

Even after the police questioned her, and when the description she gave them of the kidnapper, which was nothing, really, a glance at a stranger, was spread in whispers around the city as if her word were fact, and when she watched local officials swear the sisters would be recovered, and when her colleagues and friends drew away as if she were solely responsible for the girls' absence, and when she wondered if she was, and when she swore to herself she wasn't, Malysh lay at her feet as if the world was all right.

She touched her cell phone. For an instant, she was tempted to call Lieutenant Ryakhovsky. But if he could not find two humans over ten months, he certainly would not be able to track down a dog tonight.

The woods grew dark. She emerged to a city that had lost light. The phone was buzzing—Katya.

When her friend's car pulled up, Oksana climbed into the back. Max was in the passenger seat. His eyes were wide with apology. "I'm so sorry, Oksana, really. I don't know what could have happened."

"You don't know?" Oksana said. "I know. You let him out."

"I mean I didn't realize." They were rolling down a pitted road together. Katya's hand was on the gearshift and Max's hand was on Katya's thigh. Oksana hated this: the cozy pair, the pain inflicted. Why did she ever have Max and Katya over? Oksana grew up training herself to be independent, strong, less trusting than her mother, and still somehow she ended up inviting in those who hurt her.

She pressed her forehead to the window. "Where to?" Katya asked.

"The cross-country ski track. We spent a lot of time there this winter." Oksana stared out. "It's good it's getting dark," she said to the car. "I'll be able to spot his fur in an instant."

Malysh might have left because he, like her husband, hated Max's company. Max's boasts, Katya's laughter, their infiltration into Oksana's home. They swung through the ski base's empty parking lot, where they scanned the snowless skiing paths and the limitless forest. Oksana lowered her window to shout. No movement came from between the trees.

Through the hours Ryakhovsky interviewed Oksana at the police station in August, he had been dismayed at her inability to describe the sisters' kidnapper. "Think again," he said. "Go over it once more. You saw these children climbing into a strange man's car and you didn't pause at all?"

"How could I have seen he was a strange man?" Oksana said. "He looked common to me."

Ryakhovsky narrowed his eyes. He struck Oksana as a boy playing in a police uniform. "My superiors need you to produce something," he said. "A memory, a detail. There must have been something in the experience that stood out to you." She stared at him. "Do you try to be this useless?" he asked. "You work at it in your spare time?"

"It must come naturally to me," she said. The words were bitter on her tongue.

The long, long list of what she had not seen. All that she failed to do. At Oksana's direction, Katya turned the car back to the street, looped around the traffic circle, and headed toward the city center. Meanwhile Max described to them Malysh's behavior this afternoon. The dog had been normal, even mellow, sniffing at Max's empty hands then returning to the bedroom to rest while Max gathered the work he had left the evening before. "Malysh wants an adventure, that's all," Max said. "He'll come back when he's tired himself out." Oksana kept her eyes on the sidewalks. After some silence, Max said, "This afternoon Romanovich—"

"Please stop talking to me," Oksana said, and he did.

They passed the squat block of the library, the gold-topped church, and the pedagogical university. They slowed at the monument of a full-size tank at the corner of Leningradskaya and Pogranichnaya. The tank's armament tipped toward the twilit sky. In the blackness of every sagging bus shelter, Oksana looked for Malysh's body. The summer's missing-person posters, rippled from a year's rain and snow, were sealed with packing tape to the shelter walls. For the first time, Oksana really understood how the Golosovskaya girls' mother must feel. Because Malysh was not in the bus shelters. He was nowhere.

From the open window, Oksana called his name. Every so often some group of teenagers shouted back. The car continued south, past rows of stand-alone metal garages and the twinkling lights of the container terminal. It took more than an hour to climb from one point of their crescent city to the other. Katya and Max murmured to each other in the front seats. Once they reached Zavoyko, where Petropavlovsk's hills rose into cliffs facing the black ocean, Katya turned them around.

Oksana pictured Malysh somewhere bloody in the dirt. Could not help it—as they passed other cars, she searched between their headlights for pale fur, and when their car was alone on the road, she imagined all the places her dog might be crumpled.

You believe that you keep yourself safe, she thought. You lock up your mind and guard your reactions so nobody, not an interrogator or a parent or a friend, will break in. You earn a graduate degree and a good position. You keep your savings in foreign currency and you pay your bills on time. When your colleagues ask you about your home life, you don't answer. You work harder. You exercise. Your clothing flatters. You keep the edge of your affection sharp, a knife, so that those near you know to handle it carefully. You think you established some protection and then you discover that you endangered yourself to everyone you ever met.

Even the man she married had put her at risk. One terrible Sunday last June she and Anton parked at the foot of a little mountain outside the city and hiked to the clearing on top. Oksana sat down to settle her breath, while Anton threw a stick for Malysh. The dog's black lips were wet with excitement. Listening to Anton's voice, the joke in it suddenly surfacing, Oksana lifted her head in time to see her husband throw the stick over the cliff and Malysh run after. She screamed. She saw it: the dog's perfect body following, its arc, its vanishing, she would not be able to stop it, she would have to watch him go. The noise ripped through her. In that instant, she was so prepared for tragedy that she could not believe how Malysh gave up the game and turned back to jog toward Anton. Her hands were already on the ground. Her mouth was open and wailing.

Malysh, all dumb with life, was looking at her husband, expecting the next stick. She threw her arms around the dog's neck. He smelled like exertion, the outdoors, and her devotion. "What is wrong with you?" she shouted at Anton.

"Don't be silly, come on," he said. "He never would've jumped."

Her eyes were filled with the vision of her dog doing exactly that. "He trusts you."

"This is an animal descended from wolves. You understand? His grandparents survived in the tundra. He has a hundred times more survival instincts than you or me." She buried her face in Malysh's side. "Sana, I was fooling around," Anton said, and she cried out, "It wasn't funny."

They returned to the car that afternoon the way they so often ended up walking, with Oksana ten meters ahead and her husband letting her go. The dog ran back and forth between them—galloping up to one and turning back to the other. In the hundredth round of this, Oksana dug her hands into his fur. "Stay with me," she commanded. They were far enough ahead of her husband that she could no longer hear Anton's feet. Malysh's body trembled under her. He stuck to her side for an instant, shaking, then dashed backward to find Anton and shepherd them together again.

There were worse times of her life before that afternoon. When none of her school classmates spoke to her for three months after she bit a boy at recess. When her mother pulled out the photo albums every holiday and made Oksana stare at pictures of her father as a young stranger deployed in Afghanistan. When Oksana lost her scholarship in her third year of university, or could not get out of bed after her mother moved to the mainland, or stopped her birth control but never got pregnant, or found those strings of text messages on Anton's phone. Worse periods, yes, but no worse moment, because no other grief distilled so well into a single instant: that stick sailing off into the sky and her dog following.

Katya guided the car around a curve. The streets poured past their windows. Rising curbs, parked cars, empty intersections. Collapsed single-family houses, snapped-together prefabricated buildings. Teenagers fell away and old drunk men took their places. Apartment lights turned out on the hills.

Watching for evidence of Malysh, Oksana saw Kamchatka as it really was. The August day she walked past the kidnapping, the weather was warm, and the air in the city center smelled good, salt and sugar and oil and yeast. Anton had gotten down on his knees that morning to apologize for the other woman—at the time he swore there was only that one. And Oksana forgave him. While she left her desk, picked up Malysh, and drove the dog to the center for a walk by the water, she felt light. Hopeful. Even in the parking lot, after she secured the leash and let Malysh out of the car, the city looked beautiful to her. The sun was bright, brilliant, playing across the dark panels of freshly washed hoods. In front of her, two elf-faced girls climbed into leather seats in a big car. Oksana believed the world might be wonderful.

Those two girls were gone. Anton, too. Oksana let them all go without noticing. And if that round-faced child killer she'd walked past flagged down Katya's car at this moment, Oksana would not recognize him. Why should she? He looked just like anyone else in this ugly place. She never saw what was in front of her until it was too late.

The last time she spoke to Ryakhovsky was when the detective called to say they were winding down the investigation. "Oh," she said. "Why? Are you sure?" That was when she still had the security of her fingers buried in the warm fur on her dog's shoulders. Now she thought of calling back—not to ask for police help but to tell Ryakhovsky she understood.

She understood. There was no reason left for hope. Outside, buildings blurred against the night.

The day's adrenaline had emptied away. Katya glanced at the rearview mirror as they entered Oksana's neighborhood's traffic circle. "It's late," Katya said. "Wherever Malysh is, he's sleeping. It may be time for us to do the same."

Katya turned onto Oksana's street and slowed to navigate around potholes. Max said, "When you get home, you'll probably find him curled up on your landing."

Bottles, hubcaps, and first-floor windows turned into spots of white that could be, but never were, Oksana's dog.

"Do you want us to stay over?" Katya asked.

"No," Oksana said.

"Are you sure?"

Oksana's dry face did not move. "I'm certain."

The car bumped downhill in neutral. The phone in Oksana's lap started to buzz. She flipped the phone over, glanced at the screen, and silenced it. Max, turned around in his seat, raised his eyebrows at the interruption. "Is that Anton? Still trying to call you?"

"Are you really in a position to be asking me questions?" Oksana said. "Because, believe me, while I'm looking for my dog's body on the street, I'm thinking of many questions I'd like to ask you."

"I'm only—" said Max.

"Don't be cruel to him," said Katya. Defending that idiot.

Oksana said, "I should be nicer?"

"You should understand he made a mistake. A terrible mistake. One he wishes he could take back."

Oksana stared at the side of Katya's face. "I understand perfectly."

They rolled to a stop in front of Oksana's building, left gap-toothed by its broken entrance. Oksana climbed out, shut the door behind her, and then opened it again. The car's interior light illuminated Katya and Max, those awful dinner guests, those traitors. They waited for her to speak as though they expected her to invite them upstairs after all.

"Whatever was between us, it's finished," Oksana said. "Katya, don't text me. Max, no more lunches."

"Hold on," Max said. "I did this, it was my fault. Don't— Katya's only here to help. Don't act as though she hurt you."

"Did you not hear me?" Oksana asked. "Could I say this more clearly?"

Max, mouth open, turned to Katya, whose knuckles were wrapped high on the steering wheel. He turned back. "Are you serious? I lose weekday lunch privileges, but she loses a fifteen-year friendship?"

"You would have never been in my house if it weren't for her. I don't want your kind of mistakes in my life anymore."

"You know, you can be a real bitch," Katya said. Her eyes were shadowed. Oksana scoffed. "Truly," Katya said. "We came out tonight to help you. I know you're upset, but if you would just look outside yourself, you would see that we're here trying."

"What fine help," Oksana said. "Should I be grateful that your boyfriend murdered my dog?"

Katya shifted her car into gear. The engine got louder. "Malysh is probably upstairs. But you want to be alone, we'll leave you alone. I can't imagine how I hung around this long anyway."

"I'll be alone," Oksana said. "You've both made sure of that. You're right. Thank you."

The apartment building's stairwell was dark. The landing was empty. Oksana's security door jutted forward.

She slipped inside her double doors and called, "Malysh?" He did not come.

Oksana pressed her hands to her chest, the phone hard against her ribs as punishment. One of her doors bent onto the landing and the other hung into her home. Outside them, the building slept. In her living room, fists pressed to skin, Oksana blamed herself. Sloppy. As deliberate as she had tried to be all these years, she was sloppy, and this was the consequence. She had closed her eyes to the world around her. Walked happily past a murderer of children. Put all of herself into an animal that ran . . .

If only Malysh had jumped that day on the mountain. Oksana should have thrown the stick for the dog herself. In August, in the very first few hours of police questioning, the missing girls' mother had come to the station to talk to Oksana. Only now, months after that desperate conversation with her, did Oksana appreciate why. It hurts too much to break your own heart out of stupidity, to leave a door unlocked or a child untended and return to discover that whatever you value most has disappeared. No. You want to be intentional about the destruction. Be a witness. You want to watch how your life will shatter.

J U N E

A forest takes seventy years to recover after a fire. Out the car window, black streaked across the hills that guided Marina away from home. Limbless trunks rose from charred earth. In the front seats, Eva and Petya argued over the ending of an Australian horror movie. Eva was winning, speaking with more conviction; Petya kept falling silent as he navigated around potholes in the road. The next time he downshifted, Eva turned in her seat to make her case to Marina. "The end of it is a fantasy, like a dream sequence, don't you agree?"

"I didn't see the movie," Marina said.

Eva pursed her lips. "From what you heard us describe, though. Doesn't it seem most likely that it's a fantasy?"

Marina shook her head. "I don't know." That familiar pressure began to come down on her chest.

Petya, bringing the car back up to speed, glanced at his wife. "She hasn't seen it. Leave her alone." Eva blew out her breath and muttered a word. "She's fine," Petya said. His eyes flicked up in the rearview mirror. Marina looked again toward the window. Above them, the sky was enormous, bloated with clouds. The long tracks of dead forest looked like thousands of bones pushed up from their graves.

The weight dropped hard on her chest. Marina could not breathe. She put her head back, folded her hands in her lap, and focused on shutting off the part of her mind that insisted on leading her toward panic. The path was simple: horror movies, petrified wood, bones. Graves. Murderers.

One hand came up to press on her sternum. Her heart hurt. If Marina could peel off her left breast, crack back her ribs, and grip that muscular organ to settle it, she would. She started having these attacks last August, after her daughters disappeared. A doctor gave her tablets to relieve the anxiety. Those did not help. No prescription brought her children home.

Marina was drowning in the backseat of her friends' car. Pulling air in through her nose, she concentrated on benign knowledge instead. Seventy years for full regrowth. Where did she learn that? In childhood . . . her grandfather taught her, probably. Her family spent weekends at her grandparents' dacha when she was a girl. He showed her the difference between common and creeping juniper, how to apply a lime wash to an orchard, and the best time to tap a birch for its juice.

Her lungs inflated again. As the car bumped along, Marina counted facts. What else did she know about trees? About the formation of hills? Though now a propagandist by necessity, she was a journalist by training, and she had always had a head for information. They were on kilometer 250 of 310 along the pitted road toward Esso. Another hour and a half would pass before they reached the campground. The holiday they headed toward might draw only a few hundred people; its organizers had already transmitted a press release to the party newspaper and there was no need for on-the-ground reporting, but Marina's editor, who was soft, sensitive, encouraged her toward any opportunity to leave the city. As soon as Marina mentioned Eva and Petya's invitation, he insisted she attend to cover the event. When, toward the end of last week, she said she was rethinking the trip, he called her into his office and shut the door. "You have to go," he told her. Again, more firmly, with his shoulders hunched forward so he could catch her eye: "You have to." Not for the story, she knew, but for the comfort of the rest of the office. He wanted her to leave in grief but come back different.

The road north followed the path of a blaze so old Marina's grandparents might have heard news break about it. That was another fact. The trees still looked like death to her.

"Are you all right back there?" Eva called over the seat. "Are you hungry? Are you bored?"

Marina leaned forward. The seat belt tugged against her strained ribs. "I'm fine."

"Well, I have to get out," Eva said. She spoke sideways—maybe Marina was not meant to hear. Petya checked his watch and guided the car to the side of the road, so Eva, slamming the door behind her, could climb down off the gravel shoulder. Eva's ponytail bobbed as she unbuttoned her pants and crouched. Marina looked out the other window. The trees on that side were thick, deep, damp-looking. Old growth.

She remembered taking her girls for an early hike. In a younger forest, on a warmer day, in a neighborhood at the southern end of Petropavlovsk. Sophia so small, then, that Marina carried her most of the way in a backpack. That sweet load on Marina's spine. Sophia's fingers brushed Marina's bare arms, and Alyona pulled leaves off the shrubs they passed. Alyona was five years old, at the height of her obsession with carrots—she ate nothing but—and Marina brought a plastic bag full of them, washed and peeled and prepared, for her daughter to picnic on. The three of them climbed along a stream bank, with the sun coming through the trees in strips and ribbons. The sound of Alyona's crunching, the trickle of fresh water, the steady rush of Sophia's breath behind Marina's ear.

Marina pressed her palm to her chest. Her inhalations got shallower. Petya was doing her the kindness of pretending he did not hear.

The passenger door opened and the car chimed in greeting. "Thanks, my joy," Eva said. She opened the glove compartment, pulled out a sanitizing wipe, and leaned over to kiss her husband on the cheek. The car bloomed with the smell of rubbing alcohol.

When they were another fifteen kilometers along, rain started, falling in little patters at first, then faster, harder. Up front, Eva was talking again about a woman at the campsite she wanted Marina to meet. Marina checked her phone. No service. The police had her parents' numbers on file, so in case anything developed in the city, they would be able to contact her family, but . . . Marina hated leaving cell service. These interruptions happened so often—at the ocean, at the dacha, on one stretch of the road between the city and the airport. During the first months the girls were gone, Marina went nowhere that risked disconnection. She drove from home to work, work to home, with her cell phone clutched in one hand on top of the steering wheel.

When she called the police major general to say she was considering traveling to this campground for the weekend, he, too, pushed her toward the trip. "Take a vacation," he told her.

"It's for work," she said.

"Well, take some extra time for yourself." His voice dropped. "Marina Alexandrovna, our investigation is no longer active."

Listening, Marina rolled her chair away from her desk and bent over her knees. "I understand that. But if—"

"We will get in touch right away if any new information comes in. Of course we hope for a lead." Marina could not breathe then, either. "But take your trip. Live your life. Now is the time to move forward."

He dared to mention hoping for a lead, after she had dedicated months to combing through city news coverage, calling scattered village police stations to ask after unsolved kidnappings, tracking down the prison records of men convicted of sex crimes against minors, begging superiors in the party to bring this case to the attention of Moscow. The major general said such things to make her doubt they had ever spent a minute looking for her daughters. With him in charge, no wonder the girls had not come back, Marina thought and wanted to suffocate.

"It better clear up," Eva said. Her narrow face tipped toward the windshield. "Otherwise setting up the tent will be a nightmare."

"It'll pass," Petya said. Marina tucked her phone back in her bag.

Drops tracked across her window. She thought about surface tension, chemical composition, school science experiments. Nothing else. No recent memories.

By the time they pulled up to the fence bordering the campground, the rain had stopped. The stretch of wet, shining grass in front of their car was lined by empty booths. A stage in the middle of the clearing bore a banner: WE WELCOME VISITORS TO THIS TRADITIONAL FESTIVAL IN CELEBRATION OF THE REGION'S CULTURAL MINORITIES. HAPPY NEW YEAR—NURGENEK.

"Happy New Year," Marina said. It sounded odd in June.

"The party's not until tomorrow," said Eva. Petya slammed his door on his way to grab their things from the trunk.

Arms full of supplies, they crossed the clearing on a dirt path that took them into the forest. They heard people talking, smelled cooked meat. An ATV was parked on the path ahead of them; when they squeezed past the vehicle, they found thirty people sharing dinner around tables in the open air.

"That's her," Eva whispered to Marina, and stepped forward. "Alla Innokentevna." A gray-haired woman in the center of the group glanced up. "It's so good to see you again."

The woman put down her fork and beckoned them. Her lips pursed as Eva approached. "Don't you usually come earlier?"

"We do. This year we brought a friend"—Eva looked behind for Marina—"a journalist. She had to work yesterday so we couldn't leave until this morning."

Marina nodded at the group. Alla Innokentevna was smiling now. "A journalist. In the city? What newspaper?"

"United Russia's," Marina said.

"We sent you a press release," Alla Innokentevna said.

Marina said, "I know." Eva broke in: "When we described the holiday to her, she said she had to experience it for herself. She hasn't been up north for years. And before she worked for the party, she covered all sorts of subjects. In 2003 she won the Kamchatka Regional Prize for her reporting."

Petya glanced at Marina. "In 2002," Marina mouthed. He winked.

"Have you eaten dinner?" Alla Innokentevna asked. "No? You can set up by the big yurt." She gestured toward the trees. "Come back afterward and we'll have plates for you." The other event organizers and the young members of visiting dance troupes fell back into their own conversations.

Eva turned around, grinning. Her face shone in the blue evening. She looked ready to celebrate someone else's new year.

They put up the tent on soaked ground. Water seeped through the knees of Marina's pants while she held the tent ties in her fists and waited for Eva and Petya to finish arguing over where to put the stakes. When they got back to the tables, three dishes of boiled meat and buttered rice waited. Some of the dancers had left, but Alla Innokentevna still sat. The organizer waited until Marina took her first bite to start talking. "You're going to cover the holiday for your paper?"

Marina nodded. The meat was soft against her teeth. A few meters away, two teenagers washed dishes in a basin of soapy water.

"I run the cultural center here. You arrived late," Alla Innokentevna said. "We had a concert this afternoon."

Marina swallowed her mouthful. "I'm sorry we missed it."

"Most people come tomorrow, anyway. It's all right," Alla Innokentevna said. Her glasses turned opaque as they caught the little light left in the sky. "What did you win your reporting award for?"

"A series on poaching. Salmon poaching in the southern lakes."

Alla Innokentevna lifted her chin. The reflections slid away, turning her glasses back to transparency. "Dangerous work."

"Yes," Marina said. It had been. In those years, poaching was organized crime; poachers stripped rivers of their entire salmon runs, tanks of caviar surfaced for illegal sale, bears and eagles starved to death throughout the peninsula, international environmental groups dumped billions of rubles into Kamchatka's economy to fight the black market. Marina had been there on the water. Rowing boats out at night, no flashlights, no talking. The rangers holding rifles in the seats beside her. An emergency radio resting heavy at their feet, and her lips dry, her blood racing. Ripples off the oars. Frogs called back and forth. As they steered closer to the poaching teams, belly-up fish floated past, each one slit from gills to anus, each body gleaming from the moon.

She left investigative work to go on maternity leave. By the time Alyona took her first steps, Marina no longer missed the risk; she wanted to stay far away from night raids, gutted creatures, men who carried weapons. After Sophia was born and the girls' father left, Marina found a different way to support a family. She wrote lies for the party, which paid the bills. For a while, she kept their household safe and happy and whole.

Marina got up. She gave her plate to the dishwashing teenagers, took a rinsed mug from the stack, and fixed herself tea. The hot water came from a kettle sitting on coals. The leftover meat, fat congealing, was in a stockpot on the ground. Back at the table, Eva was telling Alla Innokentevna about their last year in the city. Marina checked her phone again. The conversation at the table quieted. When she looked up, Alla Innokentevna was staring at her, and Marina knew Eva had told the woman that her daughters were gone.

Eva kept trying to help. Last week making travel plans, and again this afternoon in the car, she had told Marina that this head organizer had a missing child, too. Eva talked about that fact as if Marina and Alla Innokentevna had something in common, but Alla Innokentevna's daughter was already a high school graduate when she vanished from Esso. Her name never appeared in public records. The girl ran away from home, Eva said. There was no comparison.

Marina poured out the rest of her tea and balanced the mug on the pile of dirty dishes. "Thank you," she told the teenagers, both of whom had women's hips already. Marina returned to the table to tell Eva and Petya that she was exhausted. She was headed to bed.

"Outhouses are down the path. The river is straight back. You can wash yourself there," Alla Innokentevna said. The organizer's voice had not changed—usually people's voices changed after they found out—but the quality of her focus had. She turned a pure beam of attention on Marina. For nearly eleven months already, people had been watching Marina, expecting details, begging for more. They wanted to know what went wrong with her family. They enjoyed feeling sorry for her once they heard.

The tent rustled as Marina crawled in and unrolled her sleeping bag against one wall. The trees above her made restless noises. Their branches threw black lines across the tent's gray dome.

A school dance troupe must be staying in the yurt beside her. Young voices floated through the air. Someone thudded on a drum, and someone else laughed, too loudly. Of Marina's two girls, Sophia had been the dancer. Her skinny limbs . . . even as a baby, she was long-legged. Whenever the culture channel was on the TV at home, Sophia imitated the ballerinas. Raised her arms, sharp elbows, and bent one knee. Lifted her face, with its high eyebrows and thin, innocent lips.

Marina curled her fingers over her sternum. She turned her face toward the plastic wall. She could not help thinking of them, she could not, except as soon as she did, she slipped too far into fantasy—pictured them coming back, both of them intact, frightened but alive. Their hair a little longer than when she saw them last. She imagined them returning in the same clothes. The three of them would huddle together, and Marina would run her hands over their backs, their worn shirts. She would press her mouth to their foreheads. Her girls would stay safe with her forever.

Or her imagination slid the other way. Finding their bodies instead.

Move forward, the major general had told her. Live. Marina would not survive another year if she pictured these things. Her pulse was deafening. The images choked her. Her hand was a claw under her neck, and she did not think about their little necks, their bodies, the stranger's hands that touched them, her daughters, she would not. She shut her eyes and screamed in silence at herself to calm down.

Calm down. Count something and calm down.

The sleeping bag she lay in was rated to zero degrees. The tent belonged to Petya and Eva, and had space to sleep four. In childhood, Marina camped in humbler conditions: her father's army tent, made of canvas and rope. Her father set their tent up in a section of the garden behind her grandparents' house. Marina cataloged the smells of those summer nights. Early grass. Fresh dirt. The bitter leaves of tomato plants.

The drum sounded again over her heartbeat. Leaves rustled. In the darkness behind her eyelids, Marina sorted through a lifetime of trivia.

She breathed normally by the time Eva's and Petya's footsteps crunched outside. The tent door unzipped. They crawled in clumsily, shushing each other, and the heavy scent of liquor followed. Eva giggled a little. Marina listened to them slide over their sleeping bags, fuss with zippers and Velcro. Petya whispered something. "She's sleeping," Eva said. He was quiet. There came the wet noises of one, then two, kisses, before they lay down.

In the morning Marina left the tent before them. The sun, up for barely an hour, blurred yellow in the mist above the tree line. Yesterday's rain was rising from the ground. The wet settled cold on Marina's skin. Down at the river, she spat toothpaste foam into the water and watched it churn away. She remembered the body the police had recovered from the city's bay in April—their many mistakes and misidentifications—they had called her to the coroner, although they knew it wasn't right. They knew. They only wanted her to release them from their duties. Spiderwebs at her feet were decorated with water droplets. Farther into the forest, birds sang.

On her way from the outhouse, she again passed the tables, now set up with stacks of paper napkins for breakfast. Alla Innokentevna, standing with two other women by the cooking fire, waved and called, "Join us."

Marina wrapped her plastic sandwich bag more tightly around her toothbrush. "It's all right. We brought food. I don't want to intrude."

"You're not intruding. I'm inviting you."

After a moment, Marina stepped off the path. Alla Innokentevna nodded and turned back to her cooks.

Marina let her fingers trail along the plank tabletops as she approached their little group. Flakes of ash, caught by the wet air, floated toward her. One of the cooks held out a plastic mug. "Take it," the cook said, and Marina hurried to do so. A tea bag was already inside. The cook said, "Here," and poured water from the blackened kettle. "How'd you sleep?"

Both this cook and Alla Innokentevna had that bouncing, northern way of speaking. "Fine," Marina said. The cook turned her attention back to the meal—rice floating in milk—but Alla Innokentevna faced Marina. Soon, the organizer would start to ask questions.

"It's lovely here," Marina said, to stop her.

"You don't come up this way too often?"

"No. I can't. I have work."

"We all have work," Alla Innokentevna said. She waved one hand, and ash fluttered in her wake. "In any case, you're here now."

Marina slid her palms around her mug, which was hot enough to light up the tender skin. The rest of Marina's body was cool, wary. Rice swam through the milk as one cook stirred the pot.

"My son and one of my daughters will be here today," Alla Innokentevna said. A mention of children. Finally the organizer was coming to her point.

"Good morning," Eva called from the path behind them. Marina turned to see her friend wave. Eva's face was fresh from being washed.

"Did you sleep well?" Alla Innokentevna called back.

Eva came over. Drops of river water were suspended on her jaw. "My husband's just getting up. He's not a morning person," she told the group. "Unlike some of us." She nudged Marina. The cooks ignored the conversation now. Eva drove talk toward the day's events, then the recent construction on the campground—Alla Innokentevna had installed a sauna with a wood-burning stove—and then incidents from around the peninsula. Global complaints: the country's downgraded bond credit rating, the interventions in Ukraine. There was always some new catastrophe to discuss.

Marina sipped her tea. The taste was bitter. The bag had steeped too long.

Once Petya joined them, Marina left the couple to eat together, with their spoons resting in half-full bowls of porridge and their knees touching under the table. She took her time around the camp.

A pen and notepad were in her jacket pockets in case the need for any award-winning journalism arose. In the woods, away from the first clearing, surprises were hidden: the sauna, a shack stocked full of canned food, a small yurt. Traces of conversation came from the eating area. Music played in the distance. Farther into the trees, Marina found a little house on stilts—a granary. Notched logs made a ladder from the ground to its door. She climbed up.

On her back on the planks, she watched dust drift from the bunches of dried grass that insulated the granary's roof. She was close enough to the river to hear water rushing. What kind of place was this? Meant to store food, obviously, but during what time, and for whom? If a grounds tour was offered later, Marina should take it. She knew too little about Kamchatka's north. Native culture was not taught in school when she grew up. There was a little more of that local history in today's lessons . . . Alyona would probably know.

The girls had now missed an entire school year. If they came back, they would have to join new classes.

Why did she do this? Couldn't she recall the past without imagining what had happened to her daughters since?

They could come back. They could not.

The last Marina knew, Alyona and Sophia were in the city center. A woman taking her dog out had seen them walking there. After that, the police lost them; investigators said at first a man snatched them, but the search teams turned up no men to hold accountable. Marina had walked the city shouting her daughters' names. She pounded on her neighbors' doors. She enlisted librarians to help scour the archives for any mention of children gone missing. For four fruitless months, she called the headquarters of the Ministry of Internal Affairs in Moscow, gasped on the phone to junior staff members, scribbled names and phone numbers that led her nowhere.

Then the Petropavlovsk police interrogated Marina and her exhusband, as though Alyona and Sophia would turn out to have been hiding in one of their apartments the whole time. Then the police said the girls drowned. In the spring, they dragged the bay for bodies.

The major general had used that excuse to scale back the investigation last month, so there would be no more organized search parties or announcements to local media. When she heard about that decision, Marina went to the station with the girls' bathing suits.

"These were still in our apartment," she said, pressing the printed nylon to his desk. "Are you thinking Alyona and Sophia went swimming in their clothes? During a cold summer? That they drowned in the center, in still water, at the height of tourist season, without anyone noticing?"

He asked her to sit. She took the bathing suits back to hold in her lap. "Do you want to know what I'm thinking?" he said. "We have not found any evidence of a kidnapper. We have not found your daughters on land. We know they were next to the water when they disappeared. It's a reasonable conclusion."

"And the witness?" Marina asked.

The major general shook his head. "At this point, we don't believe she was a witness to anything at all."

Marina started to hyperventilate there in the station. An assistant came over to help her out of her chair. The police did not believe the witness—but Marina did. She had interviewed enough liars over the years to see when someone was telling the truth. The dog-walking woman did not have much information to offer, but she was frank, when Marina met with her that first day, about what she saw: a man in a dark car with two girls.

No. Alyona and Sophia did not drown that day. They were taken.

This was the knowledge that depressed Marina's lungs. She understood how such cases took shape. Though her work now, for the party paper, was generally cheery (electricity grids humming, roads repaved, citizens turning out to the polls in record numbers), she was familiar, from her early work and her latest research, with the other side of the news. Kidnappings around the world. Police corruption. Sexual assaults. Abuse. Children murdered. Alyona's and Sophia's school pictures appeared on her own front page—their faces alike as two drops of water, their finely combed hair—and when she saw them, Marina pictured terrible things: where were those child-ish heads now? Where were their bodies? Which girl was victim first? Had they screamed?

"Are they dead?" she asked her ex-husband, when the drowning theory came out. He had moved to Moscow for a job when the girls were little, and the time difference meant Marina was always inter-rupting in some way. Still, she kept calling. Her ex was a comfort to speak to because they could share the blame: she should have never left them alone that day; he should have never left them in Kamchatka to begin with; she should have taught their daughters to stay away from dangerous men; he should have shown them what a trustworthy one looks like. He was the only person, besides the girls' kidnapper, who might deserve more guilt than Marina.

He was quiet. "I don't know," he said.

"Exactly. Because I think we would know. I think we would feel it—something different. A more permanent absence."

"Maybe."

"You don't think so?" She had wanted him to agree, or to disagree, or something. To tell her how to proceed.

"I don't know," he said again. "I would . . . like to believe that was true." He spoke carefully. This was how he talked in moments of great stress; during arguments, he became deliberate. He tried to manage her. He was hurting, she knew, but not as much as she was. She suffered more. She was the guilty one, after all. The blame did belong to her.

He said, "Maybe they really are gone," and she wished him dead in their place.

The people who surrounded Marina at home tried to do better than that. They invited her out and were gentle. This trip was not the first time she had left the city—for New Year's, she went with her parents to the dacha, coated then by ice. The stakes in the garden were black with withered vines. Marina had a panic attack at mid-night, and her mother fetched her a pill and fixed her warm vodka with honey. On Alyona's birthday in March, they came together again, nervously. Marina's mother was the wreck then, weeping for the girls. Marina cut the cake to the sound of sobs. Sophia's birthday was coming soon.

For her part, Marina survived. She went to her office, filed her scripted articles, responded to small talk. She showed up at friends' apartments when they asked her to. She called the police station in search of updates. But that was all she could manage, and sometimes even that seemed like too much. Everything that once propelled her was now gone. She used to be a storyteller, she used to have a sense of humor, she used to be a mother, but now she was—nothing. Alla Innokentevna was equipped, after her loss, to organize celebrations, but Marina was a person left purposeless.

Someone called her name in the woods. Marina's hand stayed on her chest. The planks under the curve of her head were hard and scratchy and unforgiving. She remembered Sophia's breakfast that last morning. Oats mixed with milk and freeze-dried bits of berries. A peeled orange. The girl's shoulders over the table looking as easily shattered as porcelain cups.

"Marina," Petya shouted. Closer now. She exhaled, waited, and then realized—maybe he was looking for her for a reason—maybe they had contact from the police. No. It wouldn't be. And yet she sat up.

"I'm here," she shouted back.

The log ladder rocked in place. Petya's head came into view, framed by the granary's entryway. "There you are," he said. His eyebrows rose in tenderness.

His expression made it clear he had nothing urgent to say, but still she asked, "What is it? Did anything happen?"

"No," he said. "Sorry." Brows now creased. He climbed the rest of the way up and joined her inside. "Nice little nest you found here."

"Caw, caw," she said.

He turned himself around to face the river. He had to hunch to fit under the roof. In front of her was the broad sweep of his back. She lay down again.

"Eva sent me to find you. They're about to start."

"Okay. I'll come in a minute."

"She wants you to talk to people." Marina did not respond. Eventually, he said, "It'll be a good time today."

"I know it will," she said. "I'm sure." She doubted.

The world around them was a constant buzz. The rushing water sounded louder than their breath did. Petya shifted his weight. The wood creaked.

"I'm too heavy for this," he said. "I'll see you down there." She kept her eyes fixed on the roof as he climbed out.

.

The clearing was filled with people. Yesterday's empty stalls were packed tight with trinkets and posters. Shouting over each other were narrow-eyed villagers, teenagers in neon hooded sweatshirts, pale Russians with swollen red noses, city tour guides wearing name-brand outdoors gear. Alla Innokentevna, who this morning was dressed in slacks and a turtleneck, wore a beaded deerskin tunic, and spoke into a microphone on the stage.

"We thank the Ministry of Culture for its support." The crowd, that portion facing the stage, clapped. Alla Innokentevna's teeth flashed white behind the black foam of the microphone's head. "And we thank you, dear guests, for coming to our Even New Year, Nurgenek." The words blasted from speakers on either side of the stage. "We welcome you all, indigenous, Russian, and foreign, on this final day of June, to celebrate the solstice sun."

Eva and Petya were close to the stage. Eva's yellow ponytail stood out among the dark-haired locals. Marina squeezed over to her side and gripped Eva's arm, thin in its windbreaker sleeve.

"Couldn't we use some new sun?" Alla Innokentevna asked the crowd. The ground was packed with wetness under their feet. A woman on Marina's other side tittered. "We're joined today," Alla Innokentevna continued, "by native artists from all over the country. Let's meet them." Music bumped out of the speakers. It was the same song Marina had heard in the woods after breakfast—a woman's voice trilling over a synthesizer. One by one, dancers stepped onto the stage from behind the banner, shook and stomped across the boards.

Into Eva's ear, Marina asked, "Is there information posted somewhere about what's happening?"

Without turning from the dancers, Eva pointed to the left. "Try the food stall."

Marina forced her way out of one clot of people, crossed the trampled grass, and pushed into another crowd. When she got to the front, she found the morning's cooks ladling out bowls of soup in exchange for cash. Marina waved to catch one's eye. The cook showed no recognition. "Is there a schedule for today?" Marina called over other people's orders. Seeking numbers, names, the small and neutral details that could always return her to herself. The cook nodded at the end of the counter, beyond stacks of plastic bowls and loose spoons, where scattered pamphlets carried the title "Nurgenek." Marina grabbed a pamphlet and pushed her way out.

She read as she walked past the stalls. The campground was a reconstruction of a traditional Even settlement—the granary was Even, then. Long paragraphs praised the grounds' historical accuracy. A full page of the pamphlet was dedicated to pictures of dance troupes to draw tourists. The sky in those photographs was brilliant blue, while the one above Marina looked like rain.

"Genuine sealskin caps," said one vendor she passed, turning a hat inside out to show hidden speckles. The back of the pamphlet listed the holiday's events. After this came a concert on traditional instruments, then an hour-long leatherworking demonstration by native craftsmen . . . "Pardon me, miss?" said a man from behind her.

She turned to the flat black eye of a camera. A middle-aged man in a polo shirt stood beside it, recorder in his hand. "Yes?" she said. Airless.

"Is this your first time at the festival?" Marina nodded, waiting for his next question to cut. He must have recognized her. "What are your impressions so far?" She stared at him. "We'd love a comment. Where are you visiting from?"

Beside the reporter, the photographer's camera shutter clicked. "No pictures," she said. People pressed behind her, against her, but she was trying to keep a little distance between herself and the recorder. How was it possible? This peninsula was so small that she collided with random journalists wherever she went, but so big she could lose both her girls?

The reporter pushed on. "Are you enjoying yourself?"

Instead of answering, she pointed in the direction of the stage, waved to no one over there, and mouthed, "My friends." Her throat was closing. Even not knowing about the kidnapping, he forced her to return to it. She had to get away.

These attacks always felt like dying. They came on at the thought of her girls' death, and brought her to a dead place, where her lungs shut down, her mouth dried up, her vision eventually blotted out. But she had felt like this before and lived. Many times. Every time. She plunged deeper into the crowd because she felt the reporter watching.

When she finally got to Eva, Marina's chest throbbed. Eva glanced down and looked horrified. "What's the matter?"

Marina shook her head. Petya turned to them, and Marina gave him a thumbs-up. The couple watched Marina until she could talk again. "Everything's normal," Marina said.

The leatherworkers were already filing out onstage. Old men in tool belts and baggy yellow boots. "Something happened to you," said Eva.

"A reporter stopped me." Eva spun in place, searching. "It was nothing. He wanted to know what I thought of the holiday," Marina said. She held up her pamphlet. "Look what I found."

·

The disappearance day. The search-party weeks. The cameras that crowded and the requests for quotes. While her friends flipped through the pamphlet pages, Marina remembered the sour smell of microphones held under her nose. She drank that stench and described her daughters as volunteer searchers walked by her in waders. Police boats pulled nets through the bay. Flyers with her girls' faces, their heights, their weights, their birth dates, were stuck to the plywood walls surrounding construction sites. For months, until the snow fell and the police reorganized their investigation, her former colleagues' hunger for information was bottomless, and Marina was desperate, she would give them anything. She pled and sobbed on the evening news in an attempt to bring a breakthrough in the case. She was a fish ripped open for the reporting. Her wet guts spilled out. After a while, medicated, she could hardly speak. Her parents took over. She could not open her mouth, could not comprehend, could not move, and could not breathe.

From the festival crowd, the craftsmen invited a boy onto the stage to participate. They draped a hide over his knees and showed him, and the crowd, a stone set into a wooden bow. When the boy scraped the bow across the leather once, the stone fell out of its wooden socket to the boards. In the audience, those paying attention laughed.

An artisan replaced the boy in his seat and guided the tool in long strokes. Marina's heart was more or less steady. She did not see the reporter, but he was somewhere out there. Who else would she bump into here? She saw the black humps of cameras all around her—more journalists? Strangers who might recognize her from a months-old city broadcast? This was precisely why she ought to avoid busy places. When she got back to Petropavlovsk, she had to tell her editor: no more public events. No matter where she went now, people, consciously or not, were drawn toward her tragedy. They responded to some call she was still emanating; they felt compelled to approach.

The sun was lost behind clouds. The air around them was heavy. Eva squeezed Marina's shoulder and pointed out a log bench on the right side of the stage. The three of them shuffled over to take those seats.

Alla Innokentevna called for a volunteer from the crowd for a game. She handed a lasso to a Russian woman who came forward to play, while a dancer onstage leaned on a pole with a deer skull tethered to it. At a sign, the dancer rocked that pole to make the smooth bone spin. The skull swung around him like a moon around a planet.

The goal of the game was to snare the skull in motion. The white woman took aim, clumsy with the rope, and Marina stared away at the forest.

The music thumped through her brain. Marina could tell from the hoots in the crowd that the woman was missing her mark over and over again. "Are you three enjoying yourselves?" someone said.

Marina looked up. Alla Innokentevna, in her holiday tunic, looked down. The other organizers had taken charge of the stage and were calling for a second volunteer. Up close, Alla Innokentevna's outfit showed the tracks of traditional craft. A stone rubbed over leather. "Yes," Marina said.

"So many people came out this year, despite the weather," said Eva.

"The weather doesn't matter. We're not here to sunbathe, but to celebrate our history."

Marina straightened her back. "You're all doing an excellent job. It seems like everyone's having fun."

"Are you?" said Alla Innokentevna.

"I'm a little tired," said Marina. The crowd mocked someone's latest failure to lasso the skull.

"We haven't had lunch yet," said Eva. Petya stood.

"Going for food?" Alla Innokentevna asked him. "Walk around the back of the stage. Fewer people there." The organizer sat in the spot Petya vacated.

The bench was low to the ground, forcing their knees up. Marina wrapped her arms around her shins. The three women watched in silence as the dancer slowed the momentum of the swinging skull then reversed its direction, prompting cheers.

Marina sat back a little to get a good look at Alla Innokentevna in her old-fashioned clothes. A serious face, framed by shaggy gray hair. Earrings shone silver underneath. This campground was built to emulate an Even settlement, and Alla Innokentevna, who managed it, must be Even, too, Marina decided. Though Marina couldn't tell northern people apart. Even or Chukchi or Koryak or Aleut. Her grandparents used to speak fondly about how the peninsula's natives had been pushed together, Sovietized, with their lands turned public, the adults redistributed into working collectives and the children taught Marxist-Leninist ideology in state boarding schools.

Alla Innokentevna turned from the stage to face Marina. Marina looked away.

"I heard about your girls," Alla Innokentevna said. "Eva told me. My oldest daughter told me, too, months ago. She lives in the city. She followed your news at first."

The organizer's voice was low. Marina concentrated on her own inhalations.

"How did the police treat you?" Alla Innokentevna asked. Marina shrugged. "They were fine? They kept looking for a while?"

Eva must not have mentioned the case was cold. "They're always looking," Marina said.

Alla Innokentevna grimaced. "How nice."

They sat under the roars of the crowd.

"Eva told you my girl is missing, too."

"Right," Marina said. "Your teenager."

The organizer looked over Marina's head. Her face was drawn. "Not a teenager anymore. Lilia was eighteen when she disappeared, but that was four years ago."

"Eva said she ran away."

"That's what the village police told us." Alla Innokentevna met Marina's eyes again. "The police say many things, don't they? To stop citizens from pestering them."

Marina did not want to talk about this. As if she and Alla Innokentevna had had the same conversations with the police.

"I have a question for you," Alla Innokentevna said. "About the authorities in Petropavlovsk. I heard they were very aggressive. They searched for months. And they came up with many theories, organized searches, interviewed people. Is that the case?"

"Many theories. They did. Yes."

"Are you satisfied?"

"Oh," Marina said. Cheers and hoots sounded around them. "I'm outrageously happy."

After a moment, the organizer smiled. The corners of her eyes did not crease. "Aren't we all," she said. "Then I have a second question. A request."

Wherever Marina went, people tried in this way to consume her.

Alla Innokentevna took a breath and dipped her face down, setting her earrings swinging. "Tell me, how did you influence them to stay so active? You paid them."

"No," Marina said.

"You must have paid them, I think," Alla Innokentevna said. "Otherwise what reason would they have to continue? I understand, believe me. Who did you contact there? How much did you give?"

Everyone's lurid questions. Their suppositions. Every conversation Marina had had over the past year was long, unbearable, one after the next in a rhythm as steady as dirt shoveled into a hole.

"I called the ministry in Petropavlovsk," Alla Innokentevna said. "After it happened, I went to the city police station in person. They didn't listen to me. But they listen to you. Don't you have their ear?"

Marina pressed on her chest. If there were a price for the discovery of a missing person, she would have paid it to the authorities in August, ten times over. "You're wrong," she said. "The police do what they will without me."

"I am asking you as a mother."

"Asking what? Alla Innokentevna, I can't help."

"Simply tell me how." Alla Innokentevna was close. She smelled of shampoo, lotion, ash from the morning's fire. Suffocating. "And I could do something for you, if you like. We have, for example, poachers up here to write about. There are stories I could show you exclusively."

Marina shook her head. "I don't do those kinds of stories anymore."

"No? You can ask me anything."

Eva, hands around her mouth, shouted encouragement toward the stage. The skull on the pole circled endlessly. *Anything*, the organizer said. What answers could Alla Innokentevna have for her? Marina might ask what it was like to see your child turn thirteen, or fifteen, or graduate from high school. How it felt to know, and not just suspect, that if you had been a better parent, more attentive, more responsible, then your baby would not be gone today. How to go on.

Anything? Marina would take a piece of nonsense for her editor to slot into the arts section. She focused on the warm spot of her fist over her breastbone. "Tell me," she said, "what inspired you to establish the cultural center?"

Alla Innokentevna drew away. Behind her glasses, her eyelids lowered. "Love for my community," she said. "Quote me on that in your article. They don't have that in the city, do they? No." The organizer turned back toward the lasso game on the stage, and Marina, too, faced forward.

Petya returned with three shallow bowls of salmon soup on a tray. Alla Innokentevna did not budge, so he ate standing, and Marina and Eva spooned up their own portions without any more attempts at conversation. A native boy came onstage to try his luck. He raised the lasso and rocked on his heels, waiting. The deer skull spun. As Marina ate, and even after she set her bowl and spoon on the ground, she felt the presence of the organizer weighing on her, like someone's foot stepping on her chest. Alla Innokentevna wanted to use Marina's loss of Alyona and Sophia; she had failed the first time, but she would try again.

Marina put her head down. Her hiking boots were spattered with mud. The crowd erupted in applause and she knew the boy had finally lassoed it.

When Alla Innokentevna left to introduce the next event—an hour-long dance marathon for children—Petya took his seat back. Eva asked Marina, "How are you doing? Are you going to dance in the adult one?"

"For an hour?" Marina said. "No." On the stage, schoolkids moved in thick-limbed imitation of the earlier dance ensemble. One little girl was even decked out in a tiny leather tunic with a matching strap around her forehead. The girl swayed, arms in the air.

"For three hours," Eva said. "The adult one's longer. Petya and I are going to do it—aren't we, my love?" Petya agreed. "We danced through the whole thing last year. It's fun. Think about it."

"I am," Marina said, though in truth she was thinking about her grandmother's soup recipes, her father's lessons in her childhood about chopping wood. Anything to keep out of her mind the thought of what she had not been able to do for her daughters. Marina scanned the scene for another distraction. She saw children—girls waving to their parents, smiling on the stage, arranging their arms like ballerinas.

Marina stood from the bench. "I'll be back," she told her friends and made her way toward the trees.

The forest muffled the music's high notes so only the bass came through. Marina found the tent. The afternoon was drawing on. She checked her phone—no service—and slipped it into her jacket pocket anyway. Then she crawled onto her sleeping bag.

Rain came light on the tent top. The sound was soft crackles. The distant music did not interfere. She, Alyona, and Sophia used to lie in her bed together, when the girls did not want to sleep alone. Her daughters would talk across the pillows until late. Their high, precise voices on either side; Sophia's head heavy against Marina's bare arm; the twinkling spearmint smell of Alyona's brushed teeth.

Surface tension, Marina reminded herself. The reflection and refraction of light through water. If this weather continued, she would run out of rain trivia. The raindrops made noises like a thousand parting lips.

Eventually she checked the time to make sure the kids' marathon was well over. Adjusting her hood, Marina crawled out and zipped the tent flap shut behind her.

The path took her back to the clearing. Adult couples were onstage now, with drums throbbing behind them; Marina spotted Eva tossing her head and Petya stomping to the beat. Choral singing and prerecorded gull cries played through the sound system. As Marina edged around the back of the stage, Alla Innokentevna's voice came over the speakers. "Aren't they wonderful? Let's hear you cheer." A yell went up on the other side of the banner. "How long can they last?" Alla Innokentevna asked the crowd. No one responded to that.

Marina emerged beside the food booth. One of the cooks looked at her, waiting for a dinner order. "What do you have?" Marina asked.

"Soup."

"Just soup? Fish soup?"

"Fish soup and reindeer blood soup," the cook said. Marina was already taking bills out of her pocket. "The blood soup," she said, passing the cook a hundred-ruble note.

Marina held the hot plastic bowl in both hands as she shouldered her way to a spot, twenty meters from the stage, that was relatively free of other people. The evening stank of smoke. Strong alcohol and charred meat. The broth in her bowl was clear brown, and at its bottom were countless suspended droplets, darker, solid, a heap of stones on the floor of a lake. She watched the dancers while she ate. Eva, spotting her from the stage, waved with both arms high, and Marina raised her spoon to signal back.

Getting to the dregs, she put the bowl to her mouth and drank. Slivers of green onion slid down her throat. She lowered the bowl. The comment-seeking reporter stepped in front of her. "Marina Alexandrovna."

Immediately her body began to shut itself down. "Yes."

"Your friend told us about your situation." Behind him, the photographer, who looked barely out of his teens, hung on to his camera. The reporter said, "We're very sorry for your loss."

"What friend?" Marina knew, she knew, that Alla Innokentevna had arranged this ambush. Not only had the organizer herself been after Marina all day but she had enlisted the other villagers to lay claims to Marina's tragedy.

But the reporter corrected her. "Your friend, the woman—" He pointed toward the stage.

"I see," Marina said. Eva.

"She explained what happened. I'm the editor of *Novaya Zhizn,*

Esso's newspaper. We have four hundred and fifty readers, and we can run a piece in our next edition, put the call out around the village. Do you have a picture with you of your girls?"

Marina heard the pulse in her ears. Felt the blood in her stomach. Constant, constant, these small tortures. Everyone behaving as though their offer of assistance would change her world. "On my phone," she said. "But it's back at the tent." She put the bowl on the ground, the spoon in it. Placed her hands in her pockets. "Oh. No," she said when her fingers bumped against a screen. "I have it. It's here." If she moved slowly, she could last on the oxygen left in her lungs.

The reporter said, "You just tell us in your own words, and I'll record you. Their picture?" She slid her phone out of her pocket. "Perfect. Great." He gestured to the photographer, who raised the camera to cover his face.

The reporter's recorder drifted toward her mouth. Music thumped around them. "When you're ready," the reporter said.

She lifted the phone to her collar. Glass and metal touched her there, hard over her clavicle, and she lowered the phone again. She looked into the black, strange eye of the camera. Opening her mouth, expecting to choke, she spoke.

"Please help me find my daughters, Alyona Golosovskaya and Sophia Golosovskaya, who went missing from the center of Petropavlovsk-Kamchatsky last August. August fourth. Alyona is twelve years old now. She was wearing a yellow T-shirt with stripes across the chest and blue jeans. Sophia is eight and was dressed in a purple shirt and khaki pants. They were taken by a heavyset man in a big, new-looking car that was black or dark blue. If you have any information, call Major General Yevgeny Pavlovich Kulik at 227-48-06, or contact your local police department." Marina had memorized these descriptions and numbers early on. Her face in the circle of the camera lens was a person trapped in a well.

"Would you please show us?"

She unlocked her phone, scrolled to the photo roll, and held up her older girl's school portrait. "Alyona." The shutter clicked. She flicked the screen. "Sophia." They were well lit and smiling. "We are offering a reward. If you know anything, call the police."

The camera still pointed at her. Again the shutter click. The reporter asked, "Is there any message you'd like to send your girls?" He enunciated to make his later transcription easier. This was a favor he had done her, this little feature. This transaction. One column of type in exchange for her life. "What would you like to tell them?"

"That I love them," she said. And there it was—the constriction. The weight coming down. "That I'm desperate for them. I love them more than anything in the world."

"That's good. That's enough," he said. "An awful incident. We're certainly glad to help."

She edged her body away from him and shut her mouth to draw air in through her nostrils. The air did not reach deep enough to give her relief.

The photographer said, "A big guy in a black car?" She nodded. It was all she could do to inhale through her nose. The photographer said, "A Toyota?"

"Just a big black car," the reporter said. "Black or dark blue. Isn't that right, Marina Alexandrovna?"

The photographer stared at Marina. This was the difference after people found out—the raw curiosity. "You should talk to Alla Innokentevna."

Marina said, "She already talked to me."

"What did she say?"

"That—" Marina stopped, unable to continue.

"She mentioned Lilia? Her daughter?"

The reporter broke in to stop the younger man. "They already spoke, she said."

All this year had gone this way: coworkers approached Marina at her desk, or old classmates sent her emails, or her parents' friends took her aside if they saw her grocery shopping to tell her they had figured out how to find her daughters. Meanwhile the detectives told Marina they knew nothing and expected less. *Your theories don't help me,* she no longer had the oxygen to say.

"We'll print it next Saturday," the reporter told Marina. "You never know, maybe they were taken north. This might make all the difference." She tilted her head back. "Are you all right?" he asked. "Marina Alexandrovna?"

Marina's pulse was too loud. She saw it, then, the sign from last fall that she had reached a peak of terror: the edges of her vision pulled in black. The world darkened. She tried to think of something, anything—the combination lock she used at university. Her and Eva's old locker numbers. The best time of year to pick wild garlic. Anything before her girls were born. Anything to keep them out of her mind in this moment.

The dark receded. Lowering her head, she saw the people dancing. The reporter's hand hovered a centimeter beyond Marina's jacket sleeve.

Marina turned away. She wove across the clearing until she reached the woods.

The music followed her. People shouted back and forth—the crowd was getting drunker. Marina opened her mouth to swallow air. Again her vision narrowed. Light among the trees was even dimmer than out on the grass.

A fact: the statistical likelihood that her daughters would be found at this point was infinitesimal. Wherever they went, they were there now permanently, no matter the number of search parties organized or pleas printed on a front page. Marina was not ignorant. A missing child is most likely to come home in the first hour after disappearance. Every hour after that, the chance of a happy reunion decreases; by the time twenty-four go by, a missing child is almost certainly dead. Three days into the girls' absence, the city police began to speak of recovering bodies, not rescuing children. And many hours, and many days, had passed since then.

Marina had lost them forever. She was never going to get her daughters back.

At the tent, she bent over to unzip the door and tossed her cell phone inside. The phone bounced across their sleeping bags. When she tried to stand back up, she found she could not. She could not.

They were dead. They had been dead for months. Nothing she did could save them.

The drums were thudding. Her chest was collapsing. "Marina," Petya said from behind her. His hand on her back. "Marina. Breathe. Breathe." He pulled her up to standing, as straight as she would go. Now both his hands were on her shoulders. "Calm down." His familiar face. Strong when she could not be. "Marina, breathe. Look at me," he said, and she did. He made a little circle of his lips, then pulled in air, slowly. Relaxed his mouth. Let the air out. "Do it with me." Her lungs burned, her throat was torn. She, too, made an O of her lips, sucked in oxygen, let it out. "Slower," he said. "Like me." He must have followed her from the clearing. He had lost the dance marathon because of her. She focused on the pattern of his mouth.

"There you go," he said when she got her breath back. He hugged her. Her nose pressed against his chest, and she turned her face to rest there more easily. Her hands were caught between them. She moved her lips in the way he showed.

After a long moment, he asked her, "How are you?" Marina nodded. "Can you sit down?" Nodding again, she bent her knees, and he helped her sit half in the tent with her legs propped out its doorway. He crouched beside her. She felt the phantom crush of his body, its welcome weight. She remembered Sophia's head against her shoulder. Holding her girls in her arms when each was a newborn. That warmth. She had been so alone for the last eleven months that she believed she was going insane.

He stood up. She stared ahead at the woods, and he touched her shoulder. The soft skin behind her ear. "Hey," he said. She looked up. Again he formed an O with his lips. Again she mimicked him. "Keep doing that," he said. "Eva is going to be worried. I'll be right back."

With cool air hissing past her teeth, she watched him go. Petya, whom she saw in a blue suit at his wedding. Now he was heavier and going gray. Through the years, he had remained decent, honorable. Attuned to the dangers around him. If only Marina could say the same for herself. She turned back toward the trees. Her lips moved. The river, somewhere to her right, rushed away.

She twisted at the sound of someone approaching the tent. It was the photographer, camera on a sling around his neck.

"Please go away," she said. She made an O of her lips and put her head down.

He crouched beside her in the wet leaves. "I'm sorry," he said. "I don't want to bother you. But you said a guy in a new-looking car, right? Could it have been a black Toyota Surf?"

.

There is a man who lives near Esso, the photographer said, who might look like the person she had described. "This man is strange," the photographer said. His words were low, quick. He had that northern intonation to his voice. "His name is Yegor Gusakov. He lives alone. I know he sometimes goes to the city overnight, and I know he keeps his car looking nice."

"A man who cares for his car and sometimes goes to the city," Marina said.

"It's a black Toyota Surf. An SUV."

She sat with that for a moment. "What do you mean, he's strange?"

The photographer shifted his feet in his crouch. "We were in the same year in school, and he was always by himself, people felt sorry for him. He took advantage of that."

Marina kept her eyes down. The photographer's boots were dark with rainwater above the soles.

He kept talking. Yegor had been interested in the daughter of Alla Innokentevna years before that girl disappeared, he was saying. "It was more than a crush. He was almost obsessed with her. Lilia talked about it back when we were kids."

Marina glanced up at him. He was staring at her, anticipating her response.

"Lilia ran away from home," she said. "Isn't that so?"

"Some people say that. Some people don't."

"You don't," she said.

The photographer paused to choose his next words. "Listen, did Alla Innokentevna tell you what Lilia looked like?" Marina shook her head. "She was older than your daughters," the photographer said, "but short. Small. She was eighteen but she looked younger. I . . . wonder if someone might have hurt her. She could've run away herself, but she wouldn't have stayed away like this, I think, so long."

Marina worked on the muscles in her mouth. The tent's plastic rustled under her weight.

"You think he did something to her?" she asked.

"He could have. He might have."

"Have you reported this to the police?"

"The police didn't pay any attention to Lilia. Anyway, there was never anything to report. Only suspicion. He's creepy. But then—"

"I mean about my daughters," she said. "The car."

"I just— No." His forehead wrinkled. "I didn't know about any car."

She slit her eyes at him. His anxious face, his bent knees. "You just said—"

"Those pictures you showed us, I've seen those before. There were posters up here with their faces. But I never put them together with her. There was no . . . I've never heard about any kidnapper."

She closed her lips. Then she said, "What do you mean, never heard?"

"The posters said two Russian girls in the city were missing. Nothing else."

Did no call for a kidnapper ever go out through the peninsula? What had the police been doing all this time? By winter, Marina knew, authorities were already turning their attention toward custody battles, or swimming accidents, or trafficking off Kamchatka. But before that? When had the major general first discounted their witness? Was it in the first weeks of the investigation? The first days?

"I never heard about some man who took the girls away in a black car," the photographer said.

"Black or blue," Marina said. Her head was back down.

Music filtered through the trees. The sound of the river. "I can take you to see him," the photographer said. "Yegor's house is twenty minutes away. We can drive there."

"You want me to go driving alone with you."

The photographer flushed and sat back on his heels. "No, I'm not— I understand. You're thinking of your daughters? So am I. I'm not trying to get you in a car alone." He was short-haired, solid, very young. "You can bring your friends. We can do whatever you like."

Around them, the cheers from the marathon. Marina evaluated the photographer. Eager as he was, he seemed genuine, someone sincere. Certain.

The major general, telling her the girls drowned, hadn't looked so sure of himself. "All right," Marina said. The photographer stood and held out a hand to help her up. She reached backward for her phone, tucked it into her pocket, and followed.

.

At the edge of the clearing, Eva and Petya met them. Petya had his arm around Eva's shoulders. "What's going on?" Eva said. "Petya told me the Esso reporter upset you. Do I owe you an apology?"

The drizzle was starting up again. Where the evening sun should have been, at the base of the sky, was only a bleary white spot. Marina introduced them to the photographer, who said, "I'm Sergei Adukanov. Call me Chegga. I was telling your friend—"

"Chegga lives here," Marina said. "He knows a man with a big black car."

Eva's face sharpened in the low light. Her muscles tightened enough to pull on her bones and make her eyes large. Sometimes Marina forgot, from Eva's chatter about horror movies watched and festivals attended, that Eva, too, had loved Marina's daughters. Marina almost wanted to give her own apology for offering this false hope now.

The photographer told the group about Yegor Gusakov. When he mentioned Alla Innokentevna's daughter, Petya squinted. "One minute. Please. You think this has something to do with Alyona and Sophia?"

"Lilia looked younger than she was," Chegga explained, "and this guy might be—"

"Did you just find out about this case?" Petya asked. "Because it's very easy, when you first hear about it, to jump to conclusions. But when you actually know the people involved, and when you see the steps of the investigation, you understand this is not so simple to solve."

The photographer chewed on his cheeks. "I understand that. I'm not naïve."

Petya turned to Marina. "You need to protect yourself. This sounds like village gossip."

"Maybe," Marina said. "So I want to ask Alla Innokentevna for the truth."

Couples still danced on the stage. Their arms waved in the air to the beat. As her group crossed the grass clearing, Marina counted the kilometers between Esso and Petropavlovsk, the number of seats in a Toyota SUV. Could someone have driven from the city to here without notice? The roads did empty outside city limits. She saw that yesterday. And after he took the girls in the late afternoon, he would have driven into the night, unseen . . . and if he had carried extra fuel cans in his trunk, instead of stopping at a gas station, he could've gone the whole way without talking to anyone . . .

But the police must have searched the villages. They told Marina they looked everywhere.

But Chegga said he hadn't talked with any officers. He had never heard a description of the kidnapper before. To recover the girls, the city authorities only sent out posters with Alyona's and Sophia's photos and birth dates. Alla Innokentevna had warned Marina to expect this: *To stop us, the police say many things . . .*

But it should not have mattered if the details coming out of Petropavlovsk's headquarters were false. Marina herself had called the Esso police station in August. She had called every regional branch on the peninsula. They told her then they had no record of any kidnappings or lost children.

But Marina did not ask them about any eighteen-year-old they presumed had left home.

Behind the stage, in damp shadow, they found the organizer talking to a younger woman. "Alla Innokentevna," Chegga called. "Forgive us for interrupting."

The organizer frowned from him to Eva to Marina. "Go ahead."

Hours earlier, Alla Innokentevna had said she would take any questions. She had dipped close to Marina to offer her assistance and request help. And it had taken Marina all day, all this terrible year, to understand what to ask for. Marina said, "Would you tell me what really happened with your daughter? With Lilia?"

The younger woman next to the organizer flinched. She wore no glasses, and her skin was unlined, but she looked like Alla Innokentevna—the same full lips and rounded jawline. Alla Innokentevna took her by the arm and said, "Don't get into it, Tasha."

"The police told you she ran away, correct?" Marina said. "They told me my daughters must have been lost while swimming. But someone else saw them climb into a car with a man that day—a big, dark, shiny car."

"You're the Golosovskaya girls' mother," the younger woman said.

"Alla Innokentevna, did you know Yegor Gusakov bought himself a nice car a few winters ago? A large black one?" Chegga asked.

The younger woman said, "Who? Which Yegor?"

Alla Innokentevna's eyebrows were high. She kept her hand tight on the younger woman's elbow. "You wouldn't know him. He finished school between Denis and Lilia. He lives toward Anavgai . . . You're joking," Alla Innokentevna said to Marina. "This is the favor you want from me? To chase down this boy?"

"I'm coming to you to ask for information."

"Information."

"About this man. What this man might have done."

Alla Innokentevna turned to the photographer. "Is your mother in the village or out with the herd now? What would she think, to see you mislead someone in this way?"

Chegga shifted from side to side on the wet ground. Rain droplets hung on his buzzed hair. Marina said, "I was told this Yegor spends some nights in Petropavlovsk. Is that true?" The organizer sighed. "So it could be him. It's possible."

Alla Innokentevna shook her head.

"In Esso!" the younger woman said. "No. It's not to be believed …"

Alla Innokentevna spoke in another language to her. That was Even, Marina guessed. To Marina, Alla Innokentevna said, "Has someone explained to you yet what Yegor Gusakov is like?"

Next to her, Chegga made a disapproving noise. Marina spoke over him. "I hear he's strange."

"I'm sure you do hear that. It's what people say about anyone who acts different," said Alla Innokentevna. "They talk the same way about my son—they say he's strange and they worry about danger." The younger woman said something in Even, but Alla Innokentevna continued. "They're wrong. Yegor is harmless. Not very clever. He is not a criminal mastermind, do you understand what I mean? He is just a sad boy who always wanted friends."

Chegga said, "Respectfully, I don't agree." The organizer held up both palms. "He was always watching Lilia when we were children. Maybe he wanted her for himself."

Marina had never been able to watch herself pleading on television or hear her own voice crack on regional radio. After experiencing those moments, she did not want to relive them. But here, behind a stage crowded for a dance contest, near the end of a day at a rural holiday, she saw for the first time what she must have looked like. Alla Innokentevna's expression broke open, a split fruit, exposing four years of rotten loss. Her lips parted. Devastation. Her nostrils flared. Her eyes, for a second, did not see the festival, and then they focused, and she clenched her teeth, and she shut herself up again.

"I see," Marina said.

Alla Innokentevna looked straight at her. "You want to know if Lilia ran away." Marina nodded. "No. Clearly not. She got into trouble here—she'd been getting into trouble for years—and someone hurt her."

"Mama," the younger woman said.

"And no one cared," Alla Innokentevna said. "I told the authorities. No one listened."

"I'm listening," said Marina. Seeking inside Alla Innokentevna the parent she recognized.

Alla Innokentevna said, "No. You are trying to convince me, like our police captain did, of a fairy tale. Lilia was not taken from us over a schoolboy's interest. She got into something worse."

The speakers boomed as someone on the stage made an announcement. "Chegga is bringing us now to look at this man," Marina said.

"Go look, then."

"You can come with us. If we see anything that seems—if you see anything connected—to Lilia—I'll give his name, his description, his license plate number to the city police. We can go together—"

Alla Innokentevna spat the name out. "Yegor Gusakov, of all people, is not the one who killed her."

"No one killed her!" her daughter cried. "Mama, all they're saying is that this Yegor happens to match their kidnapper's description—that maybe he frightened Lilia before she left."

"Someone killed her," Alla Innokentevna said. To Marina, she said, "Like someone killed your daughters. You fool yourself by believing otherwise. You want a different answer so badly, but it will not come."

Someone touched the base of Marina's back very gently. Eva. The crowd, beyond the banner, was cheering. Alla Innokentevna had to be right. For years, the organizer had occupied the place Marina was pushed into last summer. She had been surrounded by people who stared, whispered, asked questions, but never changed her prospects of recovering what was lost. Two or three summers from now, Marina might speak the same way; she might come to accept that they were gone, that their bodies would never be found, and that the only recourse left would be bribing the police to make up a theory with a better chance of placating her.

But not yet. "So you won't go," Marina said.

Alla Innokentevna said something in Even to her daughter. The daughter shook her head. "She won't," her daughter said. Tasha. Natasha. "But if you really think this could have something to do with my sister, I will. I'll come along."

.

Petya in the driver's seat, Eva in the passenger's, Marina and Chegga and Natasha, Alla Innokentevna's daughter, in the back. The photographer leaned forward to give directions. When he broke off, Natasha said, "So what did he do to scare Lilia? She never mentioned him, I don't think. I don't remember that name."

"Oh," Chegga said. "He left her gifts. These . . . She used to say he left things outside your house." He did not seem as confident as he had when spinning tales on the campground. Alla Innokentevna had subdued them all.

"Gifts," Natasha repeated, quieter. "I don't remember." Then: "Tell me again? What does he look like?"

"White. But built like me," Chegga said.

The sky was passing from gray-blue to gray, drizzly twilight to drizzly dusk, out the car windows. The river curved away to their left. Marina, watching it go, tallied the results of this last year: her girls abducted. Her home empty. Her simple job, chosen for the ease with which she could care for her family around it, now pointless, and her top desk drawer stocked with tranquilizing tablets. Some nights she dreamed of her daughters and woke up sobbing, and the pain then was as fresh and sharp and new as it had been in the sixth hour after they went missing, as horrendous as a knife stuck in her womb. And now she was chasing another fantasy. She was choosing to push the weapon back in herself.

"What are we hoping to do?" Petya asked. "See this man? Ask him about the girls?"

"I can ask him about my sister," Natasha said.

"See him, yes," Marina said. "See his car. Take pictures to find out if our witness can identify them."

"Shouldn't we go to the Esso police station?" Eva asked. Natasha clicked her tongue.

"They're a subsidiary of the city station," Marina said. The voice coming out of her mouth was steady, journalistic, a leftover from an earlier time. "For any real crimes, the Esso officers turn to Petropavlovsk. Only the city can organize search and rescue teams."

From the front, Petya said, "Marina. What are you expecting?"

"Nothing," Marina said. That was almost entirely true.

Petya laced his fingers in his wife's ponytail. Natasha, leaning forward to look at Marina, said, "I hope my mother didn't upset you too much."

"She spoke honestly," Marina said. "I appreciate that."

"I suppose," Natasha said. In the deepening evening, she was shadow and highlight, blue and bronze. "She's had a difficult life. Not just since my sister left, but before that, too . . . she's very strong."

"You think Alla Innokentevna is wrong, though," Chegga said. The shadow over Natasha's eyes shifted. "About this. You think Lilia ran away."

"I know she did," Natasha said. "Life in a village is not what most eighteen-year-old girls dream of. Lilia had so many reasons to go." She was quiet. "Maybe Yegor was one more."

"Could be," Chegga said.

"Maybe Lilia saw something in him that no one else did," Natasha said. "Something sinister."

The car was quiet. Eva turned in her seat to study Marina.

"I followed your case all year," Natasha said. "I have two children, too, similar ages. I would've contacted you right away if I imagined there were some connection between us—that the person who pushed my sister out of the village could've hurt your girls. But I didn't know. Lilia didn't tell me. And Esso seemed a world away from what happened with your daughters. I never thought . . ."

Marina said, "I didn't either. Nobody did."

The road bumped underneath them. On either side, the flashing woods. Dark trees and summer leaves. Marina, resting her forehead against the glass, pictured her girls. How Alyona's arms freckled in the summertime—how Sophia hooted back at the sea lions when Marina took her to the city's rookery. Rain trickled across the window. "The next left," Chegga said. "Are you ready?" Eva asked. Marina exhaled into her daughters' memories.

They crossed a bridge, went down dirt, passed a metal sign marking ten kilometers to the center of Esso. Chegga pointed out the windshield. Petya rolled to a stop on the packed ground; the road they had been traveling was empty, but he pulled over regardless, to give space for any coming car to pass. On the opposite side of the road, between birch trees, was a tended parcel of land. A narrow path made of laid planks led to the door of a two-story wooden house.

The house was painted white. It sat fifteen meters away. Its windows were shuttered and its lights were off. A small garden plot in the yard held young plants. Parked in the unpaved driveway was a black SUV, which shone under the dimming clouds like coal.

"Well? Is that it?" Chegga asked.

Petya said, "We don't know."

Beside Marina, Chegga raised his camera, snapped a picture, put it back down in his lap. No one else moved. "Is he home?" Eva said to break the silence.

"The house is dark," Natasha said.

In the front, Petya said, "Marina, you should stay in the car. Until we know more."

Chegga blew air between his lips. He lifted the camera over his neck and handed it to Petya. Then he nudged Natasha. "Let me out," he said. "I'll find out if anyone's there."

"I'll come with you," Natasha said.

Chegga shook his head. "Just wait. If he's there, we were classmates, we're familiar with each other, I'll come up with something to talk with him about. And you all can see what he looks like."

The car door opened, they both climbed out, Natasha came back, the car door shut again. Chegga was crossing the road. He followed the wooden path up to the house. Petya had his eye to the viewfinder of the camera. Eva muttered something—*do you know how to*—and he shushed her. At the house's door, Chegga pressed a buzzer, knocked. If this was him, Marina thought. If this was him. After her long struggle to breathe. How could she survive knowledge?

Chegga knocked again. No one in the car spoke. Chegga, waiting, tilted his head, considered the house. Finally, he turned, shrugged at them, and started walking back.

Marina was swinging her legs out of the car. "Please be careful," said Eva. But then she, Petya, and Natasha were getting out, following. The four of them crossed the road together. The woods and fields around them were green and brown and black. No other buildings were visible. Far away, a dog barked.

The smell in the air was smoke, diesel, wild grass, mud. Chegga met them at the edge of the property, where the plank pathway touched the road, and took his camera back. Empty-handed, Petya said, "What now?"

Natasha was looking up at the house with her brows knit. She walked a few meters onto the pathway, its boards creaking, before stopping. Eva trailed after with her hands in her jacket pockets. The six shuttered windows on the house's second story looked like eyes squeezed shut. Chegga took a picture of the building. The parked vehicle. The surrounding woods.

Marina stepped into the wet green yard. She felt the rest of them watching her. Not looking back for their confirmation, she walked across the grass. Toward the black car. She could hear the swish of Petya's feet behind her.

It was big. And it did gleam. Close up, Marina could see spatters of mud on the bottom of the trunk door, caked earth in the tread of the tires, but as a whole the car looked well maintained. She tried to picture the man who lived here washing it. A white man, Chegga had said; Marina got that far, to the skin, and no further. In her mind, his face was a smudge, a bleach mark. She took a picture of his license plate with her cell phone, then backed up to get the whole vehicle in frame—back, side, front, side. A scratch, perhaps ten centimeters long, rose from one wheel well. Marina traced one hand along the paint. She continued looking.

Petya peered into the car's trunk while Marina studied the seat belts, the footwells, trying to focus on what the car contained. The seats were leather. An icon glued to the glove compartment showed the Virgin Mary outlined in painted gold. Between the dashboard vents and the front windshield was a curled plastic wrapper off a cigarette pack. An auxiliary cord trailed across the center console.

She jabbed at a window. Pressed one flat hand there, like she could push through it, she could push in. "That's hers," she said.

"What?" Petya said.

"That's from her phone." Marina was rapping on the glass. "There. There. It's Alyona's." Hanging from the rearview mirror, a strip in the shadows, was the tiny yellowed bird charm that Alyona had had fixed to her cell phone. But no. No, it could not be. Marina tried to put both palms to the glass, but her own cell, clutched in her right hand, got in the way. She pulled back and scrabbled for her speed dial, for her daughter's number, pressed call for the millionth time this year, but nothing, obviously, no fucking service out here, and even if there were there would be no ringing. Alyona's phone had stopped ringing that first day. Marina's eyes burned. She slammed on the window so hard she heard cracking and she did not know whether it was her cell or her hands or the glass or her heart that made the noise. Was this really happening? But there it was. Petya was right behind her now and she hit again at the window—should she break it? A rock?—should she take a picture?—because there it was, Alyona's phone charm, that trinket, a carved ivory crow hanging from a black cord. There it was.

"Where?" Petya asked. He was crowding close. Marina pointed. "On the mirror," she said. "There."

He peered in. They had lost too much light since leaving the campground, so it was hard to see—why didn't they come earlier? But the charm was visible all the same. That little bird, bone-colored, that Alyona had hooked to one corner of her slim black phone. Alyona's mouth had turned down in concentration while her fingers worked over the lanyard loop.

"That gold thing?" Petya said. "That's hers?"

"The one hanging down from the mirror," Marina said. Her voice was loud. She did not recognize the sound of it.

The others were at the car, too, now, though Marina had not noticed when they crossed the yard. Eva was wiggling in next to Petya to look. Chegga was straining, camera in his hands, to see for himself, and saying to Natasha, "Can you find anything of Lilia's? Can you see?"

Natasha's forehead was pressed to a window. Chegga pushed forward. Natasha said quietly, "I don't know what to look for."

Marina's hands were fists. She had to get closer. She unwound her fingers and hoisted herself onto the hood, the car's body rocking on tires underneath her. She pulled her legs up—Petya's anxious hands boosting her—and then she was kneeling on the top of the hood, staring down now, directly through the windshield. Around the neck of the mirror was wound a thin gold chain, and looped around the mirror itself was a sliver, a charm, a nothing, a piece of tourist trash. But Alyona's. Marina said, "It's hers." She knew the thing perfectly.

She remembered when they got it. Alyona had picked it off a table of identical animal carvings last spring. At the outdoor market on the city's sixth kilometer. The three of them were there that day to find Sophia new sneakers, and Sophia was dragging her feet past the stalls, complaining, because she, too, wanted a cell phone, and also some trinket to hook on to it—*that one, Mama, please!* When you get a little older, Marina had told her younger daughter, I'll get you your own phone that you can make look however you like, but for right now, you'll share your sister's . . . After August, that argument undid Marina. She could hardly bear to tell the police what she had said, let alone what she'd been thinking. She had given her children a single device between them, an object easily destroyed, with nothing more than a chunk of fake ivory on a cord to defend themselves.

Chegga's camera was clicking. Inside the car was dark. Airless. The charm did not swing.

"Why did he take it off her phone?" Marina said. "Where is her phone?"

Eva was wide-eyed. Natasha kept her face to the window.

Alyona's phone had been off, Marina knew, since the afternoon the girls disappeared. But the desire to call her daughters was flooding her. She had to hear them. "Where are they?" Marina said. So loud. "Where are they?"

The hood was hard under her knees. "Take a minute, Marina,"

Petya said. "Look again. A thousand souvenirs like this one are sold on the streets every tourist season. This one is hers? Are you sure?"

"I'm sure," she said. Even as she said it, she thought, Am I? Am I? A thing like this, generic. But I know it. Except why would he save it? Display it? If this is true, if this is actually happening, where is Alyona? Her phone dismantled—where is Sophia? With him? Yegor? Who is that? Where is he? Did they go into this house? Are they buried in this garden? In the forest? Are they on the side of the road between here and Petropavlovsk? He might have. He. How am I still breathing? How? This charm.

Painted cottages lined freshly paved streets in Esso proper, where Petya, at Chegga's direction, had driven them. As soon as a lone bar of service appeared on Marina's screen, Petya pulled over, and Marina dialed the major general's cell number. It rang without answer, so she hung up and dialed the station. A woman picked up, took Marina's name, and asked her to hold for a transfer. A young man's voice came over the line.

"Marina Alexandrovna? It's Lieutenant Ryakhovsky."

"I need to speak to Yevgeny Pavlovich."

Ryakhovsky paused. "The major general is on a case away from his desk."

"It's urgent. You have to find him immediately."

The detective sighed and lowered his voice. "Marina Alexandrovna, may I speak honestly? It's Saturday night. The major general left work hours ago. You don't want to call him at this point. He won't be sober enough to assist you."

Eva reached for the phone to take over the conversation. Marina held up a hand to stop her. The black car, Marina told the detective. The rearview mirror. Alyona's phone charm. Yegor Gusakov. His private trips to the city and his house shuttered. Out of Marina's mouth, the journalist was speaking. She listed the facts.

"Tell him about Lilia," Chegga whispered.

Also Lilia, Marina repeated. Lilia . . . Marina looked over Chegga's shoulders at the shadow of Natasha. "Solodikova," Natasha said. "Lilia Konstantinovna."

Solodikova, Lilia Konstantinovna, Marina said. Missing four years. And Yegor Gusakov. Alyona. Sophia. The Toyota, Marina said. The color of the Toyota, the size. An SUV.

"You saw this car yourself?" the detective said, voice sharp. She said yes. "Was Yegor Gusakov there? Did you see him? Did he see you?"

The darkened windows. The car in the driveway. Had he been in the house after all? Watching them? But— No, she said. She didn't think so. No.

"Where are you right now? This very instant?"

The village streetlights flickered on above. In Esso, Marina said.

"You're alone?"

She met Eva's eyes. I'm with my friends, Marina said.

"How many friends?" Four. "They know? Have you told anyone else?"

Yes. No.

"Good. Don't." The detective was silent. "Marina Alexandrovna," he finally said, "you're sure about all this?"

She nodded. He kept waiting for her answer. Yes, she said out loud.

"Give us two hours to call back," he said. "Maybe three. I'll—we'll track down the major general. We'll send a team north by helicopter. You said this man wasn't home when you were there?" No, she said. "We don't want him to know we are coming." Marina inhaled. "I can reach you on this number? So for now—do you understand me?— for now, you will need to stay out of his way. Stay away from his house. Do not go there. Tell your friends the same. Wait somewhere and expect to hear from me."

In two hours?

"I've got to find him first. We'll start organizing the flight. Then up to Esso . . ." The other end of the line was quiet as he calculated. He said, "In three."

But you'll come.

"We're coming."

And I'll wait, she said. She was always waiting. When Eva reached again for the phone, Marina gave it over, so her friends could hear the plan from the detective's own mouth. Beside Marina, under the new yellow light, Chegga scrolled through the photos on his camera. Natasha stared ahead stunned.

·

They had decided. To the campground, to collect their things, then back to Esso where there was cell service to wait for Ryakhovsky's call. Chegga told Marina, Eva, and Petya that they should stay at his house, with his wife and daughter. Marina listened to Eva and Petya agree. As helpful as Chegga had been, he had the same quality as everyone else over this year: he wanted to put himself inside the story. As if on instinct, Natasha roused, then— "No," she said to the group. "Come to ours."

"Which is closer to Yegor's?" Petya asked.

Chegga glanced at Natasha. "They're the same, practically. The village isn't big. We're two streets apart."

"But your mother," Eva said to Natasha. "She won't mind?"

"She stays at the camp during the festival." Eva nodded. "You can meet the rest of my family," Natasha said.

Out of Esso, the houses drew farther apart, the ground under their tires grew rougher. The river alongside the road returned. Marina looked into the blackened woods. In two or three hours, just after midnight, she would hear a helicopter.

When they pulled into the rows of parked cars at the campground fence, the music coming from the clearing beyond was contemporary, electronic-sounding. "Will you come with us to pack up or would you rather wait in the car?" Eva asked.

Marina could not feel her lungs, or her throat, or the pulse in her chest or her back on the seat or her hands where they had hit the car's glass. Nothing hurt. This was a new, not unwelcome, way of existing. "You can do it," Marina said. "Please."

Between the driver's seat and the door, Petya reached back to touch her shin. "We'll be back as soon as possible," Eva said.

Natasha got out, too, to let Chegga slide from the car. He hugged Marina before he left. Marina, outside her own body, observed him doing it. Then Natasha got back in to sit again. She left her door open.

This is not real, Marina thought. This could not be her life.

The night was cool, the music loud. Marina checked the time on her phone, then put her head back and practiced making an O of her numb lips. Natasha was turned toward the clearing. She said something.

"What?" Marina said.

Natasha cleared her throat. "Almost the closing ceremony."

Drums sounded through the speakers. Long research had given Marina one more fact: a body takes ten years to decompose after burial. Alyona and Sophia are buried in that man's garden, she thought. She had practically stood on top of them an hour before. After Marina's months of horror spent gathering information, that idea neither distressed nor soothed her now. It surfaced in her like a piece of driftwood. Ten years. It floated along.

"I always wanted what you got tonight," Natasha said in the direction of the clearing. "An answer."

Marina looked again at her phone. Two hours, he'd guessed, to call back.

"Any answer," Natasha said. "I'm glad for you." Her voice was flat and far away.

The words percolated through Marina. She said, "Thank you."

The two of them sat in the parked car. The music from the campground beat on.

"My mother believes . . . My mother was right," Natasha said. "Someone killed Lilia." In the dark, she turned toward Marina. "Isn't that so?"

"Oh. I don't know," Marina said. Natasha waited. "It could have been like you thought. Yegor made your sister uncomfortable. So she left."

"But she would've called us," Natasha said. "At some point. She would have called me."

Marina had no response. There was nothing to say. Natasha had found her answer.

And should Marina feel glad about that? About at last knowing something, anything at all? Because she did not feel it. Where gladness should be, or despair, or gratitude for Natasha's presence, or desperation to acknowledge the thing they shared, there was brutal vacancy. Natasha was looking at her without expectation. Marina folded her hands and pictured three small bodies, Lilia, Alyona, Sophia, among the warm dark colors of beets and carrots, with roots winding around them and dirt packed into their mouths.

The music faded and a voice yelled for order over the speaker system. "I'm sorry," Natasha said. "I can't just sit here. The ceremony's starting. Do you want to join? Or—" She faltered. "I'll leave you, if you like. I can come back to take you to our house when it's done. I just need to get up, get out . . ."

Two hours. Or three. Ryakhovsky said the police would come. Didn't he? They would track Yegor down. They would uncover the girls where they lay. Two or three hours, and after that, an eternity.

And Marina would spend all that time like this. Sitting alone. Thinking about decomposition. Kept waiting, as Alla Innokentevna had been, for the happiness that would never again arrive.

"All right," Marina said. She heard herself speak and watched herself stand from a distance. "We can go."

When they got to the fenced border of the clearing, Alla Innokentevna was at the microphone. "We celebrate this Nurgenek on the last day of June," the organizer was calling out. "We make a circle in a tribute to the solstice sun."

Natasha clutched Marina's hand. On Marina's other side, a stranger reached for her. The whole mass of people was falling into formation. Marina looked for Eva and Petya, though the night made it impossible to spot anyone from a distance. They would have to search the circle to find her afterward. That was fine.

The drums bumped up in volume. "During these long summer

days," Alla Innokentevna said, "the old sun dies, and the new one is created. The gates of the spirit world open. This is a time when the dead walk among us. Those who are living can be reborn."

Dancers crossed the grass. The flaps of their costumes trailed behind them, distorting their silhouettes. Breaking into the circle, they remade the formation, gripping the hands of tourists, locals, children.

Natasha tugged on Marina's arm. Their circle began to revolve around the wet lawn. "Repeat after me," Alla Innokentevna instructed the crowd. "Nurgenek . . ." Marina let the Even words wash past her. She could not replicate those syllables—soft vowels all in a row. Around her, other Russians tried and failed to catch the sounds. One man was shouting. A few people laughed.

They turned faster. The grass was slippery. "Tell the neighbor to one side, 'Happy New Year,'" Alla Innokentevna said. "Tell the neighbor to your other side that you wish them peace." Marina pictured the peeling shutters on Yegor Gusakov's windows. The hanging line of Alyona's cell phone charm.

Alla Innokentevna's words rose above the drumbeat. "We pass from one year to the next. You will be given a branch of juniper and a strip of cloth. The branch represents your past worries, and the cloth is your wish for the future. When you come to the first fire, throw the branch of your worries in, and jump across." Her voice, amplified, carried no hint of irony. "Hold your wish tight as you go to the next fire. You will be walking between worlds."

Marina listened so that she would not think of the turned earth in Yegor's garden. She would not think of the likelihood her breath would not last the night. Or the impossibility of waiting hours to hear a helicopter. Or the lie that wishes could change history. She would not think of her girls' hands, smaller, hotter, of how they would feel in hers at this moment, of how Alyona and Sophia would half-run to keep up with the turning tide. If she could only get them back, how perfect Marina's life would be. She must not think of that.

"This is a powerful time," said Alla Innokentevna. "Dreams come true. You will jump past the second fire to enter the New Year. And when you tie up your cloth on the other side, your wish will be fulfilled."

No longer pulled in a loop, Marina was instead drawn straight ahead, toward the edge of the clearing, where the woods began. The trees were lit orange at their bases by twin fires. A choir of voices sang in the recording.

The line of bodies in front of Marina headed for the glow. On the far edge of the clearing, from a tangle of smoke and trees, an unbroken line wound back out onto the grass. Marina saw the first fire— a campfire, really, no taller than her knees. They were getting close. A teenager in beaded leather passed out juniper and cloth.

The air smelled spicy. Freshly snapped branches. It smelled like childhood summers, her grandfather's lessons, and rivers waded years before with her children. Natasha dropped her hand to take the two objects. Then Marina, too, grasped them, the fabric thin and swinging, the juniper scratching her palm.

Common juniper. "Your worries and your wish," the teenager called over the noise.

Her worries. Her wish was simple—Alyona, Sophia—and for a terrible moment she allowed herself to believe it, that she and Natasha and Chegga and her friends could actually make them come home, that the major general and his detectives would succeed at last, that her family would be restored. That Lilia's family would track down their daughter, their sister. That they, too, would be healed. Jump the fires, tie up the fabric, and trust in your power to shape the coming year. But no. Alyona, Sophia, and Lilia were murdered. No amount of ceremony, no prescription or intervention, no big black car could alter the truth of that. Missing children, Marina reminded herself, do not return.

She was up to the first fire. She held her false beliefs in two fists: the juniper, that she could leave suffering behind. The strip of cloth, that her daughters would come back to her.

What was she walking toward? The next year would be like the last. So would the next, and the next, and the next—there was no chance of change. The phone charm would not really be Alyona's.

Or the detectives would let Yegor slip away. Her girls could no longer be rescued. Lilia was years gone. Marina would learn to close her ears to strangers; she would return to the newspaper; she would sedate herself with pills; she would continue to survive. But if she had the choice, she would not do any of that—she would go backward. To her children, her best work, her happy fact of a childhood. Where the whole world waited to be discovered. Where everyone had something to teach her and no one had ever been lost.

She turned around. The woman behind her shouted, "Jump over."

Marina could no longer speak. The attack was on her.

The teenager stepped toward her and pointed at the flames. "You jump over. It's the fire of the old year."

Marina's hands were full. She could not press them flat to her chest, and she knew how much she needed them there, how soon she would choke without their comfort. What was the point of all this? She was trying to push out of the line but people kept coming. Eva and Petya were in the woods without her. Natasha was gone. The teenager was calling out instructions. Alla Innokentevna's voice was everywhere, booming over the loudspeakers. They were making her keep moving.

No one near Marina understood. Without her girls, all she had was this breathlessness. Terrible as it was—and it was, it was—it was all she had left to mother. She jumped.

J U L Y

Don't cry. Listen. Do you want to hear again about the girl with the golden slipper? Or the two identical palaces? Did I ever tell you there was an orphan kid in the south who was raised by a pack of wolves? Yes, she was. It's true! They found her when she was a teenager and she couldn't speak human words. She ended up getting married, living in the city, and raising a family, but for the rest of her life, she ate nothing but raw meat.

I saw it once on the news. She grew up to be one hundred years old.

Don't cry...

Sophia, look at me. What do you want to hear to go back to sleep? How about the story of the villagers, after they washed out to sea?

Yeah? You'd like that again?

Do you want to say it yourself or do you want me to? Okay.

So.

The wave scooped everyone up from the ground. It carried them, their houses, their cars, over the cliff. If the villagers hadn't been shut in on all sides by water, they would've been hurt, but they were, so they weren't. They were just locked in place like bubbles in ice. They were in the center of the wave holding their breath. Their eyes were open, and their arms and legs stuck out by their sides.

Like this. Puff out your cheeks—there you go. Like that.

This wave pulls them five hundred kilometers from where their town was. There's nothing but blue wherever they look. Only a minute's gone by since they were first picked up, but they're already halfway to Alaska. The wave slows, and then it stands still, and then . . . it collapses. All around them. The people were frozen, but now they're free.

Well, right, they're still out in the ocean. But they can swim around.

They're swimming and coughing and pushing their hair back. All the heavy things that washed out with them—their homes, the sidewalks, whole trees—sink away. Everything that was light, though, is floating. Groceries. Toys. Remote controls. What else? Pillows, blankets, and books. The people can't believe it. There are even cribs floating with babies inside.

They spend the whole first day and night just gathering. The ones who aren't as strong—the old people and the really little kids—tread water, and shout directions to the ones swimming after their stuff. Like "There's my hat! My favorite hat!" Or "Don't forget my hockey stick!" Or—

Exactly. "Two cartons of orange juice over there! To your right!"

Everyone is kind to each other. Nobody gets hurt. No. Sophia, not that. Because that can't happen there. They're taking care of each other. They pull mattresses together, so people can rest. They even find some fishing poles. It's summertime, a nice warm summer. The water isn't too cold. It's the perfect temperature. This far out, the ocean looks so clear that the villagers can see to where whales pass under their feet.

Did you hear that?

Be quiet for a second. No. You hear that, don't you?

You're okay, right? So hold on one second. One second. Hold on.

He isn't . . . it doesn't sound like him. Does it? Is he coming back up already? No—I'm sorry, shh, I'm sorry. He's not. Listen.

It's not her, either. Definitely. It came from downstairs. I don't . . . Just stay quiet until we hear her knock back.

Hold on.

Come over here. Please come over here. I know, I know that's her now. I don't know why she's banging like that. It's not for us. It's not our wall. Please don't cry. We're going to get under the bed, okay?

She's yelling for no reason. We're just going to get under the bed and listen.

Shh. Good. I know. It's dark.

You're doing a great job, Soph.

You hear it? She's yelling and she's banging but there's something else, right? From downstairs.

Like people. Like a lot of people. No, I don't think it's burglars. He might have brought . . . What I want you to do is keep very, very quiet. Are your feet under the bed?

I'm staying next to you. Don't worry. She'll get in trouble, like before, but we won't get in trouble with him. We're not the ones making noise.

Come closer. I'm going to whisper, okay? And you don't pay attention to anything else.

In that place, way out, the water is warm. Whales and dolphins and a friendly octopus. The people wait and wait and wait for someone to rescue them. Then somebody says, "It's time to start swimming." But the people are scared. Aren't they? Of course they are. They're more scared than they were at any moment since they first saw that wave coming.

Somebody says, "What about our groceries and toys and pillows?"

Somebody else says, "What if there's danger out there?"

But they decide they have to try. They can't wait in the water forever.

She'll stop soon. She's just screaming like she does but she'll stop soon. Hold my hand.

I know. I hear them. Try not to be scared.

Are you listening to me? We're going to be brave if our door opens. Even if it is burglars, or if it's other people, friends of his, we're going to be strong.

Okay? Do you remember the end of the story? What the villagers say? No one helps them but they help each other. Even though their town is gone, and all they see is water in every direction, they swim for land. We can make it, they say. We're going to help each other the whole way.

Will you remember that? We have each other. No matter who opens the door. Remember that Mama's out there. She still loves us. After they go away, we can knock to Lilia, she'll knock back. She's just on the other side of the wall. Yes. I'm here. I promise. We'll stay together. We have each other. We are not alone.

ACKNOWLEDGMENTS

This book would not exist without the hospitality, generosity, and guidance of the people of Kamchatka. I am especially grateful to Tatyana Oborskaya for bringing me to Kamchatka, Denis Piculin for taking care of me, and Anastasia Streltsova for being my friend. Thanks to the United States Fulbright program and Kamchatka State University for supporting my 2011–2012 research year. During that time, the collectives at the Beringia and the Kronotsky Reserve offered invaluable help and insight. My 2015 trip back happened thanks to Elena Lepo, Aiva Lāce, Lilia Banakanova, Martha Madsen, Bystrinsky Nature Park, OOO Olenevod, and Esso's Herd 4. Meeting these people and seeing these places changed my life.

Disappearing Earth was inspired by Russia and written in America. My thanks go to Alizah Salario, Claire Dunnington, Boo Trundle, Brittany K. Allen, Leigh Stein, Alison B. Hart, Mira Jacob and the Resistance, Jennie Baird, Mika Yamamoto, and Lena Tsykynovska for reading and believing in this novel. The space and support to write it came from Brooklyn's PowderKeg workspace, Chinelo Okparanta and the Tin House Summer Workshop, Christine Schutt and the Sewanee Writers' Conference, Dionne Brand and the Banff Centre, VCCA, Hambidge, Ragdale, and Yaddo.

Thanks to Jean Kwok for being a guardian angel. Suzanne Gluck, Tracy Fisher, Andrea Blatt, and the whole WME team have given me the happiest moments of my whole life. Rowan Cope and Jo Dickinson at Scribner UK nurtured this book's growth from across the Atlantic—I am so thankful. At Knopf, Annie Bishai, Lydia Buechler, Pei Loi Koay, Josie Kals, Kathy Zuckerman, Sara Eagle, Rachel Fershleiser, Paul Bogaards, Nicholas Latimer, and Chris Gillespie guided me through every step of the publishing process and made my dreams come true. And enormous thanks go to my brilliant, kind, unfailingly patient editor, Robin Desser. There aren't words in English or Russian that can express what she has meant to this book and to me.

So many people helped bring *Disappearing Earth* to life. I will never be able to thank them all sufficiently. Let me then dedicate this last line of gratitude to the most important one: to Alex Eleftherakis, for his love, his faith, and his suggestion ten years ago to consider Kamchatka.

A NOTE ABOUT THE AUTHOR

Julia Phillips is a Fulbright Fellow whose writing has appeared in *Glimmer Train, The Atlantic, Slate,* and *The Moscow Times.* She lives in Brooklyn.

A NOTE ON THE TYPE

This book was set in Janson, a typeface long thought to have been made by the Dutchman Anton Janson, who was a practicing typefounder in Leipzig during the years 1668–1687. However, it has been conclusively demonstrated that these types are actually the work of Nicholas Kis (1650–1702), a Hungarian, who most probably learned his trade from the master Dutch typefounder Dirk Voskens. The type is an excellent example of the influential and sturdy Dutch types that prevailed in England up to the time William Caslon (1692–1766) developed his own incomparable designs from them.

Composed by North Market Street Graphics,
Lancaster, Pennsylvania

Printed and bound by Berryville Graphics,
Berryville, Virginia

Book design by Pei Loi Koay